CW01523324

Blood Spurts:

Without pain there can be no pleasure.

Contents

To be continued… **Error! Bookmark not defined.**

Chapter One:

Mike was preparing to start a new page in his checkered life. A new job awaited him, and he meticulously planned his route to Nottingham University from his home on Cromwell Street. First, he drove his van, mapping out the roads and noting the traffic flow. Next, he took his bike, testing alternative paths and feeling the inclines in his legs. Finally, he walked the route with his two dogs, observing shortcuts, potential obstacles, and anything that could affect his timing. Each journey was precisely timed, every detail logged.

He had to report to his new manager at 09:30 on Monday morning, and there was no room for error. "A good Marine is always five minutes early," he reminded himself. Even forty years after leaving the forces, he still lived by the same values. The Seven P's—"Proper planning and preparation prevents piss-poor performance"—were ingrained in him.

Starting anew in his sixties felt surreal. He was the "FNG"—the "fuckin' new guy"—a position he hadn't been in for decades. But necessity dictated his return to the workforce. His savings were dwindling, and unforeseen expenses had forced his hand. Finding a job at his age had been an uphill battle. Employers demanded proof of continuous UK employment for the last five years, something he couldn't provide. Having spent the last thirty years working abroad, he had no recent domestic work history. He had to bend the truth to secure the role, a gamble that could come back to haunt him.

For now, though, he focused on integrating into a society that felt alien. The modern world was run by people vastly different from himself. He had heard the term— "woke"—and knew he'd have to filter his words and thoughts to fit in. The transition from military to civilian life had been jarring decades ago, but now, adapting to this new landscape was an entirely different challenge. Yet, he was determined. This was just another mission, another objective. And like every mission before, he would see it through.

Chapter Two

Mike sat in his modest living room, contemplating his next move. The van had served him well over the years, but it was bulky and unnecessary for his new lifestyle. He needed something smaller, more efficient. His mind was made up. Within hours, he had listed the van for sale, found a buyer, and secured a deal on a compact runaround car. No deliberations, no second guessing—just action. It was how he had always operated.

His reasoning was simple. By registering the car with university security on day one, he would only have to go through the process once. Besides, he hardly used the van anymore. Why keep something that no longer fit his needs?

Once a decision was made, he committed fully. That was the way he lived his life— 100% focused, no hesitation. It was this mentality that had carried him through war zones, tough negotiations, and now, the challenges of civilian reintegration. One mission at a time, one step forward. The past was behind him, and his future was taking shape, decision by decision.

Chapter Three

Mike knew the work van was a manual gearbox, and he had been driving an automatic for the last twenty years. To avoid any surprises on his first day, he bought a manual car, determined to reacquaint himself with a clutch and gear stick before starting his job.

Today, he picked up his new car. Sitting in the driver's seat, he took a deep breath and familiarized himself with the controls. The clutch felt alien beneath his foot, and he instinctively searched for a non-existent automatic gear selector. Adjusting his seat and mirrors, he reminded himself that this was just another drill—practice and muscle memory would take over soon enough.

With trepidation, he started the engine and prepared to drive off the forecourt. He pushed the gear stick into first, slowly released the clutch, and—nothing. The car lurched and stalled. A sinking feeling hit his stomach as he realized his mistake—he had forgotten to release the handbrake.

The salesman smirked from the dealership entrance, but Mike ignored him. He restarted the car, this time consciously lowering the handbrake before easing off the clutch. The engine grumbled but stayed running, and he cautiously rolled forward onto the busy Nottingham ring road.

Traffic zoomed past, forcing him to stay sharp. His hands gripped the wheel tightly as he focused on smooth gear changes. His timing was rusty, but after a few stops and starts, he began to feel the old instincts returning. The embarrassment of stalling faded, replaced by determination.

This was just another challenge, another skill to sharpen. He had tackled far greater obstacles in his life, and this was no different. By the time he reached home, he was already more comfortable. Tomorrow, he'd practice again, refining his control. Come Monday morning, he'd be ready.

Chapter Four

Mike sat at the kitchen table, sipping his morning coffee, his mind consumed by a new dilemma—what to wear on his first day. Smart or casual? An ironed shirt and trousers or cargo pants and a polo shirt? He wanted to make the right first impression, but he also had to consider practicality.

If he rode his bike and it rained, he'd arrive with mud splatters up his legs. If he drove, he'd stay clean, but parking could be a hassle. The thought of walking crossed his mind, but that would mean carrying extra shoes to change into once he arrived. The endless considerations swirled in his mind, and it was still six days before he had to start.

Was this normal? Should he even be worrying about something so trivial?

He had faced down warzones, negotiated hostage rescues, and handled high-pressure situations with military precision, yet here he was, agonizing over dress codes. It was absurd, yet another reminder of how different this new world was from the one he had known.

With a sigh, he decided to keep things simple. He'd wear smart-casual—trousers, a polo shirt, and a lightweight jacket. If he needed to adjust, he'd do so after the first day. Problem solved.

Or at least, for now.

Chapter Five

Mike sat in his front room; the radio tuned to BBC Live 5. An interview was playing, and the person being interviewed kept repeating the phrase "You know" in every sentence.

Mike muttered to himself, "No, I don't know."

His blood boiled. The way young people spoke these days infuriated him. Starting every sentence with "So" and filling conversations with "You know what I mean?" grated on his nerves. Was proper speech a thing of the past?

After a few more minutes of listening to the irritating chatter, he had enough. He reached over and turned off the radio, frustration bubbling to the surface.

"No, I don't fuckin' know!" he shouted at the empty room.

Silence followed, save for the distant hum of traffic outside. Shaking his head, he leaned back in his chair and exhaled slowly. He would have to get used to this world, but that didn't mean he had to like it.

Mike was up early. As always, the dogs were walked from 04:00 to 06:00, a routine he refused to break. But today marked the first day of his new training schedule. After his morning tea and toast, he sat on his Concept 2 rowing machine, gripping the handle firmly. He set the monitor to a steady pace and began rowing, feeling the familiar pull in his shoulders and legs.

It had been a while since he trained seriously, but he needed to be fit for his new role. His body had to adapt to an earlier schedule—no more sleeping from 06:30 to 09:00. The next three days were about pushing himself, getting his body used to the rhythm.

After rowing, he cooled down, had a quick shave and shower, then prepped his bike. He would leave home at 08:00, aiming to arrive at the university by 09:00—half an hour early, just as planned.

He was excited. Being out of work for nearly three months had left him restless. He needed goals. Now, he had them.

Chapter Six

As Mike sat in his living room, he thought back to another journey—one that had taken place decades earlier. The train ride from Nottingham to Lympstone Commando Training Centre in 1979. His first job, his first time away from home. As the train bimbled along the River Exe, he had felt both amazement and fear. The rolling hills and vast open spaces felt alien, but the knowledge that he was heading into the unknown filled him with both excitement and apprehension.

That same anxiety lingered even now at 62 years old. He had done everything he could to prepare. His routes had been mapped, his timings calculated, even his bike storage arranged. But despite his meticulous planning, the feeling remained—an eager anticipation, a nervous energy that wouldn't settle until he had completed his first day.

He thought back to his recce the day before, walking into the university building and being greeted by a blonde-haired woman at reception. She had a warm smile that made him momentarily forget his mission. "Hi, yes, I'm starting here on Monday and I'm doing a quick recce," he told her.

She smiled again. "What room or department?"

"B130," he responded.

She pointed down the corridor. "Down there to the stairs, then turn right and up one level. At the top, turn left, and it's down there on the right."

He nodded. "Thanks. One more question—where can I leave my cycle?"

"Oh, I have a code for the secure bike shed round the back if you want it," she offered.

He couldn't help but smile at her helpfulness. "That would be great."

As he turned to leave, she called after him, "See you Monday. Have a good weekend."

Her words stuck with him as he sat in his chair, staring into his cup of tea. The excitement and nerves mixed, just like they had all those years ago on the train to Lympstone. Enough recce's had been done, all routes covered. It was 'Go Time'.

Monday couldn't come soon enough.

Chapter Seven

Sunday was here, and Mike was sweating the small stuff. He was so focused on Monday that he decided not to drink at all today—an unusual move for him. He had never needed a job so much. It wasn't just about money, though he smiled when he checked his Kraken account and saw that his cryptocurrency investments had made a £6000 profit. No, the job was more than financial security—it was about life. He needed human interaction. He needed to integrate.

As he sat with his morning coffee, his eyes drifted to the bookshelf, where a copy of Don't Sweat the Small Stuff by Richard Carlson rested. He had read it years ago, but ironically, he was doing exactly what the book advised against. The book preached a philosophy of letting go of unnecessary worries, of focusing on the bigger picture instead of getting bogged down by trivial concerns. And yet, here he was, running through every possible scenario for tomorrow, overanalysing everything from his route to work to what he would wear.

Carlson's words echoed in his mind: "Ask yourself the question, 'Will this matter a year from now?'" Mike exhaled. He knew deep down that a minor hiccup on his first day wouldn't ruin his life, but the anticipation gnawed at him regardless. Was this just his military discipline kicking in, or was he simply getting old and anxious?

His mind drifted again—to the blonde receptionist. He wanted to talk to her again. Was she just being polite, or was there something more? He shook his head, chuckling to himself. He was definitely sweating the small stuff. Monday couldn't come soon enough.

Chapter Eight

Mike's first day at work had finally arrived. The anticipation of meeting his new team had left him restless the night before. His routine was in place—up at 04:00, dogs walked, tea and toast, rowing machine, shower, and out the door by 08:30.

As he arrived at the university, he locked his bike in the secure shed and made his way to the office. Walking in, he was met by Chun Jia, a middle-aged Malaysian Chinese man who wasted no time in establishing dominance. Mike recognized it immediately—'storming,' the natural phase of team development where new members were tested. Chun Jia wasn't unfriendly, but he made it clear he had been there longer and knew the ropes. Mike, ever the seasoned veteran, played along, nodding and listening without giving too much away.

Kuma, the Indian IT wizard, was far more helpful. He guided Mike through logging into Teams and other software, troubleshooting with ease. "Any problems, just give me a shout," Kuma said with a grin. Mike appreciated the no-nonsense efficiency.

Then there was Russ, the manager, whom Mike had met at the interview. Russ was a talker, firing off information at a rapid pace. Mike absorbed what he could, but a lot of it went straight over his head. No matter— he'd figure it out as he went. Experience had taught him that most workplace rules were learned through action, not words.

Work ended at 16:30, and Mike hopped on his bike for the ride home. The route was mostly uphill, except for one slight downhill stretch where the tram lines joined the road. As he picked up speed, his front wheel slipped into one of the tracks, sending him flying over the handlebars.

He landed hard, sprawling across the road in front of an oncoming tram. More embarrassed than hurt, he scrambled to his feet, grabbed his bike, and pedalled away. It wasn't until he got home ten minutes later that he registered the pain. His elbow felt wet. Pulling off his jacket, he saw blood trickling down his arm. A two-inch flap of skin hung loose from his elbow.

Without hesitation, he grasped the torn skin and yanked it off completely, exposing the raw, red layer beneath. He stared at it, feeling a strange satisfaction at the sight of his own blood. Holding the small piece of skin, he licked it before tossing it into the bin. He applied antiseptic and a dressing, gritting his teeth against the sting. His hip throbbed, deep bruising making it painful to walk, but the dogs needed their walk. Every tug on the lead sent fresh pain through his body, reopening the wound and causing blood to seep through the bandage. He wiped it away with his hand, then instinctively licked the blood from his fingers.

That night, sleep was elusive. Every movement sent fresh waves of pain through his battered body. But no matter—tomorrow was another day. He had a job to do, and nothing was going to stop him from showing up. The next morning, pain coursed through his body. His hip was so swollen that every step was agony. His elbow still seeped blood beneath the fresh dressing, and lifting his arm sent jolts of pain down his side. Yet, he had no choice but to go in. The day's task involved moving heavy IT equipment from the Chemistry school. Every lift, every bend made his wounds throb, but he gritted his teeth and got on with it.

This was his life now. No complaints, no backing down—just pushing through the pain. The mission wasn't over yet. Mike needed to focus on the job. He was in pain, but he had to push through. One thing that made the day bearable, however, was the sight of young, nubile flesh walking around campus. It was a reminder of youth, energy, and the cycle of life moving forward. The pain was temporary. The job was just beginning.

Mike sat on the edge of his bed, his body still aching from the previous day's fall. His hip throbbed, his elbow stung, but what lingered most was the taste. The coppery tang of blood still clung to his tongue, a taste he couldn't shake. He ran his tongue along his teeth, as if trying to extract more of the flavour from memory alone. It was unmistakable—metallic, sharp, almost electric.

He thought about blood, about how it tasted different depending on where it came from. A deep wound had a richer, more iron-heavy taste, while a shallow cut was lighter, mixed with the salt of sweat and skin. It fascinated him. His tongue traced the inside of his cheek, where he had bitten down from the impact of the fall. That was still fresh. He pressed his molars into the same spot, reopening the tiny wound, letting the taste flood back.

Why did humans have a taste for blood? He had read once that the metallic tang was due to haemoglobin, the protein in red blood cells that carried oxygen. The iron in the blood interacted with the receptors on the tongue, sending signals that the body registered as something primal. It wasn't just the taste—it was the reaction it triggered. Something old, buried deep in the subconscious. Blood meant survival. Blood meant life and death.

He remembered the first time he had tasted someone else's blood. A split lip in a fight, the warm, salty dribble seeping into his mouth. He hadn't recoiled. Instead, he had felt something stir inside him, something he hadn't quite understood at the time. Even in the military, when patching up wounds or taking a hit, the taste had always brought clarity rather than disgust. Blood was real. Blood was truth. There was no faking pain, no lying about injury. Blood told the story of what the body had endured.

Now, in the dim morning light, he flexed his injured arm, watching the dressing on his elbow darken slightly at the edges as the wound wept. He exhaled, steadying himself. He had to get ready for work. But the taste lingered. And with it, a thirst he couldn't quite explain.

Four days had passed since his fall, and the pain had only grown worse. It wasn't just his elbow or his hip anymore—his ribs were now a constant source of agony. At first, the shock of the impact had dulled the pain, but now, every movement sent sharp reminders through his body. This morning, as he leashed his dogs, he realized just how bad it had become. Every tug on the leads made him wince, yet deep down, he found some twisted satisfaction in the pain. It was a grounding force, a reminder that he was still alive, still enduring. Pleasure and pain had always been two sides of the same coin, and for Mike, they were starting to blur.

Today, he had been assigned to move heavy switches in the storeroom, logging each one onto a spreadsheet. It was monotonous work, but at least he would be alone—no one to witness his grimaces, no one to ask if he was okay. He preferred it that way. Suffering in silence was easier than explaining. As he lifted the first switch, his ribs screamed in protest. He gritted his teeth, pushing through the pain, feeling that familiar rush. Pain was no longer just an inconvenience—it was becoming a companion, a force that kept him focused, sharp. And somewhere deep inside, he wondered how much further he could push himself before the line between pain and pleasure disappeared completely.

Chapter nine:

The weekend arrived, and Mike had survived his first week back in work, but conflicting emotions filled his mind. The lingering pain from his cycle crash gnawed at him, but so did the experience of working with "normal" people again. On Friday, he had received a message requesting a photo and a short introduction for the university bulletin. The sender, Mary, had an attractive profile picture, which piqued his interest.

Replying with a brief sentence about himself and his excitement to join the Physical Environment team, he thought nothing more of it until his phone rang later that evening. It was Mary. "Mike, I'd like to meet you in person on Monday. Can we arrange that?" she asked, a hint of coyness in her voice.

Curious and slightly amused, he agreed. "Sure, where and why?"

She hesitated before replying, "I just want to meet you personally."

Mike smirked. "Alright, Mary. See you Monday."

Chapter 10:

Monday morning arrived, and Mike was five minutes early, as always. He seated himself in the small café, positioning himself with a clear view of both the entrance and the exit. Old habits died hard.

As Mary walked in, he was stunned by her beauty. She was tall, around 5'8", with a perfectly proportioned body. Her face, youthful yet mature, made him estimate her age at forty, but her figure suggested she could be younger. She moved with grace and confidence, taking a seat opposite him and extending her hand.

"Morning, Mike," she said, her voice smooth and confident.

As he shook her hand, he noticed a small cut on her finger, fresh and still bleeding slightly. A shiver ran through him as he caught sight of the red trickle.

"What happened?" he asked, holding her delicate hand in his rougher grasp.

"Oh, it's nothing," she said with a smile, "I caught it on my keys on the way here. Will you pass me a tissue?"

As he handed her one, he caught the scent of her perfume—subtle, elegant—but beneath it, he smelled the distinct, metallic tang of blood. A perfect combination. Mary must have noticed something in his expression because she held up the tissue, now stained with crimson.

"Look at that—so much from such a tiny cut. Do you like it?" she teased, giving him a knowing smile.

Mike felt his pulse quicken. He was drawn in, mesmerized. Mary giggled, shifting slightly in her seat.

"So, Mike," she continued, "tell me—what are you really looking for here?"

The chemistry between Mike and Mary was undeniable. It was like two magnets drawn together, an invisible force that neither could resist. The moment she walked into the café, her presence charged the air. Her beauty was striking, but it was more than that—it was the way she carried herself, the confidence in her movements. As she sat down, their eyes locked, and something unspoken passed between them.

She noticed how Mike stared at her wounded finger, the small cut still bleeding slightly. "Does blood fascinate you?" she asked, tilting her head slightly. "You seemed... enthralled."

Mike hesitated, debating how much to reveal. "It's just... interesting. Blood is life, isn't it?"

Mary smirked, intrigued. "I've read that some people have a strong reaction to blood. A mix of fear, attraction, even hunger. Which one is it for you?"

Mike felt his pulse quicken. "Maybe a bit of all three."

Chapter Eleven:

As Mike parted ways with Mary, there was an unspoken promise between them—a drink later in the week. The chemistry was undeniable, a magnetic force neither could ignore. His thoughts lingered on her as he got stuck into a spreadsheet, scanning switches to record them as they were swapped out with new ones. The tedious task should have dulled his mind, but instead, it buzzed with anticipation.

Driving around campus in his van, collecting old switches, his eyes feasted on the endless display of youthful beauty. The university was alive with energy, the students exuding vibrance and innocence. Young, nubile girls strolled between lectures, laughter ringing out in the crisp air. He was in heaven.

Mike was deep in thought, his mind drifting as he drove across campus in the work van. The sudden, piercing scream snapped him out of it. Instinct took over. Slamming the brakes, he jumped out, his heart pounding as he approached the wreckage. A student's bike lay twisted under the front bumper of a shuttle bus. A pool of crimson seeped across the pavement.

A girl, barely in her twenties, was sprawled motionless by the roadside, her limbs at unnatural angles. Bystanders gasped, some reaching for their phones. Mike moved closer, his breath shallow, his pulse deafening in his ears. He could smell the blood. Coppery, raw, intoxicating. His fingers clenched involuntarily.

Was she dead?

Chapter Twelve

Mike knelt in the growing pool of blood, his hands pressing firmly against the deep wound on the girl's neck. The thick, crimson liquid pulsed between his fingers, warm and slick, seeping through his skin like an offering. He could feel the life draining from her, each weakening heartbeat pushing against his palm with decreasing strength.

His training kicked in—apply direct pressure, keep her airway clear, stay calm—but beneath the logic, something deeper stirred. The scent of blood filled his nostrils, sharp, metallic, intoxicating. It clung to him, to the air, thick and heavy like an iron fog. His pulse matched hers, slowing, fading. He swallowed hard, forcing himself to stay focused.

Around him, a silent crowd had gathered. Faces hovered above, some in horror, others in fascination, their wide eyes locked onto the scene unfolding before them. Students, professors, passersby—nobody moved to help. They stood frozen, useless, their breath misting in the cool air.

Then, the siren.

Its wail cut through the eerie quiet, distant but approaching fast. Mike turned his head slightly, catching a glimpse of flashing blue lights reflecting off glass buildings. It wouldn't be long now.

He looked back at the girl. Her eyes were half-lidded, lips slightly parted, her breath coming in short, shallow gasps. Blood loss. Shock. His fingers flexed involuntarily, feeling the weakening resistance of her body against his grip. He leaned closer, his own breath mixing with the smell of iron and fear.

"Stay with me," he murmured, unsure if she could even hear him.

The blood had slowed, no longer spurting, but oozing sluggishly between his fingers.

He knew what that meant. The body was shutting down, conserving what little remained. His hands were soaked, his sleeves stained, his jeans sticking to his knees from the spreading pool beneath him.

She was slipping away.

Mike felt something unexpected—a pang of disappointment.

His focus should have been on saving her, on holding her together until the medics arrived, but instead, a darker thought crept in, unbidden and undeniable. The sensation of blood on his hands, the warmth of it, the way it smelled, how it looked against pale skin—it filled him with something he couldn't name. A hunger? A longing?

A memory stirred. The battlefield. The smell of cordite and copper. The way blood splashed onto dirt, turning it into something primal, something real.

Was this so different?

He blinked, shaking the thought away. No. Not now.

The ambulance screeched to a halt, doors slamming open. A paramedic rushed toward him, dropping to his knees beside Mike. "We've got it from here," the man said, but

Mike barely heard him. He forced himself to release the girl, pulling his hands away slowly, reluctantly, as if breaking a connection that had already been forged.

As he backed away, his hands hovered in front of him, palms up, coated in red.

He stared at them.

And he licked his lips.

Chapter Thirteen:

The low hum of conversation filled the dimly lit bar, the scent of whiskey and perfume mingling in the air. Mike sat across from Mary in a corner booth, nursing a double Scotch, his fingers idly tracing the rim of the glass. The soft glow of candlelight flickered between them, casting shadows that danced over Mary's delicate features. She was watching him, her green eyes locked onto his, waiting for him to continue.

"So there I was," Mike said, his voice low, measured. "Kneeling in her blood, pressing down, trying to stop the bleeding. It was everywhere, on my hands, my jeans… even my shirt was soaked."

Mary's lips parted slightly, her fingers tightening around the stem of her wine glass. "Jesus, Mike," she breathed. "That must've been… intense."

He chuckled darkly. "That's one way to put it."

She leaned in, her body instinctively drawing closer. "And the girl? Did she—"

"She made it," he interrupted, swirling the amber liquid in his glass. "Barely. The paramedics took over just in time."

A moment of silence stretched between them, heavy and charged. Mary exhaled, as if she'd been holding her breath.

"That kind of thing stays with you," she said, her voice softer now, more intimate. "The smell, the feel of it… It doesn't just wash off, does it?"

Mike's gaze flickered up to hers, a knowing glint in his eye. "No. It doesn't."

Something passed between them then—an unspoken understanding. Mary studied him, the way his jaw clenched slightly, the way his fingers drummed against the table. She licked her lips, almost absentmindedly.

"Did it…" she hesitated, choosing her words carefully. "Did it excite you?"

Mike tilted his head, a slow smirk tugging at the corner of his mouth. "Would it bother you if it did?"

Mary's breath hitched, but she didn't look away. Instead, she reached for her glass, took a slow sip, and set it down deliberately. "No," she said finally, her voice barely above a whisper. "I don't think it would."

His pulse quickened. He hadn't expected her to react this way. Most people—most normal people—would have recoiled, would have tried to steer the conversation elsewhere. But not Mary. She was leaning in, intrigued, fascinated even.

"Blood is… intimate," she mused, tilting her head slightly. "It's life. It's death. And everything in between."

Mike exhaled through his nose, his grip tightening on his glass. "You're not like most people, are you, Mary?"

She smiled, slow and deliberate. "Neither are you."

The air between them crackled with something raw, something primal. Mary reached across the table, her fingers ghosting over his hand, smearing against the faint traces of dried blood beneath his nails.

"Come home with me," she said.

Mike didn't hesitate.

Chapter Fourteen:

The dim glow of the bedside lamp cast long, golden shadows across Mary's bare skin. She lay beneath Mike, her body slick with sweat, her breath coming in short gasps. Her fingers dug into his back, nails raking over old scars, her thighs wrapped tightly around his hips, keeping him locked against her.

Mike was lost in her, in the heat, in the way her body moved with his. He hadn't expected the night to unfold this way. Their conversation at the bar had simmered with something unspoken, something dangerous, but he hadn't thought—hadn't imagined—that Mary would take it there.

"God, you feel amazing," he groaned against her throat, his lips trailing a line of kisses along her pulse.

And then she said it.

"Go. Bite me."

His body tensed. He pulled back slightly, looking down at her, at the way her pupils had blown wide, dark pools of hunger.

"What?" he rasped, unsure if he had heard her right.

Mary arched against him, wrapping her arms around his shoulders. Her voice was more urgent this time, more demanding.

"Bite me, Mike. I want to feel it."

He almost fell off the bed. He pushed himself up onto his elbows, staring at her. The woman beneath him—the refined, self-possessed, almost delicate woman he had met just days ago—had transformed into something wild. Something feral.

"Mary," he started, shaking his head, but she was already pulling him back down, pressing her lips against his, her tongue sliding against his with reckless abandon.

"Do it," she whispered, nipping at his lower lip. "I want you to."

His pulse hammered against his ribs. He had played rough before, had let passion and adrenaline blur the lines between pleasure and pain. But this? This was different.

His mouth hovered over her throat. He could feel her pulse, hot and fast beneath his lips, taste the salt of her sweat on his tongue. His teeth grazed the sensitive skin, testing, teasing.

"Yes," Mary breathed, arching her neck, offering herself to him completely.

And something inside him snapped.

A deep, guttural growl rumbled from his chest as he sank his teeth into her flesh—not enough to break the skin, but enough to make her cry out. The sound sent a bolt of electricity through him. She liked it.

Mary's fingers fisted in his hair, holding him there, urging him deeper. "Harder," she begged.

He obliged.

The taste of her, the feel of her writhing beneath him, the raw, animalistic pleasure—it was intoxicating. He could feel his control slipping, feel the familiar hunger clawing at his insides.

His teeth pressed harder, his tongue darting over the small indentations he had left on her skin. The warmth of her, the scent of her, the surrender—it was almost too much.

Mary gasped, her body shuddering violently beneath him, her nails raking down his spine as she cried out his name.

Mike barely heard her.

All he could hear was the pounding of his own heart. All he could taste was the faint, metallic hint of blood.

Chapter Fifteen:

Mike lay on his back, staring at the ceiling, his breath still ragged, his body spent. Beside him, Mary curled into his side, her fingers lazily tracing the bite marks on his chest. The sheets beneath them were tangled, damp with sweat, and speckled with crimson where their passion had blurred into something primal. The air in the room was thick—sex, blood, and something darker still.

She sighed; her breath warm against his shoulder. "That was... something else."

Mike chuckled, though it came out as more of a rasp. His body ached in the best way possible. Every muscle burned, every nerve felt raw, but it was the dull throb of the bites and scratches that lingered, keeping him anchored in the moment. "Yeah," he murmured, running a hand over his face. "I think we might have ruined each other."

Mary laughed softly, a wicked, satisfied sound. "Isn't that the goal?"

She rolled onto her stomach, propping herself up on her elbows, gazing at him with a mixture of exhaustion and hunger. Her lips were swollen from his kisses, her throat marked with faint bruises where his teeth had claimed her. She looked wild, dangerous, and more beautiful than ever.

But even as they basked in the afterglow, Mike felt the familiar pull of the comedown creeping in. The high had been exhilarating, a rush unlike anything he had felt in years. But now? Now there was a void. The sharp edge of pleasure had dulled, leaving behind an ache that wasn't just physical.

Mary must have sensed it too, because she shifted closer, resting her chin on his chest. "Do you ever feel... empty after?" she asked, her voice quiet.

Mike exhaled slowly, threading his fingers through her hair. "Yeah. Every time."

She was silent for a moment, then tilted her head to look at him. "Then why do we do it?"

His lips curved into a smirk. "Because nothing else feels as good."

She smiled, but there was something contemplative in her eyes. "And how do we get there again?"

Mike knew what she meant. The peak they had reached—it was a dangerous one. It wasn't just the sex, the biting, the pain-turned-pleasure. It was the loss of control, the surrender to something primal and consuming. But how could they top it? How could they push further?

He ran his thumb over a small welt on her shoulder, watching the way her skin reddened beneath his touch. The thought sent a shiver down his spine.

"We take it further," he said finally, his voice steady but filled with something darker. "Push the limits. Find the next threshold."

Mary's breath hitched slightly, but her pupils dilated, excitement flickering across her face. "And what would that be?"

Mike smirked. "We'll find out."

She grinned, biting her lip. "I think I'm going to enjoy this."

He knew she would. But as the night deepened and the rush faded, Mike couldn't shake the feeling that once you crossed certain lines, there was no going back.

Chapter Sixteen:

Mike walked away from Mary's house just as the first hint of dawn tinged the sky with a deep violet hue. His shirt clung to his back, damp with sweat, and his muscles ached in places he hadn't even known could hurt. Every step sent tiny shocks of pain through his body, a lingering reminder of the hours spent wrapped in Mary's arms—of the lust, the pleasure, and the exquisite, biting pain.

He touched his lip, feeling the slight swelling where her teeth had broken the skin. He could still taste the faint copper tang of his own blood. The memory sent a shiver down his spine. The things they had done, the boundaries they had pushed past—it was intoxicating, addictive. And now, in the cold light of early morning, he felt the hunger stirring again.

Where could he find more of this? More of her? More of that?

His body was exhausted, but his mind raced. He needed something, some way to chase the high that was already slipping from his grasp. Would Mary be enough, or was she just the gateway to something deeper, something darker?

By the time he arrived at work, he was still lost in thought, his hands gripping the steering wheel tighter than necessary. He barely registered the hum of the van's engine as he drove around the vast, sprawling campus, running through the motions of his job. But his mind wasn't on switches or spreadsheets—it was on them. The students.

Everywhere he looked, there they were. Young, fresh, full of life. Unaware of how much they radiated energy, how their very existence taunted him. The way they moved, their laughter, their oblivious innocence—it stirred something in him, something he didn't quite understand but couldn't ignore.

His eyes lingered a little too long on their bare legs as they crossed campus in short skirts and tight jeans. The way they tossed their hair, the easy way they smiled. His thoughts drifted, images flashing in his mind—Mary writhing beneath him, her nails digging into his skin, her breath hot against his neck as she whispered, Harder, Mike. Bite me harder.

A sharp jolt of reality snapped him back.

A girl. Right in front of him.

Mike slammed on the brakes, the van lurching to a violent stop mere inches from the young woman who had just stepped onto one of the many zebra crossings scattered throughout the maze of roads and pavements.

For a moment, neither of them moved. The girl stood frozen, her eyes wide with shock, staring at him through the windshield. Mike's heart pounded, his pulse roaring in his ears. Then, slowly, her hand lifted to her face. When she pulled it away, her fingers were smeared with red.

A nosebleed.

Mike jumped out of the van, his body reacting before his mind had fully caught up. "Are you okay?" he asked, his voice hoarse.

The girl blinked at him, dazed, then looked at her bloodied fingers. She wasn't crying. She wasn't screaming. She was just staring, as if transfixed by the sight of her own blood.

Mike swallowed hard. His mouth felt dry. The scent of iron was in the air.

And all he could think about was how much he wanted to taste it.

Chapter Seventeen:

Mike reached out, steadying the girl by the elbow as she hesitated beside the open van door. "Let me take you to the campus medics," he said, his voice calm, measured. She looked at him, dazed, her eyes flickering between trust and uncertainty. Then, with a small nod, she climbed in.

The moment she settled onto the seat, another thick drop of blood slipped from between her fingers and splashed onto her bare thigh. Mike saw it glisten under the dim light filtering through the van's windshield, a vivid red against her pale skin. His throat went dry.

She sniffed sharply, wiping at her nose again, but the blood wouldn't stop. It dribbled over her upper lip, streaking her chin, trailing down her wrist, and dripping onto her white tank top, staining it in erratic, organic patterns.

Mike circled around the front of the van, his hands gripping the wheel tighter than necessary as he slid into the driver's seat. He took a steadying breath, but it did nothing to quell the pounding of his pulse.

"You okay?" he asked, forcing himself to focus on the road as he pulled away.

She let out a soft, breathy laugh, wiping her nose again. "Yeah. This always happens when I get shocked."

Mike flicked his eyes to her briefly before focusing back on the road. "You lose this much blood?"

She nodded; her voice slightly hoarse. "Yeah. Doctors say it's something with my blood vessels being weak. Stress makes them burst."

Another drop fell, splattering against her knee. Mike's gaze locked onto it before dragging his attention back to the road. His hands gripped the wheel so tightly his knuckles turned white.

She's bleeding for you.

The thought slipped unbidden into his mind, sending a jolt down his spine. He knew it wasn't true—this was just some fluke, some bizarre biological quirk. And yet, he couldn't shake the feeling that this was meant to happen.

He reached across to the glove box, blindly fumbling for the pack of tissues he kept there. When he finally grasped it, he pulled one free and handed it to her. "Here. Try tilting your head forward a bit. Pinch your nose."

She took the tissue with a small, grateful smile. "Thanks."

The blood seeped into the soft paper almost instantly, darkening it to a deep crimson. Her breath hitched slightly, and Mike could see the effort it took for her to keep calm. But she wasn't panicking. If anything, she seemed oddly resigned, as if this was just another inconvenience to endure.

As he pulled up to the medical building, she glanced down at herself, at the smears of blood on her thighs, the crimson stains on her shirt. She let out a breathy chuckle. "Damn. I must look like a horror movie extra."

Mike didn't respond. He couldn't. His tongue felt heavy, useless.

Because all he could think about was how beautiful she looked. How utterly mesmerizing the contrast of red on white, of warm liquid against soft skin, truly was.

And in that moment, he knew.

He was living the dream.

Chapter Eighteen:

Mike leaned in slightly, his hands wrapped around the cold pint glass, his fingers tracing absentminded circles against the condensation. Across from him, Mary sipped her wine, her eyes locked onto his, dark and full of unspoken hunger. The dim lighting of the bar flickered across her face, casting shadows that only deepened her intrigue.

"So there I was," he began, his voice low, deliberate, "sitting in the driver's seat, watching her press that tissue to her nose, but it wasn't stopping. It just kept coming. Thick, deep red drops rolling down her hand, her chin, then onto her legs."

Mary let out a sharp breath, shifting in her seat. She crossed her legs tightly, her fingers gripping the stem of her glass as if grounding herself. "And she wasn't panicking?"

Mike smirked, shaking his head. "Not at all. Said it happens when she's in shock. Just something in her body, weak blood vessels or something." He took another sip of his drink, eyes watching Mary's every reaction. "But the way it looked—those white thighs streaked with crimson, the way the blood shined under the light in the van—it was…" He trailed off, the corner of his mouth twitching as he watched her.

Mary swallowed, her lips parting slightly. "Beautiful?" she whispered.

Mike nodded slowly, holding her gaze. "Yeah. Beautiful."

She exhaled through her nose, shifting again, her grip tightening around the glass. He could see the pulse at the base of her throat quicken. Her cheeks had darkened, her pupils dilating ever so slightly. He knew exactly where her mind was going.

"Did she say anything else?" Mary asked, her voice breathy now, a slight edge of desperation woven into it.

Mike leaned back, stretching the moment, savouring it. "Just laughed about looking like something out of a horror film. But I don't think she realized… how stunning she looked, covered in it."

Mary pressed her thighs together beneath the table, her breathing slightly unsteady. She set her glass down and leaned forward, her fingers grazing over Mike's on the table. "We need to go," she murmured.

Mike arched an eyebrow. "Already?"

Her nails dug slightly into his skin. "Now," she insisted.

Without another word, they stood, abandoning their drinks. The night air hit them as they stepped out of the bar, but neither of them felt the chill. Mary practically dragged him down the street toward her flat, her heels clicking aggressively against the pavement.

The second the door shut behind them, she was on him, her lips crushing against his, her fingers threading into his hair. She bit his lower lip, hard enough to draw a bead of blood, and when she pulled back, she stared at it for a moment before swiping her tongue across it.

"Tell me more," she demanded.

Mike smirked, wiping the blood from his mouth with his thumb before pressing it to her lips. "How about I show you instead?"

She groaned, pulling him toward the bedroom. Tonight, would be another descent into pain and pleasure—one neither of them would ever come back from.

Chapter Nineteen:

Mike hovered over Mary, his arms trembling as he held himself up, his body slick with sweat. The metallic scent of blood filled the air between them, thick and intoxicating. A slow, warm trickle dripped from his split lip, landing onto her porcelain skin in dark, glistening droplets. She lay beneath him, her chest rising and falling with deep, erratic breaths, her pupils blown wide with desire.

She licked her lips as she felt the warm liquid trickle down her cheek. "More," she whispered, tilting her head slightly, exposing the elegant curve of her neck. "Give me more."

Mike's breath hitched. His lip throbbed from where she had bitten down with an almost inhuman force, sending an electric jolt through his body so powerful it had sent him over the edge. He had never felt anything like it—pain and pleasure so intertwined they had become indistinguishable.

Mary reached up, her crimson-painted nails trailing down his chest, leaving faint scratches in their wake. Her fingers trembled slightly, but her grip was firm, commanding. "Let's take it to the next level," she murmured, her voice husky with need.

From somewhere beneath the sheets, she produced a single razor blade, pinched delicately between her fingers. The gleaming metal caught the dim light, reflecting against the deep red polish on her nails. She held it between them, letting the anticipation settle, her eyes locked onto his.

Mike's pulse thundered in his ears, but he didn't move away. He wanted this. He needed this.

Slowly, Mary pressed the edge of the blade to his abdomen, just above his navel. She didn't apply pressure at first—just the mere contact sent a delicious chill across his skin. Then, with a calculated precision, she dragged it downward, opening him up in a thin, precise line.

For a moment, there was nothing. No pain. Just the sensation of cool air kissing the wound. Then, the first bead of blood surfaced, welling up and spilling over in a slow, mesmerizing crawl.

Mary exhaled sharply, her eyes widening in admiration. "Perfect," she breathed, running a fingertip through the crimson flow before bringing it to her lips. She moaned softly as the taste coated her tongue.

Mike still didn't feel the pain—not until the blood started pumping freely, warm and thick, spilling onto Mary's body in rich, splattering waves. It coated her breasts, trailed down her stomach, soaked into the already ruined sheets beneath them. She writhed under him, revealing in the sensation, painting herself with him.

His vision blurred for a moment, a sudden dizziness creeping into the edges of his mind. The loss of blood was more than he had anticipated. He needed to pace himself, to rehydrate—but how could he stop? How could he deny the sheer ecstasy of this moment?

Mary reached up, pulling him down to her, smearing the blood between their bodies as she pressed her lips against his once more. The taste of iron mingled between them, deepening the intoxication.

Mike groaned against her mouth. His limbs felt heavier now, his heartbeat slower. He didn't know how much blood they had lost, but it didn't matter. Not yet. There was still more to give.

Chapter Twenty:

Mike could still feel the dull ache in his limbs from the night before as he swung his leg over his bike and pushed off into the morning chill. Rest and recuperation—R&R, as he had always known it—was something he needed, but his body wouldn't allow him to stop. Not now. Not after what had happened with Mary. His mind raced as he pedalled down Derby Road, following his usual route toward the University.

The wind whipped past his face, sharp and bracing, but the lingering exhaustion from blood loss made him feel light, almost euphoric. He looked up just in time to catch the bright glow of a speed warning sign.

SLOW DOWN

He glanced at the digital readout: 32 MPH.

A thrill shot through him. The rush of speed, the risk, the adrenaline—it was waking him up, sharpening his senses. He squeezed the brakes, feeling the tension in his arms as he forced himself under the limit. His heart pounded hard, and he smiled to himself. He hadn't expected to get such a kick from something so simple.

When he arrived on campus, he secured his bike and made his way to the facilities office, collecting the keys for his small work van. As he approached the vehicle, he hesitated, gripping the key a little tighter. When he pulled open the driver's side door, the scent hit him instantly.

Blood.

It was faint now, but still there, woven into the fabric of the seat, mixed with the lingering scent of her perfume. He took a deep breath, steadying himself as a wave of dizziness washed over him.

Closing his eyes, he pictured Mary's face last night, her parted lips, the ecstasy in her eyes as she smeared his blood across her body. The sharp sting of the blade against his skin. The heat, the rush, the taste.

A horn blared behind him, jolting him back to reality. He shook himself off and climbed inside, pushing those thoughts to the back of his mind. He had work to do.

The drive to the Tower building on University Park campus was routine—until he saw her.

The girl from the other day.

She was standing at the zebra crossing, the same one where he had nearly run her down. This time, though, she wasn't in shock. She was watching him, waiting, her body poised as if she knew he would stop for her.

Mike slowed the van, allowing her to step out onto the crossing. She moved with a deliberate grace, long legs extending with every step, her hips swaying slightly as if she knew he was watching.

She does know.

His grip tightened on the wheel. A pulse of raw, unfiltered excitement coursed through him.

As she reached the other side, he instinctively rolled down his window.

"Need a lift anywhere?"

She stopped, tilting her head slightly as if considering it. Then, with a small smirk, she nodded and made her way around the van, opening the passenger door.

The moment she saw it—the dried blood staining the seat—she froze.

Mike held his breath.

She didn't recoil. Didn't frown. Instead, she smiled.

A slow, knowing smile that sent a shiver down his spine.

She stepped inside, closing the door behind her, and fastened her seatbelt. The movement only pushed her chest forward, and Mike struggled to keep his eyes on the road.

"How's the nosebleed?" he asked, forcing himself to sound casual.

"It's fine," she replied. Then, after a beat, "It excites me."

Mike turned to glance at her, his breath catching slightly. "The incident?"

"No." She met his gaze, a dark amusement flickering in her eyes. "The smell of blood. The look on your face when you saw it."

His fingers flexed against the gear stick. "Do you like blood?"

Her tongue flicked out to wet her lips. "I love it."

His pulse quickened.

"I like the taste," he admitted. "The smell."

"So do I."

She reached into her bag and pulled out a slip of paper, scrawling something on it before pressing it into his hand.

"Here's my number." She grinned. "We should talk later."

Mike swallowed hard, his body thrumming with anticipation as she climbed out of the van and walked toward the Cripps building, disappearing into the crowd.

He exhaled slowly, staring down at the number in his palm.

Blood. Lust. Hunger.

The night ahead was going to be interesting.

Chapter Twenty-one:

Mike sat in his dimly lit flat, swirling a glass of whiskey in his hand as he stared at the piece of paper in front of him. Amy. Her number was scribbled in neat handwriting, a small heart drawn beside it. He ran his thumb over the ink, thinking about the way she had looked at him in the van. The way she had smiled at the sight of her own blood.

He exhaled sharply, reaching for his phone. Mary. He needed to tell her. She had to be involved. This wasn't something he could keep from her, nor did he want to.

The phone rang twice before she answered.

"Mike." Her voice was smooth, but he could hear the underlying curiosity. "I wasn't expecting a call so soon."

"I met someone," he said, skipping the pleasantries. "Amy."

A pause. Then, "Who's Amy?"

"The student from the other day. The one with the nosebleed."

Mary inhaled sharply. "Oh?" Her voice held something between intrigue and jealousy. "And why are you telling me about her?"

Mike smirked. He could picture her now, curled up with a glass of red wine, already trying to work out where this was going.

"Because" he said, "I want you to meet her."

Silence. Then, the unmistakable sound of ice clinking against glass as she took a sip of her drink.

"You want me to meet a student?" she asked. "Mike, you do realize I'm old enough to be—"

"—Does that matter?" he cut in. "She's… different, Mary. She's like us."

That gave her pause.

Mike leaned back, stretching his legs out. "We're meeting in town tonight. A couple of drinks at Bodega. I want you to come."

Mary scoffed. "You think this is going to work? An older woman, a university staff member, and a young student? What exactly are you planning, Mike?"

He grinned, running his tongue over his teeth. "We'll find out later, won't we?"

Another pause. Then, finally, a low chuckle.

"What time?" she asked.

"21:00."

"Do you want me to act surprised when I walk in?"

"Yes. We'll take it from there. Might be a bloody night."

Mary hummed in approval. "Now that's the kind of invitation I like."

Mike ended the call, feeling the anticipation settle deep in his chest. The thought of the three of them together—Mary's confidence, Amy's youth and curiosity—sent a pulse of excitement through him.

Tonight was going to be something special. Something new.

Something dangerous.

Chapter Twenty-two:

Mike swirled his whiskey, the amber liquid catching the dim glow of the bar lights. His gaze never left Amy, who sat across from him, her fingers playing idly with the rim of her glass. She was stunning, her delicate features lit by the soft neon of the Bodega's ambiance. Her lips, slightly parted as she listened to the hum of the bar, looked as though they had been kissed by blood itself—full, ripe, and darkly inviting.

She had that look. That knowing look.

She wasn't just another pretty face. There was something about her, something familiar, something that called to him on a level beyond words. Beyond desire.

Then, a voice cut through the air.

"Well, well, fancy meeting you here."

Mike looked up as Mary approached the table, playing her part to perfection. Her expression was one of pleasant surprise, but her eyes—her hungry eyes—betrayed her excitement.

"Mary," Mike said, acting as if he hadn't expected to see her.

Mary's lips curled into a smile as she extended her hand toward Amy. "I'm Mary. And you are?"

Amy returned the handshake, her grip warm, firm. "Amy. Nice to meet you."

Mary's fingers lingered a second longer than necessary before she let go, tilting her head ever so slightly as she took in the girl before her. She's like us, Mary thought. But what did that mean? What exactly were they?

Mike saw it. The silent moment of recognition between the two women. It was in the way Mary's pupils dilated ever so slightly as she sat down, the way Amy's breath hitched for just a second as their eyes met.

There was a connection forming, something unspoken but undeniable.

Mary signalled for a drink, keeping her body angled toward Amy as she spoke. "So, what brings you out tonight?"

Amy took a slow sip from her glass before answering. "Curiosity."

Mary smiled at that. "Curiosity about what?"

Amy let her gaze flicker to Mike, then back to Mary. "You tell me."

A slow shiver crawled up Mike's spine. This was happening. Really happening.

As Mary took her seat beside Amy, she felt something stir inside her. An emotion. A pull. A deep, dark connection. But what was it?

Was it desire? Lust? Something more primal?

What did the love of blood make them?

A word danced on the edges of Mary's mind, whispering to her like a secret she had always known but never spoken aloud.

Predators.

She met Mike's gaze, then Amy's. She could see it reflected in both of them—the hunger, the need, the understanding.

Whatever they were, whatever this was, there was no going back now.

Chapter Twenty-three:

The tension between them was electric as they stepped out of the Bodega, the cool night air doing little to dissipate the heat that had built between them. Amy led the way, her confidence intoxicating as she walked with purpose through the dimly lit streets, her heels clicking softly against the pavement. Mary followed close behind, eyes flicking between Amy's slender frame and Mike's composed yet simmering presence beside her.

Mike still couldn't believe it. This wasn't something he had planned—wasn't something he could have planned. And yet, here he was, walking toward the unknown with two women who shared a desire that had only recently begun to take shape in his mind.

Amy had surprised him. A biomedical scientist, of all things. A future haematologist. The irony was almost too perfect. She studied blood. Lived for it. Wanted to understand its secrets. Mike, on the other hand, had no scientific curiosity about it—his fascination was raw, primal, instinctual.

"You never told me," Mike said, breaking the silence as they walked. "That you were a scientist. That you study blood for a living."

Amy glanced at him with a smirk, her dark eyes gleaming under the streetlights. "You never asked."

Mary chuckled lowly. "Fate, then?"

Amy shrugged. "Maybe. Or maybe blood just has a way of bringing people together."

Mike felt his pulse quicken at her words. There was something different about Amy— something beyond her beauty, her intelligence. She wasn't just playing along; she was leading them somewhere deeper, somewhere darker.

They arrived at Amy's flat—a small, modern place on the edge of the city centre. She unlocked the door with practiced ease, stepping inside and tossing her bag onto a nearby chair. She turned back to face them, biting her lower lip as she reached for the buttons of her coat.

"Drinks first," she said, her voice smooth but charged with anticipation.

Mary and Mike stepped inside, and the door closed behind them with a soft click.

Amy disappeared into the kitchen, leaving Mike and Mary standing in the warm glow of the living room. Mary leaned against the back of the couch; her eyes heavy-lidded as she watched Mike.

"She's something else, isn't she?" Mary murmured.

Mike exhaled slowly, nodding. "Yeah. She is."

Amy returned, a bottle of red wine in one hand, three glasses in the other. She poured generously, then raised her glass.

"To new experiences," she said, her eyes lingering on both of them.

Mary grinned, clinking her glass against Amy's before turning to Mike. "And to blood sports."

Amy took a slow sip, watching them over the rim of her glass. Then she set it down and took a deep breath.

"I don't just study blood," she said, her voice quieter now. "I crave it."

Mike's fingers tightened around his glass.

Mary's pupils dilated, her tongue flicking across her lips.

"Then let's not waste any more time," she whispered.

Chapter Twenty-four:

The atmosphere in Amy's dimly lit bedroom was thick with anticipation. The wine glasses sat forgotten on the bedside table, their contents barely touched. The real intoxication came from something deeper, something far more primal than alcohol.

Amy, Mary, and Mike stood together by the bed, the soft glow of the bedside lamp casting shadows that danced across their bare skin. The sterile steel of the surgical knife gleamed as Amy held it between her fingers, her lips slightly parted in fascination.

"This is… different," she murmured, tracing the blade lightly against her own forearm.

Not enough to cut—just enough to feel the cold kiss of steel against her skin.

Mike and Mary exchanged a glance. They had to ease her in, not overwhelm her. She was new to this—new to their world, their desires. They didn't want to scare her away.

Mary stepped forward first, offering her own arm to Amy, her expression soft but urging. "Here. Start small."

Amy hesitated for only a second before pressing the tip of the blade to Mary's forearm. A delicate nick, barely enough to break the skin, but enough for a bead of red to surface. Amy sucked in a breath, transfixed.

"Good girl," Mary whispered, shivering as Amy ran a curious finger through the droplet of blood.

Mike watched, his own hunger growing. The sterile preparation—the autoclaved blade, the clean method—it was almost clinical, and for a moment, he missed the raw, feral thrill. But Amy was still learning. They had to guide her.

His turn.

He stretched out his arm, offering it wordlessly. Amy met his gaze, a silent question in her eyes. He nodded, and she pressed the blade down, just a little deeper than before. A slow line of crimson bloomed against his skin, and he exhaled sharply as the heat of the sting spread.

Amy's pupils dilated as she dipped her tongue to the wound, tasting him for the first time. Sweet. Metallic. She moaned softly, the sound vibrating against his skin.

That was all it took

The three of them moved together, a tangle of limbs and breath and urgent touches. The blade passed between them, carving tiny paths of pleasure and pain. Small cuts. Precise. Measured.

Mary gasped as Mike bit into her shoulder, teeth sinking just deep enough to bruise but not break skin. She arched beneath him, her body slick with the mixture of sweat and the thin sheen of blood that streaked their bodies.

Amy was purring, her moans turning into soft whimpers as Mary pressed her lips to the shallow cut on Amy's collarbone, suckling at the fresh wound.

Then—Amy shattered first, her climax tearing through her in a high-pitched squeal as her body trembled against them. The sound pushed Mary over the edge, her own release following swiftly, her fingers digging into Mike's back.

Mike gritted his teeth as the pleasure built, his muscles tensing, his breath ragged. The scent of blood, the heat of their bodies, the wet friction—it was too much. He came with a juddering groan, his body finally releasing its pent-up hunger.

They collapsed in a heap, their bodies slick with sweat, streaked with red, the mattress protector beneath them stained with the evidence of their indulgence.

Silence.

Then—soft laughter.

Amy turned her head to look at them both, her lips still smeared with crimson.

"I think," she murmured, "I'm going to like this."

Chapter Twenty-five:

The air was thick with the scent of sweat, blood, and satisfaction. The mattress beneath them was warm, sticky, and stained—a testament to the night they had just shared. Mike lay on his back, his chest rising and falling as he stared at the ceiling.

Mary was curled up on one side of him, tracing lazy circles on his skin, while Amy was on the other, propped up on an elbow, her eyes shining with excitement.

They had gone beyond pleasure and pain. This was something else. Something deeper.

"We need to talk about this," Amy finally said, breaking the silence.

Mary laughed softly, stretching her limbs. "Talk about what, darling? The fact that we just had the most incredible, bloody, mind-altering night of our lives?" She licked her lips, still tasting the remnants of Mike and Amy on her tongue.

Amy shook her head. "No, I mean… how do we make this work?"

Mike turned his head toward her, intrigued. "What do you mean?"

Amy sat up, hugging her knees to her chest. The dawn light was creeping through the curtains now, casting a soft glow on her bare skin. "I mean… we can't just keep this between the three of us forever. There have to be more people like us. People who understand."

Mary's eyes sparkled with amusement as she shifted closer. "Are you saying you want to recruit?"

Amy grinned. "I know people at uni who would love this."

Mike's interest piqued. "People who are into… what? Blood? Pain? The pleasure of it all?"

Amy nodded, excitement evident in her expression. "I study biomedical sciences, remember? My circle is full of people who are obsessed with blood. Some in an academic sense, sure, but others… I've heard them talk. The fascination is there. Some just don't know how to explore it."

Mary shivered in delight. "More people like us." She let the words roll off her tongue, savouring them. Then, a thought struck her, and she wiggled in place, eyes glinting. "We could form a society."

"A group?" Mike raised an eyebrow.

"Yes," Amy said quickly. "A private, exclusive society. Where we can be ourselves. Where we can indulge."

Mary giggled. "What do we call it?"

Mike smirked, running a hand through his messy hair. "The Blood Spurts."

Amy tilted her head. "Like… 'blood spurts' as in actual blood spurts? Or are we playing with words here?"

Mike chuckled mischievously. "Like 'experts'—but in blood. Ex-perts."

Mary let out a delighted laugh. "I love it."

Amy nodded, a wicked smile playing on her lips. "Then it's settled. We start with careful recruitment. People we trust. We don't want just anyone involved."

"Agreed," Mike said, already picturing what this could become. The idea of a growing pack of predators sent a thrilling shiver down his spine.

The first light of morning filtered through the window, signalling that their night of indulgence was over—for now.

Mike groaned as he sat up, stretching his sore limbs. "I should get going. I need sleep before work."

Mary smirked. "You need blood before work."

He grinned, leaning down to kiss her. Then, turning to Amy, he ran his fingers along the fading cut on her collarbone. "Text me later. Let me know if you have any candidates."

Amy licked her lips, nodding. "Oh, I will."

As Mike left, he felt a rush of anticipation. The Blood Spurts were born, and soon, they would hunt together.

Chapter Twenty-six – The First Gathering

The coffee shop buzzed with the usual sounds of steaming milk, chattering students, and the occasional grind of beans. To any outsider, the seven people sitting around the corner table looked like just another group of university friends meeting for a casual study session. But beneath the surface, an electric current of anticipation crackled between them.

Mike stirred his coffee, feeling a little out of place. He wasn't a student. He wasn't part of their world of lectures, assignments, and late-night cram sessions. He was older, more experienced, and as he looked around at the five new faces, he realized just how young they all were. He didn't feel old often, but tonight, sitting among them, listening to their introductions, he felt like a relic from another life.

Mary, ever the smooth talker, leaned forward, her presence commanding the attention of the table. "So," she began, her voice rich and inviting, "I know Amy has already given you all a little insight into what we're about, but let's make this official. First names only." She smiled, flicking her gaze between them. "Let's get to know each other a little before tonight."

The first girl, a tall brunette with sharp cheekbones and piercing blue eyes, shifted in her seat and smiled. "Jane," she said simply, tucking a strand of hair behind her ear. "I study psychology. I've always been fascinated by... the boundaries people are willing to push."

Next to her, a petite blonde with a soft, almost innocent face spoke up. "Debbie," she said, her voice barely above a whisper. "Biomedical sciences, like Amy. I suppose I've always been drawn to the visceral."

The third girl, Sue, had an edge to her— dyed black hair, dark lipstick, and an expression that was hard to read. "Philosophy," she said coolly. "And... I like to experiment."

Mary grinned approvingly before turning to the two men.

John was a lean, wiry guy with glasses that sat slightly crooked on his nose. He gave a half-smirk. "Engineering," he said. "I like figuring out how things work. Bodies are just another machine, right?"

Mark, the final addition, exuded confidence. He had the athletic build of someone who spent time in the gym but carried himself like he didn't care much about it. "Medicine," he said, his deep voice steady. "Blood doesn't bother me. It fascinates me."

Amy was practically glowing with excitement. "See?" she said, turning to Mike and Mary. "I told you I had good instincts."

Mary leaned back in her chair, running a finger along the rim of her cup. "I like this group," she admitted. "You all seem eager, curious, hungry."

A pause. The word hungry lingered in the air between them, shifting the mood from playful intrigue to something darker.

"Shall we?" Mary asked, standing up.

The others followed, exchanging glances filled with anticipation. The coffee shop's warmth faded as they stepped out into the cold evening air, but the energy between them only intensified.

The hotel was close—just a short walk down the street. A neutral ground for the night's initiation. None of them knew exactly how things would unfold, but that was part of the thrill.

As they reached the entrance, Jane exhaled slowly, breaking the silence. "So," she murmured, her voice carrying a hint of both amusement and nerves. "How does this all… start?"

Mike smirked. They were about to find out.

Chapter Twenty-seven – The Morning After

The dim morning light crept through the thin curtains of the hotel suite, illuminating the remnants of the night's dark indulgence. The air was thick with the metallic scent of blood mixed with the stale aroma of sweat and lust. Bodies lay sprawled across the sheets—some tangled together, others draped over chairs or resting on the floor. No one had noticed the time passing. No one cared.

Until the scream.

It tore through the air like a razor blade, shrill and full of raw terror. Mike shot upright, his heart instantly racing. For a split second, confusion clouded his thoughts, but the sound of Amy's voice brought him crashing back to reality.

"Oh my God! Oh my God! No… NO!" Amy stood frozen in the doorway to the bathroom, her hands trembling as they barely covered her horrified eyes.

Mary, groggy but alert, was the first to react. "Amy? What's wrong?" she gasped, grabbing the bedsheet to cover her nakedness as she staggered toward the girl.

"I can't…" Amy sobbed, her body shuddering violently. "I can't look… it's… Debbie… oh God… she's dead."

The word dead echoed around the room like a gunshot. Everyone jolted upright, their eyes wide, fear replacing the euphoria from the night before.

Mike was next to move, crossing the room in two strides. He grabbed Amy gently by the shoulders and pulled her back. "Let me see."

Reluctantly, Amy let him guide her away from the door. She collapsed against the wall, shaking uncontrollably.

Mike turned his head and looked inside.

The sight nearly made him retch.

Debbie was lying in the bathtub, naked and pale—unnaturally pale. Blood coated the white porcelain, smeared in handprints and streaks, some of it dried, some still wet. Her wrists were sliced deep, to the bone, but that wasn't what caught Mike's attention. Her throat—her throat had been opened, a wide, jagged gash that nearly severed her head from her body.

He staggered back, bile rising in his throat. "Jesus Christ…"

Mary was behind him now, peering over his shoulder. Her face drained of colour as she took in the scene. "No… no, no, no… this wasn't… we didn't do this…" she whispered. "We didn't go that far."

One by one, the others gathered, unable to stop themselves from looking. Jane gasped, turning away to vomit. John sat down hard on the floor, staring blankly. Mark just stood there, his mouth opening and closing but no words coming out.

"What the fuck happened?" Mike growled, his brain racing to process what he was seeing. "She was fine last night. We were all… fine."

Amy was still sobbing. "I woke up and… I couldn't find her. I… I thought she went to the bathroom… I didn't… I didn't expect…" Her voice broke.

"Did anyone… did anyone hear anything?" Mary asked, her voice trembling. No one answered.

The reality of the situation slammed into them all at once. This wasn't the game anymore. This wasn't their fantasy world of controlled pain and pleasure. Someone— one of them—had crossed the line.

Mike's eyes darted between each face in the room. "Nobody leaves. Do you hear me? Nobody. We figure this out before anyone calls the police."

"But… she's dead, Mike," Jane whispered. "We have to call someone."

Mike shook his head. "Not yet. Not until we know what happened. If the cops show up and see this… they'll think it was all of us. We're all covered in blood."

Silence.

The game was over.

The nightmare had begun.

Chapter Twenty-Eight – The Debrief

The atmosphere in the hotel suite was suffocating, heavy with fear, guilt, and confusion. The once passionate playground had transformed into a crime scene. Blood was no longer an aphrodisiac; it was death staring them all in the face. Debbie's body remained where they'd found it, the bathroom door now shut but still looming in everyone's minds.

Mary stood in the centre of the room, wrapped in the hotel's white bathrobe, which now seemed painfully inappropriate—pure white against the crimson stains that painted their night. Her face was hard, composed, and cold, like a teacher about to scold unruly children. She was in control now, or at least trying to be.

"Right," she snapped, her voice slicing through the tense silence. "We need to talk. Properly. If we don't figure this out, we're all fucked."

No one argued. No one even breathed.

Mary's eyes scanned the group—Jane, pale and shaking; John, silent and shell-shocked; Amy, sitting on the floor hugging her knees; Mark, staring at the carpet like it held the answers. And Mike, leaning against the wall, arms crossed tightly, his jaw clenched.

"Who was the last one with Debbie?" she asked, direct and firm. "I need the truth. No bullshit."

Mark cleared his throat, his voice weak. Slowly, he raised his hand like a guilty schoolboy. "Me," he said, barely audible. "I… I was with her. We were experimenting—cutting… shallow stuff. Nothing serious. She was… laughing, joking. Then she said she wanted a bath, to wash off, relax. That was it."

Mary's eyes narrowed. "And you just let her go?"

Mark nodded. "Yeah. I mean… we'd done everything by the book. Clean blades, controlled. I thought she was fine." He shook his head, his eyes full of regret. "She kissed me before she left. Said she needed a moment."

"Did anyone go in after her?" Mary demanded, scanning the room again.

Silence.

"No one?"

Heads shook slowly. No one could meet her gaze.

"Alright then," Mary sighed, rubbing her temples. "Could she have… done this herself?"

Jane let out a choked sob. "Why would she? She seemed so happy. She was loving it… the whole thing. She said this was the best night of her life."

Mike finally spoke, his voice low and measured. "You ever think maybe that was the problem?" He looked up at the group, his eyes hard. "Sometimes when you hit the peak, there's nowhere else to go. Maybe she… didn't want to come down."

"Or," John croaked, "maybe someone followed her in. Finished her off while we were all too drunk or too high on adrenaline to notice."

The suggestion hung in the air like a noose.

Mary took a deep breath. "Let's think. The cuts on her wrists… clean, controlled. But the throat? That was rage… or desperation. Could she have done it herself?"

Amy shook her head. "I study this shit. The angle… the depth… no way she did that on her own. You pass out from blood loss before you can finish a cut like that. Someone did it. One of us."

The words were out now. No taking them back.

Mike's fists clenched. "We need to know the truth. Because if the cops show up and figure out one of us is lying… we all go down."

The room fell silent again, every person lost in their own mind, replaying the night, wondering what they missed—or what they were capable of.

Mary's voice broke the silence one last time. "We're not leaving. Not until we figure this out."

Chapter Twenty-Nine – The Who Dunnit

The hotel suite felt smaller, suffocating, as the hours dragged on. No one had left. No one could leave. Not with Debbie's body still in the bathroom, not with the sickening uncertainty hanging in the air. Someone in the room was responsible, but who?

Mike ran a hand through his hair, his mind spinning. He had been with Debbie at one point, but so had Mark. And Amy. Especially Amy.

Amy, who had been Debbie's close friend.

Amy, who had been her casual lover.

Amy, who had been playing with her that night.

Mike glanced at her now. She sat curled up on the couch, arms wrapped tightly around herself, her usually bright eyes clouded with something unreadable. Was it grief? Or something darker?

Mark, on the other hand, looked completely wrecked. His hands trembled slightly as he picked at the fabric of his jeans, his face pale, his foot tapping anxiously against the floor. Mike could see the self-doubt in his expression, the silent questioning—Could I have done this?

But the same doubt sat in Mike's own chest, like a slow poison seeping through him. His memories of the night were hazy, blurred by the bloodlust, the adrenaline, the rush of pleasure and pain. He remembered being with Debbie, felt her warm skin against his, the sting of tiny cuts tracing along his arms. She had been vibrant, alive—so how had she ended up cold and lifeless on the bathroom floor?

Then there was Amy.

She hadn't done anything out of the ordinary. Or had she?

Mike tried to replay their interactions, searching for something—anything—that stood out.

Nothing.

Nothing, except…

A look.

A glance exchanged between Debbie and Mark. A fleeting thing, so quick it could have been imagined. But now, in hindsight, it nagged at him.

"What was that look?" Mike asked suddenly, his voice breaking the silence.

Mark's head snapped up, his expression confused. "What look?"

"You looked at Debbie at one point—when she shuddered, like something hurt. It wasn't just the usual pain-play. I saw it. You looked… I don't know, different."

Amy stiffened. "I saw it too," she murmured.

All eyes turned to Mark, who swallowed hard. His gaze darted around the room as if searching for an escape, but there was none.

"I—" He hesitated, his fingers clenching into fists. "It wasn't anything. I swear. We were just… pushing limits, you know? She wanted that. She liked the pain."

"But did she ask for more than she could handle?" Mary asked, her voice sharp.

Mark's jaw tightened. "I don't know." His voice was barely a whisper now. "She said she was fine. That she could take it. She wanted to feel everything." He looked up, pleading. "You all know what that's like, right?"

They did.

They all did.

Pain and pleasure had intertwined for all of them. But this—this wasn't just about playing. Someone had taken it too far.

Mary folded her arms. "Let's be honest here. If Debbie really was into pushing limits, if she wanted to feel everything— what if she wanted to go further? What if she asked someone to take her past the point of no return?"

Silence.

Amy spoke next; her voice strained. "She told me once, ages ago, that she wondered what it would feel like to almost die. To get so close that she could feel it hovering over her."

Mike's stomach twisted.

"She wanted to flirt with death," Amy continued, her expression haunted. "But this… this isn't flirting."

"She was murdered," Mary stated flatly. "Whether she asked for it or not."

The weight of the words crashed down on them.

Mike felt his hands curl into fists. He needed answers. Now.

And there were only five possible suspects in the room.

Chapter Thirty – Outside the Box

Mary paced the suite, her heels clicking on the cheap hotel carpet, the sound echoing like a metronome of her growing suspicion. Everyone else sat frozen, caught in their own heads, but Mary's mind raced. Something wasn't right.

They were all looking inward—pointing fingers, drowning in guilt—but what if the danger had come from outside?

She stopped abruptly. Had someone else entered the suite that night?

Her eyes swept the room. The front door was locked now, but it had been wide open during their chaotic night. People coming and going, the line between reality and fantasy blurred by blood and lust. Any one of them could have left it ajar. Anyone could've wandered in, unseen, unheard.

"We're missing something," Mary said suddenly, her voice startling everyone. "What if it wasn't any of us? What if… someone else came in?"

The group stared at her, silent.

"There's no way," Mark muttered, rubbing his temples. "We'd have seen—"

"Would we?" Mary cut him off. "Think about it. The state we were in? High on adrenaline, half out of our minds? Anyone could've walked in."

Mike nodded slowly. The thought had flickered through his mind, but hearing Mary voice it sent a chill down his spine.

"I want to know if there's CCTV," she continued, looking toward Amy. "You booked this place, right? What do you know about their security?"

Amy shook her head, her face pale. "It's just a cheap hotel. I didn't even think about it. There might be cameras… maybe in the hallway or reception?"

Mary scanned the room again, her gaze lingering on the large mirror above the dresser. It was too big, too perfectly placed. Something about it itched at her instincts.

"What if there's a camera in the room?" she said aloud. "I've read about those perv hotels—cameras behind mirrors, recording people for sick thrills."

The idea sparked immediate discomfort.

"Jesus," Mike whispered. "You think… someone's been watching?"

"Maybe," Mary said. She approached the mirror cautiously, her reflection staring back at her. "You know how to check?"

Amy stood, joining her. "Yeah. You put your finger against the glass. If there's a gap between your finger and the reflection, it's a normal mirror. If there's no gap… it's two-way."

Mary placed her finger against the cool surface. Her breath caught. There was no gap.

"Fuck," she hissed, stepping back. "It's two-way."

Panic rippled through the group.

"What does that mean?" Jane asked, her voice trembling.

"It means," Mary growled, "someone could have been watching. Maybe still is."

Mike's stomach turned. The blood, the games, the pleasure—it had all been recorded? Worse… Debbie's death might be on tape.

"We need to find the hotel manager," Mary said, her voice steely. "We need that footage, and we need it now."

For the first time since the night began, there was a glimmer of hope. Maybe the killer wasn't in the room. Maybe the truth was hidden behind that mirror—or caught by a camera none of them had seen.

And maybe… just maybe… they still had a chance to uncover it.

Chapter Thirty-one – Seeds of Doubt

Mike sat silently on the worn hotel armchair, his mind swirling as everyone argued around him. The room, once charged with erotic excitement and taboo thrills, now felt cold, heavy with the weight of death. But as his mind ran back over the events of the night, a dark thought kept gnawing at him—Amy had planned it all.

She was the common thread—the spark that lit this twisted fire. It was Amy who had first teased him at the zebra crossing, Amy who had drawn Mary into the mix, and Amy who had gathered her friends—Debbie included—for this night of blood and lust. And now… Debbie was dead.

Mike couldn't stop replaying Amy's face from earlier, that strange glint in her eyes as she talked about blood, about her fascination with haematology, about bringing others into their "society." She had been so calm after Debbie's body was discovered, almost too calm. No tears, no real panic—just that unreadable look. Was it shock… or satisfaction?

His stomach churned. What if Amy had planned this the whole time?

She'd chosen the hotel. She'd booked the suite. She was the one with the medical knowledge, the understanding of how far you could push a body, how deep you could cut before it turned fatal. She'd known. She'd known. And that mirror… Mike shivered, recalling the moment Mary pressed her finger against the glass and revealed its true nature—a two-way mirror, likely hiding a camera.

Who else could have arranged that? The hotel staff? Maybe. But the more Mike thought about it, the less likely it seemed that a random employee would risk filming something like this. No, it had to be someone who knew what would happen. Someone who set the stage for it.

Amy.

The idea horrified him, but it also made a twisted sort of sense. She knew her friends—knew their curiosities, their weaknesses. She'd lured them here with promises of dark pleasures. Had she known someone would break? Had she wanted it? Maybe she needed it—to see where the line truly was. A bloodlust masked as science; curiosity laced with cruelty.

But how could he prove it? Mike's jaw clenched. Accusing Amy without evidence would tear the group apart—and if he was wrong, it could turn her, and Mary, against him. Still, he couldn't shake the feeling.

He needed to check the hotel records, find out who requested the room, ask if any equipment had been delivered. Were there extra wires leading to the mirror? Had Amy arrived earlier that day under some excuse, giving her time to set everything up?

Mike stared at Amy as she talked softly to Mary, their heads close together. Was she confessing? Plotting? Laughing? He couldn't tell. But he did know one thing—he had to act fast. If Amy was behind this, she wouldn't stop. Debbie's death might have been a test, a first act in something darker.

He rose slowly, feeling the weight of his decision. He needed help, but not from the group. This called for someone outside—a detective, maybe. Or… a private investigator. Someone to follow Amy, dig into her past, her studies, her friends.

Because if Amy was the predator… Mike was already caught in her web.

Chapter Thirty-two – Schemes

Mary sat cross-legged on the corner of the hotel suite's king-sized bed, a glass of cheap white wine in hand, staring across at Amy, who was still dabbing at her eyes with a tissue. The suite felt suffocating now, the lingering scent of blood mingling with stale sweat and the metallic tang of fear. The thrill of the night had turned into a nightmare no one could wake from.

"Who do you think did that to Debbie?" Amy's voice trembled, breaking the heavy silence. She sniffled, wiping another tear that Mary wasn't sure was real. Amy's face was a picture of concern, her lower lip trembling, mascara running in perfect smudges down her cheeks. A performance? Mary couldn't tell, but something about Amy's grief didn't sit right.

Mary took a long sip of her wine, buying time. She had seen Amy's glances throughout the night, noticed the way she'd watched Mark and Debbie—especially when things had turned darker, rougher. Pushing boundaries, Mary thought. Testing limits.

"You were closest to her, Amy," Mary finally replied, her voice steady. "What do you think happened?"

Amy shook her head, letting out a choked sob. "I… I don't know. We were all… so caught up in it. But… Mark. I think it was Mark." Her voice lowered as she said his name, almost like she was afraid of speaking it too loudly, afraid he'd hear even across the suite.

Mary arched an eyebrow. "Mark? Why?"

Amy leaned in, her eyes darting around the room as if someone might be listening. "I watched them. Early on… before it got messy… Mark was pushing her. Hard. She wasn't into it, not really. You know when someone's just putting on a brave face? She did that. For him." Amy's voice wavered but there was steel beneath the tears now.

Mary considered her words. She'd noticed it too—Debbie had looked uncomfortable at times, but hadn't said a word. It was a fine line, wasn't it? Between pain and pleasure. Between consensual and… murder.

Amy pressed on, almost eager now. "I think… I think he followed her into that bathroom. Maybe she tried to cool off, get away… but he… he couldn't stop." Amy's breath hitched, her performance flawless, but Mary's eyes narrowed.

"Are you sure, Amy?" Mary asked carefully. "Because once this gets out… there's no going back. That's a serious accusation."

Amy nodded fiercely, fresh tears streaking her face. "I know what I saw. He was… obsessed with her. Maybe he didn't mean to go that far. Maybe it just… happened. But it was him."

Mary stayed quiet, watching Amy fall apart. But something in her gut twisted. Too clean, too perfect. The timing, the tears, the scapegoating. If Amy had planned this, Mark was the perfect fall guy. Aggressive, eager, reckless—it wouldn't be hard to make everyone believe it.

Still… it made sense. Mark had been intense, angry almost. But was that enough?

"Alright," Mary finally said, voice calm and commanding. "We don't say a word—yet. We play it cool. If Mark did this… he'll slip up. Guilt always shows itself, eventually."

Amy nodded, sniffling, but her eyes gleamed as she wiped her cheeks dry. "Okay… okay. But Mary? If we don't deal with him… he might do it again."

Mary smiled thinly. "One step at a time, Amy. First, we watch. Then… we decide what to do."

As Amy leaned back against the headboard, seemingly exhausted, Mary's mind raced. What game are you playing, Amy? she thought. And am I already too deep to get out?

The blood wasn't done spilling yet. Not by a long shot.

The room fell silent the moment John's voice echoed off the walls, snapping everyone from their dazed states. Sue blinked, turning slowly toward him, her face unreadable, while Jane barely flinched, as if his sudden outburst failed to pierce the fog clouding her mind. John's words, however, lingered in the air — sharp, logical, undeniable. The camera footage. How had they all forgotten something so obvious?

Mike felt the adrenaline kick in as the pieces started falling into place. "He's right," he muttered, half to himself, before scrambling to his feet. He tugged on his shirt with shaking hands and turned to Amy. "Get dressed. Now. We need that footage. It's the only way we're going to make sense of any of this."

Amy nodded mutely, her face pale. The events of the night had taken their toll, but this new direction — an action, a plan — seemed to give her something to cling to. She moved quickly, pulling on her jacket as Mike stormed toward the door.

Sue remained seated, her eyes narrowing slightly as she followed Mike's movements. All night she had been silent, her mind ticking over every word, every glance exchanged between the group. The philosopher of the group — that's how they'd always seen her — content to watch, to consider every angle before speaking. But something about John's reaction gnawed at her. Calm, collected, and then… explosive. Was it frustration, or something else?

Jane still sat frozen, arms folded tightly, eyes unfocused. She had studied human behaviour for years, could read a lie in the smallest twitch of a muscle, but now her knowledge offered her no comfort. She couldn't trust herself, not after what had happened. Not after what they'd found. The footage — it would show the truth, raw and unfiltered. It might even tell her what her own mind refused to process.

John paced near the window now, running a hand through his hair, as if his own outburst startled him more than anyone else. "We've wasted hours," he muttered. "Arguing. Pointing fingers. The answer was here the whole damn time." He stopped, staring hard at the floor. "Unless someone's already wiped it."

The words hung heavy, the implication sinking in. If the footage was gone, then someone in that room had already thought of it — someone who wasn't interested in the truth. Mike caught John's gaze and nodded grimly. "Then we'll know soon enough."

Sue finally stood, her voice calm but edged with something new — a quiet warning. "We're all going," she said. "Together. No one splits off. No one gets near that footage alone."

Jane stirred, her voice barely above a whisper. "You really think it's one of us?"

No one answered. They didn't have to. The silence spoke louder than words.

Mike swallowed hard and opened the door. "Let's find out."

And with that, the group moved as one —
fractured, suspicious, but bound by the
same desperate need for answers.

Chapter Thirty-two – Eyes in the Walls

The suite was eerily quiet as the group
began dressing, their movements slow,
methodical, like a funeral procession rather
than a group who had shared a night of dark
pleasure just hours before. The adrenaline
had long since bled out of them, replaced by
a thick blanket of dread. Debbie's absence
loomed large, her death turning the room
from a haven of desire into a crime scene
none of them could escape.

Amy was the first to stand, pulling on her
black jeans and hoodie with trembling
hands. Her face was pale but determined,
her jaw clenched tight. "We need to go," she
whispered, almost too quiet to hear. "Now.
Before anyone comes."

Mary nodded, already dressed, watching
Amy closely. There was something off about
how Amy took control—too quick, too
practiced. Still, she said nothing. Not yet.
Mark sat silently, his head down, the image
of Debbie's bloody body burned into his

mind. He was either guilty—or breaking from the shock.

"Where are we going?" Mike asked, his voice cracking from the dryness in his throat. He didn't want to sound weak, but every muscle in his body screamed at him to run far away.

Amy zipped up her hoodie and pulled the hood over her head. "The CCTV office. If… if anyone came in or out last night, it'll be on the cameras." She avoided eye contact as she spoke, focusing instead on lacing up her boots. "We need to know what happened. If someone else was here… we'll see it."

"And if it was one of us?" Mary asked softly.

Amy flinched but didn't answer.

They moved as a pack, silent and haunted, exiting the suite and creeping down the dimly lit corridor. The hotel was still sleeping, the early morning hours offering them a brief window of safety. The stale hallway air smelled of cheap cleaning products and regret. Every sound—their footsteps, the creak of the elevator—felt too loud, too revealing.

Amy led with purpose, moving fast but cautious. She knew the layout, the back staircases, and service corridors. Too well, Mike thought but shoved the feeling down. None of them spoke, their minds racing with thoughts of what they were about to see. Were they hoping to find proof of someone else's guilt? Praying for a shadowy figure on the tape to blame, to shift this horror off their own shoulders?

Mike's stomach twisted. What if it was him? What if the bloodlust had blurred his memory and something… snapped? Could I have done it? His eyes darted to Mark, who was pale and shaking, barely able to walk straight. Or him?

The security office sat in a forgotten corner of the hotel's lower level, the door marked Staff Only. Amy glanced back once before pushing it open. The tiny room hummed with the buzz of old computers and dusty monitors, screens flickering with live feeds of empty hallways.

"No one's here," Amy whispered, relief and fear mingling in her voice. "Quick… help me find last night's footage."

Mike's hands trembled as he leaned over one of the screens. "What the hell are we even expecting to see?"

Mary's lips curled into a grim smile. "The truth… if it exists."

They found the right timestamp, eyes glued to the screen as the grainy footage played. Their suite's hallway appeared, the door opening, shadows moving… their own figures laughing, stumbling in and out. Then a long stretch of nothing.

And then… a shape. Unfamiliar. Hooded. Approaching the door… stopping… disappearing.

"Who the fuck is that?" Mark's voice cracked.

No one answered.

Chapter Thirty-three – Secrets and Silent Motions

The footage looped again, all eyes glued to the figure on the screen. The grainy image captured a hooded man moving stealthily toward their suite door in the dead of night. He didn't knock, didn't hesitate. Instead, he bent low, slid something beneath the door, and then disappeared down the hallway like a ghost.

Mark leaned forward, squinting hard. "Who the hell is that? Do any of you recognize him?"

Mike shook his head slowly. "Never seen him before. I don't remember hearing anything at the door… no one noticed anything lying there when we left, right?"

No one spoke. They all knew what that meant. Whatever had been slipped under the door was inside the room now, handled—perhaps by Debbie.

Amy stared at the screen, her face blank but her mind racing. I know him. She could feel it deep in her gut, the unmistakable jolt of recognition. She'd seen that frame, that walk before. One of her lovers, a past mistake. Why the fuck was he here? But she couldn't say it, not yet. Not until she figured out what the envelope held—and why.

Mary was the first to break the tense silence. "What about the mirror? The one in the bathroom? If there's a camera, it would be there. Maybe it caught everything, even who was with Debbie last." Her voice was tight with suspicion, her eyes scanning the group like she already knew someone was lying.

Amy swallowed hard, forcing herself to appear composed. "We'll check, but we need help. Let's find someone who knows the building." She forced a weak smile, already knowing it was useless. At this hour, there'd be no management around—just sleepy-eyed cleaners and security staff.

Still, she had to play the part.

"Come on," she said, motioning for the group to follow. As they moved, Amy instinctively tapped the inside pocket of her jacket, feeling the slim weight of the envelope she'd swiped the moment she realized what had happened. No one saw her slip it off the suite's coffee table, unnoticed in the chaos.

It was hers now. Control the narrative, control the game.

They made their way down the back stairwell, careful to avoid the main elevator where they might be caught. The early morning was still creeping in, sunlight barely filtering through the high lobby windows. The hotel was coming alive slowly, but not fast enough to save them if someone saw their faces now—haunted, wild, full of panic.

Reaching the front desk area, Amy approached confidently, leaving the others hovering nervously behind. The young clerk on the night shift looked up, bored, barely awake.

"Morning," Amy chirped, feigning innocence. "Strange question… we think there's a faulty mirror in our bathroom, looks like it could be… I don't know, warped or something? Could we get someone to check it?"

The clerk blinked slowly. "Uhh… maintenance comes in at eight. It's barely six… I'm just covering nights."

Amy forced a laugh. "Of course, no problem." She leaned in slightly, flashing a warm smile. "We're just being paranoid, you know how it is… drunk night, bad sleep, spooky mirror."

The clerk shrugged and returned to his phone, uninterested.

Amy turned back to the group; her face unreadable. "We'll have to wait. Let's… get some air. Clear our heads."

Mike narrowed his eyes but said nothing. He could see the way Amy's hand hovered near her jacket pocket, protective. What the hell was she hiding?

They stepped out into the cool morning air, each one knowing they were being played— but unsure by who. The envelope was burning a hole in Amy's pocket. And somewhere inside, was the answer—or the death of them all.

Chapter Thirty-four – Fractured Minds

The morning air was crisp, biting at their exposed skin as the group loitered outside the hotel. Silence stretched between them, heavy and unspoken. Each of them was lost in their own thoughts, their minds racing through the possibilities of what had happened, what was to come, and most importantly—who could be trusted.

Mary stood slightly apart from the group, arms crossed over her chest, her nails digging into her sleeves. She was the oldest among them, the one who should have known better. What the hell have I gotten myself into? The weight of her career, her entire reputation, pressed against her like a vice. If word of this night ever got out, if anyone at the university caught wind of her involvement… she would lose everything. Not just her job, but her standing, her dignity, her life as she knew it.

Debbie was dead. And the university was bound to ask questions. A missing student, rumours of underground fetish groups, a night of indulgence turned to something far worse. They'll come knocking, looking for answers. And what if they find me? Mary had spent years carefully curating her life, her image. She wasn't just a respected staff member; she was an authority figure, someone students turned to for guidance. That façade would crumble in an instant if this ever saw the light of day.

And worst of all? She wasn't even sure she wanted to walk away.

Mike exhaled slowly, his military training keeping him composed, outwardly at least. His mind, however, was a battlefield. I thought I'd seen it all. Death, blood, suffering... but this? He had spent years in the Marines, witnessing horrors most people could never imagine, and yet nothing had quite prepared him for the twisted pleasure of last night—or the cold reality of a corpse in their bathroom.

He had been drawn into this world gradually, a curiosity that morphed into desire, an addiction he hadn't even realized he was feeding. But now, the lines were blurring. This wasn't just play anymore—someone had taken it too far. And for the first time in a long while, Mike wasn't sure where he stood.

One thing was certain: He needed to find out what was in that envelope Amy was so desperate to keep hidden.

Amy felt the weight of the envelope pressing against her chest, a physical reminder of the secret she now held. She needed to see what was inside, but how? If they see me open it, they'll start asking questions. If I walk away to check it in private, they'll know something's up.

But she had to know.

The CCTV footage had confirmed what she feared—someone had been outside their door; someone had left something behind. And if it was who she suspected… Shit.

She forced herself to breathe steadily, to maintain her mask of concern and confusion. If she played this right, she could control the narrative. But if she slipped up…

John shifted uncomfortably, his stomach twisting in knots. Why the fuck am I here? He had always been fascinated by blood, by the rawness of it, but what he had witnessed last night had pushed beyond fascination into something darker. He liked the sensation of a controlled cut, the sight of crimson spilling in measured amounts—but this? This was torture.

Debbie hadn't just been playing along. She had been hurt. Someone had done that to her on purpose.

For the first time since joining the group, John was considering walking away. But would they even let him?

Mark clenched his fists, his pulse still racing from the adrenaline. He had loved last night. Every second of it. The power, the pleasure, the primal rush of it all. But now, with Debbie dead and everyone looking for answers, he was starting to feel something unfamiliar fear.

What if they blame me?

Mary had already started asking questions. Mike was watching everyone closely, calculating. Amy was keeping something hidden. If fingers started pointing, Mark knew he would be an easy target. He had been with Debbie last. He had been the one experimenting with her.

But I didn't kill her. I didn't.

Did I?

The group stood in uneasy silence, each of them lost in their own spiralling thoughts.

Amy exhaled sharply, breaking the quiet. "We should get out of here before staff start asking questions."

No one argued. They had bigger problems now.

And one of them held the answer.

Chapter Thirty – five - Darkness and Escape

The moment they stepped back into the hotel suite, the lights flickered once and then died, plunging the room into absolute darkness. A second later, the hum of the air conditioning cut out, leaving only the sound of their breathing and the faint rustling of fabric as they instinctively tensed.

"Shit," Amy whispered.

"A power cut," Mary muttered, more to herself than anyone else.

Mike's instincts kicked in immediately. Years of military training had taught him to act fast in crisis situations. He scanned the room, even though he couldn't see anything. The blackout was an unexpected stroke of luck. No power. No CCTV. No electronic locks. If they moved quickly, they could get Debbie out without a trace.

"Listen up," Mike said, his voice low but firm. "We're getting out of here. Now. We wrap up the body, clean the bathroom, and we move together. No noise. No hesitation."

The group hesitated for only a second before springing into action.

Amy grabbed the bedsheets, ripping them from the mattress with shaking hands. Mary fumbled her way to the bathroom, blindly feeling around for the wet towels and any blood left behind. John and Mark stood frozen for a moment before Mike snapped at them.

"Move! We don't have time."

Mark and John moved quickly, lifting Debbie's limp body from the cold bathroom floor. She was light, barely 60kg, and her head lolled against Mark's shoulder like a doll. They wrapped her in the sheet, securing it tightly around her as if she were merely a drunken friend they were helping home.

In the dimness, Mary scrubbed at the bathroom sink with a towel, trying to clear the last traces of crimson. It wasn't perfect, but it would have to do.

"That's enough," Mike said. "We're out of here."

They opened the door cautiously, peering down the hallway. The emergency lighting in the corridors had kicked in, casting eerie, flickering shadows against the walls.

"Walk slow. If we get stopped, she's just drunk," Amy whispered.

The group moved as one, keeping a steady, unhurried pace. Mark and John carried Debbie between them, supporting her weight as naturally as possible. No one was in the hallway. No staff. No guests. Just the dim glow of exit signs leading them downward.

They reached the stairwell and descended quickly, their steps muffled against the concrete. Every creak of the stairs made Mary's heart pound. Every shadow felt like a threat.

They reached the lobby. The reception desk was empty, the power cut having forced most of the night staff into the back offices. A single security guard stood near the front doors, half-distracted, scrolling on his phone.

"Act normal," Mike hissed.

They moved past the guard without a glance. Outside, the city was still alive, but dimmer than usual. Streetlights flickered, some completely dark. The blackout had spread.

They walked toward the Arboretum, a quiet, tree-filled park just a short distance away. It was secluded enough to regroup and figure out their next move.

"We need a car," John whispered.

"I've got one," Mike said. "At my place. We just need to get there without attracting attention."

They had made it out. But the night was far from over.

Chapter Thirty-Six – The Weight of the Dead

The group huddled together in the Arboretum; the cool night air thick with tension. The body of Debbie lay still in the sheets, her form unnervingly motionless under the pale glow of a distant streetlamp. They had managed to get her out of the hotel unseen, but the real problem remained—what the hell were they going to do with her now?

Amy crouched beside the bundle, her fingers unconsciously grazing the fabric. She wasn't thinking of Debbie as a person anymore, not as the laughing, moaning girl who had writhed in pleasure just hours before. Now, she was something else entirely—a problem that needed to be solved.

"How long does rigor mortis take to set in?" Mary broke the silence, her voice clinical, detached.

John shifted uncomfortably. "It depends on… It can start within two to four hours after death. Full stiffness happens between twelve and twenty-four hours." He paused. "But she lost a lot of blood. That could slow it down… or speed it up, depending on the environment."

Amy nodded, deep in thought. "Not much blood left inside her. Her muscles might not seize up like usual."

Mark let out a shaky breath, rubbing his face with his hands. "Are we really talking about this? Like, scientifically discussing how long before she goes stiff? Jesus."

"We have to," Mary snapped, her usual composure slipping. "What's the alternative? Call the police? Tell them we had a fun little play session that went too far? We need to be rational."

A heavy silence settled over them. The truth was unavoidable—Debbie was dead, and they were all in this together.

Amy ran a hand over her mouth, thinking. "We can't leave her here. The hotel is out of the question. We need to dispose of her somewhere permanent."

"Or" Mark said hesitantly, "we… cut her up."

The words hung in the air like a curse.

Mary closed her eyes for a moment. "We have the skills," she admitted. "We know how to make incisions. We know how to avoid major arteries. We know how to be clean, precise."

"But could we, do it?" John whispered.

Amy swallowed. Could she? She had spent years studying the human body, memorizing every vein, every tendon, every delicate system that kept a person alive. She had sliced into cadavers, prodded organs, examined preserved brains in jars. But this was different. Debbie wasn't an experiment in a lab. She had been warm, alive, screaming in pleasure just hours ago.

Mark's breathing quickened. "I—I can't. I can't chop her up. That's insane."

Amy exhaled sharply. "Then what? Do we dig a hole? Dump her in the river? Set her on fire?"

The sheer weight of the situation pressed down on them.

Just then, the low hum of an approaching car broke the silence. Mike had returned.

They had a way to move the body. But what would they do next?

Chapter Thirty-Seven – The Dismemberment

Mike's old Mercedes rumbled to a stop near the edge of the Arboretum, its headlights momentarily illuminating the group huddled together in the darkness. The cold air was thick with tension, the reality of their situation pressing down like a suffocating weight.

He stepped out, hands steady, mind focused. The military had taught him discipline under pressure. This was just another mission—only this time, the enemy wasn't alive. He popped the trunk and gestured. "Get her in."

John and Mark lifted the wrapped body, their faces pale. Even in death, Debbie seemed too light, too fragile. The sheets she was wrapped in were beginning to soak through with the last remnants of her blood. It made Mike's stomach turn, but he swallowed it down. No time for weakness now.

The drive was silent. Amy sat in the passenger seat, her fingers drumming on her lap, eyes bright with something dark and hungry. She had nearly forgotten about the envelope in her pocket—the mystery slipped under the door at the hotel. But that could wait. Right now, something far more thrilling was about to happen.

They reached Mike's house, an old brick building tucked away in a quiet residential area. He led them inside, his voice calm, giving orders like a seasoned commander. "Kitchen. Lay her on the table. We'll need to be efficient."

Mary, ever the rational one, nodded. "We do this right; we leave no trace."

Amy was already moving, pulling a set of scalpels from her bag, her movements sharp and eager. "I'll handle the incisions," she said, almost breathless with anticipation.

John hesitated at the doorway, watching as the others moved like a well-oiled machine.

"Jesus Christ," he muttered under his breath. He had always been fascinated by blood, by the rush of it, the taste, the warmth—but this? This was something else entirely.

Mark took a deep breath and forced himself to step forward. "We need a saw," he said, his voice hoarse.

Mike nodded and disappeared into the garage, returning a moment later with a hacksaw and a heavy-duty cleaver. He placed them on the counter with a dull thud.

Amy grinned, eyes wild with excitement. "Perfect."

The room smelled of iron and sweat as they set to work. Amy took the first cut, slicing through the soft tissue of Debbie's arm with surgical precision. The others watched in a mix of horror and fascination.

Mark's hands shook as he took the saw and lined it up against her wrist. The first drag was the hardest—the gritty resistance of bone vibrating through his fingers. He gritted his teeth and pushed harder, the sound filling the kitchen like nails on a chalkboard.

Mary watched intently, detached but focused. "We need to do this fast. The longer we take, the more chance of a mistake."

They worked in shifts, cutting, separating, packaging the remains into black garbage bags.

When it was finally done, the exhaustion hit them. The kitchen was a mess. Blood had splattered on their clothes, their faces. The air was thick with the scent of death.

Amy licked her lips, exhilarated.

And in her pocket, the envelope burned against her skin.

Chapter Thirty-Eight – Secrets:

The garage was cold, the scent of gasoline and old wood mingling with the thick, metallic tang of blood. Mike, Mark, and John moved methodically, sealing each black bag with layers of duct tape before stacking them inside the deep freezer. The low hum of the appliance filled the space, a chilling reminder of the gruesome cargo it now held.

Amy wiped her hands on a rag, her face unreadable. "I have to go," she announced suddenly, stepping away from the group.

Mary's sharp gaze followed her. "Where?"

Amy shrugged, forcing a casual smile. "Home. Shower. I need to think."

No one stopped her as she grabbed her coat and walked out, but Mary wasn't convinced. Something was off. Amy had been too quick to suggest the hotel, too eager to introduce her friends to their darkest desires, and too unbothered by Debbie's death.

Mary glanced at Mike. "I'm going after her."

Mike raised an eyebrow but didn't argue. "Be careful."

She nodded and slipped out into the night, leaving the three men alone in the garage.

The Aftermath

Inside the house, Jane sat on the couch, her arms wrapped around herself. Her usually confident demeanour had cracked, leaving behind a woman trembling under the weight of what they had just done.

Mike sat beside her, not too close but close enough. "It's going to be okay," he said, his voice low, calm.

Jane shook her head. "How? We cut her up, Mike. We put her in a fucking freezer." Her voice broke, and tears rolled down her cheeks.

Mike reached out, brushing his fingers against hers. "Listen to me. If we stick to the same story and keep quiet, no one will ever know."

Jane looked at him, searching his face for reassurance. "What if someone talks?"

"They won't."

"You don't know that."

Mike hesitated. In truth, he didn't. But fear was dangerous. It made people slip up. "Do you trust me?"

Jane swallowed hard, then nodded.

"Good. Then we're going to get through this."

She let out a shuddering breath and wiped at her face. "I need a drink."

Mike stood, moving to the kitchen. He poured two glasses of whiskey, handing one to her. She took a deep sip, her hands still shaking.

They sat in silence for a long moment, the reality of their actions settling over them like a heavy fog.

Finally, Jane spoke. "Do you think Mary's right? About Amy?"

Mike swirled the whisky in his glass, thinking. "I don't know. But I don't trust her."

Jane nodded slowly. "Neither do I."

Outside, the wind howled against the windows, and somewhere in the distance, sirens wailed.

Chapter Thirty-Nine – Amy's Discovery

Amy sat in the dimly lit room of her student house, the glow of the computer monitor casting sharp shadows across her face. The air smelled of old books and stale coffee, remnants of nights spent cramming for exams that now felt insignificant compared to the weight pressing on her chest.

Her fingers hovered over the keyboard as she hesitated before clicking play. The file she had retrieved from the envelope—the one slipped under the hotel room door—was a video. She had a gut feeling about what it contained, but now that she was about to watch it, she wasn't sure if she was ready.

She inhaled sharply, pressing the spacebar.

The screen flickered to life. At first, the footage was grainy, but then it sharpened. It was the hotel suite from last night. The camera was positioned high—hidden, just as Mary had suspected—most likely behind the bathroom mirror. The timestamp showed it was taken just hours ago.

Amy leaned in, her breath catching as she watched herself, Mary, Mike, and the others moving around the room, their bodies tangled in the twisted ecstasy of the night. She could see Debbie—alive, vibrant, lost in the euphoria of the moment.

Then the atmosphere changed.

Debbie peeled away from Mark, touching her neck where he had bitten a little too hard. She smiled but looked uneasy as she stood and walked toward the bathroom.

Amy fast-forwarded, watching as Debbie ran the tap, washing away the blood on her arms. The water turned red as it swirled down the drain. She seemed to take a deep breath, steadying herself.

Then the door opened.

Amy froze.

A figure entered the bathroom—masked, clad in black. The intruder moved quickly, grabbing Debbie by the throat, forcing her against the cold tile wall. Debbie struggled, her hands flailing against her attacker's arms. A glint of silver flashed in the dim light.

Amy slapped a hand over her mouth as she watched the knife slide into Debbie's stomach. Once. Twice. Three times. The girl's mouth opened in a silent scream, blood spilling over her lips as she collapsed.

The figure stood over her for a moment before kneeling down, appearing to slip something into her hand—something small, like a piece of paper.

Then, as quickly as they had come, the figure left, closing the door behind them.

Amy's stomach twisted into knots. Her mind raced, trying to make sense of what she had just witnessed.

Someone else had been in that room.

Someone had killed Debbie.

And worst of all, someone had filmed it.

Her face, once filled with curiosity, twisted into sheer distress. Who had done this? Had they been watching all along? And why had they left the video for her?

A sudden knock on her bedroom door made her jump.

She stared at the screen, heart hammering against her ribs.

"Who is it?" she called, trying to steady her voice.

Silence.

Then, another knock.

Amy's blood ran cold.

Chapter Forty – The Confrontation

Amy's fingers hovered over the mouse, her pulse hammering in her throat. The knock had startled her, but now that she knew it was Mary standing outside, a different kind of fear settled in. Mary was smart—too smart. And now she was here, demanding to see the footage.

Amy narrowed her eyes at the door. "Why?" she called out, forcing her voice to remain steady. "Do you think you're in it?"

A beat of silence.

Then Mary's voice, eerily calm. "Just let me in, Amy."

Amy hesitated. The screen in front of her still showed the frozen image of the shadowy figure standing over Debbie's lifeless body. She stole a glance at the timestamp. It was impossible to tell who the killer was from the footage, but the way the figure moved, the way they hesitated before leaving—it was unsettling.

Mary knocked again, firmer this time.

Amy stood, crossing the room quickly, pausing just before unlocking the door. Every instinct screamed at her to be careful. But she had to know.

She turned the lock and pulled the door open.

Mary stepped inside immediately, her presence filling the small space. She looked down at Amy, her expression unreadable. Then her eyes flicked past her, landing on the computer screen.

Amy watched closely. She wanted to see the exact moment Mary reacted.

Nothing. No gasp. No widened eyes. Just a slow, controlled blink before she turned back to Amy.

"Where did you get this?" Mary asked, her voice cool.

Amy crossed her arms. "It was slipped under the door before we left."

Mary nodded, stepping further into the room. She moved to the desk, eyes scanning the still frame on the monitor. Her face remained neutral, but Amy saw the small twitch in her jaw.

"Someone filmed this," Amy said, testing her reaction. "Someone else was in that room."

Mary exhaled sharply through her nose. "That much is obvious."

Amy narrowed her eyes. "And yet, you don't seem surprised."

Mary's gaze snapped to hers. The tension between them thickened.

"You think it was me," Mary stated, not even phrasing it as a question.

Amy didn't answer.

Mary let out a short laugh, but there was no humour in it. "If I were the killer, do you really think I'd be standing here, asking to see the footage?"

Amy tilted her head. "Maybe you didn't expect there to be footage."

Mary smirked, but there was something dark in her eyes. "Or maybe you're playing a very dangerous game, Amy."

A shiver ran down Amy's spine.

She turned back to the screen, playing the footage again. The figure in the video was roughly Mary's height and build. The way they moved—confident, calculated—it was too familiar.

Amy glanced back at Mary, who was now watching her instead of the footage.

"You saw something, didn't you?" Amy pressed.

Mary's lips curved into a slow smile. "I saw what I needed to."

Amy's stomach twisted. "Meaning?"

Mary leaned in slightly, lowering her voice. "Meaning, we're not the only ones playing in the dark, Amy."

Amy swallowed hard. "Then who is?"

Mary reached out and tapped the screen, her finger landing on the figure frozen in time.

"That," she said, "is what we need to find out."

Chapter Forty-one – Unanswered Questions

Amy's pulse quickened as Mary's words lingered in the air.

"We're not the only ones playing in the dark."

Amy wanted to believe Mary wasn't responsible for what happened to Debbie, but doubt gnawed at her mind. The footage wasn't clear, but something about the figure's stance, their calculated hesitation before leaving the room—it didn't sit right.

Then Mary spoke again.

"Where is that piece of paper that got slipped into Debbie's hand?"

Amy blinked. "What?"

Mary's expression hardened. "The note. Whoever was on that footage, they left something behind. Someone picked it up. Who has it?"

Amy's mind raced back to the hotel suite. She remembered Debbie lying on the bathroom floor, her lifeless fingers barely curled. There had been something—yes, something small and white near her hand. But in the chaos of cleaning up and moving her body, it hadn't seemed important at the time.

"I… I don't know," Amy admitted, biting her lip. "I didn't take it."

Mary let out a slow breath, her eyes narrowing in thought. "Then someone else did."

Amy swallowed. "Mike? Mark? John? Jane?"

Mary shook her head. "If they had it, someone would've mentioned it by now. No, Amy, whoever picked up that note knew exactly what they were looking for."

Amy shivered. "What did it say?"

Mary leaned against the desk; arms crossed. "If we find out, we might figure out who really did this."

Amy turned back to the computer screen, staring at the shadowy figure in the footage. "And if the person who took it is the killer?"

Mary's smirk returned, but it was cold this time. "Then we have our answer."

Amy exhaled, her mind spinning with possibilities. "If we retrace our steps, maybe we can—"

A vibration against the wooden desk interrupted her.

Amy looked down. Her phone was lighting up with a message.

From an unknown number.

Her breath hitched as she clicked it open.

"Stop digging. You don't want to know."

Amy's mouth went dry.

Mary leaned over her shoulder, reading the text. Her face darkened.

"Well," she murmured, "I guess someone doesn't like our curiosity."

Amy's hands trembled slightly as she locked the phone.

"I think we already found who has the note," she whispered.

Mary nodded slowly. "Yeah. And they're watching us."

Chapter Forty-Two – Frozen Desires

The air in the garage was thick with the scent of oil, metal, and something far more primal blood. The cold hum of the freezer buzzed beneath them, vibrating ever so slightly as Jane arched her back against its surface, her breath shallow and eager.

Mike loomed over her, his hands firm on her wrists, pressing them into the cold steel. The contrast of heat from their bodies and the icy surface beneath them sent shivers up her spine, but it wasn't just from the temperature.

It was the thrill.

It had started as something simple. A brush of their hands while cleaning up. A lingering glance as the others left. Jane had been quiet—too quiet—since Debbie's death, and Mike had seen the way her hands trembled when she spoke. Whether it was fear, guilt, or something else entirely, he wasn't sure. But when he touched her, when he pressed his fingers against the delicate pulse at her throat, her body had responded in a way that told him exactly what she needed.

Release.

Now, here they were, in the dim glow of the single overhead bulb, caught in a fevered moment that neither had planned but both desperately craved.

Jane let out a soft gasp as Mike traced the edge of the scalpel along the curve of her hip. The sharp blade was cold, barely kissing her skin, but the anticipation sent a tremor through her.

"Do you trust me?" Mike whispered, his lips brushing against her ear.

Jane swallowed hard, nodding. "Yes."

With that, he pressed the blade just enough to break the skin, a single crimson bead forming before it slid down in a thin, trembling line. Jane moaned, tilting her head back, her body reacting as if he had set fire to her veins.

Mike watched in fascination. The way she writhed beneath him, the way her pupils dilated—she needed this.

He pressed his lips to the fresh wound, tasting the warmth of her, the salt and iron filling his senses. Jane's hands gripped his shoulders, her nails digging in, adding to the shared pain, the shared pleasure.

The freezer beneath them hummed, and for a brief second, the thought flickered through Mike's mind—Debbie was inside.

Cold. Lifeless. A silent observer to their ritual.

He should have been disturbed. Should have felt guilt or hesitation.

But instead, it drove him further.

Jane's breath hitched as Mike bit down, harder this time, her blood mixing with the sweat on his tongue. The intoxicating combination pushed them both to the edge, their bodies moving in sync, lost in a frenzy of pain, pleasure, and something darker.

Something they couldn't name.

And as Jane let out a final, shuddering cry, Mike knew—there was no turning back.

Not for him.

Chapter Forty-Three – The Dark Horse:

Mark had always been an observer rather than a participant. He preferred the periphery, lurking in the shadows where he could see without being seen. It was a habit he had developed as a child—watching, learning, waiting. People underestimated those who spoke little, those who blended in, but Mark knew better. Silence was power.

Now, he found himself moving like a phantom through the damp city streets, his eyes locked on Mary as she walked with purpose ahead of him. She was heading towards Amy's student house, a place he had been watching for some time. There was something about Amy, something he couldn't place. It made the hairs on his arms stand on end.

And then there was Mary.

Mary, the strong one. The leader. The one who had pulled them all together, given their twisted desires structure and purpose. She was clever, too clever, always thinking ahead. If anyone was going to figure out what had really happened to Debbie, it was her.

Mark had to know what she knew.

Had she seen something? Had she suspected him?

His heart pounded as he kept to the darkest parts of the street, his hoodie pulled low over his face. He had always been careful. Controlled. He never lost himself the way Mike and Jane did, writhing in their own sick pleasure. He never let the blood excite him in the way it did Amy, whose hands had trembled with anticipation as she reached for the scalpel.

No. Mark was different.

He enjoyed the chase.

The hunt.

And right now, Mary was his prey.

She stopped outside Amy's door, glancing around before knocking softly. Mark pressed himself into the doorway of a nearby shop, barely breathing. He had become a shadow, a ghost, unseen and unnoticed. He listened as the door creaked open and Amy appeared, her face half-lit by the dim hallway light.

"Mary," Amy said, her voice wary. "What are you doing here?"

"We need to talk," Mary replied, stepping inside.

The door shut behind her.

Mark exhaled slowly. He moved across the street, his footsteps silent. He reached the window, just beneath where the two women were talking. Their voices were hushed, but he could still make out snippets of conversation.

"…I saw the footage, Amy."

Mark's breath hitched.

"What footage?" Amy asked, too quickly.

"The CCTV. Someone slipped something under the door. I need to know who took it. Who was it meant for?"

There was a pause. Then Amy's voice, lower, more dangerous.

"What are you accusing me of, Mary?"

Mark smirked. This was getting interesting.

The two women continued their verbal dance, testing each other, pushing for weaknesses. But Mark didn't care about their secrets. He had his own.

Because Mark knew exactly what had happened to Debbie.

He knew who had gone too far.

And he knew it wasn't him.

Not this time.

Chapter Forty-Four – The Clip That Changed Everything

Mike and Jane stared at the screen; their bodies frozen in place. The grainy, dimly lit video played on loop—a six-second nightmare that had already spread across Instagram like wildfire. The sound of the death gurgle sent a shiver through both, the unmistakable wet rasp of someone choking on their own blood.

The clip had been edited, carefully stripped of any identifiable faces, but the setting was clear to them. It was the hotel suite. Their suite. The night Debbie had died.

Jane covered her mouth, her breath hitching in her throat. "Oh my God, Mike… this is—"

"Bad," Mike finished, his voice low and dangerous.

His Marine instincts kicked in—assess, analyse, react. His mind raced through the implications. Someone had recorded the moment Debbie died, cut it down to just a few horrific seconds, and put it out for the world to see.

But why?

Was it a warning? A threat? Or something worse proof that whoever filmed it wanted recognition?

"We have to find out who did this," Jane whispered. Her eyes were still locked on the screen, her pupils blown wide with fear and something else- exhilaration?

Mike clenched his jaw, his fingers drumming against the desk. He felt an uneasy mixture of emotions himself—rage, excitement, panic.

He rewound the clip, playing it again.

That sound.

That final, desperate, rattling breath.

He had heard sounds like that before, on deployment, in combat zones where men bled out in the dirt with no one to save them. But this was different. This was pleasure mixed with pain, a ritual turned into a murder.

And someone had been watching.

Someone had filmed it.

Jane finally pulled away from the screen, rubbing her arms as if she could chase away the chill creeping over her skin. "What does this mean for us? For Blood Spurts?"

Mike exhaled sharply through his nose. "It means we have a problem. Someone in our group—maybe even someone outside of it—has evidence of what happened that night. And they're not afraid to use it."

Jane swallowed hard. "What if they go to the police?"

Mike turned to her, his eyes dark and unreadable. "If they wanted to go to the police, they already would have. This video? It's not about justice. It's about power."

Jane shivered. "Power?"

"Yeah," he said, rubbing his chin. "Someone is playing a game. They're baiting us, seeing how we'll react."

She nodded, her face pale. "Then what do we do?"

Mike clicked out of Instagram, closing the browser. "First, we find out who filmed this. And then we deal with them."

"Deal with them how?" Jane whispered.

Mike looked at her, his face expressionless.

"However, we need to."

Chapter Forty –Five -The Reckoning

The atmosphere in Mike's living room was thick with tension, the air heavy with the scent of sweat, stale coffee, and something else fear. The seven of them sat in a loose circle, bodies rigid, faces pale, eyes darting to one another, all except Mary. She was the only one who looked composed, though her fingers tapped restlessly against the armrest of her chair.

"Well," she said, her voice slicing through the silence, "it looks like our sexual endeavours have left us in deep water."

No one responded immediately. The weight of what was happening pressed down on them like an invisible force.

Debbie was still in the freezer.

The police were investigating.

And the clips of that night—the night that was meant to be about lust, pain, and pleasure—were now all-over social media.

Mark was the first to speak, his voice barely above a whisper. "Who the hell filmed it?"

Amy shifted uncomfortably in her seat, running a hand through her dark hair. "It could have been anyone," she said. "There were seven of us. But the real question is why they're posting it now."

Mike exhaled sharply. "They're toying with us. This isn't just about exposure—someone is controlling the narrative. They've edited the clips, made sure there are no faces, no clear evidence linking us. It's like they're watching us squirm, waiting to see what we'll do next."

Jane shuddered, wrapping her arms around herself. "It's like a game to them."

"Exactly," Mike said. "And we need to figure out who's playing."

Mary leaned forward, her sharp eyes scanning the room. "There are only two possibilities," she said. "Either it's one of us, or someone outside our group knew what we were up to that night."

The implication settled over them like a dense fog.

John, who had remained silent until now, finally spoke, his voice tinged with uncertainty. "Could it be someone who was in the hotel that night? Maybe someone saw us, heard something, and recorded it?"

Amy scoffed. "You think some random guest at the hotel decided to film a death scene and post it in bits and pieces online?"

"It's not impossible," Mark muttered.

Mary let out a slow breath, tapping her nails against her knee. "We need to be smart about this. The police are involved now. Debbie is officially missing. If we don't get ahead of this, we're screwed."

Jane swallowed. "What do you mean by 'get ahead of this'?"

Mary's gaze hardened. "We need to control the situation before it controls us. We need to find out who's leaking this footage and stop them before they reveal more."

There was a beat of silence, then Mike spoke. "And what about Debbie?"

The question lingered in the air, a grim reminder of the body stored in his garage.

Amy bit her lip, eyes darting to Mary. "If the police get wind of us before we deal with her, we're done for."

"Then we deal with her tonight," Mary said coldly. "No more waiting. No more hesitation."

For a moment, no one spoke.

Then, one by one, they nodded.

Chapter Forty-Six – The Disposal

The hum of the station wagon's engine filled the silence between them as they drove through the quiet streets of Nottingham. The night was cold, and even with the heater on, there was an icy tension in the air. The bags in the back of the car were stacked neatly, wrapped tightly in thick black plastic. The weight of their crime pressed down on them as heavily as the cargo they carried.

Mike kept his hands firmly on the wheel, his eyes locked on the road ahead, but his mind was racing. He still couldn't quite grasp how they'd ended up here driving through the night, carrying the remains of what was once a living, breathing person.

Mary shifted in her seat and let out a long sigh, breaking the silence. "Well, this is not easy, is it?"

Mike scoffed, keeping his gaze forward. "No, Mary. It's not easy. None of this is easy."

Mary glanced at him, studying his expression in the dim light of the dashboard. "What are you thinking about?"

Mike exhaled sharply. "I'm thinking about how the hell we got here. How did this all start?"

Mary leaned back, looking out the window as the city lights blurred past them. "Lust," she said simply. "Desire. The need for something more than just normal life. We wanted to feel alive."

Mike gritted his teeth. "And now someone else is dead."

Mary didn't respond right away. She reached into her coat pocket, pulling out a cigarette and lighting it with a flick of her lighter. She took a slow drag before speaking. "We didn't kill her, Mike."

Mike turned his head slightly, just enough to give her a look. "Didn't we?"

Mary exhaled smoke through her nose. "Someone went too far, yes. But we all played a part in creating the situation. The question is, what do we do now?"

Mike tightened his grip on the wheel. "We get rid of her. We dump the bags, and we move on."

Mary smirked. "And just like that, we pretend nothing happened?"

Mike let out a humourless laugh. "We don't pretend. We make sure there's nothing left to find."

The river Trent was coming into view now, its dark waters reflecting the moonlight. It was a secluded stretch, one they had scouted earlier—a place where the current was strong enough to carry away evidence, where no late-night joggers or dog walkers would stumble upon them.

As Mike pulled the car to a stop on the gravel path leading to the water, Mary flicked her cigarette out the window and turned to him. "Alright, let's do this."

They stepped out, their boots crunching against the damp earth as they moved to the back of the car. Mike lifted the tailgate, and the cold hit them immediately. The black bags sat there, lifeless, motionless, frozen solid.

Mary reached in, grabbing one end of the first bag while Mike took the other. It was heavier than expected, the frozen mass inside making it awkward to carry. They moved quickly, working in silence, their breath visible in the cold air as they carried the first bag toward the edge of the riverbank.

Mary looked at Mike. "Ready?"

He nodded, and together, they heaved the bag into the water. The splash was loud in the silence of the night, the weight dragging it down, the current beginning to pull it away.

One by one, they repeated the process, their movements efficient and methodical, until the last bag was gone.

Mary dusted off her hands and looked at Mike. "So… that's that."

Mike stared at the dark water. "Yeah," he said. "That's that."

Chapter Forty-Seven – The Watcher

As the last black bag splashed into the cold, dark waters of the Trent, Mike let out a slow breath. It was done. The weight of the night—the weight of her—was sinking beneath the surface, disappearing into the currents. But just as he turned to head back to the car, something caught his eye.

A flicker. A red light.

It was small, barely visible in the dark, but unmistakable—the steady pulsing glow of a recording device.

His blood turned to ice.

He froze, staring at the source of the light, partially hidden behind a cluster of reeds further up the bank. His heartbeat thudded in his ears, his breath catching in his throat. Someone was watching. Someone was recording.

Mary was already halfway to the car, brushing dirt from her gloves, her mind likely already on the next step in their cover-up. She hadn't seen it.

Mike clenched his jaw. Is it the same person? It had to be. No outsider could have known to be here, at this exact time, on this exact night. This wasn't coincidence.

He turned, walking briskly back toward the car, his mind racing. The logical move was to investigate, to see if he could catch whoever was behind the camera. But was that a trap? Whoever had set it up was clearly watching, waiting.

Sliding into the driver's seat, Mike forced himself to breathe steadily. Mary shut the passenger door beside him and stretched her arms. "Well," she said, exhaling, "that was smoother than I expected."

Mike didn't respond right away. His fingers drummed on the steering wheel, his eyes locked on the path leading back to the riverbank.

Mary frowned. "Mike?"

He turned to her, eyes sharp. "We were recorded."

Her expression didn't change at first, but then she blinked. "What?"

Mike jerked his head toward the reeds. "Over there. Red light. Camera. Someone was watching."

Mary's entire body stiffened. Her hands curled into fists on her lap. "Did you see who?"

Mike shook his head. "No. Just the light. But it means someone knows."

Mary swore under her breath. She turned to look out the window, but there was nothing but darkness now. Whoever had been watching had either left or was still hidden, waiting.

"We have to find out who it is," she said.

Mike nodded, jaw tight. "Yeah. But not tonight. If we go looking now, we might be walking into something worse."

Mary exhaled sharply. "So, what, we just… go home? Pretend we didn't see it?"

Mike started the engine. "No. We act normal. We wait. Whoever it is, they'll make a move soon enough."

As he pulled away from the riverbank, the dark shape of the water disappearing in the rearview mirror, the weight in his gut didn't fade.

Because this wasn't over.

Not by a long shot.

Chapter Forty-Eight- The note.

The car sat idling outside Mary's apartment in the soft spill of a flickering streetlamp, the glow barely cutting through the late-night haze. Inside, silence hung like fog between Mike and Mary, both of them cloaked in exhaustion and something heavier — the unspoken weight of what they'd just done.

Mike tapped his fingers on the steering wheel, staring blankly through the windshield. The bags had sunk in the Trent, but his thoughts hadn't. They were still drifting, snagging on fragments of memory — Debbie's blank eyes, Amy's scream, the red blinking light on the riverbank. Someone had seen. Someone knew.

Mary's voice cut through the stillness.

"I have something," she said, almost in a whisper. Her hand reached into the inside pocket of her long coat and pulled out a small, folded piece of paper.

Mike glanced sideways. "What is it?"

"It was in her hand. Debbie's." Mary held it between her fingers for a second longer, as if weighing its potential to crack open the last two days like an egg. Then she passed it to him.

He took it silently.

The paper was warm from her body heat. Folded into quarters, smudged with faint brown fingerprints — blood, maybe, or just grime from the night's chaos. Mike opened it slowly.

Inside was a single sentence, typed out in old-school typewriter font, the ink slightly misaligned:

"You are being watched. Not everyone in the room is who you think."

Mike stared at the words. His brows lifted just slightly, then his expression shifted. Not fear. Not confusion.

Amusement.

A slow, disbelieving grin tugged at the corners of his mouth.

Mary saw it. "What?" she asked, leaning forward. "What the hell does it mean?"

Mike held the note up between two fingers, like it was a magic trick finally revealed. "It means," he said, "that Debbie knew something. Maybe not everything. But enough to write this and hide it. And maybe enough to get herself killed."

Mary leaned back in her seat; lips pursed. "It wasn't written by Debbie. She had it handed to her — remember the footage?"

Mike nodded slowly, his mind ticking like a watch with a cracked face. "Right… someone slipped it under the door. Debbie was the only one who saw it. And she kept it."

"Maybe she thought it was a joke," Mary said, voice low. "Or maybe she didn't know who to trust. Not even me."

"Especially not you," Mike said, looking at her. "You've been two steps ahead this whole time."

Mary didn't respond. Instead, she leaned in and kissed him, brief and hard, like punctuation at the end of a sentence she didn't want to speak aloud. Then she opened the door and slipped out into the night without a word.

Mike was left in the dim, idling hush of the car, the note in his hand, his mind racing through possibilities. Who was the watcher? What were they after?

And just how much of this night had already been recorded?

As he unfolded the note again and read it once more, a new thought crept in.

What if the watcher wasn't outside the group… but inside it?

He started the engine. The night was far from over.

Chapter: Forty-Nine "The Watcher"

The soft purr of the engine accompanied Mike as he drove slowly through the sleeping streets, the note lying open on the passenger seat like a warning label he couldn't stop reading.

"You are being watched. Not everyone in the room is who you think."

The words bled into his thoughts, replaying alongside flashes of the past two days — Debbie's blood-spattered smile before she disappeared into the bathroom; Mark's blank eyes in the debrief; Amy's carefully orchestrated chaos. And now Mary, always walking one step ahead of the group like she was guiding lambs to slaughter or protecting them from wolves.

He took a long, measured breath and turned toward home. It wasn't just paranoia now — something real was happening behind the veil of sex, blood, and thrill.

Someone was orchestrating this.

And someone else was watching.

Back at the house, Mike parked the car but didn't go inside immediately. He sat in the dark vehicle, tapping his thumb against the steering wheel while looking toward the faint glow of his front window. Jane was still inside. Probably sleeping off the horrors of the night. He wasn't ready to see her yet.

Instead, he pulled his phone out and searched for footage. Nothing new from the group chat. The "Blood Spurts" thread had gone dead silent since the Instagram clip went viral. Everyone was scared. Even Mark. Especially Mark.

Mike opened a new browser window and searched the clip again, hoping maybe something had changed.

There it was — reposted again under a new account, with a caption that twisted his stomach:

"One of them knows. #WatcherAmongUs"

His mouth went dry. One of them. Not just being observed. Infiltrated.

He stared, eyes narrowing. The grainy clip showed the same brief horror — the soft lighting of the hotel suite, the blood, the silhouette of Amy gasping. Just before it cut off, a shape moved in the background, behind the mirror.

A shadow.

Not a reflection. A presence.

Mike jolted upright. The mirror. Mary had said it could be hiding a camera. But what if it wasn't just recording? What if someone had been behind it — watching through a two-way mirror?

A sick feeling twisted in his gut.

Suddenly, his front door creaked open.

Jane stood in the frame, wrapped in a sheet, her hair tangled and her eyes bleary. "You coming in?"

He nodded once and pocketed the phone. "Yeah. Just… thinking."

She turned back inside without pressing, and he followed.

The house was heavy with tension. Jane had cleaned up, the scent of bleach still faint on the kitchen tile. No trace of Debbie but the memory of her hung in the shadows.

Over coffee, they sat in silence. Jane broke it first.

"Mike… do you think someone's setting us up?"

He looked at her. Really looked.

"I think someone's been setting us up from the beginning," he said. "This wasn't just sex or blood. This was a test. And now it's a game."

She frowned. "A game?"

He nodded slowly, that grin from the car creeping back onto his face. "Yeah. And I think we've just reached level two."

Jane's eyes widened. "What does that mean?"

"It means," he said, reaching into his jacket and placing the note on the table, "the real player hasn't even stepped onto the board yet."

Outside, a fox screeched into the night.

Inside, trust was unravelling thread by thread.

Chapter: Fifty "Through the Mirror"

Mary moved quietly through the University's east wing, the soles of her boots muffled against the worn linoleum tiles. It was well past 2 a.m., and while campus wasn't exactly abandoned — the occasional hum of cleaning machines echoed down the corridors — it was still enough to make her feel like a ghost gliding through its veins.

She'd used her access badge to get in. One of the benefits of being staff. No one would question her presence here… at least, not yet.

She took the side stairs down to the basement level, where the old AV and maintenance rooms were kept. Buried among rusting filing cabinets and disused projectors was the door she was looking for — unmarked, steel, and always slightly ajar.

Inside, the university's CCTV control room buzzed with the gentle static of a dozen outdated monitors. She flicked on a desk lamp, the warm glow revealing years of dust, stacks of labelled tapes, and the stale scent of forgotten secrets.

She took a breath.

This was where she might find the answers.

Turning on the monitors, she began fast-forwarding through the recorded footage from the night of the gathering. Though the hotel wasn't on university property, some students had used campus internet to coordinate — and Mary suspected the Watcher might have roots closer to home than anyone realized.

On the third screen, something caught her eye. A motion-activated clip — timestamped just hours before the fateful night — showed Mark slipping into a restricted access room in the biomedical building.

"What the hell were you doing in there, Mark?" she whispered, leaning forward.

He didn't seem to be stealing anything. He wasn't searching. He stood in front of a storage locker for nearly five minutes, just staring at it… then walking out. No lab coat. No gloves.

But the locker number was familiar.

Mary flipped through the staff catalogue until she found what she was looking for: Locker B-19. Haematology Research

Materials. Restricted to post-graduate researchers and staff.

Her eyes narrowed. Mark was a psychology student, not biomed. He shouldn't have had access.

She pulled out her phone, dialling a contact she'd hoped not to need.

The line clicked.

"Dr. Lister speaking."

"It's Mary."

There was a pause. Then, the voice softened with wary recognition. "Mary. It's late."

"I need access to Locker B-19. And I need to know who else has been in it. You have ten minutes to meet me. Or I go public with everything I know about your research group."

Silence.

Then: "Fine. Ten minutes. Bring coffee."

She hung up, heart racing.

As she turned back to the monitors, one screen glitched — just for a second — before showing a different feed. A live feed, not from the university. It was an image of a living room. Her eyes widened.

Mike's living room.

She saw him sitting at his kitchen table. The note she'd given him lay in front of him. Jane sat across from him, sipping coffee, pale and tense.

The feed had no audio, but Mary didn't need sound. Just the red blinking light in the corner of the frame.

They were being watched.

Not just in hotels. Not just through mirrors.

Everywhere.

Mary stared, her pulse climbing. Someone had tapped into private security, maybe even phones and laptops. This was bigger than sex and death.

This was surveillance. Or maybe blackmail.

And the real question wasn't who was watching…

…but why?

Chapter: Fifty-One "Tangled Threads"

Mike sat hunched over his kitchen table, the soft hum of the old refrigerator the only sound filling the room. The small scrap of paper lay in front of him like it had crawled there of its own volition — folded once, creased, damp with the sweat of his palm.

He hadn't spoken since Mary had slipped out of the car and into the night. She hadn't said where she was going. Only that he should read what was in the note... when he was alone.

But he wasn't. Jane sat across from him, curled in his oversized hoodie, her eyes red and swollen. She hadn't slept. None of them had.

"I can go if you want to read it," she said softly.

Mike shook his head. "No. You're in it just like I am."

He picked up the note and opened it slowly, the crinkling of the paper louder than it should've been. His eyes moved left to right, narrowing, then widening. A flicker of something passed over his face —

confusion… then realization… then an almost imperceptible grin.

"What is it?" Jane asked, leaning in, her voice tinged with dread.

Mike slid the paper over to her.

She read it silently.

"Room 203. Key hidden behind the left cistern. Watch the tapes before they watch you."

Jane blinked. "What tapes?"

"I don't know," Mike muttered, rubbing the back of his neck. "But someone knew what was coming. Someone knew about Debbie. About us."

Jane folded the note again, her hands trembling. "Is this from her?"

"I don't think so," he replied. "Mary found it in Debbie's hand, right? But this… this doesn't feel like a warning. It feels like a test."

They sat in silence for a moment.

Then Jane stood and moved to the window, brushing the curtain aside just enough to peek out into the dark street. Her voice came flat, almost hollow. "Do you think it's possible that one of us set all of this up?"

Mike didn't answer immediately. He poured two fingers of whisky into a chipped glass, took a long sip, then looked at her.

"I've seen some shit," he said. "War zones. Night ops. Black sites. But this? This is something else. This is… personal. Like we've been dancing on someone's chessboard, thinking we were leading the game."

Jane turned, her expression hardening. "Then maybe we need to stop playing."

Mike gave a tight nod.

They both knew it now — it wasn't just about getting away with what they'd done. It wasn't about hiding Debbie's body or avoiding the police. No, someone had orchestrated this. Someone was filming, watching, baiting them like rats in a maze.

And Room 203?

That was the next clue.

"I say we go tonight," Jane said. "Before someone else gets there first."

Mike stood, walking over to her. "You sure you're ready for whatever we find?"

"No," she admitted. "But I'm sick of being in the dark."

He looked at her — really looked. The fear, the strength, the quiet rage. Then he nodded once.

"Grab your coat."

Together, they moved toward the door, not knowing if they were walking into an answer, a trap, or something far worse.

Outside, in the stillness of the Nottingham night, a car engine purred into life down the street.

They were being followed.

Again.

Chapter: Fifty-Two - Room 203

The hallway smelled of bleach and stale air, a sterile contrast to the pulsing anxiety in Mike's chest. He and Jane stood outside Room 203 of the Kingsleigh Hotel, the exact same place they'd used for the night of the incident. This room, though, was two floors down. No connection. No obvious reason for its mention in the note.

But the number lingered in Mike's head like a code waiting to be broken.

"Behind the cistern," he whispered, pulling Jane into the narrow corridor that led to a shared bathroom used by the lower floors. "It said the key was behind the left cistern."

"God, I feel like we're in a spy movie," Jane muttered, but her hands were shaking. She was pale under the fluorescent light, and Mike could hear the tremble in her breath.

The bathroom was empty. Quiet. Too quiet.

Mike knelt down beside the toilet and felt behind the porcelain tank. At first, nothing — just the cold curve of ceramic. Then, a small bump under his fingertips.

His hand gripped something metal.

He pulled it out slowly. A single tarnished key, wrapped in black electrical tape.

They walked back to the room. Mike hesitated for only a second before sliding the key into the lock.

Click.

The door opened with a low groan.

Inside, Room 203 was ordinary at first glance — drab carpet, cheap bedspread, old TV mounted to the wall. But there was something unnatural about it. It was too clean. The air smelled faintly of disinfectant and plastic. There were no personal touches, no mess, no signs of recent occupancy.

And then they saw the desk.

Against the far wall sat a battered metal desk, and on it — a laptop. Still open. Its screen dimmed but not shut off. A small red USB stick protruded from the side.

Mike stepped forward cautiously. "Stay by the door," he told Jane.

"No way," she whispered, coming up beside him.

He tapped the spacebar.

The screen lit up instantly.

A video paused. A dimly lit room. Shadows of people. Moaning. A flash of red. Blood. Movement.

It was them.

It was that night.

But it was different. This wasn't from any of their phones.

This was from above.

Mike scanned the video — wide angle, distorted, maybe from a corner mirror or hidden wall cam. Multiple clips were saved on the laptop. Each with a timestamp. The filenames were labelled with initials and numbers. D-S1, D-S2, A-S1, M-K1…

"Are we… being studied?" Jane murmured.

Mike didn't answer. He clicked one of the files.

A still frame. Debbie. Alive. Laughing. Holding up a small piece of paper. The same piece Mary had found in her hand.

But here's what made Mike's heart drop.

In the corner of the frame — a face.

Blurry. Masked. Watching her. Not part of the group.

A third party.

Mike froze.

"This wasn't just us," he whispered. "Someone else was in that room."

Jane backed away from the screen.

And then, the laptop chimed.

"Upload complete."

"What the hell does that mean?" Jane asked, voice rising in panic.

Mike didn't answer. He turned to the USB stick and yanked it out. The screen flickered.

And then the laptop shut itself off.

A loud click echoed from the hallway.

They turned toward the door.

Locked.

From the outside.

Chapter: Fifty-Three -No Way Out

Mike lunged for the door and twisted the handle — it didn't budge. The dull rattle echoed in the tight hallway like a warning. Locked. From the outside. Not jammed, not broken. Deliberately secured.

Jane's eyes widened. "Did you hear that click? Someone locked us in."

Mike nodded, already scanning the room again. There was no panic on his face — not yet — but his Marine instincts were surfacing. His breathing slowed, became measured. He checked the windows: sealed. Old sash frames painted shut from years of neglect. They wouldn't open without tools.

Jane's voice dropped to a whisper. "Mike... someone's still here."

It was a whisper of dread, not paranoia. And she was right. Somewhere, in the hushed breath of the corridor outside, Mike could sense it too — a presence. Watching. Waiting.

He motioned Jane back toward the corner near the desk. "Stay low. Out of sight."

He pulled his phone from his pocket. No signal.

Of course.

"CCTV," Jane murmured, pointing to the upper corner of the room.

There, half-obscured by a fake smoke alarm, was a small black dome. The lens gleamed faintly in the dim light. Mike narrowed his eyes. "This wasn't here before. Someone's been using this room."

Not just watching them — orchestrating them.

He approached the camera slowly, picked up the heavy desk chair, and with a quick, clean swing, smashed it upward. The camera sparked and went dark, plastic shards raining down.

The laptop remained lifeless, but Mike opened it again. No power. He flipped it over — the battery was missing.

Jane turned toward the door. "Who would do this? What do they want?"

Mike was silent, but his eyes flicked toward the red USB stick in his hand. That was what he wanted now — the files. The evidence. The key to whoever had been watching them.

He didn't say it, but one thought surged in his head:

"This goes deeper than Debbie."

Jane inched closer. "Could it be someone from the university?"

"Maybe. Or someone who wants us to think it is."

Then… footsteps.

Soft. Deliberate.

Just beyond the door.

Both of them froze. The sound passed once. Twice. Then stopped. A shadow slid beneath the doorframe.

Something was pushed under.

A folded note.

Mike waited five seconds, then six, before grabbing it. Jane clutched his arm as he unfolded the paper, heart pounding in her throat.

"You're not in control anymore."

No signature.

No clue.

Just seven words scrawled in the same handwriting as the note found in Debbie's hand.

Jane staggered back. "What does that mean?"

Mike didn't answer right away. He was already pacing, thinking, calculating. This was no longer just about escape. It was about war. Someone was playing a long game. Someone had laid the trap weeks ago. Maybe longer.

"We need to get out of this room," he said. "And we need to find out who's next."

Then — the lights flickered.

The screen of the laptop lit back up on its own.

And a new file appeared.

Titled: "JANE_FINAL.mov"

Chapter: Fifty-Four - JANE_FINAL.mov

Mike stared at the screen as the file loaded. The room had gone dead silent, except for the soft hum of the laptop's fan kicking in. Jane stood frozen beside him, her eyes locked on the flickering screen that now displayed only black.

Then… movement.

The video faded in with grainy, night-vision footage — green hues casting everything in an eerie glow. The setting was familiar. Unmistakable, in fact.

It was the garage.

Mike's garage.

The freezer loomed in the background, its lid ajar. The camera angle was elevated — placed high in the corner, perhaps on a shelf or beam, overlooking the space like an unseen observer.

Mike felt the blood drain from his face.

The timestamp on the corner read: "03:42 AM – 3 days ago" — the night after Debbie's dismemberment.

The image jumped slightly as the camera focused. There was movement on the screen. Someone entering the garage.

It was Jane.

She walked in slowly, quietly, glancing over her shoulder. She was wearing a hoodie. Her hair tied back. Her face partially hidden — but there was no doubt.

Jane gasped behind him. "I… I don't remember this."

Mike didn't respond. He watched as on the video, Jane approached the freezer, reached into her pocket, and pulled out… something.

A small plastic vial.

She opened the freezer, stared down at the dismembered remains of Debbie — the bags still sealed — then crouched and carefully poured the contents of the vial into one of the bags.

The footage paused.

And then a line of red text appeared across the screen:

"Jane's Touch. Jane's Trace. Jane's Fall."

Jane's hands flew to her mouth. "Mike — I swear to you — I don't remember doing that. I didn't—! Someone's setting me up!"

But Mike wasn't looking at her anymore. He was watching the screen, thinking back to that night. She had gone back to the garage alone at one point. Said she needed air. Only a few minutes.

It could've happened.

Or… could someone have drugged her? Or manipulated the footage?

Jane grabbed his arm. "Mike, listen to me. I didn't do this. This is fake — it has to be fake."

He turned toward her, eyes dark and hard. "If that vial contained DNA, if someone finds the body…"

"They'll trace it to me," she finished, voice breaking.

Mike nodded slowly. "And if they find the footage?"

Jane's breath came in short gasps now. "We have to find out who's doing this. Who filmed this."

Mike picked up the USB drive again and plugged it into the laptop. Maybe the answers were there.

The drive loaded.

One folder.

"THE BLOOD SPURTS"

Inside — dozens of video files.

Each one labelled with names, dates, locations.

Every gathering. Every session. Every person.

Even ones he hadn't known were recorded.

"This… this is all of us," he muttered.

Jane leaned over his shoulder, trembling. "Someone's been watching us from the beginning."

The screen blinked again.

A new window opened on its own.

A chat box.

UNKNOWN:

Hello, Jane.

Hello, Mike.

Time to confess… or we upload everything.

Chapter: Fifty-Five-THE MESSENGER

Mike's jaw clenched as he stared at the message on screen. Jane took a step back, as if the words themselves might reach through the laptop and grab her.

UNKNOWN:

You have 24 hours.

Confess to the authorities.

Or the world sees what you've done.

Beneath the message, a single video thumbnail popped into view — a preview of one of their "sessions" at the hotel. It was grainy but unmistakable: blood, faces, ecstasy, chaos.

Jane whispered, "This isn't just about Debbie anymore, is it?"

Mike didn't answer. He was calculating. Running through scenarios like he used to in the Marines when ambushed in the field. Who had access to everything? Who knew the layout of the garage? The house? Who had the technical skill to capture and edit this much footage without being noticed?

And then… the most uncomfortable question of all:

Who among them had the motive to burn it all down?

He looked at Jane. Her face was pale but fierce.

"I don't think this is the police," she said, voice steadying.

Mike nodded. "No cop would play games like this. They'd knock our door down, not taunt us through a hacked laptop."

She leaned in, thinking. "Then who? One of the others?"

Mike's mind immediately snapped to Mark.

The loner. The shadow. Always watching. Always just far enough back to not be suspicious… but never truly part of the group. He had kept quiet after Debbie's death, slipping out early after the cleanup. He was the one no one really knew. And now that he thought about it — Mark had asked more questions than anyone else that night. About the freezer. About Mike's computer.

But it wasn't just Mark. There was Mary, too — her obsession with control, with power. She'd taken the note from Debbie. She knew about the mirror. She had followed Amy the night she disappeared… and came back with nothing to show for it.

"What if…" Jane started, hesitating. "What if this isn't just someone in the group?"

Mike turned to her.

"What if someone's been in the group the whole time — but not for the reasons we thought? What if someone joined to expose us?"

Mike's stomach turned.

He clicked to reply.

MIKE:

What do you want?

A pause. Then the cursor blinked.

UNKNOWN:

I want the truth.

I want the one who killed Debbie.

You find them… or everyone goes down together.

Jane's voice dropped. "They're giving us a chance to turn on each other."

Mike's reply came automatically, ice-cold:

"Classic divide and conquer."

Another message appeared.

UNKNOWN:

You started this as a game. A thrill.

But blood always stains.

Let's see who bleeds last.

Chapter: Fifty-Six

Mary stood alone in her apartment, the city lights glinting off the half-drained wine glass in her hand. Her fingers played absently with the rim as her thoughts churned like a storm.

Who slipped the note into Debbie's hand?

Who sent the footage?

Who wants to burn it all down?

She had handed the note to Mike earlier — not because she trusted him, but because she wanted to see his reaction. And what she'd seen in his eyes… wasn't guilt. It wasn't innocence, either. It was relief — the kind that comes when a puzzle piece falls into place, but you're not ready to say what the full picture is.

Behind her, the apartment door creaked softly.

Mary didn't startle.

"Mark," she said without turning. "You've been lurking outside my building for thirty minutes. Did you think I wouldn't notice?"

He stepped in slowly. Pale, lean, a presence like damp fog.

"I had to see you," he said, voice flat. "We need to talk."

Mary turned, folding her arms. "Do we?"

Mark looked ragged — eyes hollowed from sleeplessness or guilt, maybe both. But there was a sharpness to him tonight, something different. He no longer looked like a boy dragged into things he couldn't handle. He looked… focused.

"You think I sent the videos," he said.

Mary tilted her head. "Did you?"

"No," Mark said simply. "But I know someone did. And I think they want us to implode."

Mary studied him carefully. "Why are you telling me this?"

"Because I've been watching," he said, stepping further into the room. "All of you. From the start. And you've been watching too, haven't you, Mary? Watching Amy. Watching Mike. Collecting little truths."

Mary didn't respond, but her grip on the wine glass tightened.

Mark continued, "I saw you follow Amy that night. And I saw you come back… alone."

A flicker of something passed across Mary's face — annoyance? Shame?

"She went dark," Mary said. "Didn't show up again. She ghosted all of us."

"She didn't ghost us," Mark said. "She was taken."

Mary blinked.

He moved closer, voice low. "Someone is playing all sides. Someone knew about the mirror camera. About the footage. About the rituals."

Mary whispered, "You think one of us set the trap."

Mark nodded.

"And now," he said, "they're pulling strings. Turning us against each other. And if we don't figure out who it is—"

"We all go down," Mary finished for him.

Silence.

Then Mary stepped forward, close enough to smell the tension on him. "So what do you want, Mark?"

His voice didn't shake. "An alliance."

She raised a brow. "You and me?"

He nodded. "We're the only ones thinking clearly."

Mary looked down at her glass. Then she set it aside.

"Alright," she said. "Let's find out who's bleeding us dry."

Chapter: Fifty-Seven- THE TRAP SNAPS SHUT

Mike's hands were clenched so tightly around the steering wheel that his knuckles looked bone-white even in the darkness of the car interior. Beside him, Jane sat perfectly still, her jaw tense, her body alert, as if bracing for something. They had left the outskirts of the city hours ago under the cover of nightfall, circling back toward Mike's place to regroup.

But something was off. Mike felt it in his chest — a low, gnawing instinct, honed from years of discipline and danger.

The closer they got to home, the worse the feeling became.

As the car rolled quietly onto his street — Cromwell Street — Mike noticed it immediately. There was a van parked across the road from his driveway. Not unusual on its own. But its windows were fogged up. No movement. No interior lights. Still. Watching.

He didn't slow down. He drove past the house completely.

Jane frowned. "That wasn't the plan."

"There's eyes on the house," Mike muttered. "We don't go in until I know who's watching."

Jane twisted in her seat, watching the van fade into the mirror. "Could be press. Or worse."

Mike shook his head. "Not press. Press would have swarmed by now. This is quiet. Tactical."

They pulled into a petrol station two blocks away. Mike killed the engine. For a long moment, neither of them spoke.

Then Jane turned, her voice low. "They know."

Mike didn't ask who "they" were. The police? Whoever leaked the footage? Or someone closer? The group had already begun to fracture under pressure.

"I stashed the rest of the equipment in the crawlspace," he said, as if rehearsing details kept reality at bay. "No prints. No fibres. But the garage is… not clean."

Jane sighed, leaning her head back. "She's still in the freezer."

Debbie. Or what was left of her.

They were walking a tightrope of logic, each step thinner, riskier, more desperate.

Jane broke the silence. "What if it's Amy?"

Mike glanced at her, eyebrows rising. "Amy's gone."

"Or playing dead." She looked at him, eyes dark with something between fear and obsession. "She's clever. She's always been clever. And we never saw her body, Mike. Not once."

Mike didn't answer, but his pulse began to pound.

"I keep thinking about the footage," Jane continued. "The gurgling clip. No face. It didn't feel right. It didn't feel like Amy."

"You think it was a plant?"

"I think someone wants us chasing ghosts while they set the trap."

Mike exhaled slowly, his military mind beginning to map out possibilities. "We need to split. You go dark for 48 hours. I'll double back. Clean the freezer. If the van's still there by morning, I'll force a confrontation."

Jane stared at him. "You're going back there?"

"I have to," he said, jaw set. "Everything is there. Everything we are."

There was a silence between them. Heavy. Tense. Final.

Then she nodded. "Be careful."

Mike didn't reply. He was already calculating entries, exits, and contingencies.

Because now it wasn't just about secrets.

It was about survival.

Chapter: Fifty-Eight- SECRETS IN THE STATIC

Mary moved like a shadow through the narrow back streets behind the university campus, Mark trailing behind her at a distance that was neither close enough to draw attention nor far enough to be lost. She was sharp. He knew that. She'd been watching all of them since the night at the hotel, playing a long game that he hadn't yet figured out. But tonight, something was different.

Mary wasn't heading toward her apartment like he'd expected. She was heading east — toward the old media labs that had been disused for over a year. Mark's boots crunched lightly on gravel as he followed her past the rusting fence and into the shadows cast by a half-broken security lamp. The place reeked of damp insulation and forgotten memories.

Mary paused near a side entrance. Without looking back, she said calmly, "You can come out now, Mark."

Mark stiffened, caught. He stepped into view, his hands raised slightly, as if approaching a wild animal.

"You've been following me," she continued, turning to face him. Her eyes weren't angry — they were calculating.

"Had to," Mark said flatly. "You don't trust me. I don't trust anyone right now either."

Mary studied him, then turned and unlocked the heavy door with a key he hadn't seen her take out. "Good," she said. "Let's stop pretending."

Inside, the place was even darker. A generator hummed in the distance, barely keeping a handful of emergency lights glowing. The media lab was supposed to be closed — renovations halted indefinitely after a funding scandal.

And yet… the equipment had power.

Mary led him down a corridor and into a small room cluttered with tech — old monitors, cables, even a signal scanner. On one wall was a corkboard covered in printed screenshots, timestamps, maps, and candid photos of each member of the group.

Mark froze.

"You've been tracking us," he said slowly.

Mary didn't look at him. She reached for a folder sitting under a monitor and tossed it onto the table. The same piece of paper

Mike had read the night before was inside — but this time, there were annotations, highlighted sections, even scribbled equations.

"What is this?"

"It's not just a note," she said. "It's a cipher. A code. Debbie didn't just die — she was trying to tell us something."

Mark stepped closer, scanning the lines. "So what's the message?"

Mary finally looked at him, and her voice dropped into something colder. "Coordinates. Locations. Symbols used in ancient blood rites… and something else. A signature."

"Whose?"

"I'm not sure yet," she admitted. "But this—" she pointed at the string of glyphs at the bottom of the note "—this matches a symbol I found etched into the back of one of the hotel mirrors."

Mark's breath caught. "So… someone's been watching us longer than we thought."

Mary nodded. "This didn't start with Amy. Or even Debbie. We've been part of something… older. Bigger."

Mark's throat went dry. "What do we do?"

Mary turned back to the wall of evidence. "We find whoever left the note. We find the watcher. And we end this — before it ends us."

Chapter: Fifty-Nine- THE HOUSE THAT WATCHES

Mike's old M-Class Mercedes rolled quietly into the driveway, the headlights cutting across the front of the house in long, yellow beams. Jane sat in the passenger seat, silent, arms folded tightly across her chest. Neither of them had spoken much since the CCTV footage — the one with the distorted clip of Amy — had gone viral. Their shared silence now felt less like comfort and more like a pact.

The house loomed ahead, dark except for a faint blue flicker escaping from the living room window. As they stepped inside, Jane instinctively locked the door behind them, then drew the curtains. Every noise in the street — a car, a pedestrian, a barking dog — felt like a potential threat. Like someone was watching.

Mike went straight to his office at the back of the house and fired up the desktop. His knuckles were white from how hard he gripped the mouse. Jane hovered behind him.

"Think it's still up?" she asked, her voice barely audible.

Mike grunted. "If it is, we need to know what people are saying."

He logged onto a few private forums, the kind where darker content lingered longer, and ran a search.

The clip was still circulating. But now there were screenshots too — stills of the blood-smeared walls, Amy's blurred face twisted in what looked like either agony or ecstasy. Someone had slowed the footage down, enhancing every frame.

Jane's hand flew to her mouth.

"Jesus," she whispered.

"They're dissecting it," Mike said grimly. "They're guessing who the other people are. They've identified the hotel suite already. It's only a matter of time."

He clicked over to a thread titled The Nottingham Blood Cult? and began reading aloud:

"Some kind of freaky sex ritual… probably students… maybe part of a secret society.

Anyone else notice the symbols drawn in blood near the mirror?"

Mike stopped reading. His eyes narrowed. "Symbols? What symbols?"

Jane looked at him. "You mean… you didn't notice any?"

Mike shook his head slowly. "No one mentioned anything like that before."

Jane crossed her arms. "I think… someone's adding to the story. Shaping it."

Mike turned to look at her. "You think this is being manipulated?"

Jane nodded. "Maybe by the same person who left that red recording light by the river. Maybe whoever slipped that note to Debbie."

Mike leaned back in his chair, rubbing his eyes. "I feel like we're being pulled deeper into a game we didn't agree to play."

Jane didn't answer, but the silence was thick with agreement.

Then — the unmistakable ping of an email.

Mike turned to the screen. One new message. No sender name. No subject. Just a single link.

He hesitated. Clicked.

A live feed opened.

A camera. Looking into a dimly lit room. At a chair. A figure tied to it.

Jane gasped. "That's… that's Mark!"

Mike's stomach twisted. "And someone's letting us watch."

He reached for the keyboard with trembling fingers.

"They know we're involved. They want us to see what happens next."

Chapter: Sixty- THE LIVE FEED

Mike's fingers hovered over the keyboard, but he didn't type. He didn't know what to say. Jane stood behind him, her hand on the back of the chair, her knuckles white.

The livestream on the screen showed Mark — unmistakably — slouched forward in a chair, hands bound behind his back, duct tape across his mouth. The feed was grainy, the audio full of static, but the unmistakable sound of shallow breathing could be heard, as if the microphone was close to his mouth.

"He's alive," Jane said, voice trembling.

"For now," Mike muttered. "Where the hell is he?"

The room was unfamiliar. Concrete floor, exposed piping above, no windows — a basement, maybe, or an old industrial space. The lighting was dim, almost green-tinted. Someone had set this up deliberately. Professionally. This wasn't some amateur prank.

Mike leaned forward and clicked "inspect" on the browser. He wasn't a hacker, but he knew enough from his time in the Marines and various overseas assignments to recognize when something was being routed through multiple proxies.

"No IP address," he said grimly. "At least, not one that makes sense. It's bouncing all over the globe. Germany. Romania. Back to London."

Jane moved around and sat beside him, her arms wrapped tightly around her knees now, eyes wide. "Do you think he… did something to Debbie? Is this revenge?"

Mike didn't answer. Not yet. His gut had been twisting since that moment by the riverbank, when the red light flashed from the shadows. Someone had been watching. Someone had planned this.

The screen flickered — and then a second camera feed appeared. A different angle, same room. But this time the camera was slowly zooming in on something behind Mark. A message painted in what looked like blood:

"TELL THE TRUTH. OR WATCH THEM DIE."

Jane recoiled. "Oh my God…"

Mike grabbed his burner phone and snapped a photo of the screen. "This is no longer about hiding the body. Someone's playing goddamn games with us."

Jane reached forward and paused the feed.

"You think it's Amy?" she asked quietly. "You think she's still alive, and this is some twisted punishment?"

Mike shook his head. "No. That wasn't Amy in the feed. I don't think she set this up. But I do think this goes further than her. She might've known something. Maybe even suspected it was coming."

He stared at the blood message again.

"TELL THE TRUTH."

Jane whispered, "About Debbie?"

Mike said nothing. His jaw tightened, fists clenching. "There's more. More than what any of us have said out loud."

He got up from the chair and walked to a locked cabinet at the far side of the room. Jane watched, confused, as he pulled out a black duffel bag and dropped it onto the couch with a dull thud.

"What's that?"

Mike unzipped it. Inside, neatly organized: burner phones, rolls of cash, several passports, and a Glock 19.

"Contingency," he said flatly.

"For what?"

Mike's eyes met hers. "For when the past starts crawling back out of the ground."

A ding interrupted them. Another message popped up on the screen. Just three words:

"MIDNIGHT. BRING MARY."

Mike stared at it.

"We've got a deadline," he said. "And someone else is pulling the strings."

Chapter: Sixty-One THE MIDNIGHT RULE

Mike locked the front door of his house, drawing the curtains tight across the windows before flipping off all the lights. The house slipped into shadow, but he moved with the ease of habit — the instincts of an old soldier kicking in. He didn't need light. He needed clarity.

Midnight.

He kept hearing the word in his head like the second hand on a ticking clock. Whoever was behind this was giving them a time and a demand: Bring Mary.

He returned to the couch, where Jane was now pacing. Her nerves were fraying, her eyes darting toward the duffel on the coffee table.

"They know everything," she said. "It's not just Debbie. It's not even just Amy. This is about all of it, Mike."

He nodded once, eyes cold. "They want to test us. They want to see what we'll do when the heat's on."

"Bring Mary," she repeated. "Why her?"

Mike's jaw twitched. "Because she's the oldest. The one who brought authority to the group. The one they think has the most to lose."

He stood and walked back to the duffel, pulling out one of the burner phones and pressing it into Jane's hand. "Keep this with you. Don't use it unless you absolutely have to. No texting. No scrolling. It's clean. Wipe it after each use."

Jane blinked at him, then nodded, her hands trembling slightly.

"You're not going alone, are you?"

"No," he said, pulling on a dark hoodie over his T-shirt. "But I'll handle it if I have to."

She watched him move around the room gathering gear — flashlight, pocket knife, gloves, a USB stick. There was no panic in his actions, just preparation. He had been here before — not this exact situation, but the edge-of-madness tension. The anticipation of violence. It smelled the same. Felt the same.

He checked the Glock again, loaded a fresh mag, then slipped it into the back waistband of his jeans, under the hoodie. He wasn't looking to start a war. But he wasn't walking into a trap empty-handed either.

"What about Mary?" Jane asked. "Does she even know?"

"Not yet." Mike picked up his phone and stared at it. "But she will."

He called her number.

It rang twice before she answered, her voice calm, clipped.

"Mike?"

"We've got a meet. Midnight. You're invited."

Pause.

"Where?"

"I don't know yet. But they said bring you."

Another pause. Then a sigh.

"I expected this."

"You expected someone to take Mark hostage and paint a threat in blood?"

"No. But I expected this to escalate. It always does with secrets like ours."

Mike rubbed his forehead. "Get ready. Pack light. And Mary…"

"What?"

"If this goes sideways, I need to know you've got my back."

A brief silence. Then: "Always."

They hung up.

Mike pocketed the phone and looked back at Jane, who was now sitting on the edge of the couch, staring into the darkened kitchen.

"Whatever's coming," she said, "we're not all making it through this. You know that, right?"

Mike nodded, expression unreadable.

"Yeah. I do."

And then he stepped out into the night, locking the door behind him.

Chapter: Sixty-Two-A
WOMAN PREPARED

Mary stood in front of her bedroom mirror, staring at her reflection. The late-night city hummed faintly outside her window — the kind of quiet that only deep hours offered, where every noise could be a warning.

She had the phone pressed to her shoulder, cradled against her cheek, as her hands moved quickly over her dresser drawers — pulling things out, laying them neatly on the bed. Notebooks, a compact first-aid kit, her passport, and a small, black velvet pouch that hadn't been opened in years.

"I'm coming," she'd told Mike, and now every cell in her body was vibrating with a strange mix of dread and exhilaration.

She ended the call, slid her phone into the inside pocket of her coat, and zipped it up. The weight of what she was carrying — not just in her pockets, but in her history — was pressing down on her chest. All the decisions, all the dark little experiments, the erotic curiosity twisted with real pain — it had never felt this heavy before.

She walked to the edge of her bed and sat, glancing down at the envelope she had taken from Debbie's hand. The same one she hadn't yet revealed to Mike in full. She had only shown him the outside, the symbol.

Inside was something else entirely — not just a message but a map, a sequence of letters and numbers that looked like gibberish to the untrained eye. But Mary knew codes. Patterns. And what she'd seen sent a chill down her spine.

It wasn't written by Debbie.

It was for her.

A test.

A taunt.

Or maybe… a warning.

Her fingers hovered over the black pouch. She opened it and removed a thin silver chain. Hanging from it was a small, carved figure — a token from a darker time in her life when bloodletting was more than just a kink. It had been a belief. A kind of faith. She hadn't worn it in years.

She looped it around her neck.

Outside, she heard a car pull up. Not Mike — she knew the sound of his old Mercedes. This one was smoother. Newer.

She moved to the window and peeked through the slats.

A sleek black sedan, engine idling.

No one got out.

Mary narrowed her eyes.

Was it surveillance?

A message?

Her doorbell rang once. Sharp. Then silence.

She didn't move.

Not right away.

Instead, she walked back into her kitchen and opened the drawer beneath the sink. Inside was a polished steel blade — a small ceremonial dagger from her days in Berlin. When she'd taught at the Freie Universität. When she had been part of something underground.

She slipped it into a sheath inside her boot.

By the time she opened her front door, the street was empty again.

The car was gone.

But on her doorstep sat a single red envelope, wax-sealed with the same strange insignia as Debbie's message.

She picked it up, heart pounding.

Another piece.

Another game.

She walked back inside, locked the door behind her, and texted Mike:

"They're watching us. I've got something. Meet me at the old observatory. Midnight."

Then she reached for her coat.

Chapter: Sixty-Three-The Crimson Message

The envelope was heavier than it looked, and warm. Not with heat, but with tension — the kind of heat that lived in your palms when adrenaline had nowhere else to go.

Mary sat back down at her kitchen table, the old wood scarred with knife marks and candle wax burns from years ago. She'd done so many strange things at this table — dissected the motivations of students, sipped wine with fellow academics, pricked her own finger under moonlight — but tonight, this table would be the gateway.

She ran her finger beneath the wax seal. It cracked like brittle bone.

Inside was not a letter. No paper. No standard message.

There was a photograph.

A Polaroid.

Grainy. But vivid enough to freeze her heart.

It was a shot of Debbie, taken after her death — after the cutting, the cleaning, the freezing — but before she'd been wrapped. Before Mike and the others had bagged her up. Her eyes were closed, but her body lay exposed on the kitchen table in Mike's house, her limbs laid out unnaturally straight.

The camera had been close. Very close. From above.

Mary looked up at her ceiling. She felt the walls compress around her.

She turned the Polaroid over.

On the back, in a precise hand, someone had written:

"One of you lies. One of you kills. One of you watches.

The first to speak burns."

Below it, a symbol.

That same damn symbol again — like a stylized eye dripping blood.

And beneath the symbol, a date and time:

04.04 — 01:13 AM

RUINS

Mary's breath caught. The ruins — the nickname for the old chapel just off campus, half-forgotten, wrapped in ivy and mystery. A place used for drunken rituals by students, whispered about in staff meetings, but never officially acknowledged.

She stared at the image again.

Who had taken it?

Someone had been inside Mike's house. Or had access to his cameras. Or maybe… they had planted their own.

But that didn't make sense.

Unless—

Unless this had never been their game. Maybe the Blood Spurts had only ever been pieces on someone else's board. Watched. Recorded. Controlled.

And now? Threatened.

Mary placed the Polaroid flat on the table, smoothing it with trembling fingers. The message was simple, sharp, and cruel.

One of you lies. One of you kills. One of you watches.

The question wasn't just who. The question was: who knew they were being watched and who was still in the dark?

And then — the most terrifying thought of all — what if it wasn't one of them at all?

Mary stood, sliding the envelope into her coat. She picked up the blade from the counter and tucked it into her boot again. She no longer felt like a professor, or a protector, or even a player in the blood-soaked theatre of lust and death they had created.

She felt like prey.

And it was almost midnight.

Chapter: Sixty-Four- The Stillness Before the Knife

The clock on the wall ticked louder than it should have. Tick. Tick. Tick. Just past 12:43 AM.

Mike sat in the garage, the freezer humming behind him like a lazy animal digesting something dark and final. The red light bulb overhead cast everything in a strange hue — Jane's skin glowed like rusted porcelain, her eyes flickering with the reflection of the flame in the candle she'd lit. The ritual had passed, the heat of lust had died down, and now only tension remained.

He'd changed into clean clothes. Jeans, black shirt, leather jacket zipped halfway. His boots were still stained along the soles.

Maybe no one would notice. But he would. He always noticed.

He stood now, restless, pacing the concrete floor, the cold of it rising through the soles of his feet. He didn't like stillness. Not anymore. Not after what they'd done.

Jane was sitting at his workbench now, quietly flipping through an old anatomy book Mike hadn't touched since his medic days in the Marines. Her fingertips were smudged with ink from something she'd been writing earlier — a poem, she claimed. But Mike had only half listened.

His eyes kept drifting to the corner of the garage — where the camera had once been hidden. The one he'd taken down just hours before the police might've come knocking. Paranoia had crept in like mold after the rain.

He turned to Jane.

"You ever feel like we're being… steered?"

She looked up slowly. "What do you mean?"

"Like someone else is pulling the strings. Watching us. Recording us. Even before Amy's clip went viral." He scratched his beard, a nervous tick. "How the hell did someone even get that footage? That angle? That sound?"

Jane's smile faltered.

"You think someone's in the house?" she asked, half-joking, but her eyes said she wasn't.

Mike shook his head. "No. I mean—maybe. But I think we've been part of something bigger. Since the beginning."

He crossed the garage and opened a drawer near the freezer. Inside: duct tape, gloves, bleach, an old burner phone he hadn't touched in weeks. He stared at it.

No messages.

But maybe soon.

He pulled out the phone, turned it over in his hands.

Then he froze.

It vibrated.

Once. A slow, crawling hum.

UNKNOWN NUMBER. No message. Just a single image loading.

He tapped it.

It was a still image of the freezer.

From above.

From tonight.

Mike dropped the phone. It clattered across the floor.

"Jesus Christ."

Jane stood quickly, voice trembling. "Mike? What is it?"

He didn't answer. Instead, he walked over to the freezer, pressing his hand on the top. The metal was cool. Calm. Deceptive.

Then, almost on instinct, he reached beneath it — and felt something.

A wire.

Coiled. Subtle. New.

"Someone bugged this place," he whispered.

And then, like a quiet gunshot in the silence, the burner phone vibrated again.

Another image.

This time, of him — standing in the exact spot he was in now, frozen like a deer in headlights. Someone had taken the shot seconds ago.

He turned toward the window.

There was nothing but night.

Chapter: Sixty-Five- The Warning in the Night

Mike didn't waste a second.

He snatched his car keys from the hook by the kitchen door, shoved the burner phone into his jacket pocket, and left the garage light humming behind him. His boots hit the gravel hard, echoing in the silence of his neighbourhood. The cold slapped him across the face as if to jolt him into focus.

He didn't know how they were being watched — or why — but someone was playing a dangerous game. And if Mary was holding the red envelope, if she was even close to cracking what it meant, then she might be the next target.

The M-Class Mercedes coughed to life, headlights slicing through the shadows. Mike punched the accelerator and tore down the street, tires barking as he cornered too fast.

He called her phone twice — no answer.

"Come on, Mary, pick up," he muttered, heart hammering in his chest.

The streets were nearly empty, the city's usual glow swallowed by the late hour. Storefronts were shut tight, clubs and bars quieting down. Only the sodium streetlights kept company, their halos flickering like dying fireflies.

He reached Mary's apartment complex off Peel Street in under ten minutes. It was an older building, tall and narrow, like a brick spine against the sky. He parked in a side alley, engine still running, and sprinted toward the side entrance. He knew her layout, knew which windows were hers.

As he reached the stairwell, his mind was racing.

What if the footage was sent to others?

What if someone was already inside?

What if he was too late?

The hallway to her apartment was quiet, save for the hum of an old vending machine. Apartment 3B. He pounded on the door with the flat of his fist.

"Mary! Open up — it's Mike!"

No sound.

He tried the handle. Locked.

His hand slid to the lockpick set sewn into the lining of his jacket. Old habits — bad ones — but helpful now. He worked quickly, forcing the tumblers until they clicked.

The door creaked open.

Inside, the place was dimly lit — just one lamp on near her reading chair. The red envelope was open on the table, papers spread across it like spilled blood.

But no Mary.

"Mary?" Mike called out, stepping in, closing the door behind him. "It's me."

Then he heard it — the quiet creak of floorboards from the back room.

He turned, hand going to the knife clipped at his belt.

Mary stepped into the hallway. Her face was pale, but focused. Alert.

"You came," she said.

"I had to. We've been compromised." He walked to her, then gestured to the papers. "Someone sent me a photo. Just now. Of me, in the garage. From above. The freezer. They're watching us."

Mary's eyes flickered. She didn't look surprised. "I know," she said. "I think I know who it is."

Mike narrowed his eyes. "You'd better start talking."

Mary took a breath. "But not here."

She grabbed the red envelope and stuffed the contents into her shoulder bag.

"We have to go to the university," she said. "There's something in the archives. I think… this goes deeper than we thought."

Mike looked at her — then nodded.

And together, they stepped back into the night.

Chapter: Sixty-Six-Jane in the Silence

The house was quiet again. Too quiet.

Jane sat curled up on the edge of Mike's worn leather sofa, her knees tucked to her chest, a blanket draped loosely around her shoulders. The heavy silence pressed against the windows like a held breath. Only the occasional creak from the cooling pipes or wind brushing the siding offered any sound.

She had cleaned herself up — mostly. The blood was gone from her hands, but she still smelled it. Still felt it. The freezer in the garage had been humming earlier, a low mechanical moan that vibrated beneath her skin. She tried not to think about what was inside.

Tried.

Failed.

Her phone sat face-down on the coffee table. She hadn't touched it in hours. The world outside the house no longer felt real. Her timeline had shattered the moment Debbie screamed, the moment fantasy slipped into something darker, irreversible.

The memory of the 6-second video haunted her. Amy's gurgling, the red flicker, the way her face was just obscured enough. It was clever. Chilling. Viral.

She wondered if her face had shown up in any of the clips.

A sudden sound — faint, metallic — drew her attention toward the back of the house. The kitchen. Or maybe the garage door. Her breath hitched. She waited. Listened.

Silence again.

"Probably the wind," she whispered to herself, though her voice didn't sound confident.

Still wrapped in the blanket, she rose and padded slowly down the hallway. The wooden floor was cold beneath her bare feet. As she passed the door to the garage, she paused.

It was cracked open.

She was sure Mike had closed it when he left.

"Hello?" she called, softly.

Nothing.

Jane's heart thudded louder than her footsteps as she nudged the door open further. The garage was dark except for the orange glow of a workbench lamp, flickering like a candle struggling to stay alive. Tools hung neatly on a pegboard. The freezer — the big one they had used — sat quiet and undisturbed.

But the garage wasn't empty.

There was a coat on the floor. Not Mike's. A hooded one. And next to it… a single glove. Latex.

She stepped forward, almost in a trance.

Then — her phone buzzed. A message.

She turned and ran back to the living room, heart racing. When she picked up the phone, the screen flashed:

UNKNOWN NUMBER

📷 1 New Image Received

She opened it.

It was her. Standing in the garage just now. Looking at the glove. From above.

Her breath caught in her throat. She turned slowly, looking at the ceiling. Nothing obvious. No red lights.

But someone was here. Had been here. Maybe still was.

The message buzzed again.

UNKNOWN NUMBER:

"Nice to see you again, Jane. Don't go anywhere."

Her hands trembled.

Mike had said they were compromised. But Jane suddenly understood something deeper: She was being hunted.

Alone.

And the game wasn't over.

Not by a long shot.

Chapter: Sixty-Seven-The Return to Campus

The city looked different at midnight.

Fog clung low to the ground like a ghost unsure of where to haunt. Orange streetlights flickered above empty sidewalks. Mike drove in silence, hands gripping the steering wheel tighter than necessary. Mary sat beside him, her legs crossed, one heel tapping against the footwell. She hadn't spoken much since they left the river.

Neither had he.

They both knew the red light on the bank had changed everything.

"Do you think it was live?" Mary finally asked, her voice barely above a whisper.

Mike glanced at her. "Could've been. Could've been motion-triggered. Or set up in advance. Someone knew we'd be there."

Mary's lips pressed into a thin line. "You think someone's been following us this whole time?"

"I think someone's been playing a longer game than we realized," he said, slowing as the gates of the university appeared up ahead. "Amy might've known. She was too clever not to."

Mary didn't answer. Instead, she pulled the red envelope out of her coat and turned it over in her fingers. "We need to know who sent this."

"We need a lot more than that," Mike said, turning into a quiet side entrance meant for faculty access. "Security. Access logs. CCTV — if they haven't been scrubbed already."

They parked behind the biomedical building. The same building Amy had practically lived in during her third year. The labs were dark, but a single security light glowed near the side entrance. Mary reached into the glovebox, pulled out her old access card.

"I don't even know if this thing still works."

Mike raised an eyebrow. "Wanna bet?"

The card beeped against the reader. Green light. Door clicked open.

Mary smiled tightly. "Old habits."

Inside, the hallway smelled of bleach and faint disinfectant. Echoes of past experiments. Knowledge. Secrets. Blood.

Mike kept close as they moved through the corridors toward the old storage labs. Mary's mind raced. Was the footage saved on one of the lab servers? Did Amy have backups here? She had worked on research projects — it wouldn't be strange for her to stash things in the secure lockers.

They reached the locked door at the end of the hall. Mary typed in a code she remembered from when she worked here.

It didn't work.

She tried again.

Still no good.

Mike leaned over her shoulder. "Let me."

He crouched, popped open a panel near the card reader, and in seconds had a circuit bypassed. The door buzzed and popped open.

"Marine training?" Mary asked, half-impressed.

"Bad decisions," he said.

Inside, they found a dimly lit lab with humming equipment. Dust-coated monitors. One of the hard drives had been freshly accessed — Mary noticed it immediately.

Someone else had been here.

Or maybe… never left.

Mike reached toward the desk — and paused.

A note. Folded. Marked with the same handwriting from the red envelope.

He opened it.

It read:

"You buried one body. How many more are coming?"

Mary backed up toward the door. "Mike…"

A soft click echoed through the lab. The door had shut.

Locked.

A camera in the corner turned with a soft whirring sound.

They were being watched.

Again.

Chapter: Sixty-Eight-Jane in the Dark

The clock in Mike's house ticked loud in the silence, like it had grown fangs.

Jane sat alone in the living room, legs curled beneath her on the leather couch, wrapped in one of Mike's blankets. The house felt colder without the others—especially without Mike. It was too quiet. Too clean. Too still.

She had wiped down the freezer earlier, more out of guilt than fear. Her hands still smelled faintly of bleach despite scrubbing them twice. It didn't matter. She could still see Debbie's face when she blinked. Pale. Cold. Gone.

The walls around her seemed to press in with every passing minute. The shadows stretched longer than they should have.

She checked her phone again.

No messages.

No missed calls.

Just... stillness.

She stood suddenly, needing to move, her bare feet padding softly across the floor.

The kitchen light flickered as she entered—damn old wiring. Still, she opened a cupboard, poured herself a glass of water, took one sip, then set it down. Her stomach turned.

She didn't know why she stayed.

Maybe it was the thrill.

Maybe it was Mike.

Or maybe… it was too late to leave.

Her thoughts spiralled. She remembered what Amy had once whispered in her ear, just before slicing the tip of her finger and letting the blood drip on her tongue:

"You either taste it and learn to love it… or you run."

Jane hadn't run.

But maybe she should've.

The house creaked. Floorboards shifting upstairs.

She froze.

Mike and Mary were still gone.

"Hello?" she called out, voice trembling more than she wanted.

No response.

She grabbed a kitchen knife from the drawer—old habits, new fear.

"Mark?" she tried, just in case.

Still nothing.

Then: a knock on the front door.

Soft. Deliberate.

Jane's heart jumped. She crept toward the front window, careful not to make a sound. Pulled the curtain aside just a crack.

No one.

The porch light flicked on suddenly, illuminating the empty step.

But then, she saw it.

Something red.

Another envelope.

Her breath caught in her throat.

She opened the door slowly, reached down with shaking fingers, picked up the envelope and stepped back inside.

This one wasn't like the first.

No wax seal.

No handwriting.

Just a small USB stick taped to the inside flap.

Jane looked at it as though it might bite her.

She held it between her thumb and forefinger, turned it over, stared at the glint of plastic and metal.

Her hands trembled as she plugged it into the laptop still open on the coffee table.

The screen flickered.

One video file.

Untitled.

She clicked it.

Static. Then…

Grainy footage.

Her. In the garage.

With Mike.

The freezer.

Blood.

The knife.

Then a close-up.

Her face, frozen in a moment of ecstasy.

And behind her… someone watching through the window.

She gasped and slammed the laptop shut.

Footsteps now. Outside. Gravel crunching.

She backed away from the door, heart hammering in her chest.

Who was filming them?

Who left the USB?

How long had they been watched?

And most terrifying of all—what did they want?

Chapter: Sixty-Nine-Into the Depths

The university's maintenance building sat quiet at this hour, long after faculty had gone home. It was a forgotten corner of campus, a squat brick box on the edge of the science block, lit by a single flickering light above the staff entrance. Mike parked in the loading bay behind it, and Mary stepped out, her coat pulled tight against the chill.

She didn't speak as she led him around to the back. Her eyes were fierce, locked in a storm of calculation. Mike followed, the red envelope still tucked in his jacket pocket. His mind buzzed with the words he'd read— Debbie's note, hastily scrawled and cryptic.

"He wears a face that isn't his.

Look to the mirror.

He is one of you, but he was never with you."

It wasn't just a warning—it was a riddle. A cipher to the madness they'd found themselves drowning in.

Mary swiped a keycard at the side door. It beeped and unlocked with a heavy clunk. Inside, the hall was dark but familiar— janitorial supplies, maintenance tools, and access to systems usually unseen by students. This was how she knew to come here. Her long tenure at the university had its privileges. And secrets.

"What are we looking for?" Mike asked, voice low, footsteps echoing.

Mary didn't answer right away. She led him down the hall, stopping in front of a metal panel locked with a code. She keyed in a sequence from memory. The door clicked, and they stepped into a hidden corridor, narrow and dimly lit. Pipes ran along the ceiling.

"CCTV archive," she finally said. "Live feeds, backups. If we're being watched, this is where we'll see it."

Mike gave a slow nod. "And if someone tampered with it?"

Mary glanced back. "Then we'll know we're already too late."

The corridor opened into a control room, small and cluttered with monitors, servers, and filing cabinets. The hum of electronics filled the space. One monitor showed a rotating feed from different cameras around campus and the surrounding streets.

Mary sat at the console and began typing furiously. Mike stood behind her, watching as she navigated through menus, timestamps, and access logs.

"There," she whispered, stopping on a feed from two nights ago.

The angle showed the rear exit of the hotel they'd stayed in. Grainy black-and-white footage. A figure—hooded, face obscured—stood just beyond the light, placing something under the door. Not the same figure they'd seen on the suite hallway camera.

"This is someone else," Mike murmured.

Mary didn't speak. She rewound. Played it again.

The figure paused. Glanced toward the camera. Held up a single hand and waved.

Waved.

Like they knew they were being watched.

"I think this is bigger than we thought," Mary said quietly. "This isn't just about Debbie. This is someone watching all of us."

"Maybe orchestrating it," Mike added, brow furrowed. "Whoever left that note—Debbie trusted them enough to take it. But they didn't stop what happened."

Mary's jaw tightened. "Or they weren't trying to stop it. Just… document it."

She turned in the chair, staring up at him.

"We're part of something now, Mike. Whether we want to be or not."

From his pocket, Mike unfolded the note again, eyes scanning its warning.

He is one of you, but he was never with you.

Could it be Mark? John?

Or someone else entirely?

Mary switched monitors, pulling up the interior feeds from that night in the suite.

She froze.

Mike leaned in.

There. In the mirror above the bathroom sink.

For a split second—one frame only—someone else's face, watching.

"Pause it," he whispered.

She did.

They stared at the screen, heartbeats racing.

The face was half-covered by shadows, but there was no mistaking it.

It wasn't anyone from the group.

And it definitely wasn't supposed to be there.

Chapter: Seventy-The Watcher

Somewhere, in a space that didn't exist on any university blueprint, the mysterious figure sat cross-legged in front of a wall of screens. A solitary desk lamp cast a circle of yellow light across tangled notebooks, old photographs, and scattered USB sticks marked in black ink with names and dates. The room was silent except for the faint hum of the surveillance system and the occasional scratch of a pen on paper.

The figure leaned forward.

On the centre monitor: the paused frame from the hotel mirror—his reflection. A fraction of a second, barely perceptible. But enough. He hadn't meant to be seen.

Or maybe he had.

A gloved hand reached out and dragged a control wheel backward, rewinding the footage just before that moment, then playing it again in slow motion.

He watched them all: Mike pacing, Mary inspecting the mirror, Amy whispering to herself before slipping away to her room.

Every movement catalogued. Every interaction timestamped.

Subject Red — Amy.

Subject Blue — Mike.

Subject Green — Mary.

The figure's pen hovered over a page titled Blood Spurts. Below it were crude diagrams—circles of names, branching lines, strange signs and old symbols— connecting them all. A web of desire, control, secrecy.

He flipped to another page: a photocopy of Debbie's university ID, now stained with something dark. A sticky note was attached:

"Debbie: Failed containment. Unreliable. Disposal permitted."

He stared at it for a long moment before tearing the page from the book and burning it in a metal dish beside him.

One less variable.

A monitor on the far left blinked. Movement detected. The camera outside Mike's house. The group was still active—still together. He didn't like that.

He zoomed in.

Mary and Mike. Back from their detour to the university. They looked shaken.

They'd seen the footage.

That wasn't part of the plan.

The figure stood up, stretching. He moved like liquid in shadow—graceful, deliberate. On the shelf above the desk were rows of labelled vials and small leather pouches. He chose one, marked with an "M," and tucked it into the inside pocket of his long coat.

There was more work to do.

He pressed a button on the keyboard. One of the monitors switched to live feed: Mary's apartment door. The timestamp blinked— 22:56.

He smiled behind his mask.

"Time for another visit."

The camera feed flickered briefly.

Then went dark.

Chapter: Seventy-One- Into the Dark

The Watcher stepped out into the night.

The city clung to silence like a secret. Streetlights buzzed softly overhead, casting long shadows that bent unnaturally as he passed. He moved without haste, his coat brushing against the edges of brick walls and alley corners, face obscured beneath the wide brim of a hat and the folds of a dark scarf. A ghost in the machine. A shadow no one noticed.

Mary's apartment wasn't far.

He took a longer route—not out of fear of being seen, but to check the signal strength of the mirror cams. Four were still active. One had gone dark... the one in Jane's student flat.

Interesting.

He took note.

At the corner of Cromwell Street, he paused to open a small, old-fashioned flip phone—completely off-grid. No GPS. No internet. Only a blinking message icon. He clicked it open and read the text.

"SUBJECT M ASKING QUESTIONS. RED ENVELOPE CONFIRMED MISSING."

He tilted his head.

Mary had the envelope. That wasn't unexpected, but the fact she'd shown it to Mike was a deviation.

He looked up at the glowing apartment window two stories above. Mary's. Shadows moved behind the thin curtains—shapes of conversation, conflict, plotting.

They still thought they were running the game.

The Watcher reached into his coat and removed a small rectangular device—flat, matte black, with a single switch. When flipped, it let out a barely audible chirp, then settled into a low pulse. It was a scrambler—temporarily disabling local Wi-Fi and jamming short-range audio recording equipment.

No calls. No recordings.

He slipped around the side of the building, boots making no more noise than a falling leaf, and approached the fire escape. He'd used it before.

Climbing in silence, he reached the second-floor landing just beneath Mary's bathroom window. He stopped, crouching.

Inside, he could hear voices. Mike. Mary. Tension. Something about the paper. Something about Amy.

He reached into the pouch marked "M" and removed a small piece of thread-thin filament—almost invisible unless caught in the right light. He stretched it across the window frame, anchoring it with a light press. As soon as someone opened the window from inside, the signal would trip.

Then he'd know.

He leaned back, satisfied.

And waited.

A cat slinked across the alley below, pausing to stare up at the figure crouched in the shadows. Its ears twitched. Then it darted off into the dark.

Above, the curtain fluttered. Mary's shadow moved toward the window.

A test.

The filament held.

Not yet.

The Watcher stood, stepped back onto the ladder, and began descending. He had a new objective.

Find the envelope. Intercept Jane. End the experiment.

He didn't walk away.

He melted back into the city.

A whisper of movement. A breath of air.

Gone.

Chapter: Seventy-Two- Tangled Threads

The soft click of Mary's apartment door echoed as she locked it behind her. She didn't notice the gentle resistance in the window frame moments earlier, nor did

Mike—who stood rigid in the living room, staring down at the slip of paper Mary had handed him not long before.

His knuckles were white around the edges of the red envelope now folded in half, the contents burned into his brain.

"DO NOT TRUST HER.

She knows more than she's told.

Watch the mirrors.

They're watching back."

Mary emerged from the small kitchenette, holding two mugs of coffee, her face lined with fatigue but her movements deliberate.

"You haven't said much," she said quietly, handing Mike one of the mugs. "What's in that paper got you all locked up?"

Mike looked at her, searching. "You didn't write it?"

"No." Her answer came too fast. Too crisp.

He narrowed his eyes. "Then why was it in your possession? You said you pulled it from Debbie's hand… but now I'm wondering if it was left for someone. Not found."

Mary stiffened. "You think I planted it?"

"I think…" He sipped the bitter coffee. "I don't know what I think anymore. I've killed people before. In war. Clean. Surgical. But this? This is chaos. We don't even know who's running the show anymore."

Mary's lips curled slightly. "If anyone's running this show, Mike, it's you and me. We're the only ones still thinking clearly."

"Are we?" He took the envelope, unfolded it again, and set it on the coffee table between them. "Because whoever wrote that… they knew we'd come looking. They knew about the mirrors. About Amy. About you."

Mary sat down slowly. "What exactly do you want to ask me, Mike?"

He stared at her. Hard. The air between them was heavy, like wet smoke. "Where were you… really… the night Debbie died?"

Mary blinked. For just a second, something flickered across her face—annoyance? Pain? A flash of uncertainty?

"I was in the suite with the rest of you."

"Until you weren't. You said you left to check the corridor. That the scream woke you."

"And it did."

"And you came back through the front door?"

She nodded.

He leaned forward. "Then why wasn't your face caught on any of the mirror reflections? I've watched the clips—multiple times. Everyone shows up, Mary. Except you."

Silence.

Mary looked down, her finger tracing the rim of the coffee mug.

"Maybe," she said finally, "maybe I knew something was wrong before the scream. Maybe I was already looking. Maybe I saw something I haven't told you yet."

Mike didn't speak.

Mary met his gaze. "What if Amy knew this would happen? What if she was watching us all night?"

Mike sat back. Slowly. "Then why'd you let her leave?"

Mary smiled, but there was no warmth in it. "Because letting someone leave doesn't mean you're not following."

For a long moment, they sat like that—two predators trying to decide if they were allies or enemies.

Outside the window, across the street, something flickered and vanished.

Chapter: Seventy-Three-Jane in the Quiet

The bathroom light buzzed quietly overhead as Jane sat curled on the closed toilet seat, a towel draped loosely over her shoulders, her skin damp and pink from the hot shower. Her dark hair clung to her neck in tangled strands, and her eyes, ringed with red, stared into the middle distance like she was trying to remember the shape of normalcy.

She hadn't gone back to her student housing. She didn't want to. The thought of being surrounded by the things of her everyday life—textbooks, unfinished laundry, the smell of old incense—was revolting. Like pretending nothing had happened. Like erasing Debbie.

Debbie.

Her stomach turned. Her phone buzzed on the sink beside her. A single notification:

@bloodverse_unbound tagged you in a reel.

Her blood froze. No. No, no, no…

Jane snatched it up, her thumb shaking as she opened Instagram. The tag had vanished—removed. Already. The page that had posted it was gone too.

But not before she saw the thumbnail image.

A hand. Debbie's. Pale, limp, blood slicked.

The scream caught in her throat. She slapped the phone face down and pushed herself off the toilet, pacing the cramped bathroom. She was breathing hard, her chest rising and falling rapidly.

How many people have seen it now? How long before someone recognizes me?

The others kept saying they'd be fine. Stick to the story. Lay low. But Jane didn't believe that anymore. People weren't fine. Not Amy. Not Debbie. Not even Mike, no matter how cool he acted.

Jane stumbled back into the hallway, wrapping her arms around herself. Mike had been kind, sure. Gentle even, when she cried. And the thing in the garage… it was intense, visceral, necessary in a twisted kind of way. But now?

Now she wasn't sure if it was compassion or calculation.

Does he care… or is he just making sure I don't talk?

Her eyes flicked to the office door. Closed. Locked, probably. Where the videos had been viewed. Where Mike kept his files. His tools. The gear he never let anyone else near.

I should leave.

But where would she go? If she left now, she might never get the full story. Might become the scapegoat. Or worse—might end like Debbie.

She moved to the living room window, pulling back the curtain an inch. Across the street, the amber glow of a streetlamp flickered… and for a second, she could've sworn she saw someone leaning against the post.

Watching.

A black hoodie. Face obscured.

She gasped and stumbled back. When she peeked again—the figure was gone.

Jane's breath shook.

There were too many secrets. Too many eyes. And too few people she could trust.

She had to make a choice.

Stay with Mike and try to survive the storm?

Or run—and hope she wasn't already too deep to get out.

Chapter: Seventy-Four-Jane's Choice

The air in Mike's house felt heavier now, dense with the scent of old wood, copper, and something darker—like memories left to rot. Jane hovered near the living room window, still watching the place where the figure had stood, the afterimage burned into her mind like a ghost in the glass.

She hadn't imagined it.

She never imagined things. That was Amy's domain—wild, impulsive Amy who had flirted with danger like it was her lover. But Amy was gone now, and Jane was still here, caught in the fallout.

She slid her phone into the pocket of her hoodie and crept toward Mike's office door.

Still locked.

He doesn't trust you either, a voice whispered in her head. Maybe he never did.

Her fingers hovered over the doorknob, but she knew better. There'd be cameras inside. Or a mic. Or both. Mike was ex-military, and paranoid as hell. He probably had a motion sensor by the desk. She would've laughed if her stomach weren't in knots.

Instead, she turned and walked silently to the kitchen. Her boots made almost no sound on the wood flooring. It was early—still dark outside—but the digital clock above the stove read 04:43. Too late for sleep. Too early for escape.

She pulled open the fridge and stared inside. A bottle of water. Half a loaf of sourdough. A sealed container with a crimson sticker marked "Pet Food – Do Not Touch." Her gut flipped. She shut it quickly.

Jane turned to the garage door. Locked too.

Of course.

The freezer was out there.

Debbie was out there.

Jane rested her forehead against the door, listening. The distant hum of the freezer was faint but present, a constant low buzz behind the silence. Like a whisper. Like a heartbeat under the floorboards.

She pressed her hand against the cold door. What would it take to make it right again?

She should leave. She should run.

But she needed something first. Proof. Leverage. A way to survive when the house of cards collapsed. Because it would. All the fake calm in the world couldn't stop it.

Her thoughts swirled—about Amy, about Debbie, about that red blinking light Mike had seen by the river. About whoever had slipped that paper into Debbie's hand. And about the figure in the streetlight, who could be a stranger… or someone already on the inside.

She needed to know what was really going on.

Jane grabbed her coat and keys and quietly slipped out the back door. She moved like a ghost, sticking to the shadows, her mind racing as her boots hit the frost-tipped grass.

If Mike woke up now, she'd say she needed fresh air.

If he followed her—she'd know for sure.

But there was a name she hadn't said aloud in days.

A name from the edge of her past, before all this.

Sarah.

Her cousin.

Second year med student.

Her one clean thread.

Jane picked up the pace. If anyone could help her make sense of what was happening—and what was coming next—it was her.

Chapter: Seventy-Five- Past

Jane walked with her coat collar turned high, the late-night chill biting at her cheeks as she passed dim shopfronts and shuttered pubs. Nottingham after midnight was a strange kind of quiet — like the city held its breath, afraid to wake the ghosts. She walked fast, clutching her phone tightly in one hand, a note scrawled on the screen:

"Sarah M. — Hidden Oak, 44 Wilton Rd."

She hadn't heard that name since before Debbie died. Back then, Sarah was just another face in the society, one of Amy's earliest recruits. But something had happened to her. She vanished after a night of "play" got out of hand. Rumours whispered she'd been taken to a psych ward. Others said she left the country. But now… someone had tipped Jane off. Sarah was back. And maybe she knew more than anyone.

The building on Wilton Road was low and unassuming, wedged between an abandoned deli and a pawn shop. A simple black sign above the door read: "Hidden Oak Recovery House." Jane hesitated at the gate, anxiety chewing through her stomach.

She buzzed the intercom.

A voice crackled through. "Yes?"

"I'm looking for Sarah. Sarah M. She was here before," Jane said quickly, glancing behind her. "She'll know me. My name is Jane. Tell her… tell her Amy's dead."

There was a pause, then the door buzzed open.

Inside was warm and sterile. Too clean. A woman with silver-streaked hair and tired eyes approached. "Follow me. She's not usually allowed visitors, but if this is about Amy, she'll want to see you."

They walked in silence through a long hallway lined with security cameras and faded wallpaper. The door to Sarah's room was metal. Heavy. Jane's heart pounded as it opened with a slow click.

Inside, Sarah sat cross-legged on a bed by the window, reading a medical textbook. Her hair was shorter now, buzzed on the sides, eyes sharper than Jane remembered — like a woman who had seen too much and then learned to live with it. When she looked up, there was a flicker of recognition.

"Jane?" she said, blinking.

Jane nodded. "It's true. Amy's dead. But there's more. Way more."

Sarah's jaw clenched, and she gestured to the chair across from her. "Tell me everything."

Jane sat and leaned forward. "Debbie's gone too. We… it got out of hand. And someone's watching us. Recording us. I think they want to tear us apart from the inside."

Sarah exhaled slowly, closing the book.

"They're still doing it," she said quietly. "Still feeding the hunger. I warned Amy to stop. I warned all of you."

"You knew?" Jane whispered.

"I knew," Sarah nodded. "Because I helped start it. But we weren't the first. There's a name, Jane. One I buried years ago. The real founder. The one who doesn't bleed, just watches others do it."

Jane stared. "Who?"

Sarah leaned in.

"The one they call Father Crimson."

Chapter: Seventy-Six- Father Crimson

The name sat between them like a third person in the room—heavier than the silence that followed it.

Jane blinked. "Father… Crimson? Is that real or just one of Amy's weird fantasy aliases?"

Sarah shook her head slowly, her eyes distant now, like she was watching memories spool past behind her eyelids. "No. It's real. And it predates Amy. Predates all of us."

Jane felt her skin prickle. "You mean… this wasn't her invention?"

"Amy was smart. Manipulative, yes, but brilliant. She didn't create the Blood Spurts — she inherited it," Sarah said. She stood from the bed and began pacing slowly. "There were whispers even before my time. At first, I thought they were just urban legends floating around dark corners of the university. Secret clubs. Rituals. Pleasure through pain. A society obsessed with blood. But then I met him."

Jane sat straighter. "You met him?"

Sarah stopped and turned. "I didn't know who he was at first. Just a guest speaker at a fringe medical conference I was dragged to by a professor who thought I had 'edge.' Tall. Silver hair. Mismatched eyes — one brown, one so pale it almost glowed. He had this presence. Like he could walk through you. I only heard the name 'Father Crimson' much later, from Amy, during one of her darker spirals."

Jane felt her stomach twist. "You think he's the one watching us now?"

"I don't think," Sarah said. "I know. And if he's involved, it's already too late."

That sentence hit Jane like ice water.

Sarah continued. "He doesn't kill, not directly. That's not his pleasure. He pushes people to do it themselves. He orchestrates. Manipulates. Films. Documents. Collects. He's not just watching us — he's curating us."

Jane buried her face in her hands, trying to make sense of it. "And you think this all started again when Amy reached out to those of us who were… compatible?"

"She was the perfect host," Sarah said quietly. "She had the charisma, the hunger, and no sense of limits. She found old files — likely recordings or instructions left behind by Crimson. She told me once that she had dreams. Visions. I thought she was spiralling, so I left. But now, with everything that's happened…"

There was a knock at the door.

Both women froze.

Sarah stepped toward it cautiously, peering through the peephole.

"No one's there," she said, confused.

She opened the door slowly.

At her feet, laid out like a gift, was a single red envelope. Just like the one Amy had carried.

Jane stepped forward, her breath catching. "Another one?"

Sarah knelt and picked it up, turning it in her hands. "He knows I'm awake again," she whispered. "And he's welcoming me back."

Without another word, she opened it. Inside was a photograph — grainy, black and white, surveillance style.

It showed Mike and Jane in Mike's garage, bent over the freezer.

"We're being hunted," Sarah said. "And he's just getting started."

Jane backed away. "What do we do?"

Sarah looked up, her eyes cold steel now. "We don't run. We find him. We end this."

Chapter: Seventy-Seven-Whispering :

The car engine idled low as Mike and Mary sat parked beneath a skeletal tree on a forgotten backroad near the river. The air between them was thick tension layered over fear, fear lacquered with regret. Mist rolled like breath from the earth, swirling under the headlights. Neither spoke for a long time.

Mike finally broke the silence. "Do you think it's done?"

Mary didn't answer right away. Her hand was still clenched around the piece of paper she'd shown him earlier—the one taken from Debbie's hand the night she died. Her mind hadn't left that moment.

"You saw the light on the bank," she murmured. "We're not alone in this, Mike. We never were."

Mike exhaled hard, gripping the wheel. "Who? Who the hell would be out there filming us? For what? Why?"

"I've been asking the same questions. But something's been off since the beginning, hasn't it?" Mary turned to look at him. "Amy. The way she orchestrated things. The people she invited. You think she didn't know about the camera in the mirror? You think the footage leaking online was a mistake?"

Mike frowned, jaw flexing. "I want to say yes. I want to believe this was just some night gone too far. But I can't anymore. Not with the envelope. Not with Debbie. Not with those damn videos."

He glanced at the passenger seat where Mary had dropped the red envelope earlier.

The contents burned in his memory —
coordinates. A date. Midnight. And a line of
text typed in stark, bloody red:

"Come see your creation."

Mary rubbed her eyes, suddenly looking
tired, far older than her years. "I haven't told
you everything."

Mike gave her a sharp glance. "Now would
be the time."

She hesitated. "I knew Amy before any of
this. Years ago. Not well. But well enough to
know she was obsessed. She talked about
blood as though it had a voice. Like it told
her things. I thought she was just darkly
poetic, maybe a little disturbed… but
harmless."

"She wasn't."

"No," Mary said flatly. "She wasn't."

Mike looked back toward the road. "And
now we're caught in her web. Or his."

"You know who she was working with, don't
you?"

"I'm starting to," he said. "The way things fell
into place. Her obsession with surveillance.
The ritualistic aspects of everything. It
wasn't just play. It was grooming. Like we

were being shaped for something. And now… now we're being watched. Judged."

Mary's eyes met his in the dark. "Then we need to make a choice. Run, or confront it."

Mike nodded slowly. "Midnight. That's what the paper says."

"And the coordinates?"

"A place I know," he said, a chill running through him. "A warehouse on the edge of the industrial estate. Abandoned for years. We used to train there sometimes. It's secluded. Perfect for… whatever this is."

Mary reached for the envelope and tucked it inside her coat. "Then we go. Together."

Mike started the car properly now, pulling onto the wet road. "And if it's a trap?"

Mary didn't blink. "Then we spring it."

As the car disappeared into the mist, the camera lens watching from the trees adjusted its focus. A red light blinked once… then vanished.

Chapter: Seventy-Eight-The Warehouse

The M-Class Mercedes rolled to a crawl at the edge of the abandoned industrial estate, its headlights cutting swaths through the rising mist like searchlights across a haunted stage. The warehouse loomed before them—a crumbling beast of rusted corrugated iron and shattered glass windows. The roof sagged under years of neglect. Vines crept up its flanks like fingers. This place didn't just feel forgotten. It felt forsaken.

Mike cut the engine and looked over at Mary, who sat silently beside him, the envelope tucked in her coat, her face pale but determined.

"Last chance to turn around," he said, his voice low and steady.

Mary glanced at him; one eyebrow raised. "We passed last chances a long time ago."

Mike smirked grimly. "Fair."

They stepped out, the cold air biting at their skin. Mary zipped up her coat. Mike checked his pockets: flashlight, pocketknife, burner phone, and the military-issue compact pistol he kept hidden in his glove box. Just in case.

The coordinates on the note led them around the side of the building. They passed old crates, rusted barrels, and a forklift that looked like it had been abandoned mid-shift twenty years ago. Finally, they reached a steel side door, padlock still intact—but as they approached, it clicked open with a soft, metallic sigh.

"It's unlocked," Mary said, frowning.

Mike said nothing, just opened the door slowly. The hinges moaned in protest.

Inside was darkness layered with the stench of old oil, damp, and something fainter beneath—coppery, familiar. Blood.

Their flashlights flicked on simultaneously, cutting through the gloom.

They stepped inside.

The main warehouse floor opened before them like a stage. Shadows danced as their beams swept across the space: graffitied walls, dust-covered pallets, chains hanging from ceiling supports. But in the centre, a table stood under a single swinging bulb, already lit. On it: a box, wrapped in red cloth. Next to it, a folded piece of paper.

Mary approached first, every muscle in her body tensed.

She unfolded the note.

"You've come to see. But what will you learn? Truth is flesh. Show yours."

Mike opened the box.

Inside was a portable monitor.

The screen flickered to life.

Static.

Then—footage.

A video from inside Mike's garage. The night they carved Debbie. Jane standing at the edge of the table. Mark holding her legs. Mike wielding the saw. Their faces, clear. Their voices, unmistakable.

"Jesus," Mike whispered. "This is... everything."

Mary stepped back, stomach flipping.

"This was recorded," she said. "Someone's been in your house. Someone has been watching us from the beginning."

On the screen, the image shifted.

Now: a live feed.

A room. Dimly lit. Chains on the walls. A figure hunched in the corner.

Mike leaned forward. "Is that—?"

Before he could finish, the figure on the screen lifted its head.

It was Amy.

Eyes blackened, mouth bound with tape.

And behind her, in the shadows… movement.

Another figure. Clad in black.

Mike's blood went cold.

"They have her," Mary whispered.

"But who's they?"

The screen went dark.

Then one last message appeared in red text:

"Midnight was only the beginning. We're not finished with you yet."

Mike backed away from the monitor, his mind spinning.

"Now what?" Mary asked, voice hard but shaky.

Mike turned toward the door. "Now we get Jane. We find Mark. We regroup."

He paused.

"And we end this."

Chapter: Seventy-Nine- Jane Finds Sarah

The streetlights buzzed overhead, casting long, sickly-yellow shadows across the quiet residential lane. Jane pulled her coat tighter around herself, her boots clicking steadily against the pavement as she neared the old row of student houses near Lenton Boulevard. It had taken her two phone calls and a whispered name at the back entrance of the library archives to find Sarah's address. But she was here now.

The house was dark, save for one soft light on the second floor. Jane paused at the gate, her breath fogging in the cold night air. She didn't knock immediately. She watched, waiting, wondering if Sarah would sense her presence before she even reached the door.

She did.

A curtain shifted. Then the porch light blinked on.

Jane stepped up and knocked.

Sarah opened the door slowly. Her hair was tousled like she hadn't expected company, but her eyes—sharp, alert—said otherwise.

"I was wondering when someone would come," Sarah said.

"I'm Jane," she replied, stepping inside without being formally invited. "You knew Debbie. You were close."

Sarah shut the door behind her, locking it with an audible click.

"I knew a version of her," she said carefully. "The side most of you never saw."

Jane sat, uninvited again, on the edge of a worn armchair. "I think someone is trying to pin what happened on us. I think you might know why."

Sarah moved to the window and pulled the curtain tighter. "Debbie was in deep. Too deep. She started filming things… not just your group. Others. Old footage. Some of it from before you even joined."

Jane blinked. "Before?"

"She was obsessed with power. Influence. She liked watching people lose control." Sarah turned to face her fully. "And someone else liked watching her."

Jane's heart thumped loudly in her chest. "Who?"

Sarah just pointed upward. "The attic. There's something up there you'll want to see."

Chapter: Eighty-Into the Attic

The stairs creaked under Jane's cautious steps as she ascended into the narrow, slanted hallway. Sarah followed behind her, holding an old flashlight that buzzed weakly, casting flickering shadows on the walls. The house smelled of wood rot and damp paper—like secrets had been soaked into its bones.

At the end of the hall stood a pull-down ladder. Sarah reached up, tugged the cord, and the attic steps groaned open like a yawning mouth. A draft of cold air spilled down, carrying with it the scent of dust, old metal, and something... faintly metallic. Jane didn't ask what. She already knew.

Sarah climbed up first, the flashlight beam bouncing. "Watch your head," she called softly, "and your assumptions."

Jane followed.

The attic was cluttered. Boxes. A cracked mirror leaning against the back wall. A small desk with an outdated laptop still faintly humming, despite the chilly air. And on the walls, like trophies or memories—or maybe warnings—were printed stills. Photographs. Frames from videos.

Jane stepped closer.

There she was. Debbie. In half-light. On a bed. Her eyes wide with the kind of pleasure that looked too close to pain. Another shot: Mike. Shirtless. Standing beside her, unaware of the lens. Then Mary. Then others. Jane herself.

"How long has this been here?" Jane asked, her voice catching.

Sarah didn't answer right away. She crouched beside the desk and opened a drawer. Inside were rows of USB drives labelled only by symbols: triangles, crescents, a red dot. Sarah picked up one marked with an hourglass and held it out.

"This one changed everything," she said. "This is why Debbie got scared. Why she started writing things down."

Jane took the drive but didn't plug it in yet. Her fingers were trembling.

"Do you think it's still going?" she asked. "Whoever's behind the recordings?"

Sarah tilted her head. "You're asking the wrong question."

Jane turned sharply. "What is the right question?"

Sarah's gaze narrowed. "Why were you invited?"

The attic seemed to shrink around her.

Jane opened her mouth to protest, but then remembered something—something Amy had once whispered to her at a party, long before any of this madness had truly begun.

"You have the look," Amy had said. "They'll come for you."

Her hands closed tighter around the USB drive.

Down below, the doorbell rang. Once. Then twice.

Sarah didn't move.

Jane whispered, "Are you expecting someone?"

Sarah answered without blinking. "I was. But it's not who I thought it would be."

Outside, footsteps crunched slowly on the gravel path. Another knock, softer this time. A silhouette moved past the frosted windowpane on the lower floor.

Someone else was watching the watchers.

And they were getting closer.

Chapter: Eighty-One-Smoke, Fog, and the Fire Beneath

Mary sat on the hood of Mike's car, a cigarette between her fingers trembling ever so slightly. She hadn't smoked in years. Not since her early twenties—when rebellion still had a romantic hue. But tonight wasn't about rebellion. It was about survival.

Mike stood a few feet away, staring out over the field where they had parked. Fog drifted low, creeping like it had weight. He hadn't said much since they left the riverside. But Mary knew him. The silence wasn't emptiness—it was calculation.

"We need to talk," she said, her voice sharp, slicing through the quiet.

Mike didn't turn. "About what?"

Mary rolled her eyes and slid off the car. "About what the hell we've done. About what's coming."

He finally looked at her then. His expression was unreadable—part soldier, part wolf. "I'm thinking more about who's coming."

"Fair enough," she said, tossing the half-finished cigarette into the wet grass. "But let's not pretend this is something we can keep outrunning. There are photos. Videos. Evidence. People are talking. And we've got no clue who's behind the camera, let alone how deep this goes."

Mike leaned against the car; arms crossed. "You think it's Amy?"

Mary shook her head. "I used to. Now I'm not so sure."

"You saw her like I did," he said. "In the beginning. She was the spark. The obsession. The one who kept pushing boundaries."

"True," Mary admitted. "But I also saw fear in her eyes before she died. She was being followed, watched. And now Jane's gone quiet. Sarah's back in the picture. Marks disappeared. And you and I? We're in the open. Together."

Mike tilted his head, considering that. "You think we're being herded?"

"I know we are," she said, pulling the small, folded piece of paper from her coat pocket. The same one she had shown Mike earlier. "And I think this is part of it."

He took it again, unfolding it slowly, rereading the strange symbols, the fragmented Latin, the message scribbled in red ink:

"Carnem sacrificii erit clavis. Et oculi eos qui spectant, videbunt omnia."

"The flesh of the sacrifice will be the key. And the eyes of those who watch shall see all."

Mike exhaled through his nose. "A riddle. Or a threat."

"Or both," Mary muttered. "Either way, we're on the edge. And I don't think we're the ones holding the knife anymore."

From the darkness, a faint whirring sound caught their attention—soft, mechanical.

Mary turned sharply. "You hear that?"

Mike nodded, already drawing a flashlight from the glove box. He flicked it on and pointed it toward the hedgerow.

There. A red dot. Flickering. Watching.

"Same one as before?" Mary asked, already moving toward it.

"No," Mike said, jaw tightening. "This one's closer."

And just beneath the blinking eye of the lens, a folded note taped to the base of the post.

Mike stepped forward, tore it free, and unfolded it.

It read only:

"You're next. Midnight. Come alone."

Mary paled.

"We've got less than an hour," she said. "What now?"

Mike looked up at her, his expression colder than she'd ever seen. "Now we stop running."

Chapter: Eighty-Two

The ripples on the River Trent had long since swallowed the night's secrets, but Mary and Mike remained in the car, silence draped over them like a second skin. The air was thick with unspoken fears and unresolved guilt. Mary's fingers drummed softly against the window, eyes locked on a patch of reeds swaying under the pale moonlight.

"We're not out of this," she said finally.

Mike glanced at her. "You think I don't know that?"

She reached into her coat pocket and pulled out the small red envelope again. Her fingers hesitated as they brushed the seal. "I didn't show you everything," she said quietly.

Mike turned in his seat, giving her his full attention.

"I found this tucked in the lining of my coat," she continued. "It wasn't on Debbie. Someone planted it. Someone wanted me to find it."

Mike leaned closer. "What's inside?"

Mary opened it slowly this time, unfolding the contents with care. It wasn't a note. It was a photograph — old, worn, and grainy. It showed a group of people standing in a forest, their faces blurred, their postures rigid. But one thing was clear: one of them was unmistakably Amy.

And beside her... was someone Mary recognized all too well.

"That's the Chancellor," Mary whispered, her voice trembling. "From the university."

Mike's eyes narrowed. "This is bigger than us."

Suddenly, a phone rang — not Mary's, not Mike's. It was hidden beneath the driver's seat. Mike reached for it, pulling out a burner phone he hadn't seen before. The screen blinked: UNKNOWN CALLER.

He answered. Silence at first... then a voice, distorted and low:

"You shouldn't have dumped the body."

Click.

Mary stared at Mike, breathless. "They're watching us."

He tossed the phone onto the dashboard and started the engine. "We're going back to my place. We need to regroup. And you need to tell me everything you've been hiding."

As they drove through the sleeping city, shadows seemed to press against the windows — watching, waiting.

Chapter: Eighty-Three- Threads of the Web

The alley behind the museum was still slick from the rain that had fallen earlier. Jane kept her hood up, her breath rising in visible wisps as she scanned the narrow passage. Sarah stood beside her, arms crossed, looking less nervous than Jane expected her to be.

"So this is the place?" Jane whispered.

Sarah nodded once. "He said to meet here, midnight sharp. I've never seen his face. Just calls. Messages. Nothing traceable."

Jane was still trying to wrap her head around how Sarah had managed to get tangled up in this. She'd always seemed so removed from everything—the drama, the secrets, the blood—but now she was the one leading Jane through the maze.

"Who is he, exactly?" Jane asked.

"I don't know his real name," Sarah said, looking over her shoulder. "But he knew about Amy. Knew about Debbie. And he said… it's happened before. Not just once. A string of disappearances. Covered up. Silenced."

A shape moved in the shadows, and both women tensed. A tall man emerged, face mostly hidden by a scarf and low cap. He didn't speak right away—just looked at them both, sizing them up.

"You brought the envelope?" he finally asked, his voice deep, calm, but with a cold edge.

Jane exchanged a quick glance with Sarah. "No," she said. "We want answers first."

He seemed unfazed. "Fine. Amy wasn't who you think she was. She was working for someone. Watching you. All of you."

Jane's stomach twisted.

"She wasn't the first," he continued. "There were others before her. All bright. All curious. All drawn into something they couldn't control. Debbie wasn't the plan. That was chaos. But someone used it."

"Used it for what?" Sarah asked.

He leaned against the brick wall. "To flush you out. The ones who survived. The ones who could be… valuable."

"Valuable?" Jane echoed; her voice sharp.

"Smart. Ruthless. Willing to go past the edge and not fall apart. You're all test cases."

Jane's breath caught. "Tested for what?"

He tilted his head slightly. "Control. Influence. Blood isn't just a fetish for some—it's a language. And you're learning to speak it."

Sarah took a step forward. "Who are you really?"

But the man was already backing away into the darkness. "Bring the envelope tomorrow night. Same place. Midnight. Or you'll never know what's written between the lines."

And then he was gone.

Jane and Sarah stood in stunned silence, the city suddenly feeling too quiet.

Sarah finally broke it. "We need to get that envelope."

Jane nodded, but her thoughts were already racing to Mike… and Mary… and the secrets that had followed them all from the very beginning.

Whatever was going on—it wasn't over.

It was just starting.

Final Chapter: The Reflection

The air in Mike's house was dense with silence. The group had fractured. Trust was fragile. Mary paced near the front window, her eyes tracking every passing car. Jane hadn't returned. Sarah was out there somewhere. And Mark… no one had heard from him in hours. The events of the past few days had stretched reality, morality, and sanity to their limits.

Mike sat on the edge of the kitchen table, hands still stained faintly with blood no matter how hard he scrubbed. He could feel the weight of the river on his shoulders—the bags, the splash, the red blinking light. Someone had seen. Someone had been waiting.

"They'll come for us," he said aloud, not looking at Mary.

Mary turned sharply, her voice hushed and razor-edged. "Then we need to be ready."

Mike's eyes drifted to the folder on the counter. Inside was the paper Mary had handed him days ago. Its meaning was clear now—coordinates, time stamps, initials. It was a message. But from who?

Suddenly, headlights washed over the living room. Mary dropped low, peering over the window ledge. A small car rolled to a stop. From it, Jane stepped out, alone, her face pale and determined.

Mike opened the door before she knocked. "Where the hell have you been?"

Jane didn't answer immediately. She walked past him into the room, her presence cold and quiet. "It's over," she said. "Or…it will be."

Mary narrowed her eyes. "What do you mean?"

"I found the original footage," Jane said. "The one before it was edited. The one from the mirror."

Mike's blood ran cold.

Jane opened her phone and placed it on the table. She played the clip.

It showed the suite—Debbie alive, laughing, twirling slightly with a glass in her hand. Then a shadow. A figure entered the room—masked, gloved. Not Mark. Not Mike. Not anyone they knew. The footage cut out seconds before the scream.

"No one from our group?" Mary asked, barely breathing.

"No," Jane whispered. "Someone else was there. Watching."

"Who?"

Jane looked at both. "I think Amy knew."

They all paused.

Mary nodded slowly. "That red envelope… I think it was bait."

Mike looked between them. "So… what now?"

Before anyone could respond, the house lights flickered—then went out.

Darkness swallowed the room.

A low hum filled the airpower returning, or something else.

Then a knock. One, two, three—slow and deliberate.

Mary stepped to the window. No one was there.

The knock came again—this time from the back door.

Mike grabbed the torch from the drawer. Jane's breathing quickened. They moved together to the back of the house.

Nothing.

On the step, a flash drive lay in a clear case.

Mike picked it up.

No note. No label.

Mary stared. "Do we play it?"

"We don't have a choice," Jane said. "Not anymore."

Two Days Later

A university spokesperson confirmed the disappearance of several students, citing ongoing investigations. Police had declined to comment on specifics, but sources hinted at disturbing digital evidence emerging from a private group chat tied to a now-defunct social collective called Blood Spurts.

An anonymous blog post surfaced online, written in an oddly personal tone. It detailed the events of a night where fantasy blurred with ritual, and where one participant never woke up. The blog ended cryptically:

"We wanted something primal. Something true. We found it. And something found us back."

Mark stood in the Arboretum, the Polaroid trembling in his hand.

Somewhere, just beyond the trees, a soft click echoed in the still night — the shutter of another camera.

He didn't run. He didn't scream.

He simply whispered to himself:

"Who's watching now?"

Book Two Title: Crimson Veil

Truth bleeds deeper than guilt.

Contents

Chapter One: The Net Tightens

The morning news buzzed from the outdated TV perched above the bar in the corner of the station. Grainy footage played on a loop—students dancing under red lights, shadows twisting, faces blurred, but not entirely unrecognizable. Debbie's face flashed up again: "Missing: Last seen near city centre. Any information, please call—"

Detective Inspector Laura Halstead stood silently, coffee in hand, eyes fixed on the screen. There was something about this case that itched beneath her skin. The students were closing ranks. Faculty was tight-lipped. Something had gone wrong in Nottingham, something darker than a missing person.

Across the city, Mike sat at his kitchen table, still in his boots from the night before. The house was quiet, save for the slow hum of the fridge. The spot where Debbie had once lain was now scrubbed raw, the scent of bleach still faint in the air. He hadn't slept. He hadn't even tried.

Mary had called earlier, but he let it ring. He didn't want calm voices or clever planning. He wanted action. He wanted the silence to break.

A knock at the door made him flinch. He reached for the blade he'd started keeping in the drawer.

"Mike," came a familiar voice. Jane.

He opened it cautiously. Her face was pale, her dark eyes alert. "They were at the Uni today. Questioning students. Looking for inconsistencies."

He stepped aside and she entered. "How bad?"

"Bad," she said. "They've asked for phone records. CCTV pulls. One of Amy's friends was talking—loose-lipped, scared. Said something about blood rituals, some kind of secret society. They're getting close."

Mike let out a low exhale. "And what about the video?"

"It's everywhere," Jane said bitterly. "Clipped. Muted. Just enough to stir the pot. The press is hungry."

At that moment, his phone lit up. A message from Mary: "Emergency meet. 6 PM. Same place."

"They're circling us like wolves," Jane said. "And we've got no pack leader."

Mike stared at her. "Then maybe it's time someone stepped up."

Across town, Mary was already at the meeting spot—a dusty, disused room above a shuttered bookstore they'd used for their original gatherings. She paced, tapping her phone against her palm, thinking, planning.

The door creaked and Mark entered, hoodie pulled up. He didn't say much, just nodded.

They were trickling in, one by one, faces tighter than before, eyes hollower. The unity they once celebrated felt fractured. The thrill had turned sour.

When Mike arrived, the room shifted. He walked in with purpose. Not the reluctant participant anymore. Not the bystander.

"We need to be smart," Mary began.

"No," Mike interrupted. "We need to be ready." He scanned the group. "The police aren't going to stop. We all know that. So we have a choice. Run. Or fight."

"Fight how?" Jane asked, arms folded.

"Information," Mike said. "We find out what they know, how far they've come. We take control of the narrative."

"And if they already have too much?" asked Mark.

Mike's eyes darkened. "Then we make sure they don't live long enough to use it."

Silence.

The game had changed.

Chapter Two: Through the Cracks

Detective Inspector Laura Halstead rubbed at her temples as the overhead lights of the incident room flickered slightly. Sleep had become a stranger in recent days, replaced with caffeine and a dogged determination that only the truly obsessed could understand.

Across the table, Detective Sergeant Arun Malik was scrolling through security footage, eyes glassy from hours of screen time. Halstead walked over and handed him a second coffee. He took it with a grateful grunt.

"We're missing something," she muttered.

"No signs of forced entry at the hotel," Malik replied. "And none of the staff remember seeing Debbie that night. But…" He tapped the space bar, pausing on a frame. "There's this."

The image was grainy but clear enough: a man in a hooded jacket, walking away from the suite door. Time stamp: 03:17 AM. No face. No sound. Just a flicker of movement, and a shadow sliding something under the door.

"Envelope?" Halstead guessed.

"Looks like it. Can't tell who picked it up, though. No interior footage."

"Still," she said, "we have someone on the outside involved. That changes everything."

She returned to her board—a collage of printed stills, timelines, and scribbled notes. At the centre: Debbie Farrell,

22, third-year student, missing seven days now. Around her, a slowly growing web of names, locations, and digital evidence. A few had been officially questioned Amy, before her mysterious disappearance. Mark, who offered too little and too smoothly. Mary… That one didn't sit right. Too controlled.

"Where are we with the university records?" she asked.

"They're dragging their feet," Malik said. "Something about student privacy. Legal red tape."

"Then we lean harder. Someone's going to crack."

She turned to a new addition: a printed screenshot of a viral video. A short, six-second loop with blood, muffled cries, and a shrouded figure. No faces. Just implication. It had surfaced four days ago and exploded online. The tech team was working backwards, trying to trace the upload point.

"Anything from the metadata?"

"Wiped," Malik said. "Professionally."

Halstead's brow furrowed. "They've got someone smart on their side."

A knock on the door interrupted. A young officer entered, breathless. "Ma'am. You're going to want to see this."

He led them into the adjoining tech room. One of the forensic analysts had a laptop open, fingers poised dramatically above the space bar.

"We decrypted part of the message in that envelope," she said.

Halstead's pulse quickened.

The screen showed a scan of a torn piece of paper. Barely legible script. The analyst zoomed in and enhanced the text. Four words:

"She chose the knife."

Silence.

"Is that a confession?" Malik asked. "Or a taunt?"

"Could be either," Halstead said. "Or both."

She stared at it. The phrase was too calculated to be random. This wasn't about sex games or misguided rituals anymore. This was a game of power and control. Someone was orchestrating this like a play. Carefully. Sadistically.

"And get this," the analyst added. "We found a matching phrase posted anonymously on a dark forum three days ago. Same words. Same handwriting, scanned and uploaded."

Halstead didn't move. "They're playing with us."

"They're inviting us," Malik added quietly.

Halstead looked back at the photo wall. The faces, the timelines, the lies.

"No more cat and mouse," she said. "I want all of them on watch. Full surveillance. Let's see how they act when they feel the walls closing in."

Chapter Three: Pressure Points

Mike stood with his back to the kitchen sink, arms folded, eyes fixed on the group gathered around his dining table like students facing a final exam. The lights were dimmed, curtains drawn, and the air inside was thick with tension—cigarette smoke, unspoken thoughts, and a growing sense of dread.

"They've made it official," Jane said, breaking the silence. "Debbie's now listed as a missing person on the university site. Her picture is everywhere."

John swore under his breath and poured another drink. "It was only a matter of time."

"No," Mary said, coldly precise. "It was too late the moment we let that body hit the water. Now, it's just fallout."

Mike exhaled slowly. "And you think we can't manage the fallout?"

"Some of us aren't made for this," Mary replied, eyes flicking to Jane and Mark.

Jane looked small in her oversized hoodie, her leg bouncing nervously under the table. She hadn't been herself since Debbie disappeared. Gone was the flirtation, the hunger for pain and power. What was left was fragile, frayed.

Mark, as always, sat slightly apart from the others. He was hunched forward, fingering a torn beer label, not meeting anyone's eyes.

"We need a new plan," John said, pacing. "The cops are on us. I got stopped outside campus yesterday. Routine questions, they said. Bullshit."

"They're watching all of us," Mary agreed. "And they've probably linked us through Amy. She's vanished, which only makes us look worse."

"She hasn't vanished," Mike said sharply. "She's hiding. There's a difference."

"Doesn't matter," Mary snapped. "Every second she stays away, we look more guilty. They'll use her absence to divide us."

A moment of silence.

Then Jane spoke, voice trembling but clear. "What if someone talks?"

All eyes turned to her.

"I mean… what if they offer a deal? To one of us. If we turn on the others."

"They won't," Mike said.

"They will," Mary corrected, her tone icy. "They always do."

Mike walked to the table, his presence looming larger than the walls around them. "Let me make one thing clear," he said. "We're in this together. If any one of us cracks, the rest go down too. You think they'll show mercy? We're not just talking murder—we're talking desecration. Conspiracy. Obstruction."

"Jane didn't mean—" John started, but Mike raised a hand.

"She meant exactly what she said. And she's not wrong to be afraid. But if fear starts running this group, then we're already finished."

Silence.

Mark finally looked up. "So, what do we do?"

Mike's eyes narrowed. "We wait. We listen. We stay clean. That means no phones, no public meetups, no more mistakes. If any of you feel the need to confess your sins, do it to a priest. Not a detective."

Mary stood, gathering her coat. "Waiting won't save us. We need to get ahead of this. I've been following Amy's trail."

Mike's eyes narrowed. "You found her?"

"Not yet. But I'm close. She has the rest of that message, Mike. You know she does."

The room grew colder.

"If she turns it over to the police—" Mary didn't finish the sentence.

She didn't have to.

Mike looked around at the people he'd once trusted with blood and secrets. Now, he wasn't so sure any of them could hold under pressure.

"We find Amy," he said. "Before they do."

Chapter Four: Shadows and Smoke

Amy's boots slapped against wet pavement as she ducked down an alley off Mansfield Road, breath misting in the early morning chill. The city was still half-asleep, but she wasn't. She hadn't slept more than a few hours in days.

Not since the first video clip had surfaced.

Not since she realized someone else had been watching them too.

Nottingham was a familiar maze to her, but today it felt hostile. Every bus stop ad with Debbie's face on it. Every glance from a stranger that lingered too long. Every flashing blue light in the distance. It all set her nerves on fire.

She'd changed hostels twice. Paid in cash. Used stolen Wi-Fi from coffee shops to track mentions of her name online. So far, nothing direct—no formal charges. But the web was tightening.

And now, she was headed to Derby.

Not because it was safer—because it wasn't—but because she had a stash there. A burner phone, a hard drive, and the second half of that letter Debbie had been clutching when she died. She couldn't afford to leave any loose ends. Not anymore.

The 6:45 a.m. train to Derby was half-full. Construction workers, students, an old couple asleep by the window. Amy took a seat near the rear and kept her hoodie up, earphones in with nothing playing, just to signal silence.

She watched the countryside blur past and tried to slow her thoughts.

Who had sent that letter?

Who had recorded the video?

And most importantly—who else knew?

She was still asking those questions when she arrived in Derby. The city was waking up fast, people spilling into the streets like ants from a disturbed nest. Amy moved quickly through the back roads, avoiding cameras where she could, reaching the small storage locker she'd paid for months ago under a fake name.

Inside the locker was a black rucksack, dusty and untouched. She unzipped it and checked the contents:

A burner phone with one unread message.

A small, encrypted drive.

A clean set of clothes.

And the folded note she hadn't dared read until now.

Amy sat cross-legged on the cold concrete floor and stared at the envelope for a long moment. The same red wax seal. No name. Just a symbol—a crude drawing of a broken eye.

She peeled the wax away and unfolded the letter.

The handwriting was the same as the one Debbie had received. Sharp, elegant, and threatening in its precision.

"You've all played your parts well. But not everyone has been honest. The mirror sees what you deny. And the eye? The eye never forgets."

Amy felt her stomach twist. She read it again. Then a third time.

What the hell was this?

She powered on the burner phone. The unread message popped up in seconds.

UNKNOWN: You're running out of time, Amy. We see everything. You need to choose a side.

Her hand trembled. Not with fear—but with something close to rage. She was done running. If someone wanted to play games, fine. She could play too. And she knew exactly where to start.

Back in Nottingham.

She had one last stop in Derby—a cheap internet café near the university. There, she sent an encrypted message through a secure channel. Just three words:

"Meet me. Midnight."

She didn't sign it. Didn't need to.

If they were watching, they'd know where.

She stood, grabbed the rucksack, and stepped into the cold Derby air. Clouds loomed overhead, grey and swollen, ready to burst.

It was almost poetic.

Because Amy wasn't hiding anymore.

She was hunting.

Chapter Five: The Watcher

He watched them all.

From the quiet confines of his windowless flat, the Watcher leaned back in a worn leather chair surrounded by walls of monitors. Their faces blinked across the screens—Mike, Jane, Mary, Mark, and now, Amy.

Each one had played their role beautifully.

Each one had bled—some figuratively, some far more literally—for the cause.

The Watcher sipped from a chipped tea mug, the words Best Dad Ever faded to a soft blur. A memento from a life that had ended years ago. A past burned to ash by grief, betrayal, and one catastrophic night that no one else remembered anymore.

But he remembered.

He always remembered.

That's why the mirror in his flat was covered in black cloth.

Because what he saw when he looked at himself wasn't the man he used to be—it was the thing he'd become. The architect of this twisted ballet. The silent puppeteer pulling strings through coded letters, ghost accounts, and edited videos timed with surgical precision.

Amy had been easy to manipulate.

She always wanted to be seen.

Mike was predictable—military men always were. Guilt, pride, the need for control. He was the hammer.

Jane? Jane was the crack in the glass. Fragile but sharp when broken. And break, she would. Soon.

But it was Mary who fascinated him most. The queen on the board. Calculating, restrained, willing to do what the others wouldn't—because she believed she was above the rest. Because she'd buried her own sins deep in university corridors, hiding behind a polished smile and an old Oxford accent.

The Watcher ran his fingers across a keyboard, bringing up a live CCTV stream from the River Trent. He rewound two nights, paused, enhanced.

There.

The red glow of his decoy cam blinking on the bank.

They had seen it. Panicked.

And that had been the point.

Fear drives people to reveal themselves faster than truth ever could.

He opened another window—an email draft he had yet to send.

Subject: The Final Round

To: undisclosed recipients

Body: You've seen the warnings. Heard the whispers. Now it's time to choose. Tonight at midnight, the eye opens fully. One of you will not survive it.

He didn't send it.

Not yet.

First, he needed to check on the girl.

Amy.

He tapped a key and brought up a hidden camera feed—her student house in Lenton. Amy was packing. Nervous. Determined. He admired that about her. Despite the blood and lies, despite everything, she still had fight in her.

He respected fight.

But respect wouldn't save her.

He leaned forward, brushing aside a newspaper to reveal a carefully arranged set of items: a scalpel, a burner phone, and an ID card from the university. Not his own. Someone else's. Someone who hadn't been seen since last term.

Someone no one was even looking for yet.

"Time to finish the story," he whispered to himself

The story he had started years ago.

The story about how pain creates power. And power demands sacrifice.

He reached under the desk and pulled out a slim black case. Inside was an envelope—identical to the ones Amy and Debbie had received. Red wax, eye symbol, no return address

But this one wasn't going to any of the usual players.

This one was for someone new.

A wild card.

Someone no one expected

With a sharp flick of his wrist, the Watcher sealed the envelope and wrote a single name across the front.

SARAH.

Then he smiled, leaned back in the chair, and waited for midnight.

The hour of judgment was coming.

And this time, the blood would run deeper than ever before.

Chapter Six: The Rendezvous

Amy's boots slapped against the wet cobblestones of Nottingham's Lace Market, her breath fogging in the early evening chill. She pulled her coat tighter, the red envelope pressed to her chest beneath the fabric like a second, frenzied heartbeat.

The city glowed around her in puddles of amber and neon, but none of it felt safe. Every step echoed too loud, every passerby a possible tail. The messages had been cryptic—burn after reading stuff—but they all led her here.

"7:30. Beneath the old sign. Come alone."

She arrived outside the abandoned textile mill, the rusted iron sign still clinging to the brickwork like a rotted crown: ROWLEY & SONS — EST. 1881.

The place had been gutted years ago, a haven now for graffiti, rats, and—apparently—clandestine meetings.

Amy hesitated at the threshold.

Something about this felt… final.

She slipped inside.

The scent hit her first—wet wood, mold, and the iron tang of old metal. Shafts of moonlight spilled through gaps in the boarded windows, casting skeletal shadows across the floor. Her boots crunched over debris, but there were no voices. No sign of anyone.

"Hello?" she called, her voice too loud, too thin.

Then she saw it.

A single folding chair sat beneath a flickering utility lamp rigged to a power bank. On it, a mobile phone, face up, already recording. Amy stepped closer, heart thudding, and reached for it. As she touched the screen, it sprang to life.

A video began to play.

It was her.

Not from tonight. From the night everything went wrong.

The camera angle was high, maybe a ceiling corner—grainy, black and white—but there she was, straddling Debbie, the silver scalpel in her hand. Laughter from the group echoed in the background, blurred bodies moving in rhythm. Amy was smiling.

Until she wasn't.

Until Debbie's eyes rolled back, and the smile died.

Amy dropped the phone as if it had burned her. It clattered to the concrete.

A whisper drifted from the shadows.

"Do you remember what came next?"

She spun.

A figure stepped forward, cloaked in shadow, face obscured beneath a hood. Not police. Not Mike. Not Mary.

Not anyone she knew.

"What is this?" Amy demanded, her voice cracking. "Who are you?"

The figure stepped closer, hands open and unarmed. "I'm the one who's been watching. Guiding. Testing."

"Testing?" she barked. "Debbie's dead. We're being hunted. The group's falling apart."

"And yet, here you are. Alive. Resourceful. Dangerous."

Amy shook her head, stepping back toward the exit.

"You orchestrated this," she said, almost choking on the words. "All of it. The letters. The footage. Even the red light by the river."

"You all played your part," the Watcher said simply. "But only a few of you deserve to move on to the next phase."

Amy swallowed, her hand finding the envelope in her coat.

"What's in this?" she asked. "Why did you want me to have it?"

He gestured to the phone. "The key to your survival. If you're willing to use it."

"And if I'm not?"

A pause.

Then: "Then you'll be next."

The threat wasn't shouted. It didn't need to be. It was cool, absolute.

Amy stared at him, trembling. Not with fear— but fury.

"You have no idea who I am," she said. "I don't just survive. I endure. And I learn."

The Watcher tilted his head, like a curious animal.

Then, silently, he turned and walked back into the shadows.

Leaving Amy standing in a derelict building, phone still recording, red envelope still unopened, and her world tilting on the edge of something far worse than guilt or grief.

This was war now.

And she intended to win.

Chapter Seven: The Envelope

Sarah stood in her quiet kitchen, the hum of the old refrigerator the only sound.

The house had never felt more silent — or more threatening. She had just returned from her shift at the campus medical centre when she found the envelope tucked under her front door. No name, no return address. Just red wax, a stamped insignia she didn't recognize, and her heartbeat, picking up speed as she peeled it open.

Inside was a single photograph. Blurred. Grainy. But she recognized the faces. Hers among them — laughing, eyes lit in the glow of that infamous night at the hotel. A second image followed. Debbie, moments before she was found.

A note was scrawled beneath in dark ink:

"They all lied. Who will you protect?"

Her throat tightened. Sarah hadn't spoken to the others in days. Jane had gone quiet. Amy was missing. Mike — distant and harder than ever. Mary, always composed, now sending short, clipped replies.

Her fingers trembled as she picked up her phone. She started to type a message to Jane... then deleted it. What if this was a trap? What if someone was trying to pit them against each other?

A knock at the back door startled her. She jumped, heart slamming in her chest. She crept over, pulling the curtain back just a sliver.

No one.

But a second envelope had been left on the step.

She didn't open it right away.

Sarah stared at the second envelope like it might detonate if she touched it. Her breath came shallow and fast, her body frozen in place. The red wax was identical to the first— unmistakable. The same insignia pressed into its surface. A symbol she still couldn't place, though it stirred something in her memory, like a half-remembered dream—or a nightmare.

She finally opened the door, snatched the envelope, and slammed it shut again, locking it quickly behind her. Her fingers fumbled at the edge of the paper, and this time, the contents weren't photographs but typed pages. Five of them, carefully folded.

She laid them out on the kitchen table, her eyes scanning the first few lines. What she read made her stomach twist.

"The story you think you know is not the story that happened. The night Debbie died, you were all being watched. There are files. Recordings. Transcripts. What you did was only part of the performance."

"Check your inbox. They've started releasing pieces."

Sarah blinked, then sprinted to her bedroom and powered up her laptop. Her email loaded slower than usual—probably her nerves. Her university inbox showed a single unread message, subject line: The Curtain Rises.

The sender was anonymous, but the email body contained a single hyperlink and nothing else.

"No," she whispered. "This can't be happening."

Her fingers hovered over the mousepad. She clicked.

A browser opened to a private site with no branding, only a black background and a streaming video player.

The video began to buffer. Sarah's eyes widened as the image resolved: it was a timestamped video from inside the hotel suite. Low-light, grainy night vision. But the shapes… the outlines… the voices. She could recognize them.

There they all were. Amy. Mark. Jane. Herself. And Debbie.

There was laughter. Drinks. Tension.

Then a shadow moved across the screen— someone not in the group.

She gasped. "Who the hell is that?"

The figure's face never showed, but they moved with precision. Confident. Like they belonged there. The video skipped forward: Debbie entering the bathroom. Another skip. The shadow slipping in behind her.

Then… static.

The screen went black.

Sarah slammed the laptop shut, the sound echoing like a gunshot in the still air.

Her hands trembled. Her mouth was dry.

Debbie hadn't died from a game that went too far.

She was murdered.

And someone had been filming it all.

The knock at the front door nearly made her scream.

She grabbed a kitchen knife without thinking and crept slowly toward it.

Another knock. Soft. Three gentle raps.

She pressed her eye to the peephole.

Mary.

Sarah opened the door, just a crack.

Mary stood there, calm as ever, her coat dusted with rain. But her eyes were hard.

"We need to talk," she said.

"I just saw—" Sarah whispered.

Mary held up a phone. "I know. It's spreading. Someone's leaking the footage. Not just to us. But to everyone."

Sarah opened the door wider. "Why now?"

Mary stepped inside; her face grim. "Because someone wants to finish what they started."

Chapter Eight: The Reckoning

Mary slipped inside Sarah's house like a shadow, shedding her rain-slick coat and hanging it neatly by the door as if she had all the time in the world. But Sarah could feel it — the urgency in her bones, the ticking of an unseen clock growing louder by the second.

They moved to the kitchen without speaking, the weight of everything unsaid pressing against the silence like a storm about to break.

Sarah offered tea out of habit. Mary declined.

Instead, Mary placed her phone face-down on the table, her eyes never leaving Sarah's.

"I saw the same clip," she said. "But not just that. I've been receiving fragments. Files. Some audio. Some... surveillance. Someone's been collecting on us for a long time."

Sarah nodded, jaw clenched. "Who sent them?"

Mary exhaled slowly. "I don't know. Not yet. But they know what they're doing. They're controlling the narrative. Feeding us just enough to turn us on each other."

Sarah picked up the envelope again — the first one — and laid the photo of Debbie on the table beside it. "She didn't die by accident."

"No." Mary's voice was quiet. "She was executed."

The word sat heavy between them.

"And now someone's putting on a show," Sarah added. "One clip at a time."

Mary leaned forward, her fingers tapping once against the table. "We have to ask the right questions. Not just who's behind this, but why. Why wait until now? Why leak it piece by piece?"

Sarah thought for a moment. "Because they're building something. A spectacle. We're not just witnesses anymore—we're characters. Cast in a play we didn't audition for."

Mary smiled, but there was no joy in it. "Exactly. And we need to figure out who's directing it before the curtain falls."

Silence again, then Sarah whispered, "I think Jane's already broken. She hasn't replied to me in days."

"She's fragile," Mary said, matter-of-fact. "But she won't talk. Not yet. What about Mike?"

Sarah hesitated. "He's unravelling. He was already at his edge. This? This is going to push him over."

Mary's expression darkened. "Then we need to get ahead of this before he does something stupid."

The lights flickered overhead — just for a second — but both women looked up, reflexes on edge.

"Power glitch," Sarah said, trying to sound braver than she felt.

Mary was already pulling a small flash drive from her coat pocket.

"I've downloaded everything I've received so far," she said. "There's more than just the suite footage. They had access to the university servers. Emails. Security feeds. Someone even tapped into our messaging apps."

Sarah's eyes widened. "They've been watching us since before the hotel?"

Mary nodded. "This wasn't just a night that went wrong. It was a setup. And now it's a slow burn. They're seeing who cracks first."

Sarah stood. "We need to find Amy."

Mary's eyes narrowed. "You think she's still alive?"

Sarah's silence was answer enough.

Mary stood too, slipping the flash drive into her coat pocket again.

"Then let's start pulling threads," she said. "And pray the whole thing doesn't unravel before we do."

Mary and Sarah left the house just before dawn. The streets were damp from a light drizzle, and the city was beginning to stir — delivery vans humming past, a jogger in a neon windbreaker slicing through the fog. Normal life moved forward, oblivious to the danger lurking beneath its surface.

They didn't speak much during the drive.

Mary had insisted on taking her car — a low-profile grey saloon with no identifying features. She didn't trust ride shares or taxis. Paranoia? Maybe. But she called it preparation.

They parked in a multi-story garage on the edge of the city. Sarah followed Mary up three flights of stairs to a private office block, most of which was closed or dark this early in the morning.

A security keypad guarded the door at the end of the hall. Mary punched in a code, and the door clicked open.

Inside, the air was stale. A single desk with two chairs. A laptop. A corkboard on the far wall covered in pinned photos, post-it notes, printouts of CCTV stills and messaging app logs — all mapped out in spiderweb lines of red thread.

Sarah stopped just inside the doorway, her eyes widening. "You've been building this for weeks?"

Mary didn't answer right away. She pulled the blinds shut and turned on the desk lamp.

"I started the moment the first clip leaked," she said. "Because I had a feeling it wasn't just an accident. And now you know why."

Sarah moved closer, scanning the board. A name caught her eye — one not part of the group.

"Who's this?" she asked, pointing to a grainy photograph of a man leaning on a motorbike, partially obscured by a hood.

"Unknown," Mary said. "But he's popped up three times — outside the hotel, at the university gate, and just across from Mike's house. Always in the background. Always watching."

Sarah swallowed. "And you think he's our director?"

Mary crossed her arms. "If he's not directing, he's at least holding the camera."

A sharp knock at the office door startled both of them.

Sarah's heart leapt. She reached for the desk instinctively.

Mary raised a hand to silence her, then moved to the door slowly, checking the security cam feed on her phone.

The hallway was empty.

But when she opened the door, a third envelope had been left on the floor.

This one was black.

Mary picked it up carefully, peeled the seal, and inside was a single card — no photos this time.

Just a short line printed in bold serif font:

"You're getting closer. But at what cost?"

She folded the card, slipped it into her coat, and turned back to Sarah.

"Time to escalate."

Chapter Nine: Mike

Mike's knuckles were white around the steering wheel, the hum of his old M-Class Mercedes the only constant as he tore down the country lane. The city lights behind him felt distant, muffled — like another life.

He hadn't slept. Not since the second clip leaked.

It had shown Debbie again. Closer. Slower. The angle was wrong — from above. Not the suite's cameras. A drone?

And then, a frame of Jane. Just her face. Flashing in and out, like an accident or... a warning.

Mike had destroyed his phone an hour ago, slamming it into the kitchen floor until the screen gave way, then dunking the pieces in bleach. But it didn't make him feel safer.

It made him feel watched.

They were all unravelling. And it wasn't just guilt. Someone was orchestrating this. Keeping them paranoid, sleepless, fractured.

And Mike — well, Mike was done waiting.

He pulled off the road and parked at an abandoned quarry he used to visit during his military years, a place no GPS tracked and no signal reached. From the back of the car, he pulled out an old duffle bag — tools, maps, burner phones, and something else he hadn't used since Kandahar.

He dropped the bag at his feet, crouched in the gravel, and took a long breath.

Then he opened the burner phone, dialled a number burned into his memory.

It rang once.

Twice.

Then: "It's been a while."

Mike didn't waste time.

"I need you," he said. "This thing's bigger than I thought."

There was a pause. Then a gravelly voice replied, "You always did pick the complicated ones."

The call ended.

Chapter Ten: The Gathering Storm

Mary sat opposite Sarah in the modest living room of Sarah's rented house, the atmosphere thick with unsaid thoughts. The envelope Sarah had received was now spread open on the coffee table between them like a piece of evidence in an interrogation. The grainy photo. The scrawled message. The image of Debbie, frozen in time.

Mary didn't speak right away. She sipped her lukewarm tea, her eyes drifting to the edges of the room as if half-expecting it to start closing in. Her usually calm demeanour had been slowly unravelling since the second envelope was found.

Sarah broke the silence. "Why me, Mary? Why now?"

Mary blinked, then leaned forward, her fingers steepled in front of her. "Because you're the last neutral party. You weren't in as deep as the others. You kept one foot outside the madness."

Sarah shook her head. "That's not true. I was there. Maybe not the worst of it, but I didn't stop it either."

Mary sighed. "None of us did."

The photograph still sat there, challenging them both. The group had splintered since Debbie's death, paranoia seeping in like damp through old wallpaper. Everyone seemed to suspect everyone else.

Mary reached into her coat pocket and slid something else across the table — a third envelope. "I found this outside my flat last night. Same wax. Same handwriting."

Sarah hesitated, then peeled it open. Inside was no photo this time, but a list of names. Every one of them connected to the group. Her own. Mary's. Mike. Jane. John. Amy. Mark. All neatly typed.

And one more name at the bottom, underlined.

Edward K. Morrison.

Sarah frowned. "Who is this?"

Mary looked grim. "That's what we need to find out."

There was a pause as both women stared at the paper, unease settling over them like fog. Whoever was behind these messages wasn't just playing games anymore — they were orchestrating something much bigger. Something with layers none of them had yet seen.

"Do you think this Morrison is behind it?" Sarah asked.

"I think," Mary said slowly, "he's either behind it — or he's the next target."

Meanwhile, Jane sat alone in a quiet corner of a café across town, a half-drunk latte cooling on the table beside her. Her eyes scanned the article on her phone, the headline blinking in bold:

UNIVERSITY AUTHORITIES ASSIST POLICE IN INVESTIGATION INTO MISSING STUDENT.

A chill crept up her spine. Debbie's name wasn't mentioned, but the timing, the location, the description — it all pointed in one direction. The net was tightening.

She glanced over her shoulder.

Everyone in the café looked normal, indifferent — but then again, so had they once.

Her phone buzzed. A blocked number.

She hesitated, then answered.

A distorted voice crackled on the other end. "You saw the list, didn't you?"

Jane froze. "Who is this?"

"You're being watched. All of you. It's time to choose a side, Jane. Before someone chooses it for you."

The call ended.

Jane sat motionless, heart hammering.

Across the street, in a parked car, a figure watched her through the tinted windshield.

Mike stood, the wind cutting across the quarry floor. He wasn't just preparing anymore. He was going to hunt.

Chapter Eleven: The Watcher

The engine was off, but the car's interior remained warm, humid with the breath of someone who hadn't moved in hours. The figure in the driver's seat sat still, obscured by the tint and a strategically low baseball cap. A long-lens camera rested in the passenger seat, capped for now. The figure's gloved fingers tapped slowly on the steering wheel, rhythmic and patient.

Across the street, Jane still sat in the café. She looked shaken. Good. That was the point.

The figure's phone buzzed — not a call, but a silent notification from a secure messaging app. A single ping.

"She took the call. It's working."

The figure smirked. In the rearview mirror, a second reflection hovered — not a person, but a small red light blinking from the mounted dashcam. It wasn't recording traffic. It was synced with something else.

Fingertips reached for the glove compartment. Inside: a small collection of envelopes, identical to the ones delivered earlier. Red wax seals, crisp parchment, and a printout labelled:

"Phase Two Targets."

The figure rifled past Jane's name, then Sarah's. Then came Mike's.

Next to his name was a symbol. A circle with a horizontal line through it.

Unpredictable. Dangerous. Watch closely.

The figure leaned back, eyes narrowing. Of all the group, Mike was the one most likely to act — not think. He had the military background, the nerves, the tendency to snap. That made him both a threat and a potential tool.

Still watching Jane, the figure spoke softly into a voice recorder:

"Jane responded to prompt. Fear confirmed. Message was received. Subject is now destabilized. Recommend Phase Three to commence by end of week. Further surveillance of Mike begins tonight."

The phone buzzed again. Another message. This one contained a location pin.

"Morrison is moving."

The figure sat up straighter.

Edward K. Morrison. The name at the bottom of the list.

The man no one in the group had ever mentioned aloud — because only a few had ever heard of him. But he knew them. Knew their secrets. Knew Debbie.

Knew the game.

The car started without a sound, electric and near silent. It pulled away from the curb slowly, unnoticed by Jane, who was now paying for her drink with distracted fingers. The figure took one last glance at her through the mirror.

"Your time's coming."

And then the car slipped into the traffic like a phantom, en route to a location only two people in the city even knew existed.

Chapter Twelve: The Rendezvous

The rain began as a whisper against the windshield — fine, misty droplets that blurred the streetlights into long streaks of gold and white. The figure kept the car steady, weaving through the quiet side roads of Nottingham, away from the university, away from the noise. The GPS pinged softly, the blue route line shrinking with every turn. Final destination: a forgotten industrial yard near Colwick, locked behind rusted fences and shrouded by trees that had grown wild from neglect.

The car pulled into the gravel lot, tires crunching beneath. The engine shut off. Silence reclaimed the night.

The figure stepped out, coat drawn tight, head down against the drizzle. The building ahead loomed like a husk — three stories of broken glass and blackened brick. But the rear door had been replaced. Reinforced. There was a keypad beside it, small and new.

A practiced hand entered the code. The lock clicked.

Inside, the air was cooler, drier. The light flickered to life overhead. Just one bulb. Bare. Harsh. A hallway stretched forward, lined with steel doors, numbered but unmarked.

At the end: a door slightly ajar. Through it, a voice.

"You're late."

The figure stepped in. Removed the hat. Droplets slid off the brim. Beneath it, a woman's face — sharp, angular, focused. Her eyes didn't blink as they landed on the man seated behind the desk.

Edward K. Morrison.

He was older than expected. Silver at the temples. His hands bore the calluses of someone who'd once worked with them, but everything else about him was polished. Sharp suit, a blood-red tie. A man who once moved in circles far above academia or underground orgies. Now? He was the architect of something more sinister.

"Traffic," she said flatly.

He gestured to the seat across from him. "Sit. Tell me what you've seen."

She sat. The envelope she carried was placed on the table between them — sealed, unopened.

Morrison picked it up and cracked the wax with a fingernail. Inside: a memory stick. And a single photo.

Jane. Standing at the café window. Looking back, as if she sensed someone watching.

Morrison studied the image and nodded.

"She's folding. Good. And Mike?"

The woman leaned forward. "He's slipping. Doesn't care anymore. That makes him the easiest to provoke — or the hardest to control."

Morrison's lips twitched. Not quite a smile. "Both are useful."

He turned to a monitor on the wall and clicked a button. Grainy footage flickered on. The river. The bags. Mike and Mary.

"It's going to unravel," the woman said. "Even Mary's questioning things now."

"That's what we want."

She raised an eyebrow. "And when it does?"

Morrison's gaze was cold.

"Then we start collecting."

He reached into the drawer beside him and pulled out a black folder marked with a gold emblem — the same insignia from the red wax seal.

Inside: files. Photos. Diagrams. Surveillance logs. Debbie's name, circled.

And beneath it, another:

"Target: Sarah."

Chapter Thirteen: A Thread Unravels

Sarah stared at the wall of notes and photographs she'd pinned above her desk — it had started with just the image from the envelope, but now it had grown into something that looked like a conspiracy theorist's fever dream. Strings of red yarn connected blurry surveillance stills, hand-scribbled notes, and maps of Nottingham and Derby. Her once-comfortable flat was now a nest of obsession, lit only by the glow of her laptop and the occasional flicker from the streetlamp outside.

She had spent days combing through every shred of information she could gather. Facial recognition tools. Image metadata. Even amateur forums where true crime fanatics dissected real events like murder mystery novels. And somewhere between the whispers of urban legend and academic scandal, Sarah had found a pattern.

Names. Places. Dead ends.

But something — or someone — connected them all.

She sat cross-legged on her bed, the second envelope Morrison's spy had left still unopened on the bedside table. She had kept it sealed deliberately, fearing what it might confirm. But now… she needed answers. Carefully, she sliced it open with a scalpel from her old med kit.

Inside were three items:

A flash drive.

A folded paper map of Nottingham, circled in three locations: the hotel, the riverbank, and Colwick Industrial Park.

And a third photo. This one made her stomach drop.

It was of her. Alone. Sitting on a park bench. Yesterday.

Someone had been watching her — was still watching her.

She plugged the flash drive into her laptop and clicked open the only file. A video loaded. Grainy, silent surveillance footage. A man and woman entering a building. The timestamp: 2:13 AM. Location: Colwick.

The door behind them had a small keypad.

Sarah's eyes narrowed. The woman's walk — it was familiar. Something in the posture, the tension of her shoulders. She couldn't quite place it.

She scrubbed through the video. A second file auto-played. This time, a voice.

"Mike's slipping... even Mary's questioning things now."

Sarah's blood ran cold.

It was that woman's voice again. Smooth. Controlled.

And then:

"That's what we want."

"Then we start collecting."

She paused the playback and zoomed into the folder Morrison had opened. There — the top page of the dossier.

TARGET: SARAH

She backed away from the desk instinctively, bumping into the chair. They were planning something. She wasn't just a loose end — she was next. The puzzle that had haunted her since Debbie's death now made cruel sense.

This wasn't just about the group anymore. Someone had orchestrated this. Manipulated them. Pushed them toward destruction while recording every move.

The others needed to know. Jane, Mary… even Mike. But who could she trust now?

A noise from the hallway snapped her head around. The floorboard. The third one from the end. It always creaked.

She hadn't moved.

Sarah grabbed the scalpel from her table, her back pressed to the wall as the shadow under her door shifted slightly — pausing.

Someone was outside.

Chapter Fourteen: A Knock at the Edge

Sarah's breath caught in her throat.

The shadow outside the door didn't move again, but the weight of its presence seemed to press against the very air in the flat. She tightened her grip on the scalpel. Her heartbeat pulsed loudly in her ears, every beat a countdown.

She forced herself to breathe slowly. Think. React, don't panic.

The logical part of her brain whispered: Maybe it's just a neighbour. Maybe the floor creaked on its own.

But deep down, she knew better.

Someone was here. Watching. Waiting.

Sarah stepped quietly, barefoot on the wood, slipping across the room toward her wardrobe. She didn't need to open the door to leave — her bedroom window faced the fire escape. If she could just get outside, disappear into the night—

The knock came. Soft. Deliberate.

Not the confused tapping of a delivery driver. No announcement. No voice.

Just that sound.

Three sharp raps.

Sarah froze mid-step.

A moment passed. Then another.

She moved. Fast.

Pulling the wardrobe door wide enough to grab her hoodie, she shrugged it on and reached for the window, unlocking it with a practiced twist. Cold air bit at her cheeks as she slid the pane upward. She swung one leg over the sill and winced at the metal chill of the fire escape beneath her foot.

That's when she heard it.

The click of her front door unlocking.

Someone had a key.

Her heart jumped into her throat as she scrambled through the window, landing harder than she intended on the grating. She kept low, crawling past her bedroom window as she heard the door creak open behind her.

She didn't wait to see who it was.

Down the ladder. One rung at a time. Fast, but silent. She hit the pavement in seconds, eyes flicking across the street. Nothing. No headlights. No movement. The streetlight above her buzzed weakly.

Then a figure appeared in the window — silhouetted. Still. Watching.

They didn't call out. They didn't try to follow.

Sarah didn't stop running.

She didn't go to the university, or Mike's, or even to Jane. Every instinct screamed stay unpredictable.

She ducked into a side alley, heart hammering, breath visible in the chill. Only then did she allow herself to pull out her phone. No signal. She muttered a curse.

But she had the map. She still had the flash drive. And more than anything else — she had the knowledge that someone inside the group was playing a much bigger game.

They all lied. Who will you protect?

That question burned in her mind.

Who had the others sided with? Were they pawns like her, or worse — willing participants?

One thing was certain. She couldn't run forever. She needed to move first. Strike, not hide.

And she knew just the place to start.

Colwick Industrial Park.

Chapter Fifteen: Closing Circles

The morning broke cold and grey over Nottingham. A thin mist hung above the rooftops like something unspoken, suspended in the air. Inside Mike's house, the heavy blinds were drawn, but the atmosphere wasn't hidden — it was tensed, thick with unsaid words and fraying nerves.

Mike sat at the kitchen table; a cup of black coffee untouched in front of him. His fingers drummed an uneven rhythm against the wood grain. Jane paced. Her movements were tight, calculated — not the same woman who had once revelled in danger. Now, there was calculation in her eyes. Survival mode.

"She's gone off the grid," Jane said for the third time, chewing her nail. "No phone. No socials. Nothing. That's not like Sarah."

Mike looked up, eyes shadowed with sleeplessness. "She's smart. Maybe she knows someone's watching."

"She knows more than that," Jane muttered, stopping her pacing. "The envelopes, Mike. That wasn't some prank. That was a message."

He didn't respond. Just stared at the coffee until it cooled. Then, finally, he spoke:

"Mary's not answering either. She left me a voicemail last night. Said something cryptic about debts coming due."

Jane raised an eyebrow. "You think she's talking to the cops?"

"No. Mary wouldn't go to the police." His voice was sure. "But she might be working her own angle."

A knock at the door sliced through the silence.

Jane froze. Mike stood, quietly and quickly moving to the wall to retrieve the Glock he kept behind the framed photo of his Marine unit. He motioned for Jane to stay back and crept toward the door.

He opened it a crack, gun tucked behind his thigh.

No one was there.

Just an envelope on the doorstep.

Red wax. No name.

Jane reached for it before Mike could stop her. She held it up, inspecting the seal.

"A different insignia," she said. "Not the same as Sarah's."

Mike's jaw twitched. "Open it inside."

Back at the table, they peeled it open.

Inside — a USB drive. No note. No threats. Just that.

Mike inserted it into his laptop and let the screen flicker to life. A video file began to play. Low-quality footage, but unmistakable.

It was from that night.

Not the hotel hallway. Not the CCTV from the elevator.

This was inside the room.

The camera was hidden. Possibly inside the bathroom mirror. It showed grainy but clear footage of the group. Of Debbie. Of what followed.

Jane covered her mouth. "Someone's had this… this whole time?"

Mike's fingers curled into fists. "And now they're using it."

He paused the video. On the screen — Mary, stepping forward, saying something to Amy, before turning away. The timestamp put her there minutes before the panic started. Just moments before everything spiralled.

Mike and Jane looked at each other.

"It's not over," she whispered.

"No," Mike said, standing. "It's just beginning."

Chapter Sixteen: Mary in the Silence

Mary had always known how to disappear.

It wasn't a skill learned overnight, but rather over years — long before the incident at the hotel. Before Debbie. Before the envelopes. Before they began to turn on one another like desperate animals in a cage.

She stood now in a disused railway tunnel just outside the Nottingham city limits, the cold biting into her coat. Moss clung to the bricks around her, and overhead, the arching tunnel framed the world like a forgotten entrance to something more ancient than the city above.

A figure approached from the far end, coat long, hood low. Mary didn't flinch. She simply checked her watch. The timing was precise.

"You're late," she said, voice low.

The figure removed their hood — a woman, early forties, sharp eyes. "And you're playing a dangerous game."

Mary nodded once, folding her arms. "Aren't we all?"

The woman handed over a small brown case. Not an envelope. Not a USB stick. This time, something more tangible — papers, files, something old-school. Mary flipped it open briefly, scanning. Her lips tightened. She snapped it shut again.

"You were right," the woman said. "Everything that night — the hotel, the camera, even the original booking — was flagged by someone in internal surveillance. Someone higher than campus security."

Mary's mind raced. "That footage wasn't just being watched... It was being fed somewhere."

The woman nodded grimly. "Whoever's pulling the strings wanted every move documented. From the beginning. And someone in your circle helped them."

Mary took a breath, steadying herself. "Amy?"

"Maybe. Or Mike. Or both. But there's something else."

She hesitated before pulling a second envelope from inside her coat. It was identical to the others, down to the wax seal.

"This one never made it to its intended recipient. It was intercepted. That's why I called you."

Mary opened it slowly.

Inside: a photograph. Sarah — not from the party. But more recently. At a café. Alone. Taken from across the street.

A simple note:

"She's next."

Mary stared at the handwriting. It didn't match the others. This was messier. Almost frantic.

"This isn't just about leverage anymore," Mary whispered. "This is… escalation."

The woman shifted her weight. "You need to decide where your loyalties lie, Mary. Because something much bigger is in play. And this time, it won't be as easy to vanish."

Mary didn't reply. She turned, case in hand, and started back through the tunnel, the cold not bothering her now.

She had questions — too many. But one thing was becoming clear:

Someone had orchestrated the chaos of that night. Someone with reach, with resources, with an eye on them before Debbie's death.

And now, as her former allies scrambled in the dark, Mary knew what she had to do.

Find the origin.

Cut the strings.

And silence the puppeteer.

Chapter Seventeen: Tracing the Source

Mary sat alone in the dim back corner of the university archives room, the overhead light flickering above her as though hesitating to illuminate the truth. Her laptop was open, casting a pale blue glow against her face as her eyes scrolled through files — some official, some not. What she was doing wasn't technically legal, but after everything that had unfolded… she couldn't trust the system to deliver answers.

She hadn't told anyone where she was going. She'd disappeared off the grid for the last few days. No contact with Jane. None with Mike. And definitely not with Sarah. But she hadn't been idle.

It had started with the red seal. That strange insignia stamped into wax — she'd seen it before. Months ago, while reviewing alumni files during an internal audit. A man named Gideon Rourke. He'd donated anonymously, under a shell trust that bore the same symbol — a stylized serpent coiled around a chalice. It was subtle. Intentional.

And now it was showing up again.

She scribbled the name onto the edge of her notebook and drew a line beneath it. Gideon Rourke. The name sounded like something from a novel. But this was no fiction.

Mary leaned back in her chair and cracked her knuckles. She had access to restricted directories through her university credentials — perks of her long career. Rourke had been expelled as a student in the early 2000s. Not for academic misconduct, but for something buried deep: rumours of "unauthorized psychological experiments" during a student retreat. The official report was redacted. He'd vanished shortly after.

She opened the university's hidden archive — a digital cold room, housing reports never meant for daylight — and input a string of search terms. The results were fragmented, but a few threads emerged.

There had been another incident years ago. Another girl. Another cover-up. Same symbol.

Mary swallowed hard. Was this all repeating itself?

Her phone buzzed — not a number she recognized. Just a message:

"He's watching. You're close."

Her blood ran cold.

Someone knew she was digging. But who? And how?

She shut the laptop and gathered her notes, slipping them into her worn leather satchel. She had to move. Not just to stay ahead — but because she now believed something she hadn't allowed herself to accept until this moment:

Debbie's death wasn't an accident.

And worse — the group hadn't been random. They'd been chosen.

Mary exited through the back of the library, the door clicking softly behind her. Outside, the air was thick with mist. Every step felt heavier now, as though the weight of the knowledge she carried slowed her down.

But she wouldn't stop. Not now.

Back in her car, she turned the key and pulled away from the curb. She had one name. One direction.

It was time to find Gideon Rourke.

Chapter Eighteen: The Architect

Mary had always trusted logic. It was her compass in the chaotic seas of human behaviour. But now, that compass spun wildly. The deeper she dug, the less sense the world made — and the more convinced she became that someone had laid the groundwork for this descent long before the first blood was spilled.

The name Gideon Rourke had surfaced like a rotten log breaking the still surface of a black lake — uninvited, ominous, and impossible to ignore.

A man whose name hadn't been spoken around the university in years. Once a prominent psychology professor with a reputation for unconventional — and at times unethical — research into group dynamics, ritual behaviour, and pain thresholds. Dismissed quietly, no charges filed, no official scandal — just vanished into obscurity. But now, his name echoed from the lips of frightened students, whispered in buried campus archives, and found etched into the margins of notebooks that once belonged to Amy.

Mary parked outside the ruins of an old academic retreat centre just north of Derby. It had been shuttered after a fire over a decade ago — supposedly an electrical fault. But the building still stood, half-collapsed and covered in ivy. And someone had been inside recently. The chain on the side gate had been replaced. Fresh cigarette butts lay by the door.

She stepped inside carefully, torchlight sweeping the dust-streaked hallways. Each creak of the floorboards beneath her felt like it could wake the ghosts of the place. But she wasn't here for ghosts. She was here for Gideon.

A faint hum buzzed from deeper inside. Something running. A generator?

Mary followed the sound, descending narrow stairs into the old basement level. Here, the air was cooler, stale, and carried the coppery tang of mildew and decay. Her torch illuminated a door at the end of the corridor. Half open. Beyond it — light.

She eased it open slowly.

Inside was a makeshift office — cables running from a generator in the corner, hooked into old CRT monitors, hard drives, notebooks stacked in towers, and photographs pinned to every wall.

Her stomach dropped.

Photos of the group — from years before. From weeks ago. Some taken in secret. Others from that night. Debbie's face stared back at her in several frames. So did Amy's. Jane's. Her own.

And in the middle of the room sat a man in his sixties, balding, with intense eyes and fingers yellowed from tobacco. He didn't look up when she entered — he was writing in a journal with furious speed.

"Gideon Rourke," she said flatly.

He glanced up, as if mildly inconvenienced.

"You're not supposed to be here," he replied, voice gravelly.

Mary stepped further into the room. "You're the one who started this?"

"No," Gideon said, setting the pen down slowly. "I just opened the door. They walked through it willingly."

"You manipulated them. All of them."

"I showed them who they are beneath the layers of polite society. That was always the goal. To witness the unravelling — the return to instinct."

Mary stared at the wall, at her friends, at the twisted shrine to chaos. "Debbie's dead."

"I know," he said, with no remorse. "I didn't kill her."

"Then who did?"

He shrugged, leaned back in his chair. "Does it matter? She was always going to die. They all are. That's the point."

Mary's hands trembled with rage. "You used us."

"I observed you," he said. "You chose your roles."

She took a step closer. "I'm choosing a new role now."

Gideon smiled. "Are you, Mary? Or are you just another mask, still pretending this isn't exactly what you wanted?"

Behind them, the monitor crackled. A new image blinked onto the screen — someone else watching. Not Gideon. A third party.

Mary turned sharply.

"Who's that?" she asked.

Gideon didn't reply. His face had finally changed — the smug confidence replaced by something that looked like fear.

Mary felt her blood chill.

They weren't alone in the game.

They never had been.

Chapter Nineteen: The Tipping Point

Sarah stood on the rooftop of the campus library, wind tangling her hair as she stared across the sea of buildings cloaked in late-night mist. The envelope from earlier still burned in her jacket pocket like a brand. She hadn't shown Jane everything. Not yet. Not until she could confirm what she feared.

Because one of the photos in the envelope hadn't been taken on the night Debbie died — it had been taken the day before. In it, Sarah was walking alongside Amy in Derby. A moment she didn't remember, wearing clothes she didn't recognize, her own face partially turned away.

A fabricated image?

Or something much worse?

She'd started doubting herself. Her memory. The timeline. And now, with Jane growing more distant and Mary completely off the grid, the only person she could trust was herself — and that felt increasingly dangerous.

The campus below was quiet. Too quiet. She knew the police were circling. Detectives had been to her flat twice now, asking about Amy, about Debbie. They had that look — like they already knew more than they were saying. Like they were waiting for her to slip.

But what if someone wanted her to?

Sarah had begun noticing things: shadows moving where no one should be, people watching her from cars parked too long outside her building, messages erased from her phone, emails she didn't remember writing. Paranoia was no longer just a possibility — it was survival instinct.

She stepped back from the edge, phone clutched in her hand, the screen glowing with the name of a secure contact: A. F. — someone Amy had once trusted, someone who'd helped her with past... projects.

With trembling fingers, Sarah tapped a message:

"I think we were part of something bigger. I need to know what Amy knew. Before she disappeared. Before Debbie died."

She hit send.

A response came almost instantly:

"Meet me. Tonight. You're already being watched."

Her blood ran cold.

She spun, suddenly hyper-aware of the open rooftop. But no one was there.

She took the stairs down two at a time, exiting through a side door and into the chilled air of the car park, where only a few lights flickered against the fog.

That's when she saw it — a figure across the lot, leaning against a lamppost, hood up, unmoving Not Gideon. Not Mike.

Someone else.

They didn't approach.

But they were waiting.

Sarah didn't move either. Her instincts screamed to run, but something deeper kept her rooted. Because for all the fear, there was a pull to this moment — a strange gravity, like finally stepping into the frame of a painting she'd spent weeks circling.

Her phone buzzed again.

"You're close. Just follow the lights."

The lamppost nearest the figure flickered. Then the next. A path illuminating toward a side gate near the edge of campus.

Sarah took one step. Then another.

She didn't know who was leading her anymore — but she knew she couldn't turn back.

As she passed the figure by the lamppost, they didn't speak, didn't even lift their head.

But she could feel it.

They knew her name.

And they knew exactly what she'd done.

Chapter Twenty: The Circle Narrows

Sarah's footsteps echoed softly against the cold, tiled corridor beneath the abandoned wing of the university. She'd followed the instructions from the latest message—no phone, no bag, just the note tucked inside her coat lining and the steady thrum of adrenaline. The hallway smelled of old bleach and damp stone, a forgotten artery of the building she'd passed a hundred times but never truly noticed.

A security door stood at the far end, slightly ajar, its keypad blinking amber. No code needed. Someone wanted her inside.

She hesitated. Her reflection in the dusty glass showed more than tiredness. She looked hunted. Her eyes, once sharp with clinical precision, now flickered with uncertainty.

A voice called from within. Male. Calm.

"Come on, Sarah. You're late."

She stepped through.

The room was dim, lit only by a cluster of overhead projectors casting old photographs onto whitewashed brick walls. The images shifted every few seconds—shots from hotel corridors, CCTV captures, blurred faces laughing, crying, recoiling. Her own face appeared. Mark's. Mary's. Jane's. Mike's. Debbie's.

At a long table, a man stood with his back to her. His silhouette was tall, deliberate. He was placing papers into a leather-bound folder, methodically.

"Who are you?" she asked, her voice low, wary.

He turned. Not young, but not old—somewhere in that ambiguous middle, with sharp eyes that didn't miss a flicker of movement. His voice was calm and practiced, like someone who'd delivered too many bad truths in rooms like this.

"My name is Morrison. I'm not the one pulling strings. I'm just the one who still knows how to tie them."

Sarah didn't move. "You've been watching us."

"For a long time."

"Why?"

"Because one of you was never supposed to survive that night." He met her gaze. "And now someone wants to finish what they started."

Sarah's pulse surged. "Debbie?"

He nodded. "And not just her."

The projectors clicked to another image—this one recent. A man in a car. Another of Amy, in a disguise she thought had fooled everyone. A third image—Sarah herself, entering this very building just ten minutes ago.

Sarah's breath hitched. "Are you the one sending the envelopes?"

"No. But I've intercepted a few. Enough to know you're not safe, and neither is anyone else connected to that night."

He slid a file across the table. "Inside, you'll find names. Accounts. Surveillance logs. Even connections to someone higher—someone no one in your group knows is involved. Yet."

Sarah opened the folder slowly. The first name nearly made her knees give out.

Mary Winton.

Morrison watched her reaction with a grim satisfaction.

"She's not who you think she is."

Sarah looked up. "And what do you want from me?"

He leaned forward. "Help me stop what's coming next. Because if we don't, this won't be about a single body in a river or a cover-up. This will spiral into something far worse. And you'll all be at the centre of it."

She stared at the names, the evidence, the photos. Her hands closed around the folder.

"Then let's begin."

Chapter Twenty-One: The Marionette's Hand

Mary's breath hung in the cool, dry air of the subterranean chamber beneath the chapel ruins outside Nottingham. She moved like a ghost through the underground catacombs, each footstep echoing against walls that hadn't heard a voice in years — at least not one that didn't whisper secrets.

She held the flashlight low, the beam skimming across dusty floors and the cracked remains of mosaic tiles. Her phone had no signal. She wasn't surprised. This place wasn't on any map.

Ahead, a heavy iron gate groaned open before she could reach it.

"Mary," said the voice. Soft. Male. Elegant. Like silk draped over a knife.

He was waiting.

Gideon Rourke.

She had pieced the name together from fragments—old university grants, shell charities, obscure footnotes in funding records for experimental psychological studies. She traced the financial shadows from Amy's application all the way back to a defunct think tank connected to an elite network once exposed in a brief investigative report. The reporter vanished before publishing part two.

Mary stepped forward into the light of the chamber.

Rourke stood with perfect posture, tall and precise, in a tailored coat. His hair was silver at the temples, and his smile didn't reach his eyes.

"You've come far," he said.

"I had help," Mary replied, calm but alert.

He gestured to the circle of books, scrolls, and old reels of film that surrounded the room's centrepiece — a low table bearing the red wax insignia she'd seen too many times to ignore.

"The others think they were playing a game of guilt and secrets," Rourke said. "They don't understand they were being played."

Mary stayed silent.

He stepped closer. "But you—you knew there was something more. A reason each member of the group was chosen. That night wasn't an accident, Mary. Debbie's death wasn't collateral damage. It was a test."

Mary stiffened. "A test?"

Rourke's smile curved, serpent-like.

"Your reactions. Your loyalties. Your fears. We placed each of you into that room not for what you'd done—but what you might do, when pushed far enough."

Mary's voice was steel. "Why?"

"Because we're preparing for something bigger. And people like you—smart, adaptable, willing to lie, to cut— you're candidates."

Mary's heartbeat faster, but she kept her face still.

"And Debbie?" she asked. "Was she a candidate too?"

"She was the spark," Rourke said. "But she was never meant to survive. You were always meant to choose."

Mary looked down at the red wax symbols scrawled in patterns across the table — not just sigils, but coordinates. Locations. Dates.

"What are you planning?"

Rourke leaned in, his voice now a whisper.

"Awakening."

The lights flickered, as if the chamber itself trembled at the word. Mary's jaw clenched.

"You'll never get them all to join you," she said.

Rourke's expression didn't change.

"They already have."

From behind her, a second set of footsteps approached.

Mary turned. Mike stood in the doorway, his face unreadable.

"Hello, Mary," he said quietly.

Mary's eyes widened — not in shock, but confirmation

She had feared this moment.

Now it was here.

Chapter Twenty-Two: Bloodlines and Blind Faith

Mary didn't move. The air between her and Mike was colder than the stone beneath their feet. The low flicker of candlelight painted shadows across his face — shadows she hadn't seen in him before.

"How long have you known?" she asked, keeping her voice steady.

Mike didn't answer right away. His eyes, once hard with instinctive defense, now brimmed with something else. Not remorse. Not pride. Resignation.

"Long enough," he finally said. "Long enough to stop asking questions."

Rourke watched them both from behind his steepled fingers. "He was one of the first. Recruited for his loyalty. For his... adaptability."

Mary's lip curled. "You used us. All of us."

"No," Rourke said gently. "We gave you an opportunity. The world you thought you lived in? A fabrication. A surface-level distraction. We pulled back the curtain."

"You killed an innocent girl," Mary snapped. "You called it a test."

Rourke leaned forward. "And you passed it, Mary. Don't forget that."

Mike took a step closer, voice low. "You think I wanted it to go that far? That any of us did?" His jaw flexed. "But once it started, it couldn't stop. We couldn't stop."

She looked at him, searching his face. "So what now, Mike? You hand me over too? Offer me up as proof of your loyalty?"

He shook his head. "No. I brought you here so you could see it for yourself. The truth. Everything you thought you understood — the university, the grants, the research — it was all the first layer. The real program runs deeper."

Mary's fists clenched at her sides.

"The others — Jane, Sarah, even Amy — they've seen flashes of it," Mike said. "But you've seen the shape of it. You're closer than any of them."

Rourke stood slowly, the chamber darkening behind him. "We can offer you a place at the table. All the questions that keep you awake at night? We can answer them. But you must let go of what you think justice looks like."

Mary's heartbeat thundered in her ears.

"You're offering me power," she said. "At the cost of my soul."

Mike looked away.

Rourke smiled thinly. "You'd be surprised how quickly ideals fade when the alternative is irrelevance."

Silence hung, thick and weighted.

Then Mary stepped forward. "Show me. Everything."

Mike blinked. "What?"

"I want to know what you've been hiding," she said. "But don't mistake this for loyalty. I'm not here to join your cult. I'm here to understand it."

Rourke chuckled. "Curiosity. The first step to conversion."

Mary turned to him. "It's the first step to exposure."

The tension cracked, electric.

Mike opened a steel door embedded in the stone. A faint hum echoed from within — something mechanical, something alive. Mary followed, her steps sure.

Behind them, Rourke whispered into the shadows. "She's the one. Watch her."

A figure moved in the dark.

The puppet master's grip tightened.

Chapter Twenty-Three: The Vault Beneath

The heavy steel door groaned as Mike pushed it open, the thick scent of ozone hitting Mary's senses immediately. The chamber beyond was unlike anything she had expected.

Rows of servers lined the walls, cables snaking along the floor like veins. Low, pulsing blue lights illuminated a central structure — a glass-walled vault suspended in the centre of the room by thick steel chains. Inside the vault, something glowed faintly, a steady rhythmic pulse, almost like a heartbeat.

"What is this?" Mary whispered, stepping over the threshold.

Mike didn't answer immediately. He motioned for her to follow him across the narrow catwalk leading to the central platform. Their footsteps echoed, hollow and eerie.

"This," Mike said at last, his voice carrying a strange mixture of awe and regret, "is what they've been building for years. Data. DNA. Surveillance. They've been collecting everything. Not just from us — from the entire city. The university was just a front."

Mary frowned, feeling the chill seep deeper into her bones. "Collecting for what?"

Rourke's voice drifted in from behind them. "Prediction. Control. Evolution."

Mary turned to face him. His silhouette loomed in the doorway, calm and unhurried.

"You think wars are fought with guns now?" Rourke said, stepping onto the catwalk. "No. The real wars are fought here. Control information, control the future. Control the bloodline, control destiny."

Mary swallowed hard. Her mind raced. This wasn't just about a sadistic group covering their tracks — it was about something far larger. They had plans for them. They had plans for everyone.

Inside the glass vault, Mary could now see objects pinned like grotesque trophies — blood samples, personal effects, even fragments of memories. Tiny flashes of faces, voices, moments — all captured, digitized, and archived.

Debbie's locket glinted from one corner.

She stepped closer, her fists tightening. "You're building a weapon," she said. "One made of flesh and secrets."

Mike looked down. "They call it The Mosaic. Piece by piece, creating something... unstoppable."

"And what about us?" Mary asked. "Were we just experiments too?"

Rourke's smile was almost tender. "You were catalysts. Test subjects. Proof of concept."

Mary's jaw set hard. "You underestimated us."

Rourke raised an eyebrow. "Did we?"

For a beat, the only sound was the hum of the vault and the distant clicking of cooling fans.

Mary turned to Mike, voice low and urgent. "We have to destroy it."

Mike's expression flickered — fear, doubt, hope — all warring beneath the surface. "It's not that simple.

"It never is," she said. "But we have to."

From the corner of her eye, Mary spotted movement in the vault — a shadow. A flicker of something alive. She stiffened.

Rourke saw her look. "You're not the first to want to bring it all down," he said. "And you won't be the last."

Mary squared her shoulders. "Maybe not. But I'll be the one who succeeds."

The overhead lights flickered. Somewhere deep below them, a siren began to whine — a low, mournful sound like the world itself crying out.

Mike stepped forward, determination sharpening his features. "Tell me what to do."

Mary met his eyes. No more half-measures. No more fear.

"We take the whole system offline," she said. "Tonight."

Behind them, unseen in the darkness, the puppet master leaned forward, watching.

Smiling.

Chapter Twenty-Four: Sabotage

Mary moved with urgency, her boots slamming across the catwalk as she surveyed the vault's inner workings. Everything depended on speed. Rourke might have let them glimpse the truth, but he wasn't about to stand back and watch them destroy it.

Mike peeled open a panel along the wall, revealing a tangle of coloured wires and glowing circuit boards. "Overload the server's coolant systems," he muttered, yanking a multi-tool from his belt. "It'll fry the processors and cause a chain reaction."

"How long do we have once it starts?" Mary asked, already scanning the room for other vulnerabilities.

"Ten minutes tops before it blows. Less if the failsafe's kick in."

Mary nodded grimly. That was enough. It had to be.

Behind them, Rourke watched with maddening calm, as if he were observing a play he had written long ago. "You really think collapsing this little node will stop the greater machine?" he said, voice almost soft.

"No," Mary said without looking back. "But it'll send a message."

Rourke chuckled under his breath. "Messages are for the living."

Mike didn't answer — he was working too fast now, sweat starting to bead on his forehead.

Mary dashed toward the nearest control station, scanning the readouts. She caught sight of a master override code blinking in red — an emergency shutdown sequence that could be manually triggered if they cut the right circuit.

She shouted over her shoulder, "I need you to kill the primary security feed! Now!"

Mike cursed under his breath but obeyed, sparking a blade across the wiring.

Sparks showered down as a screen flickered and went dead.

Immediately, the room dimmed.

The heartbeat-like pulse inside the vault stuttered.

Mary felt the air shift — like the vault was waking up.

"No turning back now," Mike muttered.

The sirens intensified. From deeper within the complex, Mary heard the pounding of boots — reinforcements on their way. The organization wasn't going to let this go without a fight.

Rourke stepped forward, hands up. "Stop this madness," he said. "You don't know what you're doing. You're ripping apart the future!"

Mary stared at him, feeling the fury rise in her chest. "The future isn't yours to control."

She turned back to Mike. "Hit the coolant lines now!"

Mike jammed the blade into a coolant mainframe. Instantly, a high-pressure hiss filled the room as supercooled vapor burst into the air.

The vault's glass began to crack, spiderwebbing fractures shooting outward. The glowing objects inside the chamber flickered, like dying stars.

Sirens, shouting, the creak of collapsing machinery — the chamber was turning into chaos Mike grabbed Mary's arm. "Time to go!"

As they ran back across the catwalk, a deafening rumble shook the room. The servers along the walls began exploding one by one, bursts of fire and sparks lighting up the darkness.

Behind them, Rourke stood motionless, watching it burn, a strange smile on his lips.

Almost... proud.

Mary and Mike burst into the stairwell as the first explosions rocked the chamber.

Concrete dust filled the air. Pipes burst. Alarms screamed.

They didn't look back.

At the top of the stairs, they stumbled into a narrow service corridor lit by flickering emergency lights. Mary's chest burned, but she forced herself forward.

"Where's the exit?" Mike shouted over the din.

"This way!" Mary yelled, dragging him toward a hatch door labelled 'Maintenance - Surface Access.'

She spun the wheel. The door groaned, stuck.

Mike slammed his shoulder against it. Once, twice.

It popped open with a shriek.

Cold night air rushed over them like a blessing.

They emerged into the dark, deserted woods behind the university's industrial labs. Stars wheeled overhead in a black sky. Somewhere far behind them, the ground shuddered again — a muted whump as the chamber collapsed into itself.

Mike bent over, gasping for breath, his face streaked with grime.

Mary stood tall, her heart still pounding. She stared back toward the faint glow of the fires.

It was done.

At least... for now.

Mike wiped his mouth with the back of his hand. "You think we bought ourselves any time?"

Mary shook her head, solemn. "No. We just moved up their list."

From the shadows, another figure watched them.

A different puppet master.

And the real game was only just beginning.

Chapter Twenty-Five: Ghosts Rising

Smoke curled above the treetops, drifting toward the cold stars.

Sarah watched from the crest of a nearby hill, her breath steaming in the night air.

She had seen the explosions light up the forest floor like a heartbeat, one blast after another until the ground seemed to ripple. She hadn't been close enough to be caught, but she had been close enough to understand.

Mike and Mary had pulled the trigger.

She should have felt relief — a twisted, vengeful satisfaction at the thought of Rourke's secret empire burning to the ground. But instead, a sick knot tightened in her gut.

The burning vault hadn't ended anything.

It had started something much worse.

Her phone buzzed quietly against her thigh.

A message. Unknown number.

"New players inbound. Watch your back. -G"

Gideon Rourke.

Still alive.

Still moving his pieces.

Sarah swore under her breath and pocketed the phone. She pulled her jacket tighter around herself and started down the hill toward the city lights.

Somewhere, someone was filling the vacuum the Blood Spurts had left behind.

Someone worse.

Across the city, deep underground, the puppet master moved quietly through an old service tunnel that hadn't seen maintenance in decades. A black-gloved hand slid across a sealed steel hatch, tapping a code into a recessed keypad.

The door hissed open.

Inside, a new nerve centre buzzed to life — fresh servers, fresh personnel. Men and women in dark clothes moved with clinical precision, ready to pick up where Rourke had fallen.

The puppet master — not Rourke, but someone Rourke had only ever feared from afar — smiled beneath their mask.

"Phase Two is green-lit," they said into a headset.

A voice crackled back: "Targets?"

"Primary: Blood Spurts survivors.

Secondary: University and city infrastructure.

Tertiary: All liabilities."

The puppet master's hand hovered briefly over a series of live feeds — blurry surveillance footage of Mike, Mary, Jane, and Sarah moving separately through the night.

Then the hand closed into a fist.

"No loose ends."

Mike and Mary stumbled across the frost-rimmed parking lot behind the industrial labs, still running on adrenaline and sheer stubbornness. Every muscle in Mike's body screamed for rest, but he knew better.

They were still in the crosshairs.

"We need a new plan," Mary gasped.

Mike shook his head. "No. We need to disappear."

Mary shot him a look — fierce, almost wild. "Disappear? After everything we've learned? After what they did to Debbie?"

Mike closed his eyes for a second, the weight of it all crushing him.

"I'm not talking about surrender," he said finally. "I'm talking about war."

Mary's lips curved into a cold, dangerous smile. "Good."

The faint howl of sirens echoed across the distant streets.

They needed allies. Resources. Time.

They had none.

But they still had one advantage:

They knew the truth now.

And maybe — just maybe — they could weaponize it.

Sarah ducked into a side street, instincts prickling.

Someone was following her.

Not Rourke's old goons. These steps were too careful. Too quiet.

Professional.

She slipped her hand into her pocket, wrapping her fingers around the cold metal of the tiny switchblade she had carried since the night Debbie died.

Not today, she thought grimly.

Not without a fight.

Back at the ruins of the vault, fire crews battled the flames.

A man in a clean black suit stood on a nearby ridge, watching.

He adjusted his cufflinks, speaking into a hidden mic.

"Subject Zero has been terminated," he said calmly. "Proceeding to secondary acquisitions."

Far beneath his feet, something stirred in the wreckage — not dead, but waiting.

The Blood Spurts thought they had burned the sickness out of the system.

But all they had done was light a fuse.

And the real explosion was still to come.

Chapter Twenty-Six: Hunters and Hunted

The night bled into early morning; the cold biting deeper as Sarah kept moving.

Every shadow seemed alive now. Every silence loaded with unseen threats.

Down the alley. Across the desolate park.

No place felt safe anymore.

She needed to find Mike and Mary — she needed to regroup before she picked off like an easy target.

But even as she thought it, Sarah knew: the old alliances were shattered. Trust was a dying currency.

Her phone buzzed again. Another unknown number.

"Corner of Wilton and 8th. 10 minutes. Come alone."

A shiver passed through her. No name, no reassurance.

But something inside her — the same stubborn core that had survived everything so far — clicked into place.

She wasn't going to run anymore.

Tucking the blade tighter into her sleeve, Sarah disappeared into the waking city.

Mike crouched beside a battered black SUV, breathing hard, eyes scanning the horizon.

Mary stood behind him, arms crossed, jacket torn and streaked with dirt.

"Something's wrong," she muttered, checking her battered burner phone for the tenth time. "Sarah should've called back by now."

Mike wiped a smear of blood from his forehead. "Sarah's smart. If she's silent, it's because she's trying to stay alive."

Mary nodded grimly but didn't look convinced.

Far off, a siren wailed — not police, but something worse.

Private security. Hired guns.

Mike leaned closer; voice low: "We stick to the plan. Meet at the fallback spot if we get separated. No heroics."

Mary gave a bitter laugh. "We stopped being heroes the night Debbie died."

Mike didn't argue. He just tightened the straps on the stolen backpack — cash, burner phones, forged IDs — everything they needed to vanish if the worst came

"Ready?" he asked.

Mary smiled a humourless smile. "Born ready."

They slipped into the misty streets like wraiths, hunted and hunting all at once.

Sarah's boots crunched against broken glass as she approached the meeting point.

Wilton and 8th — a half-abandoned industrial zone, grim and silent.

A flicker of movement ahead caught her eye — a figure, hooded, standing perfectly still beneath a flickering streetlamp.

No backup. No obvious weapon.

Sarah didn't hesitate. She moved forward, knife ready, heart thundering.

"Sarah," the figure said — low, female, almost familiar.

Jane.

Sarah blinked, thrown off for a split second.

"What the hell are you doing here?" she demanded.

Jane's face was pale, eyes hollowed out with exhaustion. "Same as you. Trying to survive."

"That message — was it you?"

Jane shook her head. "No. Someone else set this up. They want us in the open. Vulnerable."

Sarah's stomach twisted.

A sharp crack rang out — the unmistakable sound of a suppressed gunshot.

Both women ducked instinctively, sprinting toward the shattered remains of a warehouse across the street.

Inside, darkness swallowed them.

Sarah's mind raced:

Who else knew they'd be here?

And why hadn't Jane warned her sooner?

In the control van a block away, the new player — the one who had inherited Rourke's scattered empire — leaned over the monitor bank, watching the feeds.

"Target One and Target Three in play," an operative reported.

"Hold fire," the leader said. "Let them sweat."

Another operative hesitated. "Orders on the man and woman at perimeter?"

The leader smiled coldly.

"Capture alive if possible. But if they fight..."

A casual shrug.

"End them."

The Blood Spurts survivors were valuable. Their suffering, even more so.

Mary pressed herself against the SUV's frame, one hand on Mike's arm, freezing him mid-step.

"You hear that?" she whispered.

Mike tilted his head.

Helicopter blades. Distant, but closing fast.

"We need to move," he growled.

But before they could retreat, headlights slashed through the darkness — three black SUVs fanning out across the abandoned lot.

Doors opened. Men in tactical gear spilled out, weapons raised.

Mary's mouth went dry.

Mike gave her one hard look.

"No surrender," he said.

Mary nodded grimly. "No mercy. Together, they dove into the shadows, hunted animals fighting for their lives.

Sarah and Jane crashed through the warehouse's rotting side door, lungs burning.

They stumbled into a cavernous space filled with ancient machinery, rusted beams, and shattered glass.

Jane gasped, pointing: "There! A service hatch!"

They ran — just as more gunfire shredded the air around them.

Sarah slammed her shoulder against the hatch. It groaned open, revealing a narrow staircase spiralling down into darkness.

Without hesitation, they plunged into the depths.

Above them, heavy boots pounded closer.

Sarah didn't look back. She just kept moving, deeper and deeper, into the guts of the city — hoping that somewhere ahead, there was a way out.

Chapter Twenty-Seven: Into the Dark

The staircase twisted downward into pure blackness, the air growing colder, damper, heavier with every step.

Sarah's heart hammered in her chest. Each breath felt like dragging ice into her lungs.

Jane stumbled behind her, one hand gripping the back of Sarah's jacket to stay upright in the darkness.

Somewhere above, they heard boots striking concrete.

The hunters weren't giving up.

Sarah reached the bottom first, groping for a wall, a door, anything. Her fingers brushed cold steel — an industrial access door, battered but still solid.

"Help me!" she hissed.

Together, she and Jane forced their weight against it. It groaned, then snapped open with a violent screech, spilling them into another underground tunnel — this one even older, crumbling with age.

Old maintenance lines, Sarah guessed. Forgotten by the city. Perfect for disappearing — or dying.

"We have to keep moving," she whispered, pulling Jane forward.

They didn't dare use a light. They stumbled through the dark, following the stale breath of air that hinted at another way out.

Behind them, the thudding boots paused. Voices murmured. Orders were given.

Sarah knew what came next — they'd send trackers. Dogs maybe. Heat sensors.

We're running out of time.

Across the city, Mike and Mary fought their own desperate battle.

Mike led them through the twisted alleys, ducking between broken fences and abandoned shops. He kept his head low, movements quick and sharp. Mary matched him stride for stride, gun drawn from the stash Mike had kept hidden under the SUV's seat.

"They're herding us," Mike said between breaths. "They want us boxed in."

"Good luck with that," Mary muttered.

Ahead, the way narrowed — a dead-end alley.

Mike swore under his breath.

From the rooftops, a laser sight danced briefly across Mary's shoulder. She ducked instinctively, firing a shot upward without hesitation.

Glass shattered.

A cry of pain.

"Down!" Mike barked, dragging her into a side door half hanging off its hinges.

Inside, they found a maze of back corridors, once offices, now just hollowed-out husks.

"We can still make it," Mike said, voice low and tight. "Get to the fallback."

Mary nodded grimly. "And if we can't?"

Mike gave a brutal grin.

"Then we take as many of them with us as we can."

Underground, Sarah stumbled over a fallen pipe, catching herself just before she hit the floor.

She realized suddenly that Jane wasn't behind her anymore.

"Jane?" she hissed, turning back.

Silence.

"Jane!"

A faint scuffing noise. Sarah spun — and saw Jane slumped against the tunnel wall, clutching her side, blood seeping through her fingers.

"No, no, no," Sarah muttered, rushing back.

"I'm fine," Jane gasped. "Keep going."

"Like hell," Sarah snapped. "Come on."

She hoisted Jane's arm over her shoulder. Jane was weaker than she let on, every step slower. But they moved.

They had to.

At the far end of the tunnel, a faint light glowed.

An exit?

Or another trap?

Sarah didn't care anymore. She just knew they couldn't stay here.

The figure in the control van — the one orchestrating the night's hunt — watched the monitors with clinical detachment.

"They're splitting up," the tech murmured. "Standard survival pattern."

"Predictable," the leader said, leaning back, fingers steepled.

"Let them run a little longer. The deeper the fear, the sweeter the fall."

Mike and Mary burst into a wider street — briefly illuminated by flickering neon from a boarded-up diner.

The SUVs were nowhere in sight.

For now.

Mike checked his watch.

Five minutes until the rendezvous time with Sarah — if she made it.

"You trust her?" Mary asked, reading his mind.

Mike didn't hesitate. "With my life."

Mary gave a grim little smile. "Then let's go earn that trust."

They took off again, disappearing into the maze of a city that no longer belonged to them.

Sarah and Jane finally staggered into a maintenance shaft — a battered ladder leading up toward a manhole cover faintly outlined by streetlight above.

"Freedom," Sarah whispered hoarsely.

A shout echoed behind them.

The hunters were coming.

Jane started to climb. Sarah followed, heart pounding in her throat.

Halfway up, a shot rang out — sparking off the ladder, inches from Sarah's foot.

Another. Closer.

Sarah didn't look back.

She just climbed faster, muscles screaming, every instinct yelling at her to survive.

Jane reached the top, pushed against the manhole — and it gave way.

Fresh, freezing air rushed in.

They tumbled out into a side street —
cracked pavement, broken
streetlights.

No time to rest.

No time to think.

Sarah dragged Jane to her feet.

From the shadows ahead, she saw a figure
moving — fast, purposeful.

Mike.

And Mary.

Relief flooded Sarah so hard she almost
dropped Jane.

Mike skidded to a halt when he saw them,
shock flashing across his face.

"Come on!" he barked, waving them forward.

Behind them, more figures spilled from the
tunnels, dark shapes, weapons
glinting under the sickly streetlights.

No time left.

Together, the battered survivors ran — into
the heart of the city's ruins, into the jaws of
whatever came next.

Hunters. Hunted.

No more difference between them now.

Only who could outlast the night.

Chapter Twenty-Eight: No More Running

The city around them was a skeleton, hollowed and broken, the streets cracked and empty.

Mike led the group, weaving through alleyways and crumbling industrial lots, one hand steadying Sarah as she half-carried Jane along.

Behind them, the hunters moved like shadows, always just out of sight — but never far enough.

Mike pulled them into the shell of an old textile factory. Huge iron beams loomed overhead, the roof sagging and riddled with holes where moonlight poured through in thin silver streams. Dust danced like spectres in the light.

They crouched behind a rusted loom, catching their breath.

Jane slumped to the ground, blood staining her side. She was fading fast, every breath a shallow rasp.

"We can't keep running," Sarah said, wiping sweat from her forehead. Her voice was low, furious. "They'll pick us off."

Mike nodded grimly. "Then we stop running."

He rose to his feet, drawing a heavy black pistol from inside his jacket — the last of his personal arsenal.

"If they want a war," he said, voice steady and cold, "we'll give them one."

Mary, leaning against a cracked pillar, cracked a grin despite the bruises mottling her face.

"About time," she said.

Sarah hesitated.

Fighting meant killing. Fighting meant losing any chance of slipping away quietly.

But looking at Jane — looking at all they'd lost already — she realized they were past that now.

She stood. "I'm in."

Mike glanced at her, approval flickering briefly in his hardened eyes.

"Good. Because here they come."

Footsteps.

Lots of them.

The hunters moved into the factory with calculated precision, spreading out, weapons raised.

A voice boomed from the shadows — amplified by a handheld speaker.

"Give up. There's nowhere left to run."

Mike stepped into the open, his silhouette framed by the broken windows and the sickly city lights beyond.

"You first," he called back, raising his weapon.

The hunters hesitated.

Just for a second.

And that second was all Mike needed.

The first shot echoed like a thunderclap through the dead city.

One of the hunters dropped, weapon clattering from his hand.

Chaos erupted.

Mary rolled into cover, firing short, disciplined bursts. Sarah grabbed a metal rod from the floor and smashed the nearest attacker's knee, sending him sprawling. Mike moved like a machine, his shots brutal and precise, forcing the hunters back step by step.

But it wasn't enough.

They were too many.

From a high catwalk above, a shadow moved — different from the others. Not just another mercenary. Something else.

A sharp voice cut through the gunfire.

"Enough!"

The hunters froze instantly, weapons dropping to low ready.

From the shadows stepped a man in a dark coat — face hidden under a pulled-down cap.

Sarah recognized him immediately.

Gideon Rourke.

The true hand behind the Blood Spurts chaos.

The spider at the centre of the web.

"You don't understand what you've stumbled into," Gideon said, voice smooth as oil.

Mike didn't lower his gun.

"Try me."

Gideon smiled — a slow, sad thing.

"You think you're fighting for survival. But you've already lost. This was never about you. Not really. You're pieces on a board you can't even see."

Mary stepped forward, weapon steady.

"What do you want?"

Gideon's eyes glittered in the half-light.

"Truth," he said.

"And blood. Always blood."

From the rafters, more shadows gathered — not mercenaries.

Other survivors. Other victims.

Faces they recognized: people from the University. From the streets.

Recruits.

Slaves.

Followers.

The Blood Spurts had grown far beyond a twisted game.

It was a movement now.

And they were caught in its storm.

Mike realized it then, deep in his bones:

There was no winning.

Only surviving.

Only burning it all down.

He turned to Mary, to Sarah, even to the barely-conscious Jane.

"One last stand," he said quietly.

"Or we die on our knees."

Mary raised her pistol. Sarah gripped the metal rod tighter.

Jane, pale but conscious, nodded weakly.

They were bloodied.

They were broken.

But they weren't finished.

Not yet.

Mike smiled grimly at Gideon Rourke — and opened fire.

Chapter 29: The Circle Narrows

The flickering light above them buzzed with static as Mike leaned against the cold wall of the chamber, eyes locked on Mary. Her expression was unreadable, yet her fingers tightened around the worn edge of the folder she'd recovered from Gideon's vault.

She had opened it only moments before, but her silence since had been louder than any scream.

"You're going to have to say something," Mike said, voice low, the tension between them thick enough to choke on. "I've seen men freeze up under fire, Mary. But this?"

She turned the folder slowly toward him, and his eyes scanned the pages: surveillance photos, transcripts, university documents... and a list. Seven names. One of them crossed out in red: Debbie Holloway.

Mike's jaw clenched. "They were targeting us?"

Mary nodded. "Not just us. The society existed long before we stumbled into it. But someone started watching — cataloguing our behaviour. This isn't just about Debbie. This is about leverage. Control."

Mike stepped back, the walls of the chamber seeming to close in tighter. "And Gideon?"

"He's not the architect. He's an archivist," she said bitterly. "Someone else is pulling the strings. This—" she tapped the list, "—was a grooming operation. Psychological experimentation wrapped in pleasure, wrapped in secrecy."

Mike ran a hand through his hair. "So who's the real target?"

Mary looked up at him, her voice sharp. "All of us."

A door creaked somewhere behind them — not the main one they entered through.

Both froze.

Footsteps echoed down a hallway they hadn't seen before, concealed behind a panel Gideon had never mentioned. A new voice floated through the dark, precise and cold.

"You were never meant to come this far."

A figure emerged from the shadows — not Gideon. Older, clean-cut, suited. A glint of recognition crossed Mary's face. Her knees went weak.

"Dr. Lennox," she whispered. "From the Ethics Board?"

"Ah," the man said, smiling faintly. "So you do remember."

Mike stepped forward, instincts kicking in. "You're the one who funded the research. The behavioural studies. You sanctioned it all."

Lennox stepped fully into the light now, revealing an ID badge — not from the university. Private Sector Intelligence Liaison — Albion Group.

"We didn't sanction murder," Lennox said coolly. "But we certainly observed your choices. You were all given freedom. How you used it? That was the test."

Mary's voice cracked. "What about Debbie?"

Lennox's eyes darkened. "Debbie was an unfortunate catalyst. But her death revealed what we needed to know. Who breaks. Who leads. Who buries the truth."

Mike moved protectively in front of Mary. "So this was all some kind of simulation?"

"No," Lennox said. "This is reality. You made your choices. Now we decide how the world remembers them."

A humming noise rose — hidden cameras shifting, locking onto their faces.

"Consider this your final question," Lennox said. "Will you hide… or expose the truth and take everyone down with you?"

Mary looked at Mike.

Mike looked at the folder.

Everything they thought they understood was gone. And now, the final move would be theirs.

Chapter 30: Beneath the Surface

Sarah sat alone in her living room, blinds half-closed, laptop screen glowing dimly against the dusk outside. Her hand hovered over the mouse as her browser finished refreshing.

The decrypted server access code had worked.

She wasn't sure what she expected to find. Maybe more surveillance footage. Maybe a log of messages. What she got instead was worse.

Case File #E-2197

Title: Experimental Cohort: Voluntary Subjects — Group Seven

Keywords: Psychological Stress Index, Groupthink Analysis, Pleasure-Aggression Cycle, Subject Compliance Threshold

Her throat tightened as she scrolled through the headers. Every one of them was marked with the names of her friends. Hers. Amy's. Jane. Mike. Mary. Debbie.

They hadn't just been watched. They had been profiled. Manipulated. Studied.

Each folder contained clinical assessments — personality inventories they had taken during university orientation, archived therapy transcripts, even data from their fitness apps and campus key cards.

It wasn't paranoia anymore. It was real.

Sarah clicked open a file tagged Subject #E7–04: Sarah Ellison.

Emotional variability: High

Resistance to group pressure: Moderate

Capacity for dissociation: Significant

Liability index: 71%

She gasped and closed the window, chest heaving. Her hands shook as she grabbed her phone.

Jane hadn't responded in over 24 hours.

Mary had gone dark since the last cryptic message: "If I don't come back, trust your instincts. Find Rourke."

And Amy... Amy was likely lost or worse.

But she couldn't sit idle anymore. Not after reading what was really going on. This wasn't about guilt. Or morality. It was about control. These weren't accidents. Debbie's death had exposed a nerve in a much larger operation.

Sarah stood, grabbing her coat, stuffing a USB copy of the files into her pocket.

As she opened her front door, she stopped cold. A black sedan sat at the curb. No plates. Windows tinted dark. The engine idled, but no one got out.

Was it surveillance? Or something more direct?

She turned back, locking the door behind her, breathing harder now. The walls were closing in. Her next step had to count.

Back in the underground chamber, Mike looked at Mary, both flanked by shadows as Dr. Lennox waited, his hands calmly clasped behind his back.

The folder still sat on the table between them — the truth, laid bare in ink and blood.

Mary's voice cut the silence like a blade. "If we release this, they'll bury us."

Mike didn't hesitate. "Then we give them something they can't bury."

He reached forward, picked up the folder, and tore the camera from its bracket with his other hand.

Lennox didn't move. "You're making a mistake."

"No," Mike said. "You did."

Mary's fingers brushed the USB drive in her pocket — the backup she'd made before they came down here. Her expression hardened.

"Time to flip the experiment," she whispered. "Let's see how they like being watched."

Together, they turned toward the chamber door.

Whatever came next, they were ready.

Chapter 31: The Ripples

The world didn't erupt all at once. It cracked — in whispers, posts, and headlines that felt at first too absurd to be real.

A late-night drop on a whistleblower forum. Encrypted folders. Academic logins. University headers. Scanned memos stamped "CONFIDENTIAL — Experimental Ethics Board."

The file was titled simply: "Spur."

A journalist at The Independent picked it up first. Then a blogger in Leeds. Within six hours, it had hit Reddit and was trending on X. By the next morning, major outlets were circling like sharks.

The revelations read like a conspiracy thriller — only worse. A clandestine psychological experiment, allegedly sanctioned by a covert ethics division within several academic research institutions, targeting students in a "stress-response enhancement program."

Terms like "behavioural escalation," "group delusion," and "pleasure-aggression thresholds" were used in official reports. Dozens of names were redacted, but some leaked through: subject numbers cross-referenced with student ID numbers, vague but damning. It didn't take long for Internet sleuths to match timelines and identities.

And at the centre of it all? A girl who had vanished — Debbie Langford.

Photos of her circulated. One image — Debbie, arms around a group of students at a club, hours before her disappearance — was everywhere.

Theories spread fast.

"MK Ultra 2.0?"

"A government black-ops psy test?"

"Mass psychosis disguised as academia?"

Even those who didn't believe were glued to the story. TikTok was flooded with speculative clips. YouTubers dissected timelines. A student-led protest had already begun forming at the university gates by dusk.

The university issued a flat denial. A spokesperson called the claims "a fabricated smear campaign" based on "maliciously doctored documents."

But the more they denied it, the more people believed it.

Because the leak had included video.

Blurred. Distorted. But unmistakable: a group in masks, in a hotel bathroom. A girl lying prone. A red spatter pattern. No faces, but enough to make anyone watching feel the burn of proximity.

The public didn't need certainty — they needed a target. The university became one. The department heads another. Rumours swirled of a "Subject Zero" still alive and hiding in the city.

And in the shadows, those who had once orchestrated the game now scrambled.

Data had been scrubbed. Files deleted. But it was too late. The exposure had cracked the shell.

Somewhere in the Midlands, in a shuttered office beneath a research building long since renamed, a man stared at a monitor showing real-time sentiment analysis from across social media.

A heatmap glowed red across England.

"They triggered the failsafe," he muttered, rubbing his temples. "They're not subjects anymore."

A voice from the dark asked, "What do we do?"

The man didn't answer immediately. Then, finally:

"We adapt."

Chapter 32: Jane in the Fire

Jane stood by the window of her flat, curtains half drawn, as the city below buzzed with unease. Helicopters passed overhead more frequently now. Sirens felt less like background noise and more like a countdown. Outside, students gathered in protest — some shouting with handmade signs, others livestreaming the scene.

Inside, Jane felt like a ghost drifting through a collapsing dream.

She hadn't slept properly in days

The apartment smelled like stress — sweat, old coffee, takeout boxes that hadn't made it to the bin. Her phone buzzed relentlessly. Anonymous numbers. Journalists. Former classmates asking cryptic questions.

And beneath it all, her inbox taunted her with one unread message:

"You still think you're in control?"

No sender. No header. Just a link that, when clicked, led to a short looping video.

A figure. Masked. Standing at the edge of a dark canal.

In their hand: something small, round.

Then — the splash.

Jane had closed the browser immediately. But the image wouldn't leave her.

Was that Mike?

Was that Debbie?

Her thoughts spiralled again.

She hadn't spoken to Mike or Mary since the story broke wide. Sarah had sent one word — "run" — and nothing more.

Even the safe places didn't feel safe anymore. The pub on Derby Road, the campus café, even Mike's garage. All compromised. All surveyed, probably.

She paced.

Her laptop was open on the coffee table. Dozens of tabs filled the screen. News stories, livestreams, Reddit threads dissecting her life in terrifying detail. She didn't remember that photo being taken — the one with her laughing on someone's lap — but it was there now, shared, reposted, twisted.

"Are these the new Manson Kids?" one comment read.

"That one on the left — looks like she's loving it."

Jane flinched. She clicked away.

Her own face now felt unfamiliar. Foreign. A version of her that only existed in rumours and screenshots.

A knock at the door snapped her out of it.

She froze.

Three short raps. One long.

The signal.

She crept to the peephole. A shadow. Then a whisper through the crack:

"Jane. It's me."

Sarah.

Jane hesitated, then unbolted the door. Sarah slipped in like smoke.

She looked worse than Jane had expected — her eyes wild, hoodie soaked from the rain, a backpack slung over one shoulder like she hadn't stopped moving in days.

"You saw it?" Sarah asked immediately.

Jane nodded. "It's everywhere."

Sarah dumped her bag and pulled out a folded piece of paper.

"I followed the trace," she said. "The digital trail. Whoever leaked the files — it wasn't random. It was curated. Targeted. Someone wants us found."

Jane's mouth was dry. "Why now?"

Sarah hesitated. Then:

"Because someone broke the chain. There was a handler. And now they're gone."

Jane blinked. "Gone?"

"Murdered. Or disappeared. Either way, someone's cleaning house. And we're next."

The flat seemed to shrink around them. Rain began to fall outside, tapping against the glass.

Jane's voice was barely a whisper: "So what do we do?"

Sarah looked up, her expression hardening.

"We stop running."

Chapter 33: Blood and Echoes

The chamber walls seemed to breathe around them — damp stone pulsing with memory, the faint hum of unseen machinery vibrating beneath their feet. Mike stood at the far end of the room, staring at the ancient mural that had once seemed like myth and now felt too real. Mary was beside him, arms crossed, unreadable as ever.

He turned toward her, the air between them thick with everything they hadn't said.

"So this is it," Mike said finally. "The heart of it all."

Mary nodded. "And we're not alone in here."

The lights buzzed. Somewhere behind the steel-grated corridor, movement echoed. Not footsteps. Not mechanical. Breathing. Watching.

The platform beneath the mural had revealed more than just carvings. A panel had slid away, exposing old technology — tape reels, data drives, a console built into the stone like it had always been there. Modern wires met ancient architecture. The fusion was unsettling.

Mike gestured to the control console. "This wasn't built by hobbyists."

Mary knelt beside it, fingers gliding over buttons. "No. This predates even Morrison's network. The symbols here — they're Sumerian. But the tech? Looks like something DARPA buried in a lab back in the '80s."

"You're saying this was military?"

"I'm saying," Mary said, "we were never the first. Just the latest fools to think we were in charge."

Silence.

The weight of their decisions — the rituals, the blood, the manipulation — now looked less like deviance and more like orchestration. What they had stumbled into years ago hadn't been found. It had been left for them.

A trap.

Mike walked the room's perimeter, stopping at a wall that bore a single embedded lens — a camera. Still active. Blinking.

"We've been watched this whole time," he muttered.

Mary didn't look surprised. "And now the watchers are tightening the leash."

He exhaled, rubbing a hand down his face. "Sarah and Jane are in the wind. Mark hasn't checked in. Amy... she might already be gone."

Mary finally stood. "That's why we finish this."

Mike turned. "How? "We broadcast. Everything. What happened. Who pulled the strings. We use their equipment against them. Then we vanish before they can shut us down."

He stared at her, surprised. "You're serious?"

Mary's eyes gleamed. "We might be monsters, Mike. But I'll be damned if we're their monsters."

He smiled, faint and grim. "Alright then. Let's give the world a show."

Mary moved toward the console. Her hands moved quickly now, typing in codes pulled from memory — ones she had stolen from Morrison years ago when she still believed knowledge equalled control.

As the chamber lights dimmed, a soft chime rang out.

System Online. Broadcast in 90 seconds.

They stood in silence, the countdown ticking between them.

Finally, Mike spoke.

"When this goes out — it's war."

Mary nodded. "Then we fight."

Chapter 34: The Watchers React

The room was low-lit, bathed in a cold bluish hue cast from a bank of monitors. Seven screens played simultaneously, each looping footage from different locations — Sarah's quiet kitchen, the riverside trail Mike had walked days earlier, a grainy feed from the underground chamber. In the centre of the room stood him — the Watcher. Known only by a codename, "Rourke" was a phantom on every intelligence list and a ghost in every formal investigation. No fingerprint. No official presence. Only whispers.

Behind him, a panel of silent figures observed, faces hidden in shadow. Their silhouettes shifted only when the audio feed crackled — a whisper caught from inside the chamber where Mike and Mary stood surrounded by relics and records of events they didn't understand. Yet.

"They're close," said a woman in the panel, her voice clipped, military. "He's pushing for the truth."

Rourke didn't move his eyes from the monitors. "Let them. They'll dig where I need them to. Just like Sarah."

Another screen flickered — Sarah, her hands trembling as she held the envelope she'd just discovered in her flat. Her face was pale, sweat beading on her upper lip. The note inside had been planted days earlier — part of the push. Not to terrify her. To force her. To awaken her.

"She's beginning to see it now," said Rourke. "The whole story's never been about Debbie. That was only the start."

One of the other watchers shifted uneasily. "If they go public—"

"They won't," Rourke interrupted calmly. "They're fractured. Paranoid. And we've seeded enough doubt between them that they're just as likely to turn on each other as seek help."

He walked slowly toward a wall-mounted file cabinet and retrieved a folder. Inside: redacted reports, old Polaroids, police files with faded stamps, and a photo of a much younger Mike, not in military gear, but behind a desk labelled Psychological Operations – Deep Studies Division.

"Mike doesn't even remember this version of himself," Rourke said, laying it on the table. "But he's about to."

From one of the screens, Mary's voice crackled again — frustrated and sharp. She had found something. A ledger. A confession? Rourke's eyes narrowed.

"She's close," one of the watchers warned.

"She is," he agreed. "But it won't save them."

Silence settled over the room. The watchers knew what that meant. It was already too late for salvation. The game was simply shifting boards. Secrets were unravelling, yes — but not the ones anyone had expected. Sarah wasn't just a bystander. Jane hadn't disappeared. Mike and Mary were being guided, shaped, driven toward a confrontation with truth so twisted it might consume them.

And in the shadows, the watchers prepared for Phase Two.

Chapter 35: The Meeting Place

Sarah stood beneath the skeletal frame of the old bandstand in the Arboretum, the iron canopy rusted and flaking above her like something out of a forgotten war. Wind danced through the trees, their bare branches casting tangled shadows over the cracked concrete beneath her feet.

She checked her phone again: 10:59 p.m.

Still no sign of Jane.

The park had a strange weight tonight, as if it knew what was coming. Sarah had kept her movements discreet—switching buses, circling blocks—but she knew full well if someone wanted to track her, they already had. Still, she'd come alone, just like Jane had asked.

A footstep.

She turned sharply

Jane emerged from the trees—not from the main path, but from the shadows, her coat drawn tight around her like armour. Her face was drawn, sleepless. But her eyes, when they met Sarah's, were focused. Determined

"You came," Sarah said quietly

Jane nodded. "Because I think we're all running out of time.

They stood in silence for a moment, not quite sure how to start. Jane reached into her coat and pulled out a flash drive, holding it in her palm like it might bite

"This was in my mailbox. No return address. No note. I didn't open it at home. I didn't want to risk it.

Sarah took it gently, turned it over. Unmarked. Cold to the touch. "Do you know what's on it?

"Not yet," Jane replied. "But it's tied to Debbie. And to us.

They sat down on the edge of the platform. Sarah pulled a small tablet from her bag, powered it up, and inserted the drive

The screen flickered to life

First, a list of names. Not just theirs—but professors, admin staff, visiting scholars. Some crossed out. Others highlighted. Among them, in bold

Deborah Lowe – Status: Expunged

Sarah Blayne – Status: Pending

Jane Holloway – Status: Escalating

Sarah's throat tightened

"What the hell is this?" she whispered

Jane shook her head. "There's more.

A video file loaded next. Grainy security footage from the night Debbie died angles no one should have had access to. Camera shots from inside the corridor, the stairwell, even from what looked like a hidden lens embedded in the mirror of the hotel room

Whoever had compiled this footage… they'd been watching all of them for much longer than any of them realized

Sarah's voice was barely a whisper. "This isn't just surveillance. It's control.

Jane exhaled. "Someone's been orchestrating this. Pushing pieces. Eliminating risks. Which means… we're still on the board.

Before either could say more, Sarah's phone vibrated. One message. No number

"Your window is closing. They won't be alone next time.

No signature. Just dread

Sarah looked to Jane. "They're trying to force our hand.

"We need to warn the others," Jane said, already standing. "But not all at once. We don't know who's already compromised.

Sarah stared at the tablet screen, the cursor blinking like a metronome counting down. "Then we start with Mary."

Chapter 36: The Reckoning Plan

Inside the dim-lit living room, silence ticked like a time bomb. Sarah sat on the edge of an old armchair, Jane stood by the window peeking through the slats of the blinds, and Mary laid out three burner phones, a stack of documents, and the old leather folder.

They had everything they needed to bring down a giant—except for time.

"This," Mary said, tapping a photo of Gideon Rourke from the folder, "is the man behind it all. He orchestrated the experiments, the disappearances, the manipulation of the Blood Spurts. He seeded the myth and then weaponized it."

Sarah raised an eyebrow. "And the university covered it up?"

"Not all of them knew," Mary replied. "But enough. Rourke was one of their darlings until he went rogue. When he resurfaced last year—quietly—they brought him back under a different title. Research Consultant. Independent. Funded through private grants."

Jane shook her head. "Let me guess— those grants are just fronts."

"Exactly," Mary said. "One of them ties back to an offshore trust owned by the Everswell Foundation. And that's where we strike."

"Remind me," Sarah said slowly, "why does a philanthropic medical trust have black site servers hidden behind university firewalls?"

Mary smiled without humour. "Because it's not really medical. It's behavioural. Control. Obedience. Conditioning. Blood is just the start."

Jane turned from the window. "So what's the move?"

Mary slid a flash drive across the table. "We get this into the right hands. A journalist named Ava Linnell has been circling this story for months. She just needs proof. Real proof. Video. Documents. Audio. Everything on this drive."

"Where do we find her?" Sarah asked.

"She's staying off-grid in Newark," Mary said. "An old friend's bookstore. And if we don't get this to her by tomorrow, I guarantee someone else will silence her first."

Sarah stood. "Then we move now."

But just as they turned to leave, Jane held up a hand. "Wait."

The burner phone on the table vibrated. A single message lit the screen:

YOU HAVE ONE HOUR. STOP DIGGING. OR WE FINISH WHAT DEBBIE STARTED.

They all stared at it.

"Is this a bluff?" Sarah asked.

"No," Mary said, her face hardening. "It's a warning."

Jane picked up the drive and tucked it into her coat. "Then let's make sure it's their last."

Mary locked the door behind them as they stepped back into the night, unaware that two figures had already taken positions across the street. One on the rooftop. One in a car with tinted windows and a laptop open, watching every move.

Chapter 37: The Silent Feed

The rooftop gravel crunched faintly under the weight of the watcher's boots as he adjusted the lens on his scope. From his vantage point above the derelict pharmacy across the street, he could see the women clearly through the slit in the blinds. His breath fogged the scope for a moment— then vanished, just like everything else he touched.

"Three targets. All accounted for," he murmured, barely audible, his voice carried through the micro-comms transmitter embedded in his collar.

Down below, in the parked car with windows tinted darker than regulation, the second figure sat back in the leather seat, fingers tapping out patterns on a thin, matte-black keyboard connected to a satellite uplink. A cracked screen showed heat signatures moving in the house. No sound—just the movements.

"They've received the drive," said the voice in the car, female, sharp-edged. "They'll try to move. Should we intercept?"

"No. Let them run," replied the rooftop agent. "They're doing our work for us."

In the car, the watcher glanced sideways at a faded manila folder marked OPHELIA / ACTIVE THREADS. Inside were old photographs, snippets of surveillance transcripts, and one blood-smeared envelope sealed in plastic. She didn't need to read them again. The contents were burned into her memory.

"What about Ava Linnell?" she asked aloud, already typing in geo-coordinates. "If they're heading to Newark, she'll be next."

"She's being watched," came the answer.

A soft beep interrupted the silence. An alert lit the screen.

[ALERT: NODE BREACH ATTEMPT—SOURCE: EXTERNAL | CLASSIFIED SECTOR 7]

The woman's fingers stopped mid-keystroke.

"They're not just running," she said. "They're hacking. Mary's trying to open a backdoor."

The rooftop agent tensed. "Do we shut it down?"

"No. We trace it."

She ran a tracing algorithm, watching as the map bloomed outwards — the connection routed through six countries before looping back to a private satellite node housed in a dormant university server. Whoever Mary had recruited to help her, they were damn good. Not good enough.

"Trace complete. I've got a physical location on the uplink: northern perimeter, sector H, beneath the engineering annex. Guess where Mary used to lecture?"

The rooftop agent chuckled, dry and cold. "Poetic."

Then came silence between them. Not the quiet of failure—but the silence of anticipation. They weren't worried. They were patient. And their leash was longer than anyone suspected.

Inside the car, the woman finally tapped a single key. A command line opened:

ENGAGE SUB-PROTOCOL: INITIATE OPHELIA (PHASE II)

"Let's see how far the rabbit hole goes," she said.

And with that, the watchers didn't just observe.

They acted.

Chapter 38: Ava Linnell

Ava Linnell hadn't meant to vanish. It just became easier than explaining why she was still alive.

The laboratory lights flickered overhead as she shut down the final monitor in her private unit — buried three floors beneath the University of Nottingham's defunct biomedical wing. Above ground, the building was a carcass of shuttered halls and vandalized lecture rooms. But here, below the noise, Ava had kept working long after her name was wiped from the faculty directory.

She'd seen the signs earlier than most. The night Debbie West disappeared, Ava had been in the next building over. Her sensors — unofficial, experimental — had picked up anomalous thermal spikes, blood oxygen disruptions, and panicked vocal frequencies. She reported it once. Only once. And then, just like that, her funding vanished. So did her student researchers.

And her flat was broken into without anything being taken.

So she went dark.

Tonight, however, the silence cracked. Her laptop pinged. A code buried in a string of diagnostics blinked twice, then resolved itself into a name:

SARAH M. // OPHELIA THREAD 2

Ava stared at the line of code. Someone had activated the protocol she built to trace classified experiments — the ones buried under a program nicknamed Ophelia, a project she'd helped design before she understood what it really was.

How did Sarah get this key?

Before she could process the answer, her secondary terminal hissed to life. Grainy security footage, intercepted from a private feed — three women in a kitchen. One of them, Sarah.

She watched them argue in hushed voices. Then came the envelope. Ava's breath caught when she saw the red seal. They'd found it.

Someone was lighting fuses again. And that meant her time was up.

She swept her hand across the desk, gathering two encrypted drives, her notepad, and the small silver case she kept locked in the freezer — not blood, not tissue samples. But something worse: a cloned neural mapping drive marked "Subject X — Pre-Breach."

She slid it into her backpack and locked the room down.

As she climbed the emergency stairwell, boots echoing in the shaft, Ava's mind raced. The others — Mike, Mary, Jane, Sarah — they were all players now. But none of them knew who had been behind the original research directive. Or what Subject X really was.

It wasn't Debbie.

It was someone else.

Someone no one had noticed had gone missing.

By the time she reached the garage exit, a cold drizzle slicked the pavement. She could feel eyes on her. She knew surveillance when she sensed it. But she also knew how to vanish.

Ava slid into her rusted Saab, keyed the engine, and whispered:

"You shouldn't have sent Sarah that file. But now that you have—fine. Let's finish what we started."

The car peeled away from the curb.

Destination: the northern perimeter.

Goal: find Sarah before they did.

Chapter 39: The Watchers React

In a dimly lit boardroom nestled deep beneath a nondescript building on the edge of Nottingham, the Watchers sat in silence, eyes fixed on the wall of monitors before them.

Ava had resurfaced.

Her appearance in the Derby station's surveillance feed earlier that day had triggered every alert the system was programmed to recognize. Her face — long thought scrubbed from every traceable record — blinked back at them now with terrifying clarity.

"She's not hiding anymore," muttered Dr. Ellory, her fingertips drumming against the table.

"Or," said the man beside her, "she's making a move."

The Watchers — not a government unit, but something more covert — had spent years manipulating power behind the scenes. Universities, research labs, social behaviour studies, even surveillance networks — all seeded with their influence. Ava had been one of theirs once. A brilliant researcher, a gifted manipulator, and ultimately… a traitor.

"She's inserted herself into the mess," said another watcher, leaning forward. "The Blood Spurts group is fractured. Amy's vanished. Jane is unstable. Mike and Mary are on the verge of exposing us — and now Ava walks right into the fire?"

Dr. Ellory turned to the others. "She's not walking into the fire. She is the fire."

They all knew what that meant. Ava didn't resurface unless she had leverage — or a plan.

A different screen flickered — Sarah and Jane, walking through a shadowed corridor in the old university archives. The Watchers' access into those feeds had been spotty at best since Ava's appearance. Someone was scrubbing data in real time.

"She's already inside our systems," someone muttered.

Dr. Ellory rose from her seat and approached the wall of monitors. "This ends now. If Ava means to expose us, then we'll burn the entire project to the ground before she gets the chance. I want eyes on Mike and Mary. We need to know if they've opened the chamber."

The words were chilling — and final.

One by one, the Watchers rose. Quiet. Methodical. Ready to dismantle what they had spent years building.

Because Ava's reappearance wasn't just a signal.

It was a declaration.

Chapter 40: The Quiet Truths

The corridor smelled of forgotten paper and cold dust. Sarah's flashlight beam swept across boxes stacked high and marked only by coded symbols. The old university archives hadn't been accessed in years, maybe decades—another part of the campus swallowed by bureaucratic neglect and the passage of time.

Jane walked just behind her, one hand gripping the envelope Sarah had brought. She hadn't spoken much since they entered the building, her mind still processing Ava's reappearance, the anonymous photos, and the spiralling consequences of everything they'd done—or been caught in.

"What exactly are we looking for again?" Jane finally whispered, her voice echoing softly against the stone walls.

Sarah stopped, crouching beside a long, steel filing cabinet. "Answers. Or leverage. I think Ava knew we'd come here."

She pulled open the drawer. Inside were dusty folders—personnel files, old research proposals, and something marked Project Veil.

Jane's breath hitched as Sarah flipped it open. "Wait. That was Morrison's signature," she pointed out, jabbing a finger at the bottom of a funding proposal.

"Exactly. Morrison. Gideon Rourke. Ava. It's all tied together." Sarah laid the papers out across a nearby table. "They weren't just funding behavioural research. They were testing control. Psychological compliance. Surveillance conditioning."

Jane leaned in. "And it started with us?"

Sarah shook her head. "It started before us. But we were the latest… trial."

The sound of creaking wood echoed through the room. They both stiffened.

Footsteps. Slow. Deliberate.

They killed the flashlight. Darkness swallowed them whole.

Sarah's heartbeat thundered in her ears as the steps drew closer. Then stopped.

A single voice—deep, composed—spoke from beyond the shelves.

"Curiosity can be fatal. But perhaps it's time someone knew the truth."

The lights buzzed on. Fluorescents flickered to life.

Standing on the other side of the room was a man in a grey suit, thin-framed glasses perched on his nose. He held up his hands, palms open.

"I'm not here to hurt you. My name is Lucan. And I'm here because the Watchers have made a mistake."

Jane stepped protectively in front of Sarah.

Lucan continued, "Ava isn't your enemy. Nor am I. But what's coming—what's already in motion—needs your help to stop."

Sarah narrowed her eyes. "Why us?"

"Because you survived the experiment. And because you're the only ones left who can still think for yourselves."

He reached into his coat slowly and pulled out a sealed flash drive, setting it gently on the table.

"Everything you need to know is on this. But you only have a few days before the veil drops for good."

He turned to go, then paused. "Tell Mike and Mary to meet me. Midnight. Arboretum gate."

He vanished into the hallway, leaving behind the flickering buzz of fluorescents and a silence now thick with purpose.

Sarah reached for the flash drive.

Jane stopped her. "You sure about this?"

"No," Sarah whispered. "But it's the only real lead we've got."

Chapter 41: Between the Pines

Mike stood in the dim yellow wash of his garage light, hunched over the workbench, pretending to be busy with tools he no longer needed. His thoughts were elsewhere — circling the name Lucan like a hawk. The message from Sarah had been brief, but it was enough to stir something dormant in him.

Mary sat cross-legged on the back steps, her phone in hand, thumb idly flicking through news headlines. The world outside seemed so distant now. The scandal was spreading — whispers of disappearances, altered records, encrypted footage leaked to fringe outlets. People didn't know what they were seeing, but the fear was contagious. The Watchers had gone too far. Or they'd lost control.

"You think it's real?" she asked, not looking up.

Mike didn't answer immediately. He set down a screwdriver, then turned, wiping his hands on a rag already stained from a thousand other messes. "Real enough for Sarah and Jane to risk contact again. That says something."

Mary nodded. "Lucan. Midnight. Arboretum. Feels like a trap."

Mike gave a dry chuckle. "Everything's felt like a trap since the moment Debbie walked into that room."

That silenced them both. The weight of it hung between them like smoke.

Finally, Mary stood and walked over. "So we go in blind?"

"No," Mike said. He opened a locked drawer and pulled out a thin folder — not university files, not surveillance footage. It was his own collection, something he'd built in secret over the last few months. Scraps of data. Schedules. Intercepts. Faces and names that didn't appear in any official record.

"You've been tracking them," Mary said, surprised.

"I had to know who we were up against," Mike replied. "And now, thanks to this Lucan character, we might finally get a name behind the curtain."

Mary flipped through the pages. One name stood out: A. Kessler — a ghost in nearly every document. Approvals. Signatures. Always in the margins.

"Who is Kessler?" she asked.

"Maybe the one pulling the Watchers' strings. Or maybe just another puppet. But either way, I want to look him in the eye."

They drove through the still, cool night in Mike's car. No music. No small talk. Just the hush of the engine and the knowledge that this meeting wasn't just another step — it was a turning point.

The Arboretum loomed ahead, its skeletal trees reaching skyward under a moon-blanched sky. The iron gate was already ajar.

Mike parked and killed the headlights. They sat in the dark a moment before stepping out.

Footsteps approached.

Lucan emerged from the shadows, the same thin-framed glasses glinting in the moonlight. "You came," he said simply.

"We're not here for games," Mary said. "What do you want?"

Lucan raised his chin. "To show you where this really began. And what's coming next."

He gestured toward a hidden path between the trees.

Mike hesitated, then glanced at Mary. She gave a small nod.

They followed him into the woods.

The real story, it seemed, had only just begun.

Chapter 43: Threads of Doubt

The warehouse echoed with the sound of distant machinery—old, irregular, like the heartbeat of something asleep but dreaming. Jane stood at the edge of a metal catwalk overlooking the floor, her voice quiet.

"We're being watched again. Not just by the cameras. I can feel it."

Sarah didn't reply right away. Her gaze was locked on the wall of monitors, each screen flickering between angles of the campus, a hotel hallway, the River Trent. A looping video played silently: Debbie laughing. Debbie glancing toward the mirror. Debbie vanishing from frame.

Jane finally turned to Sarah. "That envelope you received... the note said They all lied. Who's they, Sarah? Who's lying?"

Sarah hesitated. "All of us."

She stepped forward, placing a flash drive onto the table. "I traced the metadata. Every leaked video online, every clip that showed up on Reddit or Instagram—it all passed through the same server node. Guess who's behind it?"

"Gideon?" Jane asked.

Sarah shook her head. "Ava."

Jane's heart pounded. "That's impossible. She disappeared months ago."

"She was silenced. But not dead. She's been pulling the strings from the shadows—using us as test subjects. And now she's made herself known again. That footage? That wasn't to expose us. It was bait."

Sarah turned. "To see who'd react. Who'd try to cover it up. She's watching how far we'll go."

Jane looked back at the screens, the eerie flicker casting harsh shadows across her face. "Then she already knows."

Sarah nodded. "It's a game. But it's more than that. Ava wants someone to win. She's waiting to see who cracks… and who endures."

Outside, thunder cracked, rolling over Nottingham like a warning drumbeat. And far away, a message pinged on Sarah's phone. Untraceable sender. One line:

"Next moves yours. Clock's ticking."

Chapter 42: The Clockmaker's Hand

Ava watched from the shadows of her borrowed flat, its windows blacked out, the hum of a dozen screens filling the silence. The city pulsed beyond the curtains, unaware of the storm she had released.

In front of her, five displays glowed. Each one showed a different figure: Sarah, Jane, Mike, Mary, and Mark. Their movements were logged, analysed, patterned. Every text message, every flicker of doubt—they were all part of her script now.

This wasn't revenge.

This was a reckoning.

Ava leaned forward, her fingers tapping commands into her keyboard. The timeline adjusted. New footage queued up—some real, some artfully altered. She'd learned from the best. From Morrison. From the Watchers.

But she wasn't their puppet anymore.

They thought she'd drowned in the cleanup after Debbie's disappearance. A digital ghost swept away by corrupted data and falsified police reports. But they underestimated her. She had watched from the sidelines. Listened. Waited.

Then she'd started to pull threads.

She'd seen how quickly the group fell apart under the weight of shared guilt. Not from law enforcement. From fear. From each other. No blade could carve like paranoia.

Ava clicked on Jane's feed. Paused it. Jane, pacing a warehouse office. She was close to breaking. Sarah, too—but differently. Sarah was connecting dots, sensing the larger network at play. That made her dangerous.

Mike, meanwhile, had shifted into survival mode. Still protective, still pretending to lead. But he didn't realize the camera in his garage—the old dash cam he'd forgotten to disconnect—was still transmitting.

She opened a new message.

To: The Watchers Internal Node

Phase Two complete. Activation parameters confirmed. Group under duress. External leak planted. Awaiting final response from Subject Sarah.

She hesitated. Then added a line.

Morrison compromised. Remove or observe?

A slow exhale followed as she hit "encrypt" and "send." The message dissolved into a secure packet, vanishing down the dark net's deepest corridors.

Then her burner phone buzzed.

Unknown ID. A number only three people had ever used.

She answered.

A man's voice. Measured. Cold.

"You've gone off script."

Ava smiled. "That's the point."

Static. Then:

"You realize they'll come for you now."

"They already are."

She ended the call.

Behind her, on the largest screen, the image shifted—grainy CCTV footage of Mary walking down a narrow alley, following a lead Ava had planted. The bait had been taken.

Ava leaned back, lacing her fingers behind her head.

Let them chase ghosts. Let them fight shadows.

She was the clockmaker now.

And the clock was ticking.

Chapter 45: Into the Hollow

Mary's boots echoed down the alleyway, her breath puffing white in the chill April air. The city was deceptively quiet tonight—

Nottingham's usual Friday thrum dampened by drizzle and dread. She tightened the coat around her shoulders, the envelope clutched inside its lining like a talisman.

The message had been brief:

"If you want answers, come alone. 11:13 p.m. Kingswell Alley. Bring what she gave you."

The "she" had to be Sarah. Or Ava. Or maybe Debbie, if the dead could send invitations.

Mary had told no one. Not Mike. Not Jane. Not even Sarah, who'd been growing increasingly erratic since receiving her own envelope days ago. The group was fraying fast. Everyone believed someone else was cracking.

She wasn't going to wait for another ambush.

At the mouth of the alley, her steps slowed. Her fingers hovered over her pocket— where the old USB drive Sarah had recovered now rested. A drive containing footage, names, numbers. Half decrypted. Half a curse.

The back wall of the alley was marked with a red symbol—stylized, intricate. A

Watchers' insignia, if she remembered Morrison's notes correctly. She ran a finger over it. Fresh paint.

She stepped closer.

The brick behind it shifted with the pressure of her palm, revealing a recessed handle. She pulled. A narrow steel door creaked open, revealing a descending stairwell dimly lit by a single bulb swinging from the ceiling.

She hesitated.

Then descended.

The door clanged shut behind her.

Below, the stairwell gave way to a wide chamber—half-underground, slick with condensation, the smell of rust and old electronics thick in the air. Banks of outdated surveillance equipment lined one wall. CRT monitors hummed to life as motion sensors triggered her presence.

On the largest monitor, Ava's face appeared. Static-draped. Blurred.

Mary froze. "Ava?"

The voice that responded wasn't just Ava's. It was layered, synthetic. Altered.

"Hello, Mary. I wondered if you'd come. Most people don't like seeing their file."

One of the monitors flickered. Mary's face. Then a timestamped series of images. From campus. From her flat. From that night in the hotel.

Ava continued:

"They kept tabs on you long before you met Mike. Before Jane. You were a perfect mark. Smart. Loyal. Morally flexible."

Mary's hands balled into fists. "Why are you showing me this?"

"Because you're the only one left who might still choose truth over survival."

Another screen lit up. Sarah, pacing her apartment. Mike, sharpening something in his garage. Jane, crying in her car. Mark— missing, again.

"You can burn it all down, Mary. Or help cover it up forever."

The chamber lights dimmed. A panel in the far wall slid open, revealing a pedestal. On it: a second envelope, and a keycard.

Ava's final words echoed as the feed crackled and cut.

"One door leads to the truth. The other leads home. You have five minutes to decide."

Mary stepped forward, her mind spinning. The envelope. The keycard. The offer.

Above her, somewhere in the city, her phone vibrated. A missed call from Sarah.

She didn't reach for it.

She reached for the keycard.

Chapter 46: The Quiet Pact

The rain ticked gently against the roof of Mike's station wagon as it idled on the edge of the old canal road, headlights off, hazard lights blinking like a nervous pulse. Inside, the air was heavy. Damp. Tense.

Jane sat in the passenger seat, arms folded tightly across her chest, her hair slick with rain from the sprint to the car. She hadn't said a word since Mike picked her up from the safe flat in Beeston. She hadn't needed to.

Both of them were thinking the same thing:

Who's next?

Mike adjusted the rearview mirror, catching a flash of his own eyes—red-rimmed, restless. He looked a decade older than he had three weeks ago. "We're not going to make it through this if we don't talk," he said finally.

Jane's gaze didn't shift. "Talk about what? The cameras? The envelopes? The fact that someone has footage of Amy's last breath and Debbie's last scream and is leaking it like episodes of a show they directed?"

Mike flinched, but nodded. "Yeah. All of that."

A moment passed. Then Jane pulled something from her coat pocket. A small metal USB stick. She placed it in the centre console between them. "I found it in the lining of the red envelope. Hidden."

Mike stared at it. "Have you plugged it in?"

She shook her head. "I'm not sure I want to see what's on it."

Mike reached slowly toward the dash where an old, battered laptop sat closed. He opened it. The screen flared to life, waiting.

"I think we have to."

Jane inhaled, then nodded.

He inserted the drive.

A folder appeared. Titled:

THE EYRIE.

Inside: dozens of videos. Some raw surveillance footage — of the group, of Morrison, of rooms filled with cultic imagery and ritual-like gatherings.

But one file caught Mike's eye.

"JANE_RITUAL_CAM3.mov"

His hand hovered over the mouse.

"Don't," Jane said suddenly.

He paused. Looked at her. "You don't want to know?"

"I already do." She met his gaze. "I remember more than I've let on. About that night. About the room. About Debbie."

Mike sat back, tension knotting his shoulders. "Then why hide it?"

"Because it's not just us they're after. It's not just our story. It's generations of secrets. Families. Institutions. This thing — whatever The Eyrie is — it doesn't just want to expose us. It wants to rewrite everything."

She turned to face him fully now. "And I think Mary just found the door."

Mike's eyes narrowed. "You've been talking to her?"

"No. But I got a text. One word. Kingswell."

He exhaled. "That alley?"

"She's already there. Or was. Whatever's happening next, it's already in motion."

The rain outside picked up, wind howling against the windshield.

Mike started the engine.

"Then we follow it," he said.

Jane looked back at the laptop screen. The video was still there. Unwatched. Waiting.

She closed the lid. "Let's finish this."

Chapter 47: Kingswell

The wheels of the station wagon crunched over broken glass and old gravel as Mike pulled the car into a narrow alley marked only by a rusted sign: KINGSWELL STORAGE – UNITS 1-19. Jane leaned forward in her seat, scanning the shadows cast by a flickering streetlamp. They were somewhere on the east side of the city, the kind of place long forgotten by planners and gentrifiers alike.

"Are you sure this is it?" Mike asked, cutting the engine.

Jane nodded slowly, pulling out her phone. The text from Mary was still there — one word, timestamped three hours ago. No follow-up. No location drop. But Jane had remembered the name. Kingswell had come up in one of Debbie's old notes, scrawled in the margins of her criminology textbook: "They meet beneath Kingswell. Always beneath."

Mike stepped out into the chill night air, his boots echoing on the wet concrete. Jane followed, jacket zipped, eyes scanning every shadow.

Unit 6's overhead light was out, but the padlock on the door looked recently cut. Mike bent to inspect it.

"Someone's been here tonight," he murmured.

Jane pulled the door slowly. It groaned open to reveal nothing but darkness inside. They hesitated only a second before stepping in together.

A musty, chemical scent clung to the air — mold, old oil, dust. The unit was empty at first glance, but in the far corner, behind an overturned filing cabinet, Jane spotted something half-buried in the dust: a brass trapdoor. No handle. Just a shallow indentation.

Mike crouched, tracing its outline. "This isn't on any floorplan."

Jane retrieved a small metal rod from her pocket. "Mary gave me this. Told me not to use it unless I was ready."

Mike looked at her. "Ready for what?"

Jane stared at the trapdoor. "To find out who started this."

The rod fit perfectly into the indentation. With a metallic click, the panel shifted, rising slightly with a hiss of displaced air.

They exchanged one final look before Mike pulled it open.

Stale air poured out, cold and dry, and a narrow iron staircase descended into darkness. Jane went first, flashlight from her phone illuminating the steps.

The passage spiralled for what felt like forever. Graffiti gave way to old brickwork. Then symbols — carved, painted, some modern, others ancient. Each step down felt like a descent into another era.

Finally, the stairwell opened into a vaulted chamber. What light there was came from old Edison bulbs strung along the ceiling, flickering faintly. On the walls: photos, documents, red string maps — all names they recognized. The group. The faculty. Even the watchers.

And in the centre: a wooden table, and on it — a reel-to-reel tape recorder, still running.

Mike stepped forward, heart racing. He pressed stop. Then play.

A voice crackled to life. Male. Measured. British, but aged.

"If you're hearing this… the cycle has already turned again. And you've either become part of it… or you've come to stop it. Either way, you must understand: none of this began with Debbie." Jane clutched Mike's arm as the voice continued.

"This goes back to the 1974 incident. The ritual at Godshaw Quarry. We buried it. But the descendants… they kept the fires lit."

A pause.

"The Eyrie is not a cult. It is a contingency. For those who believe society must sometimes bleed to survive."

The tape clicked. Rewound automatically. Then stopped.

Jane whispered, "We weren't the first."

Mike's voice was barely audible. "And we won't be the last."

From the far end of the chamber, another light flickered on. A second reel. Another message — or another voice?

But before they could move, a sound echoed up the stairwell behind them.

Footsteps.

They weren't alone.

Chapter 48: The Man in the Dust Coat

Mike saw him first — a figure breaking through the mist, a silhouette in a dust-coloured coat moving with the unhurried precision of someone used to being watched. Jane stiffened beside him, her hand instinctively brushing the grip of the compact pistol she'd stolen weeks ago and barely remembered how to use.

The man stopped ten feet from them, the streetlamp above casting a fractured glow across his face. Mid-fifties, hollow cheeks, a scar bisecting one eyebrow. He looked like he hadn't slept in days. Or years.

"I figured I'd find you both here," he said, voice as gravelly as the cracked pavement beneath them.

Mike squared his shoulders. "You're Rourke."

The man smiled — not warm. Not even amused. Just tired. "One of them."

Jane's eyes narrowed. "Them?"

Rourke nodded toward the boarded-up church behind them, its spire a jagged tooth against the city's skyline. "You think you're running from the law, from guilt, from your own mistakes. But this goes deeper than the night Debbie died. Deeper than the videos, the bodies, the secrets you've buried."

He pulled a folded envelope from inside his coat. "This was never about any one of you. Not Sarah. Not even Amy. You were chosen because you were flawed. Willing to follow. Easy to provoke."

Mike didn't take the envelope. "What do you want?"

"To warn you," Rourke said. "Something bigger is coming. The watchers — the real ones — have activated the next phase."

Jane looked from Rourke to Mike, then back again. "What does that mean?"

"It means that after tonight, sides will no longer be a choice. They'll be survival."

Then, as suddenly as he'd appeared, Rourke tossed the envelope at Mike's feet, turned, and vanished back into the fog.

Jane stepped forward, crouching to retrieve it. The wax seal was cracked. The inside held only a list — names, dates, locations. Hers was on it. So was Mike's. So was Sarah's.

At the bottom, scrawled in red:

"Phase Two: Exposure. Let the world see what we made."

Mike clenched his jaw. "We don't run anymore."

Jane stared at the names. "Then we go to war."

Chapter 49: The List

Sarah had barely closed the curtains when the first ping came through.

One New File Received.

She stared at the screen. No sender. Just a blinking download prompt. Not a text, not an email — something deeper. Her laptop stuttered under the weight of the data.

For a moment, she hovered — then clicked.

A folder opened, revealing dozens of subfolders. All titled with familiar names.

Sarah. Mike. Jane. Mary. Amy. Debbie. Morrison. Rourke. Ava.

Her stomach twisted.

Each name opened to audio recordings, surveillance stills, redacted documents, even receipts. Not just of that night. But going back years. Conversations she'd long forgotten. Incidents she never even witnessed but had somehow been tied to.

Then she saw the last folder.

PROJECT LAMIA

Her pulse thudded in her ears as she clicked. Inside was a single video. The timestamp was the same night Debbie died, but it wasn't taken by anyone in their group. It was aerial. Infrared. High-resolution.

They were being watched.

From above.

In the corner of the screen, a watermark blinked: ARGUS SYSTEMS // ACTIVE OBSERVATION UNIT 17B.

Sarah backed away from the desk like the thing might explode. This wasn't just blackmail. This was military. Intelligence-grade. Someone had been running operations around them. She glanced out the window. Were there drones now? More watchers?

Then the message came — not on the laptop, but on her phone.

Unknown number. No text. Just an image.

It was her. Right now. Standing by the window. Taken from outside.

The caption read:

"You are the only one not compromised. Yet."

She swallowed hard. Her chest felt tight. What the hell did that mean?

Was it a warning? Or a threat?

She paced the room, breath catching. Then, against every ounce of better judgment, she opened a secure browser and started digging. "Project Lamia" wasn't something on the surface web. But in a dark database of forgotten whistleblower caches, she found one reference:

Project Lamia: Psychological contagion testing. Subject pools drawn from university populations. Controlled trauma events. Monitoring group ethics under escalating stress.

Underneath, a redacted report dated five years ago:

Primary goal: test susceptibility to ideological infection in young adult populations. Ideal environment: urban universities. Method: immersion in ritualized events, managed conflict, and manufactured moral dilemmas.

Sarah stumbled back, bile rising in her throat. They were lab rats. Debbie had been bait. The others—test subjects. The entire "Blood Spurts" chain of chaos wasn't accidental.

She thought of Jane, of Mike, even Mary. None of them had known. But someone had. Maybe Amy. Maybe Ava. Maybe whoever was still pulling the strings.

Her phone buzzed again.

MEET AT 12:00. SAME PLACE. BRING NOTHING. COME ALONE.

Beneath that, an address she hadn't seen since freshman year: the old student union basement — sealed off after a fire.

Sarah didn't wait. She grabbed her coat.

Whatever this was, it had to end.

Chapter 50: The Meeting

The room was quiet except for the low hum of the ventilation system. The industrial lights above flickered as though protesting the weight of the moment. Jane's eyes darted from the entrance to the man seated across from them — Mike, his jaw clenched tight, eyes calculating. They were waiting. For him.

A shadow moved across the glass. Then the door opened.

The figure stepped in — not masked, not armed, but calm. Dressed in a pressed charcoal coat, scarf tucked neatly, posture composed. He looked… almost unremarkable. But both Mike and Jane felt the shift in the air the second he entered.

"You're early," Mike said.

The man gave a faint smile. "Or maybe you're late."

He stepped closer, eyes resting on each of them in turn. "Jane. Mike. I expected more chaos."

"You brought it," Jane said, her voice dry.

The man — who had introduced himself as Gideon Rourke only hours before through an encrypted message — removed a folded sheet of paper from his coat. "This city is cracking open. You feel it, don't you?"

Mike didn't respond.

Jane stood. "You've been orchestrating this—watching us. The footage. The letters. The bodies."

"No," Gideon replied, "I didn't orchestrate. I accelerated what was already decaying. You're not victims. You were the match before I ever touched the fuse."

Mike's fists curled on the table. "You want to act like you're in control, but you've got your own mess coming."

Gideon paused. "Possibly. But you're still trying to outrun your own."

He dropped the paper on the table. A blurry image of Sarah and Mary — both near the edge of a river, both unaware of the lens capturing them. Scribbled beneath it: "She's not who you think she is."

Jane leaned in, heart skipping. "What are you saying?"

"I'm saying you've been focused on the wrong threats," Gideon said. "And if you want to survive what's coming next, you'll need to choose wisely."

Then he turned and left.

Silence returned.

Mike picked up the paper, staring at the image. His eyes narrowed. "Mary knew about the envelope. About Debbie. About everything."

Jane looked toward the door Gideon had exited through. "And Sarah's been hiding things, too."

Mike leaned forward, lowering his voice. "Then we stop reacting. We move first."

Outside, thunder rolled low across the sky. Rain tapped against the windows like the ticking of a clock running out.

Somewhere across the city, Sarah stood staring at another envelope. And Mary? She was no longer hiding.

Whatever came next would shatter what remained of their loyalties.

To be continued…

Final Chapter – Chapter 51: The Clearing

The fog was thick in the woods behind the abandoned observatory where the group had once gathered for their strangest rituals. Now, it had become their reckoning ground.

Mike stood at the edge of the clearing, arms crossed, watching as Mary and Sarah approached. The light from their torches carved gold out of the mist, throwing shadows that danced like spectres.

Gideon Rourke was already there — calm, hands folded, standing beside a small metal box resting atop a stone pedestal. Behind him, two masked Watchers stood guard. Silent. Unblinking.

"We're all here," Mary said, her voice hard.

"No," Gideon replied. "Amy isn't."

"Because she's dead?" Sarah asked.

"No," said Gideon, his smile almost gentle. "Because she chose her side long ago."

Mike tensed, feeling Jane shift beside him. Jane's eyes hadn't left the box. She whispered, "What is that?"

Gideon placed one hand on the lid. "The archive. Copies of everything — footage, recordings, documents. All your secrets. But more importantly... the truth about what was started, and why."

"Why are you showing us this now?" Mary asked.

"Because the game ends here," Gideon said. "You all thought this was about one girl's death. But that night... it was a door. You opened something. The consequences were never just yours."

He flipped open the box. Inside were labelled flash drives, envelopes, and a blood-red journal.

"The Watchers," he continued, "aren't monsters. They are curators. They keep records of humanity's hidden urges, failings, darkness. You all made yourselves part of the exhibit."

A beat passed. Mike stepped forward. "What happens now?"

"That depends," Gideon said. "You can expose it all. Burn it down. But understand this — the fallout will swallow everyone. Yourself included."

Mary looked to Sarah. "We could still walk away."

"No," Sarah said, stepping forward. "Not again."

She picked up the journal and thumbed through the pages. Names. Events. Dates. Not just about them — but generations. Patterns. Cycles.

"We've been part of something sick," Sarah murmured. "But maybe we can end it."

Jane touched Mike's arm. "We decide."

He looked at her. Then to Mary. And finally, Gideon.

"We bring the whole thing into the light," Mike said.

Gideon didn't flinch. "Then may you have the strength to survive the truth."

From a distance, sirens began to wail — growing louder. Police. Authorities. Or someone else entirely.

Mary closed the box. "We run out of time."

Sarah stuffed the journal into her coat. "Then let's finish what we started."

As the group turned and disappeared into the fog, the clearing emptied. Only Gideon remained. He turned to one of the masked figures.

"Activate the second archive," he whispered.

The Watcher nodded and stepped into the trees.

Because stories… never truly end.

Contents

CHARACTER RECALL: THE SURVIVORS OF BLOOD SPURTS

Mike Halston

Then: A former Royal Marine turned student under a special veterans' program. He was the protector, the enforcer, the one who kept the group "safe" during their underground game nights. In Book 1, he became the unofficial leader when the fantasy crossed into murder.

Now: Hardened by guilt. Obsessed with truth. But still haunted by what he didn't see coming. Mike's greatest fear: he enjoyed the control too much.

"In the Corps, we hunted ghosts. But this? This was a ghost that hunted back." — Mike, Book 1

Mary Elson

Then: The university receptionist — not a student but drawn into the group via Debbie. Mary was older, quieter, the group's anchor — and the one who cleaned up the aftermath when things got messy. Her calm masked her secrets.

Now: Mary has doubts. About her past, her role, and her own memories. She thought she was just playing the game. Now, she wonders if she was always part of something much worse.

"I only kept the keys. I never asked what they opened." — Mary, Book 1

Debbie Lang

Then: The vibrant, reckless ringleader of the games. She created Blood Spurts — an underground dare system mixing truth-or-dare with pain, secrets, and escalating risks. She died in the hotel bathroom, throat slit — the first casualty of something darker.

Now: A ghost. A trigger. A symbol. Everyone sees her differently: martyr, manipulator, or first sacrifice.

"You play the game, or the game plays you." — Debbie, last known message

Sarah Lin

Then: The quiet one. An honours student, always watching. She never spoke much during the games, but she never missed a detail. When Debbie died, Sarah disappeared for days. When she returned, she knew things she shouldn't have.

Now: Sarah is the closest to the truth. She's the only one left un-compromised — for now. Her inbox is full of surveillance drops, whisper files, and encrypted warnings. The Archive has taken an interest in her — and she's not sure why.

"They didn't record me by accident. I was always part of the test." — Sarah, Book 2

Amy Velasquez

Then: The empath. The caretaker. Amy kept the group together emotionally — until she saw Debbie's body. She was the first to scream. The first to break. And maybe the first to be turned.

Now: Vanished. Either dead… or part of something else entirely.

"Pain was never the point. What we confessed under pain — that's what they wanted." — Amy, Book 2

Jane & Others

Then: Part of the peripheral players. Students, bystanders, dare-takers who never realized how far things had gone. In Book 1, some ran. Some were silenced. Others were "recruited."

Now: A few remain. Watching. Waiting. Or already compromised.

Chapter One: The Morning After

The dim morning light crept through the paper-thin curtains of the Briarwood Inn suite, brushing against empty bottles, ashtrays, and smeared glasses like a silent judge. The air was a slow, heavy fog of blood, sweat, and stale perfume. The floor was littered with cards from last night's game, red string bracelets, and half-scribbled dares that now seemed absurd in the quiet aftermath.

Bodies lay draped across furniture and tangled sheets—silent, still breathing, but far from peace.

No one noticed the time.

No one noticed the absence.

Until the scream.

It cleaved the silence like shattered glass.

Amy's voice tore through the room, brittle with hysteria. "Oh my God! No… NO!"

Mike bolted upright, instincts flaring. For a moment, disorientation dulled his reaction—until he saw her. Amy, framed in the bathroom doorway, shaking, her hands fluttering like broken wings over her mouth.

Mary stirred next, wrapping a sheet around her body. "Amy? What's wrong?" she croaked, already moving.

"I can't…" Amy choked, stumbling back. "It's… it's Debbie… she's dead."

The word rang out, stark and final.

Mike was on his feet instantly. He pushed past Amy gently but firmly. Her knees gave out, and she collapsed to the floor, sobbing.

The moment Mike stepped into the bathroom, he stopped cold.

Debbie lay in the tub.

Naked. Still. Blood soaked the porcelain, smeared in strange patterns, some dried like symbols, others still fresh enough to glisten.

Her wrists were slashed — deep, clean, like someone had done it with intention.

But that wasn't what made Mike stumble backward.

It was her throat — torn open, ragged and wide. Not a slice. A rending. Her head hung unnaturally sideways, nearly severed.

Mary appeared beside him. One look and her face drained of life. "No… no, we didn't… we didn't do this."

Behind them, the others gathered.

Jane gasped, turned, and vomited into a trash bin.

Mark stared blankly, lips moving without sound.

John slid to the floor, eyes glazed.

"What the fuck happened?" Mike growled, voice trembling under the surface. "She was fine last night. We were all fine."

Amy was hugging her knees now, eyes wide with trauma. "I woke up and she was gone. I thought she went to the bathroom… I didn't hear anything…"

"Did anyone?" Mary asked.

Silence.

The kind that thickens into guilt.

This wasn't the game anymore.

This wasn't a dare or a show of courage.
This was real. Cold. Irrevocable.

Someone had crossed the line.

Mike turned to the group, eyes hard.
"Nobody leaves. Do you understand me?
Not until we figure out what happened. If we
call the cops now—like this—they'll think it
was all of us."

Jane looked up, her voice a broken whisper.
"But she's dead, Mike. She's dead."

He nodded once. Grim. Steady.

"And if we don't get ahead of it, we all go
down with her."

Outside, the first siren in the distance barely
registered.

Inside, the game was over.

And the nightmare had begun.

Chapter Two: The Rules Were Never Real

Before the blood, there was a game.

They called it Blood Spurts. What started as a late-night dare between philosophy students and outsiders evolved into something much stranger. A social experiment. A cult of adrenaline. A closed loop of carefully managed chaos.

It was meant to test limits — physical, emotional, ethical. A mixture of truth-or-dare and ritual. Rule-bound. Secretive. Dangerous.

But not deadly.

Or so they believed.

It began during Mary's late shift as a university receptionist. She was older than most of the students, smart, careful, and a little too intrigued by the group's raw energy. She watched from the sidelines at first. Then she joined. She brought structure. She enforced boundaries.

Mike entered next. Former Royal Marine. Quiet. Watchful. Drawn in by his younger cousin Debbie, who was always chasing extremes. Mike was supposed to be her tether. Instead, he became something else. The one who watched when others looked away. The one who saw things even he didn't want to understand.

Debbie was the nucleus. Bright, magnetic, reckless. She found a dusty folder in an abandoned psychology lab titled "Project Lamia." Inside: redacted studies, bizarre questionnaires, and notes on behaviour under duress. She turned it into a game. She made it theirs.

By Book Two, things had gone sideways. The group fractured. Surveillance footage emerged — of them, of others, of nights none of them remembered. A shadow figure named Gideon Rourke contacted Sarah, the quietest of the group, revealing that Blood Spurts had been monitored from the beginning.

It wasn't just a student game. It was a social contagion study. They were the data.

There were others. Watchers. Observers. Archivists. People with masks and cameras and silence. The group's rituals, pain-sharing challenges, even their supposed choices — all catalogued. Measured. Adjusted.

Debbie's death wasn't a fluke.

It was an escalation.

Book Two ended in the fog outside an abandoned observatory, where Gideon presented a metal box: The Archive.

Footage, confessions, psychological profiles — even predictive models of their behaviour.

Mike, Sarah, Jane, and Mary chose to expose it. To break the cycle.

But when they left that night, Gideon whispered to his masked companion: "Activate the second archive."

Because this wasn't just about them anymore.

The experiment had grown.

Wider.

Darker.

Deeper.

And somewhere in the background, someone had rewritten the rules — not just of the game, but of what reality they were allowed to believe in.

Now, in Book Three, the fallout begins.

Chapter Three: We Were Never Meant to Survive This

The rain hadn't stopped in three days.

Sarah crouched beneath the collapsed eaves of the burned-out train depot, soaked to the bone and clutching the journal like it was still warm with blood. Somewhere behind her, a siren wailed — not police. Something higher, deeper. She'd heard it before.

It meant they'd found someone.

She just didn't know who yet.

Mary paced in the shadows, arms crossed tightly over her chest. Her coat hung from her like a funeral shroud. "They're closing in," she muttered. "We're not ghosts anymore."

Sarah said nothing. Her fingers had found a name in the journal again — Jane Elwell: Subject E4-03. Next to it, a note in tight, clinical handwriting: "Projected breach: 84%. Disposition: Redirect."

Mike emerged from the underpass, breath steaming in the air. "North access is clear. No movement. But they've got drones near the canal. Infrared. We're on a grid now."

"What about Jane?" Mary asked.

Mike looked down. "She's not answering."

Sarah felt the cold move deeper into her bones. Jane had always been the hinge. Brave enough to question, fragile enough to hide. If she'd gone dark, something was wrong. Worse than wrong.

"She wouldn't run," Sarah said.

"She might not have had a choice," Mike replied. Then softer: "Not all chains make noise."

They had tried to blow the lid off the Archive. Book Two ended with fire and fury — encrypted files sent to journalists, rogue data dumps across fringe servers, a desperate scream into a world that didn't want to listen.

But the story hadn't gone viral.

The Archive had absorbed the blow, silenced the leaks, swallowed the evidence. And now, the experiment wasn't just continuing.

It was adapting.

There were new players in the game. Smiling professors. Hollow-eyed interns. Anonymous tipsters pretending to be whistleblowers. And always, always the Watchers — standing still just long enough to be seen, just long enough to haunt.

Mary sank down beside Sarah. "We need to disappear. Change names. Erase ourselves."

Sarah shook her head. "That's what they want. Witnesses who go quiet. Survivors who become myths."

"So what then?" Mary asked. "We keep playing?"

"No," Sarah whispered. She opened the journal, revealing the final page — blank, except for a single line written in red ink:

"The infection spreads when truth is suppressed."

Mike glanced at it and nodded. "Then we make it louder. Ugly. Unignorable."

He looked at them both. "We go to the press again. But this time, we don't stay anonymous."

Mary flinched. "You're saying we expose ourselves?"

Sarah's eyes were steel. "We already were. From the start."

A crack of thunder split the sky above them.

Somewhere, a camera lens blinked.

They stood together now — hunted, haunted, and fully awake.

Because this was no longer about secrets.

This was about survival.

And whoever had built Project Lamia was about to learn:

You don't control the fire once the match decides to burn.

Chapter 4: The man in the room

The rain struck the windows like fingernails tapping to be let in.

Sarah sat alone in her apartment, lights off, blinds closed. The only glow came from the cracked screen of her laptop, paused on an image she couldn't stop looking at: Gideon Rourke, captured mid-step outside the university's burned-out archives building. The timestamp read three days before Debbie died.

She'd seen him again last night — in person this time.

Not just some name buried in redacted documents. Not just a watermark at the corner of a surveillance feed. Gideon Rourke was real. And he had spoken her name like they'd met before.

But they hadn't… had they?

Two years ago —

The hotel suite had reeked of sweat, cologne, and expensive bourbon. Laughter spilled out of the room like static, wild and senseless. Sarah had stayed near the wall, always watching. Debbie had just finished her "Seven Blade Dare." Even the hardened ones — Mike, Jane, even Mary — looked shaken.

That's when the door opened.

No knock. Just a quiet, deliberate click. And in walked a stranger in a tailored charcoal coat, far too composed to be drunk, far too still to belong there.

Debbie's smile faltered. "Uh… you lost?"

The man said nothing at first. Just looked at them. One by one. Measuring.

Then he said it: "You've gone further than expected."

Sarah remembered the shift in the room — the sudden silence. As if something sacred had been broken.

Mike stepped forward. "Who the fuck are you?"

The man smiled. "You'll know me when it matters."

He turned to Debbie. "It's almost time."

Then he left, just as calmly.

They laughed it off later, mostly. Said it was probably a dare Debbie had set up, one more twisted layer to the night.

But Sarah never forgot his face. That precision. That knowledge.

Now —

She stared at his image. Older, but barely. Same suit. Same quiet authority.

Gideon Rourke.

He was no longer a mystery. He was a name attached to Project Lamia, to the ARGUS surveillance initiative, to the strange Blood Archive they'd uncovered beneath the university.

She reached for her phone and dialled Mary.

"Did you ever see him before that night?" Sarah asked.

Mary was quiet. Then: "Yes. Once. At the registrar's office. He was talking to the Dean, but… they never said his name. Just called him a 'consultant.'"

"From what?"

"I didn't ask." A pause. "Maybe I should have."

Sarah closed her laptop. She already knew the answer. Gideon wasn't from any department. He wasn't a student. He was the observer. The handler. The instigator.

He was the reason none of this had ever really ended.

And now… he was back.

Waiting.

Chapter 5: The hollow

Mike hadn't slept in two nights.

He'd tried. God, he'd tried. But every time his eyes closed, he saw it again — the tub, the blood, Debbie's lifeless grin. Her throat torn open like a confession scrawled in flesh.

And beneath it all: the rhythm of that first night. The game.

"Blood Spurts" had been a dare once. A twisted thrill between kids too clever and too bored for their own good. A secret society of scars and control. He'd told himself it was about limits — about owning pain instead of running from it.

But now?

Now it felt like a gateway drug to something older, sicker, and never meant for them.

He stood alone in his flat, shirtless, staring at the scar above his left collarbone — the one Debbie had carved herself. It used to feel like a badge. A memory of something electric. But now it just burned. A brand from a life he couldn't justify anymore.

He'd once been proud of what he called "tactical deviance." The ex-Royal Marine in him had believed pain was a pathway. That trauma, when chosen, forged bonds deeper than brotherhood.

But that night had broken something. Not just in the group. In him.

He could still hear the things Gideon Rourke had said in that fog-covered clearing. The man had spoken with the calm of someone who'd seen too much — or worse, engineered it. You were the match before I ever touched the fuse.

Mike didn't want to believe it. But part of him… knew it was true.

Because deep down, he'd liked it. All of it.

The blood. The hierarchy. The power.

And what did that make him?

Flashback — 18 Months Ago

The hotel suite was buzzing. The lights were low, and the dare wheel spun with a dizzying clack. Mary poured tequila shots with one hand while blindfolding Jane with the other. Debbie laughed — high and sharp — from where she stood atop the table, blade pressed to her thigh. The first cut always drew applause.

Mike sat on the edge of the couch, already drunk, already gone. But it was the adrenaline he'd been chasing — the crackle just beneath the skin when pleasure and danger brushed against one another.

That was the night he kissed Debbie. Right after she finished her third blood rite.

She'd tasted like metal and secrets.

"You're worse than me," she'd whispered.

And maybe she was right.

Now

Mike splashed cold water on his face, gripping the sink like it might run away.

"Focus," he muttered.

The group was unravelling. Sarah had gone dark. Mary was no longer playing defence. And Gideon? He was baiting them into something much bigger than they understood.

But Mike still had training. He still had muscle memory. He could protect them. If there was anything left to protect.

He looked up at the mirror. His reflection looked older, hollower.

He didn't recognize the man staring back.

Still, he whispered the same line he'd used on the battlefield — years before Blood Spurts had ever existed:

"Don't flinch. Don't look away. And never let the shadows move first."

It was time to call Sarah.

And it was time to finish this.

Chapter 6: The eyes that stayed open.

Sarah's POV

They were called the Watchers, but the name didn't do them justice.

To watch implied passivity — observation from a distance. But what the Watchers did… was curate.

Sarah stood beneath the flickering light of the underground archive vault, Gideon's box now cracked open in front of her. The metallic scent of old data — reels, tapes, USBs sealed in wax — filled the air with sterile rot. She flipped through the red journal again, its margins packed with notes in languages she didn't recognize, dates that stretched back decades, maybe longer.

This was where the rot had started.

This was where they had kept score.

Flashback // Excerpt from the Red Journal

London, 1972

"Initial tests successful. Psychological erosion occurs most rapidly between 18–26 years. Youth still believes in consequence, but has no immunity to myth. The introduction of 'The Game' catalysed spontaneous hierarchies, cruelty disguised as intimacy. We recorded everything."

"Phase One complete. Six candidates destabilized. Three retained."

The Watchers hadn't emerged in the first Blood Spurts. Not in the way Sarah now understood. Back then, their presence was background noise — a flicker of static in a forgotten corner of a recording, a streetlight that stayed on too long. Shadows that didn't quite match the figures who cast them.

But by the time Debbie died, the signs were there. Jane had mentioned strange emails that vanished after being read. Mike once caught a glimpse of a man in a charcoal coat watching from the rooftop. And Sarah… Sarah had found the first mirror glitch in the hotel hallway.

Only in Crimson Veil did the curtain begin to lift.

Gideon Rourke had given them names, but no identities. Only masks. Only rules. The Watchers didn't intervene. They provoked. They tested. They refined.

And worst of all: they kept everything.

Every twisted decision. Every whispered secret. Every drop of blood spilled in the name of thrill, ego, or desire. Archived. Categorized. Reviewed.

She turned to the adjacent wall where photos were pinned like insect specimens: blurry images of students, of them, caught in half-lit moments, unaware they were being studied.

What made it worse — what twisted the knife — was how subtle the manipulation had been. The game hadn't started because someone told them to. The Watchers had just made sure they wanted to.

Present Day

Sarah pulled the journal to her chest and stepped back into the cold hallway. The lights buzzed like hornets above her. Her breath clouded in the air. Somewhere above, a vent clicked open.

"They were never watching," she whispered to herself. "They were waiting."

And now?

They'd stopped waiting.

Chapter 7: The things we Bury

Mary's POV

She hadn't wanted to come back.

Not to the city. Not to the memories. And certainly not to the hotel.

But here she was again — five years later, standing at the edge of the same parking lot beneath a cloud-thick sky, staring up at the building where everything had gone wrong.

The windows on the fifth floor were dark now. Empty. Forgotten. But in her mind, that suite was still full of music, laughter, bad wine, and the giddy cruelty of young people who believed they were untouchable.

They called it a game.

Blood Spurts — part dare, part seduction, part ritual. It had started in whispers around campus. A challenge for those willing to play on the knife's edge of pain and pleasure. But by the time it reached Mike and Jane, by the time it reached *her*, it had already evolved into something more dangerous.

Something curated.

She knew that now.

But back then? Mary had just been the receptionist in the admin office, older than the rest, invisible to most of them. Until one day, she overheard Debbie talking about it — the "sessions," the "rules," the way people started to feel *changed* after playing.

And then she'd gotten the envelope.

No name. No return address. Just a folded card that read:

You've been selected. Curate or be consumed.

Inside was a list. Not of participants. Of *roles.*

Debbie — "the Catalyst."
Mike — "the Guardian."
Jane — "the Fracture."
Sarah — "the Observer."
Mary — "the Gate."

She didn't understand what it meant. Not until Gideon called her, not until he showed her the first file — footage of Debbie weeks before the game even began. Watching. Recording. Smiling into the wrong camera.

"She volunteered," Gideon had said. "But she didn't understand the weight. You can help guide the process. Minimize the damage."

Mary had agreed.

She told herself it was to protect them. She told herself she was a buffer, a failsafe. She told herself a lot of things.

But on the night Debbie died, Mary had stood in the hallway outside the suite for twenty-two minutes before entering.

Listening. Waiting. Knowing *something* was wrong.

And doing nothing.

She hadn't known Debbie was already bleeding out in the tub. She hadn't known the Watchers were recording. But she knew the game had gone too far. And she knew Gideon would bury it, just as he always had.

Until now.

Now, Sarah had the journal. Now, Mike was asking questions. And the Watchers weren't hiding anymore.

Mary leaned against the wall of the hotel, heart hammering in her chest.

She had been the Gate.

But maybe it wasn't too late to shut it.

Chapter 8: Cracks in the Wall

Sarah's POV

Sarah found Mary on the rooftop.

She knew she'd be here — same place Mary always came when the weight of things grew too heavy. The cold wind tugged at Mary's coat as she leaned over the ledge, staring down at the shimmering city below.

"Do you ever think about jumping?" Sarah asked quietly, stepping up behind her.

Mary didn't flinch. "I used to. Not anymore."

Sarah folded her arms, watching the older woman. "You know why I'm here."

Mary let out a long, tired breath. "You want answers."

"I want the truth," Sarah said, her voice hardening. "No more circles. No more lies."

Mary straightened, finally turning to face her. "It wasn't all a game, Sarah. Not even in the beginning."

Sarah's jaw clenched. "You were there that night, Mary. You knew something was wrong before we did. Before Debbie…" She faltered, the word still sharp after all these years.

"I didn't kill her," Mary said softly.

"I never said you did."

Mary's lips curved into something bitter — halfway between a smile and a grimace. "But you wonder if I let it happen."

Silence hung between them.

Sarah looked down at the rooftop gravel beneath her boots. "We were just stupid kids."

"You were," Mary agreed quietly. "I wasn't."

There it was — the raw crack in the wall.

Sarah's fists clenched. "Why, Mary? Why did you get involved? You weren't like the rest of us."

"I was lonely," Mary admitted, voice thin. "I watched you all, every day, from my little desk in the admin office. You were alive, Sarah. Messy, wild, reckless… and alive. I was thirty-five and invisible."

Sarah's throat tightened unexpectedly.

Mary's eyes glistened in the dim rooftop light. "So when Gideon came to me — when the Watchers offered me a place at the table — I said yes. I told myself I'd be protecting you. Guiding the group."

"But you didn't," Sarah whispered.

Mary shook her head. "No. I just watched."

The word sat heavy between them.

Sarah stepped closer, her voice lowering. "The journal says there was another phase after Debbie. That the experiment didn't stop with us. Do you know what they're planning, Mary?"

Mary's shoulders stiffened. "They're not just watching anymore, Sarah. They're preparing. You need to understand — Gideon was never the architect. He's just the curator."

Sarah's pulse quickened. "Curator of what?"

Mary's eyes darkened. "Human collapse."

Sarah's breath caught.

Mary placed a trembling hand on Sarah's arm. "We need Mike. We need Jane. And you need to decide right now — are you willing to burn it all down, even if it means burning us too?"

For a long moment, Sarah didn't answer. She stared past Mary, at the glowing skyline, at the faint wail of sirens below.

Finally, she whispered: "I don't think we have a choice anymore."

Chapter 9: The Curator

Gideon Rourke sat alone in the dim chamber beneath the old library.

The room smelled of cold stone and ancient paper, the walls lined with shelves holding dusty ledgers, reels of surveillance footage, and delicate red notebooks stamped with the Watchers' symbol — the closed eye.

He poured himself a small glass of whiskey, savouring the way the amber light caught in the cut crystal.

The Watchers had been here long before him. He was no founder — just another in a long chain of stewards. His job wasn't to command but to curate. To preserve. To document.

In Book One, Blood Spurts, the players thought they were acting on their own dark urges, chasing the thrill of pain, seduction, and risk. Gideon had been there in the shadows, nudging them along, recording the social breakdown, taking notes as each moral thread frayed.

When Debbie died, Gideon's original assignment was supposed to end. But something changed. The group hadn't shattered. They'd clung tighter. And when Sarah started digging, when Mike's military instincts kicked in, when Mary slipped behind the curtain, the Watchers saw an opportunity.

Book Two, Crimson Veil, escalated the game.

That phase tested not just individual collapse but ideological infection. Could Gideon introduce new fractures — through fear, through loyalty tests, through carefully planted lies? Could he push the group into destroying itself?

They had resisted.

Oh, they had broken plenty — but not in the ways the Watchers wanted.

So now came Book Three. The final phase.

He sipped his whiskey slowly, watching the monitor on the far wall.

Sarah and Mary on the rooftop.

Mike and Jane reassembling their fractured alliance.

The younger ones — Amy, Mark — drifting in and out of the edges, already half-lost.

Gideon knew the archive Sarah carried wasn't the archive. It was bait. It always had been.

The real treasure — the true experiment — was unfolding now. Could these humans, these fragile, clever, self-destructive creatures, choose truth over survival?

Could they expose everything, knowing it would destroy them?

His phone buzzed on the desk. A message.

Activate final protocol. Ready the second archive.

Gideon smiled faintly. The Watchers were ready to pull the curtain back entirely. Not just on this group — but on the whole system.

He stood, straightening his cuffs, feeling the weight of his carefully constructed mask settle over his face again.

For two books, he had been the man in the background, the cold observer. But in this final act, Gideon knew his own role was shifting. He was no longer just a curator.

He was the final test.

And when the last page turned, when the last betrayal fell like a hammer, Gideon Rourke intended to walk out of the ashes — not as the Watchers' servant, but as their master.

Chapter 10: The Trap

Mike crouched low behind the rusted-out car, his breath sharp in his ears.

The warehouse loomed ahead, its windows broken, its concrete walls slick with rain. The message had been clear:

Midnight. Come alone. Bring the journal.

But Sarah hadn't trusted it. Neither had Mike.

Now they were here, together, waiting in the dark.

"I don't like this," Sarah whispered beside him. Her fingers trembled slightly on the journal she clutched to her chest — the same blood-red book that had driven them this far.

Mike scanned the rooftop. No obvious sentries. But the tension in his gut told him they were walking straight into something.

"This isn't Gideon's style," Mike murmured. "He'd want to face us himself."

Sarah shook her head. "Unless he wants us to think that."

Lightning flashed distantly, briefly illuminating the cracked asphalt, the long-dead power lines sagging above.

Mike remembered the beginning — the allure of Blood Spurts, the high that came from stepping over moral lines, the feeling that they were untouchable. Back then, he'd been a thrill-seeker, a soldier still hungry for the edge.

Now? He felt hunted. Not by Gideon. Not even by the Watchers.

By something worse.

Sarah tensed. "Movement."

Mike followed her gaze. A figure had emerged from the side door — tall, hooded, face hidden. Not Gideon.

Another figure appeared behind the first. Then another.

Within seconds, five shapes stood at the warehouse entrance, forming a silent wall.

Sarah's breath caught. "That's not just Gideon."

Mike swore under his breath. "It's the inner circle."

The ones they'd only heard whispers about — the real architects, the ones even Gideon answered to.

Suddenly, the ground under Mike's boots felt very thin.

Sarah gripped his arm. "What do we do?"

Mike exhaled slowly. "We walk in."

Sarah's eyes widened. "Mike —"

He met her gaze. "If we run, they'll hunt us. If we stay, they'll crush us. But if we walk in — we might get one shot to break this."

Her jaw clenched. Then she nodded.

Together, they rose from cover, stepping into the open. The rain soaked through Mike's shirt in seconds, the cold biting down to his bones.

The five figures didn't move. They just watched.

When Mike and Sarah reached the door, one of the figures finally spoke — a woman's voice, low and cold.

"Mr. Bennett. Ms. Carter. You brought the journal."

Mike's hand hovered near his belt — no weapon, but the tension in his muscles felt like a drawn blade.

"Who are you?" Sarah demanded. "Where's Gideon?"

The woman's hood tilted slightly.

"Gideon was never the trap," she said softly. "You are."

Before Mike could react, the door behind them slammed shut.

The last thing he saw before the lights went out was the faint gleam of cameras — dozens of them — hidden in the walls, the ceiling, the floor.

They hadn't been walking into a confrontation.

They'd been walking onto the stage.

Chapter 11: The Council's Truth

The room was silent except for the faint hiss of air through hidden vents.

Mike and Sarah stood at the centre of a wide, circular chamber — walls lined with black glass, the ceiling a dome of dull steel.

They could feel the eyes on them, though they saw no faces.

Suddenly, the room dimmed further, and a thin ring of light illuminated the platform where they stood.

A voice echoed, amplified, but unmistakably human.

"Michael Bennett. Sarah Carter. You've come far."

Sarah's fists tightened at her sides. "Where's Gideon?"

Another voice, softer, male. "Gideon has served his purpose. As have you."

Mike's jaw clenched. "What do you want?"

A panel on the far wall slid open, revealing a long table, and behind it, seven shadowed figures seated — the Council.

The inner architects of the Watchers.

One figure leaned forward slightly. "Do you know what this was ever about?"

Mike scowled. "Control."

Sarah spat, "Power."

The council figure gave a soft, almost amused laugh. "No. Understanding."

A second figure spoke, her voice sharp as glass. "For centuries, we've observed how humans unravel when tested. When presented with chaos, most collapse. But a few… reveal extraordinary patterns."

Sarah shook her head. "You murdered Debbie. You shattered lives."

The woman answered calmly. "We revealed what was already there. Blood Spurts, Crimson Veil — they weren't games. They were instruments. Trials to separate the noise from the signal."

Mike took a step forward. "And what signal are you looking for now?"

The first speaker stood, the light catching his pale, lined face.

"You, Mr. Bennett. You, Ms. Carter. You survived every phase. You adapted, you resisted, you fought. You were never just participants. You were candidates."

Mike froze. His heart pounded.

Sarah's voice shook. "Candidates… for what?"

The man smiled faintly. "For integration."

Behind them, the walls shifted, revealing massive screens flickering with data — faces, locations, live feeds of thousands, maybe millions.

"We are no longer content to observe from the shadows," the man continued. "The Watchers must evolve. We will shape, guide, and embed into the social bloodstream. And to do that, we need vessels. People the world believes are real. People with scars and stories — like you."

Mike's stomach turned. "You want us to be your front?"

Sarah's voice hardened. "Your puppets."

The council leader's eyes glinted. "Our avatars."

Suddenly, the floor under their feet vibrated. Mike instinctively reached for Sarah, pulling her close.

"We've mapped your networks, your habits, your drives," the woman said smoothly. "Everything you are has been recorded — replicated. Even now, we're already deploying the next phase."

Sarah's breath caught. "You don't need us."

The man smiled. "No. But imagine how much cleaner it looks if you stand on the stage and say you chose this."

The chamber doors sealed shut.

Lights pulsed on the far end of the room — dozens of Watchers stepping forward, masked, silent.

Mike squared his shoulders, heart hammering. "We're not giving you what you want."

The council leader's smile faded.

"No," he said softly. "But the world will."

The lights surged, and the Watchers closed in.

Chapter 12: The Breakout

Mike's pulse thundered in his ears as the masked Watchers closed in, their black-gloved hands reaching, their boots eerily soundless on the cold floor. He and Sarah were trapped.

They were under the old observatory, the original site where Blood Spurts' twisted experiments had begun years ago — but this was no abandoned ruin anymore. Beneath the crumbling dome, an entire hidden facility had been built, one they hadn't seen coming.

Sarah's breath hitched beside him. "There's no door," she hissed.

Mike scanned the walls — smooth black glass, no visible seams. The council sat calmly behind their glowing table, watching like scientists observing lab rats in a maze.

Mike's fists clenched. He wasn't going to die here.

"Sarah," he murmured, his voice low. "Remember the access tunnels they used in the early tests?"

She blinked at him. "The fire tunnels?"

"Yeah. There has to be one below this floor."

Sarah's eyes darted to the edges of the room — the faint lines where floor panels met. She'd been here before, years ago, as a test subject. She knew there were emergency passages, hidden out of sight.

But they'd have to get there.

Mike turned, meeting the gaze of the nearest Watcher. The masked figure was less than two meters away. Mike raised his voice.

"You know," he called to the council, "for people who claim to predict human behaviour, you've made one mistake."

The lead council member leaned forward slightly. "Oh?"

Mike grinned, teeth bared. "You forgot what happens when a cornered animal fights back."

Then he lunged.

His shoulder slammed into the Watcher's chest, knocking the figure back into another. Chaos erupted — the room flashing red as alarms blared, the Watchers trying to regroup, shouting commands into hidden earpieces.

Sarah dropped low, darting between two guards. She grabbed one of the metal rods from a belt holster and slammed it across the back of a knee. The Watcher fell with a sharp grunt.

Mike yanked another down by the mask, ripping it clean off — the young man beneath barely older than twenty, eyes wide with shock.

"Where's the floor access?!" Mike barked.

The kid shook his head furiously, terrified. But Sarah was already moving — she had spotted it.

"There!" she yelled, pointing to a maintenance hatch half-hidden beneath the council table.

Together, they ran.

Behind them, the council members rose in a slow, coordinated motion, watching with cold detachment as their prey scrambled for escape.

Mike grabbed the edge of the hatch and heaved — the metal groaned, the panel shuddering, but finally popped open. A narrow shaft yawned below, lit by faint emergency lights.

He shoved Sarah forward. "Go!"

She dropped in, sliding down the ladder as shouts echoed above.

Mike swung his legs over — but before he followed, he turned and locked eyes with the lead council member.

"We're not done," Mike growled.

The older man gave the faintest nod. "No," he murmured. "You're not."

Mike dropped.

The hatch slammed shut behind him.

Down in the maintenance shaft, Mike caught up with Sarah, their breath ragged in the tight space.

"Where does this lead?" he panted.

Sarah wiped sweat from her brow. "If the maps are right? Back to the surface tunnels.

But we'll need to move fast — they'll be rerouting guards."

Above them, the faint sound of boots striking metal echoed down.

Mike took Sarah's hand. "Then we move. Now."

Together, they plunged into the dark.

They weren't just fighting to escape the council.

They were running to expose everything — before the Watchers could close the net for good.

Chapter 13: Gideon's Move

The night air was sharp atop the ridge overlooking the observatory. Gideon Rourke stood in the shadows, his long coat stirring in the wind, eyes fixed on the crumbling dome below.

His earpiece crackled softly.

"They've made contact," a voice murmured. "They're inside."

Gideon allowed himself the faintest smile. "Of course they are."

He checked his watch — a sleek black military model, synced to the countdown running in the background. The window was narrowing. If Mike and Sarah didn't break out within the next twenty minutes, the council's extraction teams would lock down the tunnels permanently.

He paced slowly, hands clasped behind his back.

For years, Gideon had played both sides. On paper, he was an independent operative — part consultant, part fixer, part saboteur. To the Watchers, he had been an external agent, brought in when things threatened to spill too far into public view.

But Gideon had never been fully loyal to the council. Not really.

He understood the original mission: monitor, test, push human boundaries. But over time, the council had turned into something else — an entity obsessed with control. No longer content to observe, they had started shaping events directly, curating chaos like curators arranging exhibits in a private gallery.

Gideon had seen enough.

He had picked his side months ago — and tonight, it was time to show his hand.

A soft footfall sounded behind him. He turned slightly as Ava emerged from the trees, her dark hair tied back, a pistol holstered under her jacket.

"They're in the south tunnels now," she reported quietly. "We can meet them at the secondary exit."

Gideon nodded. "Good. The council will block the main shafts first. We'll need to intercept before they flood the outer passageways."

Ava hesitated. "And the council itself?"

Gideon gave a thin smile. "They'll stay seated. They always do. They think they're untouchable in that room — but tonight, the data Mike and Sarah carry is the real threat."

His eyes flicked toward the glowing dome.

"Once they surface, we get them out of here," he said. "Then we leak everything. Names. Experiments. Locations. The whole archive. No more hidden hands."

Ava let out a slow breath. "You really think they'll let us live after this?"

Gideon's jaw tightened. "I don't care."

He checked his watch again. "Time to move."

Together, they slipped back into the forest, moving quickly down the ridge, following a narrow, overgrown path that led toward the old maintenance shafts.

Gideon's mind raced.

Mike had changed. Sarah had hardened. Even Mary — the old receptionist turned survivor — had learned to see past the lies. They were no longer just pawns in a twisted experiment.

But Gideon knew the council had one last card to play.

He could feel it in the air — that electric tension right before the storm.

As he and Ava reached the treeline, the first dull thud echoed from the tunnels below. Explosives. Forced blockades.

They were out of time.

Gideon clenched his fists.

"All right," he murmured, voice steeling. "Let's bring them home."

Chapter 14: Breaking Through

The air inside the tunnel was stifling, heavy with dust and the sharp scent of old stone and rusted metal. Mike's shoulders burned as he pushed a fallen beam aside, clearing the narrow crawlspace for Sarah to slip through.

She coughed, waving a hand in front of her face. "Mike, we don't have time to clear the whole passage. They're closing in behind us."

Mike turned, wiping sweat from his brow with a grimy sleeve. His chest heaved, muscles straining — but not just from the physical effort.

He could feel it: the old hunger, the pulse that once thrilled through him like fire in his veins.

In the early days — back in the first Blood Spurts — Mike had thrived on the edge. Former Royal Marine, adrenaline junkie, the guy who ran toward violence when others flinched away. The games, the blood, the sharp taste of control — it had fed something raw inside him.

But now?

Now he was tired.

Not physically — though the bruises and scars had accumulated — but in his soul.

He wasn't chasing the thrill anymore. He was running from the wreckage.

"Mike!" Sarah grabbed his arm, shaking him. "Snap out of it — I can hear them back there."

He blinked, shaking himself free of the spiral. "Yeah. Yeah, I'm good."

He wasn't good.

He was worn down.

They scrambled forward, squeezing through a side shaft, the old metal walls groaning as they brushed past. Somewhere deep in the tunnels, the Watchers' operatives were sealing exits, flooding passages. They had to be two steps ahead — or they'd end up trapped like rats in a maze.

Sarah glanced back at him. "You used to love this, you know."

Mike grunted. "What?"

"The danger. The edge. Back then, you'd have been smiling." She didn't say it cruelly — just an observation.

Mike let out a slow, shaky breath. "I know."

He paused, pressing his forehead briefly to the cool wall. "I used to think the blood was the point. That it made me sharp, made me alive."

He straightened, meeting her gaze.

"But now? I just want out. I want us out. No more deaths. No more games."

Sarah gave him a small, tired smile. "You're not the same guy anymore."

"No," Mike murmured. "I'm not."

A loud metallic thud echoed behind them — too close. Sarah jumped. Mike's eyes snapped wide, instincts kicking in.

"Move," he ordered, grabbing her hand. "Now."

They ran, ducking through the broken maintenance archway, lungs burning, footsteps echoing in the confined space.

The tunnel forked ahead — left or right. Mike hesitated for only a second before pulling Sarah right. He knew the layout better, remembered the old escape routes from long ago.

As they sprinted, his mind raced.

He wasn't hunting blood anymore. He was fighting for survival.

For Sarah. For the others.

For himself.

Ahead, a faint light glimmered — not the cold, sterile glow of the Watchers' equipment, but real light. Outside light.

"We're close," Sarah gasped.

Mike nodded; teeth clenched. "We just have to live long enough to reach it."

And as they surged forward, hand in hand, the echoes of his old self — the man who craved the crimson rush — faded behind him, step by painful step.

Chapter 15: The Pursuit

In the control van parked at the mouth of the tunnel system, a row of monitors flickered with grainy black-and-white feeds. Figures moved on the screens — two blips marked in red, deep inside the labyrinth.

"They're moving faster now," the lead Watcher murmured. His voice was smooth, almost detached. He tapped the glass gently. "Sector Four cleared yet?"

A younger agent at the console nodded. "Sealed five minutes ago. They're boxed in on three sides. Only one viable exit left."

The lead Watcher — codename PHANTOM — gave a small, satisfied smile. "Good. Herd them to the surface. Gideon wants eyes on them before they breach."

Behind them, another figure stepped into the van, rain dripping from the hood of her black jacket. Ava. Her eyes, sharp and calculating, swept the monitors.

"They're smarter than you gave them credit for," she murmured.

PHANTOM didn't flinch. "They're rats in a maze, Ms. Ava. They'll scramble, they'll run — but they'll still hit the traps."

Ava's mouth tightened. "Don't underestimate them."

Inside the tunnels, Watcher teams advanced methodically — helmets gleaming under headlamps, weapons lowered but ready. Their boots crunched over debris as they moved through the narrow shafts.

One team leader keyed his comm. "North approach secure. Negative on visual — target may have doubled back."

PHANTOM's voice crackled through the earpiece. "Negative. Keep pressure. Push them east."

In the shadows, a pair of agents paused at an intersection. Faint echoes rippled down the corridor — hurried footsteps, breathing, scuffing against the walls.

"Movement," one whispered.

The other raised his hand, signalling the team.

With surgical precision, they split into flanking positions. This wasn't the chaos of Book One, where brute force ruled — nor even the occult manipulations of Crimson Veil.

No, the Watchers had evolved.

They had refined their methods, honed their craft.

They were no longer observers.

They were predators.

Inside the van, Ava leaned closer to the monitors, watching Mike and Sarah's markers dart through the digital map. Her jaw clenched.

"They're heading for the south tunnels," she said quietly. "They know the old infrastructure better than you predicted."

PHANTOM tapped a screen, pulling up thermal overlays. "We predicted every variable. It's a controlled test."

Ava gave him a sharp look. "You're not the only one testing, Phantom."

The Watcher gave a faint smile but said nothing.

In the tunnels, the two figures kept running, unaware that the walls were closing around them.

Above ground, more Watcher units spread out, forming a loose cordon near the collapsed maintenance yard. Night vision scopes scanned the crumbling ruins, while drones hovered silently overhead.

The order was simple.

No escape.

Inside the van, a new voice crackled over comms — one that froze Ava mid-step.

"Council orders," the voice rasped. "Do not engage directly. Observe final interactions. Confirm subject parameters before retrieval."

PHANTOM's face darkened slightly. "Copy."

Ava exhaled slowly, her mind racing.

She had seen this before. Mike and Sarah weren't just running from death — they were running into something worse. Something the Watchers had been waiting to unleash.

Chapter 16 – Fracture Point

The cold air inside the maintenance tunnels stung Mike's lungs as he sprinted, Sarah close behind. Concrete walls flashed by under the flicker of their stolen flashlight, the echo of footsteps behind them no longer distant.

"They're closing in," Sarah hissed, clutching the satchel tighter against her chest — the satchel carrying the archive they'd risked everything to steal. "We can't outrun them forever."

Mike shot a glance back, his face pale but determined. "We don't need forever. Just five more minutes. Gideon said the hatch leads out by the river."

She almost laughed — not because it was funny, but because it was insane. Trusting Gideon Rourke had never been part of their plan. Not in the beginning, not even midway. And yet here they were, running on a breadcrumb trail laid out by the one man who knew more than he ever let on.

Above ground, Gideon watched the treeline from the edge of the abandoned parking lot, breath curling in the cold night air. His coat hung loose, one gloved hand holding a slim communication device.

"They're pushing too fast," he muttered into the mic. "Pull back the perimeter teams. Give them a path."

A voice crackled in his ear: "The Council won't like this."

"They never do," Gideon smirked. "But they hired me for a reason." He lowered the mic and glanced toward the blinking signal on his handheld tracker — two blips, moving fast, heading right toward the exit. Good. Let them reach it. Let them think they were ahead.

In the shadows across the lot, the Watchers waited. Masked figures, cloaked in heavy garments, their eyes reflecting the faint glow of infrared lenses. They were patient, calculating. The Council had grown them over two decades — evolving from mere observers into full enforcers, trained to monitor, extract, or erase as necessary.

Where once they'd only watched, now they shaped outcomes.

Inside the tunnels, Mike's legs burned, his heart pounding in his ears. For the first time in months, maybe years, the old hunger — the thrill he'd once chased in the Blood Spurts days — was silent. No rush. No taste of violence on his tongue. Only fear. Only purpose.

He slammed his shoulder into the rusted hatch, the metal screeching as it gave way. Cold night air rushed in, and beyond it, the gurgling river stretched out under a moonless sky.

"We're out!" Sarah gasped, her eyes shining with raw hope.

Mike reached to pull her through when a figure stepped from the trees — Gideon.

"You're late," Gideon said, smiling faintly. "But you made it."

Mike's fists clenched. "You sold us out."

"No," Gideon said softly, holding up a hand. "I'm the only reason you're still breathing. Behind them, shadows moved — Watchers closing in, their steps soundless. On the ridge above, more figures emerged, and just beyond, a sleek black vehicle approached with two members of the Council seated inside, watching everything unfold.

Sarah's breath hitched. "What do we do now?"

Mike's voice was low, steady. "We end it."

The final confrontation had arrived — every choice, every betrayal, every buried secret now rising to the surface.

And the night had only just begun.

Chapter 17 — The Break

Mike's muscles tensed as the first Watcher moved into view, a sleek figure in dark combat gear, face hidden behind the silver mask.

"Hand it over," the figure said — voice modulated, almost inhuman.

Sarah gripped the satchel tighter. "Like hell."

Behind them, Gideon lifted a hand slowly, his eyes flicking between Mike and the Watchers. "Careful," he murmured, "if they wanted you dead, you'd already be on the ground."

Mike's heart pounded so hard he could barely hear. He knew that. He knew it. These weren't just enforcers — they were handlers. Trappers. The Watchers didn't move without purpose.

Sarah whispered, "Mike… what if he's part of this?" Her eyes darted to Gideon.

He shot her a look. "I know."

But they had no choice.

Suddenly, the sleek black vehicle pulled up closer, headlights snapping on. Mike shielded his eyes as the rear door opened — and for the first time, they saw her.

Amy.

Alive.

Her hair was shorter now, her face pale, sharper somehow — but unmistakably Amy. She stepped out, her thin hand raised calmly.

"Mike," she said softly, "Sarah. You weren't supposed to get this far."

Sarah's mouth dropped open. "Amy? You're… you're with them?"

Mike's stomach flipped. No.

Amy smiled faintly, stepping toward them. "There's always been more going on. Debbie's death, the Blood Spurts games, even Crimson Veil — all of it was curated. We were chosen."

Chosen. The word slammed into Mike like a punch.

"We were the experiment," Amy continued, voice steady. "But not all experiments fail. Some of us… graduated."

Sarah staggered back, shaking her head. "You're lying."

"I'm not," Amy said, her eyes glinting. "And the real twist? Gideon works for me."

Mike whipped around — Gideon gave a small, regretful shrug.

"I warned you to choose wisely," Gideon said softly. "You just kept chasing the wrong threat."

A ripple passed through the Watchers, a subtle shift as they raised their weapons — not to kill, but to seize.

Mike's blood roared in his ears. For a heartbeat, the old urge surged inside him — the hunger, the edge. But he forced it down. No. Not this time.

He grabbed Sarah's hand, squeezing hard. "We run."

Before she could respond, he pulled her sharply sideways — into the river.

Cold slammed into them, water dragging at their limbs, but they pushed through, fighting against the current.

Behind them, the Watchers hesitated — not wanting to risk the chase in unfamiliar terrain.

Amy's voice echoed faintly across the water. "Let them go. They'll come back. They always come back."

On the riverbank, Gideon watched them vanish into the dark. His jaw tightened.

Because in the end, the trap wasn't just physical.

It was psychological.

And the next phase had just begun.

Chapter 18 — Beneath the Surface

The cold bit into Mike's skin like knives. His lungs burned as he and Sarah broke through the river's surface, gasping for air. The night pressed heavy around them, the moon a pale smudge behind thick clouds.

Mike pulled Sarah toward the shore, both of them scrambling up the muddy bank, panting hard. His arms were scraped raw, but he barely felt it — the adrenaline drowned everything else.

Sarah collapsed onto her back, coughing water out of her lungs. "God… dammit, Mike…" she rasped. "You didn't even warn me."

He dropped beside her, chest heaving. "Didn't have time."

She shoved at his shoulder, weakly but angry. "You never give me time."

For a moment, they just lay there, staring up at the night sky, their bodies shaking. The river gurgled behind them, swallowing the noise of the Watchers regrouping on the far bank.

Mike turned his head toward her. "You okay?"

Sarah gave a shaky laugh. "Define okay."

Silence settled between them — but it wasn't comfortable. Not anymore.

Mike could feel the old fractures. Back when Blood Spurts started, Sarah had been a thrill-seeker, eager to push limits, always hungry for more. Mike had been drawn to that, pulled into the sharp energy between pain and pleasure, blood and control.

But now? Now, Sarah's eyes were different. Hardened. Not just thrill-seeking — battle-worn.

"You're mad," he muttered.

Sarah let out a humourless laugh. "Mad? I'm furious, Mike. We're up against an organization we don't understand, betrayed by people we trusted, running for our lives — and you still act like you have to shoulder it all alone."

Mike bristled. "You think I wanted this? You think I planned for any of it?"

"No," Sarah snapped, pushing herself up, "but you always act like you have to be the hero. Like the rest of us can't carry weight."

Mike's fists clenched, then slowly relaxed. His shoulders sagged. "I'm just trying to keep you alive."

Sarah's face softened — just a flicker. "I know."

For a beat, the space between them pulsed with everything unspoken — the regrets, the buried anger, the history that tied them together tighter than they admitted.

Finally, Sarah said quietly, "We can't keep running. We have to outthink them."

Mike nodded. "Agreed."

They sat in the wet grass, shivering, listening to the distant hum of engines and shouts across the river.

Sarah drew in a slow, shaky breath. "You think Gideon let us go?"

Mike's jaw tightened. "No. He's counting on us coming back."

Sarah gave a bitter smile. "Then maybe it's time we stop playing the part they wrote for us."

Mike looked at her, something sparking in his eyes — the old soldier's fire, tempered now by something heavier: resolve.

"Then let's flip the game," he murmured.

In the distance, thunder rolled low.

And somewhere far away, the Watchers began setting their next pieces on the board.

Chapter 19 — Ghosts We Left Behind

Mike's fingers tapped out a rhythm on the cracked burner phone as Sarah paced the length of the damp motel room.

Outside, a neon sign buzzed faintly, casting sharp blue light through the dirty window. The room smelled of mildew and cigarettes, the kind of place where no one asked questions — perfect for fugitives.

"Are you sure about this?" Sarah asked, voice low, arms crossed tightly.

Mike didn't look up. "No."

She let out a frustrated breath. "You didn't answer back there when I asked if Gideon let us go. You don't think we escaped, do you?"

Mike finally raised his eyes. "He's still pulling strings. But if we're going to rip this out at the root, we need more than just the two of us."

Sarah sank onto the edge of the bed, hands clasped. "Who, Mike? Who's left?"

He clicked the last number, hesitating a heartbeat before hitting send. "Jane."

Sarah stiffened. "You trust Jane?"

"I trust she hates Gideon more than she hates me," Mike said grimly.

The line crackled, ringing once… twice…

"Mike?" The voice on the other end was sharp, familiar, layered with both exhaustion and suspicion.

"Jane, it's time."

A pause. Then a bitter laugh. "Didn't think you'd live long enough to say those words."

Sarah leaned forward, whispering, "Put her on speaker."

Mike clicked it over. "Sarah's here."

Another pause. "Well, well, the golden girl survives. Colour me shocked."

"Jane," Sarah cut in sharply, "this isn't a reunion call. We need help. We're going after Gideon, but the Watchers are closing in fast."

Jane's voice hardened. "You're just now figuring out they never stopped watching? The council's been moving assets for weeks. You two are just the last to realize the walls are closing."

Mike rubbed a hand over his face. "Then come in. Help us crack this open."

A long silence on the line.

Finally, Jane spoke quietly. "You're not the only ones left, you know. There are others.

Ones who broke away, who've been waiting. But you'll have to convince them you're not leading the Watchers straight to their door."

Sarah exchanged a look with Mike. "We're past convincing. We're down to desperation."

Jane gave a short, grim laugh. "Good. Desperation is the right place to start."

She rattled off a meet location: an abandoned subway entrance two cities over. Midnight. No weapons visible. No surprises.

As the call ended, Sarah exhaled slowly. "Do you think they'll actually show?"

Mike stood, tucking the burner into his pocket. His face was hard, but his voice was steady.

"They'll show," he murmured. "Because if they don't, Gideon wins."

He crossed to the window, looking out into the cold night. For the first time in a long time, his chest felt lighter — not because the threat was gone, but because for the first time, they weren't alone.

Behind him, Sarah rose, pulling on her jacket.

Together, they stepped back into the storm.

Chapter 20 — Crossroads at Midnight

The abandoned subway entrance yawned open like a mouth swallowing the city. Broken tiles littered the cracked concrete steps, and rusted gates sagged on twisted hinges.

Mike scanned the shadows. Midnight sharp. No sound except the drip of water somewhere deep below.

Sarah shifted beside him, her eyes flicking nervously over the graffiti-scrawled walls. "I don't like this."

"Neither do I," Mike murmured.

A sudden flicker — movement near the tunnel mouth.

Jane emerged from the darkness, her silhouette sharp, coat flaring behind her like a blade. She wasn't alone. Two figures flanked her, faces hooded, silent, watching.

"You made it," Jane called softly. Her voice echoed.

Mike stepped forward, hands raised. "We came alone. Just like you said."

Jane gave a small, bitter smile. "For once, you follow instructions."

Sarah narrowed her eyes. "Where are the others?"

Jane shrugged. "Waiting. Watching." She gestured to the two hooded figures. "These two came as… insurance."

Mike's gut tightened. He didn't like this.

Jane tilted her head. "You know, it's funny. All this time, you thought Gideon was the master behind the curtain. But here's the truth, Mike — the real master has been sitting inside your little circle since the beginning."

Sarah froze. "What are you talking about?"

Jane smiled wider. "You still don't get it?"

One of the hooded figures stepped forward, pulling back their hood.

Amy.

Alive.

Sarah's breath caught. "But… you died. Debbie… you were…"

Amy's eyes glittered cold. "I survived. And I learned. Gideon? He's not the only one pulling strings. He was just phase two. I'm phase three."

Mike felt the bottom drop out of his stomach. "You were working with the Watchers."

Amy smiled softly. "Not working with. Leading."

Jane gave a small, mock-apologetic shrug. "Surprise."

Sarah's fists clenched. "Why?"

Amy stepped closer, her voice almost tender. "Because none of you ever understood. The game was never about survival. It was about evolution."

Suddenly, floodlights blazed on around the tunnel mouth. Dozens of masked figures — Watchers — emerged from the shadows, weapons raised, surrounding them.

Mike spun, heart hammering. Sarah grabbed his arm.

Amy's smile widened. "You were never running from the Watchers, Mike. You were running straight to me."

Jane's voice turned cold. "Welcome to the final phase."

For the first time, Mike felt something crack inside his chest. Not fear. Not rage.

Betrayal.

He locked eyes with Sarah.

And in that breathless second, they both knew — they were going to fight.

Even if it meant burning everything down.

Chapter 21 — The Breaker's Edge

Mike's fists curled, every muscle coiled tight. Sarah's hand tightened on his arm, her breath ragged.

All around them, masked Watchers closed in, weapons glinting in the harsh white floodlights. Jane stood to the side, calm and smiling like a snake. Amy stepped forward, head held high, eyes glowing with triumph.

"You really thought you'd outplay us?" Amy said softly. "All your scrambling, all your running — we've been ahead of you since the hotel. Since before Debbie."

Sarah's voice came out low and sharp. "Debbie died because of you."

Amy's smile faltered for half a second. "She was… necessary."

Mike felt his vision narrow, rage pounding like a war drum in his chest. He shot a glance at Sarah — a silent agreement passed between them.

No more running.

No more games.

Without warning, Mike lunged.

He slammed his shoulder into the nearest Watcher, knocking the man off balance. Sarah moved with him, sweeping low to grab the dropped weapon. She fired — the crack of the shot slicing through the stunned silence.

Chaos exploded.

The Watchers surged forward, weapons raised. Mike grabbed a baton from the ground, swinging hard, cracking it across a masked face. Blood sprayed. Sarah spun, dropping another guard with a clean shot to the leg.

Jane cursed and ducked back, pulling out a radio. Amy's face twisted in fury.

"Take them down!" Amy screamed.

Mike grabbed Sarah's wrist, yanking her toward the side tunnel. "Move! Now!"

They sprinted, boots slamming against the concrete, ducking under rusted beams and leaping over old debris. Behind them, gunfire erupted, bullets sparking against the walls.

They burst into an old maintenance room — metal lockers, shattered lights, dust thick in the air. Mike shoved the door shut, jamming a pipe through the handle.

His chest heaved. Sarah's eyes were wide, hair plastered to her face with sweat.

"They were never going to let us walk," Sarah gasped.

Mike slammed his fist against the wall, frustration roaring in his veins. "We're outnumbered. Outgunned."

But Sarah was shaking her head, her lips curving into a tight smile. "Not outsmarted."

She pulled something from her coat — the small black device Gideon had slipped to them back at the river.

Mike's eyes widened. "The detonator."

Sarah nodded grimly. "Gideon said… if we ever needed a real distraction."

Outside, they heard the shouts, the pounding of boots.

Mike looked at Sarah, something fierce sparking between them.

"Ready?"

Sarah's thumb hovered over the button.

"Let's burn their whole damn game down."

She pressed it.

A low rumble shook the walls.

Outside, muffled shouts turned to screams.

Mike grabbed Sarah's hand, pulling her through a back hatch as the floor buckled. Behind them, fire bloomed — a roar of light and heat tearing through the tunnels.

The old subway collapsed in on itself, the Watchers' command centre reduced to rubble.

As they emerged, breathless, into the night air, Mike turned to Sarah.

"This isn't over," he said, eyes fierce.

Sarah nodded, her smile grim. "No. But it's our turn now."

Somewhere far off, Amy watched the smoke rise, her eyes narrowing.

Phase three had failed.

But she wasn't done yet.

Not by a long shot.

Chapter 22 — Ghosts in the Ash

The night air bit cold against Mike's skin as he and Sarah moved quickly through the shadows, their breath clouding in the dark. The flames behind them were still crackling, the Watchers' stronghold buried beneath smoking rubble.

But Mike knew better than to believe it was over.

Sarah touched his arm gently, her face pale but determined. "They'll regroup. Amy… she's not the type to go down with the building."

Mike gave a tight nod. His pulse was still pounding, adrenaline searing through his veins. "She's always three steps ahead."

As they crossed a narrow bridge, an old warehouse loomed ahead — the place where Gideon had told them to meet if things went south.

But the windows were dark.

The door hung slightly open.

Mike motioned for Sarah to stay back, creeping forward with a practiced carefulness, his old Marine instincts humming to life. He pushed the door slowly, slipping inside.

The smell hit him first: smoke, metal, something faintly chemical.

Then he saw them.

Bodies.

Two Watchers — masks shattered; throats slit clean.

Gideon was gone.

On the far wall, a message was scrawled in blood-red paint:

"Too slow."

Mike's fists clenched. His jaw tightened.

Sarah slipped in behind him, eyes going wide at the scene. "No… Gideon…"

Mike touched the edge of one mask, flipping it over. The hollow black eyes stared back.

He felt the weight settle heavier on his shoulders.

"We're not just running from Amy now," he said grimly. "She's started cutting away the pieces she doesn't need."

Sarah shivered. "She's cleaning house."

A sudden sharp noise made them both whirl — the soft crunch of a boot on gravel.

They spun around, weapons raised — only to see a figure step calmly from the shadows.

It was Gideon.

Alive.

Barely.

His face was pale, blood streaking down one side. He limped forward, clutching his side. "They knew," he rasped. "Amy knew I'd meet you here."

Sarah rushed to his side, helping steady him. "We thought you were dead."

Gideon gave a thin, grim smile. "Not yet."

Mike narrowed his eyes. "Why spare you? Why not finish it?"

Gideon's expression darkened. "Because she wanted to send a message. And because she's already setting up the final stage."

Mike's heart sank.

"The final stage?" Sarah asked, voice tight.

Gideon nodded slowly. "She's planning to broadcast everything — every tape, every archive, every dirty secret we ever thought we buried. Not just about the Watchers. About us."

Mike felt the weight of it hit his chest.

The hotel. Debbie. The games. The blood.

If Amy unleashed it, they were all finished.

"We stop her," Mike said quietly, his voice like steel. "Whatever it takes."

Gideon smiled faintly. "Then you'd better hurry."

Because somewhere, not far away, Amy stood before a bank of monitors, her finger hovering over the control panel, the countdown already ticking.

Chapter 23 — Countdown

Amy's reflection shimmered faintly in the polished glass of the control room, her pale face lit by the flicker of dozens of screens. Across every monitor, the same image pulsed — a spinning countdown clock, glowing red against black.

00:29:59.

She smiled, tapping one manicured finger against the console.

Outside the reinforced glass, the last of her loyal Watchers were fanning out, securing the perimeter. She could hear their muffled voices through the headset, calm and certain.

They had no idea she was about to leave them all behind.

Amy stepped closer to the terminal. She reached into her coat pocket, pulling out a small silver device — a modified pulse key. One touch, and every archive, every file, every corrupted secret from the last three years would flood onto the public net.

The governments wouldn't be able to bury it. The Watchers wouldn't be able to spin it.

And Mike?

He'd burn with the rest of them.

Her fingers hovered above the activation pad.

At the edge of the compound, Mike crouched behind a shipping container, sweat beading down his back despite the cold. Sarah pressed close behind him, her breath sharp in his ear.

"She's in the main control room," Gideon whispered over the comms. "But listen, Mike — this isn't just about stopping her. It's about what comes after. If you take her down, you'll be the face they turn to."

Mike gave a bitter smirk. "Yeah, well, I'm not sure I'm leadership material."

Sarah touched his arm. "We're with you. Always."

Mike closed his eyes briefly. That warmth — that anchor — it steadied him in a way no weapon ever could.

Then he snapped his eyes open. "Let's go."

Inside, Amy watched the final seconds bleed away.

00:02:11.

She inhaled slowly, savouring the moment.

"Do you know," she murmured, her voice soft as silk, "what it's like to control the story?"

The door behind her slammed open.

Mike.

Sarah.

Amy turned, her eyes glittering. "You're too late."

Mike lifted his weapon — but Amy only smiled, holding up the pulse key between two fingers.

"Shoot me," she said, "and this drops. The broadcast triggers automatically."

Mike's muscles coiled, his mind racing.

Sarah's voice was low, urgent. "Mike… think."

Amy's smile widened. "You never learned, did you? This was never about survival. It was about transformation."

00:00:30.

Mike took a slow step forward.

Amy's hand twitched, hovering over the final button.

"Did Debbie scream?" Mike asked softly.

Amy's eyes flashed. "She sang."

Sarah gasped.

And Mike moved.

Not forward — but sideways.

He slammed his elbow into the main console, driving it down with all his strength. Sparks exploded; the panel burst in a shower of light. Amy shrieked, jerking back — but the pulse key flew from her hand, skittering across the floor.

Sarah dove.

Caught it.

The timer froze —

00:00:03.

Amy's breath hitched.

Mike stepped closer, his face grim. "It ends here."

But Amy's smile came back — slow, feral.

"Oh, no, Mike," she whispered. "You just triggered the real game."

Above them, the ceiling split open — metal grating peeling back to reveal rows of black drones, eyes flickering red, humming to life.

Mike's stomach turned to ice.

Sarah's voice cracked. "Mike…"

And somewhere across the compound, Gideon's voice cut through the comms, sharp and panicked:

"RUN!"

Chapter 24 — Firestorm

The first drone shrieked as it dove, a spear of red light slicing through the smoke-filled control room. Mike yanked Sarah down just in time, the heat of the beam searing past his cheek.

The room erupted into chaos. Sparks rained from the shredded ceiling, cables snapping like whips, alarms blaring in a rising, hysterical chorus.

Amy was gone — she'd bolted the second the drones came online, slipping through a side exit before Mike could stop her.

"Get up!" Mike barked, hauling Sarah to her feet. She was clutching the pulse key so hard her knuckles were white.

They dashed through the control room's side door, skidding into the dark corridor beyond. The compound's walls shook as the drones swarmed, crashing through the air vents, tearing through the reinforced security layers like paper.

"Gideon!" Mike shouted into his comms. "Where are you?"

Static.

Then Gideon's strained voice: "Evac point — west platform — move, NOW!"

Mike grabbed Sarah's hand, pulling her into a sprint. The corridor pulsed red with emergency lights, shadows flickering in the corners.

Behind them, a drone smashed through the steel door, twisting and shrieking, eyes blazing.

Mike spun, firing — one, two, three sharp bursts — but the rounds barely dented the machine's armoured chassis.

"We need heavier firepower," he growled.

Sarah yanked him toward the far end of the hall. "Storage room. I saw it earlier — come on!"

Inside the storage room, they slammed the door shut and braced it with a steel bar. Sarah darted to a crate, yanking it open. Inside: a stash of old Watcher tech — EMP grenades, pulse disruptors, specialized rounds.

Mike grinned, teeth flashing. "Now we're talking."

He loaded a disruptor shell into his rifle, shoving an EMP grenade into Sarah's hand.

The door shook violently.

Mike raised his rifle, took a breath — and nodded.

Sarah yanked the door open, hurling the grenade down the hall. A blinding pulse of blue light lit the corridor, and the pursuing drones faltered, their systems sparking wildly.

Mike charged out, dropping two more drones with precise shots. Sarah followed, heart hammering, lungs burning.

On the west platform, Gideon was waiting, flanked by two battered Watcher defectors.

"You're late," Gideon said coolly, though his sharp eyes flicked nervously to the sky, where the drone swarm was circling.

Mike strode up, tossing the pulse key into Gideon's hands. "We've got maybe five minutes before this whole place goes up."

"Good," Gideon murmured, pocketing the key. "Let it burn."

Sarah stared at him. "What?"

Gideon smiled thinly. "The only way to break the Watchers is to destroy their roots. We end it tonight."

As if on cue, Amy's voice crackled over the platform loudspeakers — cool, triumphant:

"Leaving so soon? Oh, come now — I've got one more surprise."

The platform rumbled. Beneath their feet, the floor split open, revealing a vast, black chamber — and rising from its depths, a monstrous machine, bristling with weapons, its core pulsing like a heartbeat.

Mike's blood turned cold.

Sarah gasped.

And Gideon whispered, almost in awe, "She built a failsafe."

The machine's eyes flared red.

Amy's voice purred: "Let's play."

Chapter 25 — Detonation

The monstrous machine roared to life, gears grinding, limbs unfolding, weapon arrays locking into place. Its core pulsed once, twice — then unleashed a blinding arc of energy that tore across the platform, shearing steel like paper.

Mike tackled Sarah, shoving her behind a concrete pillar just as the blast ripped past.

"Gideon!" Mike bellowed.

But Gideon was already moving — sprinting across the open space, coat whipping behind him, a small device clutched in his hand. He darted between the machine's scanning beams, heading straight for its exposed flank.

Sarah scrambled up beside Mike, breathless. "He's insane — that thing will kill him!"

"No," Mike growled, eyes locked on Gideon. "He's betting everything on one shot."

Above, Amy watched from a glass control room, her face illuminated by glowing panels.

"Poor Gideon," she murmured, her fingers dancing over the console. "Still thinks he's the hero."

She leaned closer to the microphone.

"Mike… I know you're listening."

Mike stiffened, teeth clenched.

Amy's voice was soft, almost regretful.

"You were always the best player. I really did admire you. But you should've walked away when you had the chance. " Gideon reached the machine's flank, slamming the device onto its armoured plating. A green light blinked. One second. Two.

Suddenly, the machine twisted, slamming a massive mechanical arm down. Gideon rolled aside — barely — but the device was crushed under the blow.

Mike's heart stopped.

Gideon looked up, blood on his face.

Their eyes met across the platform.

And Gideon smiled.

He raised one hand — revealing a second detonator.

Click.

The ground shuddered. Deep below, a chain of buried charges erupted, shaking the entire facility. Explosions roared through the walls, tearing through foundations.

The monstrous machine reeled, systems faltering. Sparks shot from its joints, its red eyes flickering wildly.

Mike grabbed Sarah's hand. "We run. NOW."

Together they sprinted, dodging falling beams and shattering glass as the platform buckled.

Gideon, bleeding and staggering, limped after them.

Overhead, Amy slammed her fists onto the console, screaming.

"No! NO!"

Behind her, the control room's windows cracked, fire licking up the walls.

Mike, Sarah, and Gideon burst out into the open night just as the entire compound erupted in a towering fireball, the shockwave hurling them to the ground.

For a moment, there was only silence — the sky above glowing with smoke and burning debris.

Mike pushed himself up, coughing hard. Sarah lay beside him, dazed but alive.

Gideon knelt a few feet away, face streaked with ash, shoulders shaking.

Mike staggered over, gripping his arm. "Did we do it?"

Gideon looked up, eyes hollow.

"I don't know."

From the burning wreckage, a dark figure emerged — walking calmly through the flames.

Amy.

Alive.

And she was smiling.

Chapter 26 — The Final Confrontation

The heat from the burning compound washed over them, waves of blistering air that made Sarah's eyes sting and Mike's skin crackle with sweat.

Amy stood at the edge of the inferno, her silhouette sharp against the pulsing firelight. Her once-pristine blouse was torn, hair wild, but her eyes — those cold, calculating eyes — gleamed with triumph.

"You really thought you could outplay me?" she called, her voice smooth, almost amused. "After everything we've been through, Mike, you still don't understand."

Mike squared his shoulders, stepping forward. "I understand you killed them. All of them. You used us. You made us pawns."

Amy tilted her head. "You were pawns before I ever arrived. I just made you see the board."

Sarah hissed under her breath, fingers tightening on the small pistol she'd scavenged from the wreckage. "She's stalling."

Mike nodded once. "Yeah. But why?"

Gideon, limping up beside them, grimaced. "Because she's not finished yet."

Suddenly, the earth trembled — a low, rumbling vibration. From the ruined compound, a massive shape emerged, dragging itself free from the rubble.

The Watcher Prime.

A towering construct, larger than anything they'd faced before. Its body was a grotesque fusion of steel and bone, mechanical limbs bristling with weapons, its central core a pulsing, crimson eye.

Amy turned slightly, smiling at the monstrous machine. "Meet the next phase."

Mike's stomach twisted. "You've got to be kidding me."

Sarah raised her gun, but Gideon put a hand on her arm. "That's not going to scratch it."

Amy stepped forward, lifting a sleek control device. "You see, Mike, you were the test. The rest of them? The students? Mary? Even Debbie? Just proof of concept. But you…" She smiled. "You made it real."

Mike clenched his fists.

Sarah whispered, "We need a plan."

Gideon's eyes flicked across the burning wreckage. "There's only one."

The Watcher Prime roared to life, weapons locking onto the three of them.

And Mike ran.

Straight at Amy.

Sarah shouted, "Mike, WAIT—!" but he was already moving, sprinting at full speed, every muscle straining.

Amy's eyes widened — just for a split second — before Mike slammed into her, sending both of them crashing to the ground.

The control device skittered from her hands, bouncing across the dirt.

Gideon dove, snatching it up. "I hope you're ready to gamble, Mike!"

The Watcher Prime charged, engines howling.

Gideon jammed the device into its frequency port.

Mike pinned Amy to the ground, their faces inches apart. "Checkmate."

Gideon hit the button.

A high-pitched shriek filled the air — a piercing electronic wail that split the night.

The Watcher Prime convulsed, limbs jerking wildly. Sparks exploded from its joints, its crimson eye flickering, fading…

…and then, with a final grinding howl, the machine collapsed, shaking the earth as it fell.

For a heartbeat, everything went still.

Amy's smile was gone.

Mike let out a long, shuddering breath, feeling the weight of everything they'd survived.

Gideon stood beside him, face pale, eyes haunted. "It's over."

Sarah joined them, slipping her hand into Mike's.

Amy lay in the dirt, defeated, her eyes burning with quiet fury.

But somewhere in the shadows, unseen, another figure watched — one none of them had noticed.

And it smiled.

Because some games never truly end.

Chapter 27 — Burn It All Down

The sky roared with fire.

Flames licked up into the black night, towers of orange and gold twisting into the clouds like the arms of some angry god. The compound — once a fortress, once a sanctuary, once the heart of the Watchers — was now a smoking ruin.

Mike ran, Sarah right behind him, heart hammering in his chest like a war drum. Every breath tasted like ash. Every heartbeat thudded like a countdown.

Gideon sprinted alongside them, clutching the data drive against his chest — the drive that contained every secret, every lie, every betrayal going back decades.

Behind them, the wreckage of the Watcher Prime collapsed in on itself, each metallic groan echoing like the death knell of an empire.

"We have to move!" Sarah shouted, coughing through the smoke. "It's going to blow!"

"Almost there!" Mike barked, eyes fixed on the perimeter gate.

A sudden blast behind them sent a wave of heat screaming through the air. A piece of burning metal whistled past Mike's ear, slamming into the ground with a hiss of steam.

"We're not going to make it!" Gideon yelled.

Mike grabbed Sarah's arm, yanking her forward. "We MAKE it!"

They burst through the shattered gates just as the earth shuddered violently beneath their feet.

A rumbling roar, deeper than anything human, rolled up from the compound. Mike turned just in time to see the ground split open, a final explosion ripping through the central core.

The blast surged upward, a monstrous pillar of flame punching into the night sky, lighting up the horizon like a second sun.

Mike flung himself over Sarah, shielding her with his body as the shockwave slammed into them.

Gideon hit the dirt beside them, arms wrapped around the drive, gritting his teeth as the heat scorched over his back.

The world became a storm of light, noise, and fury.

Minutes — or maybe hours — later, Mike lifted his head.

His ears rang. His mouth tasted like blood and smoke.

Beside him, Sarah groaned softly, blinking through soot-streaked lashes.

Gideon coughed, rolling onto his back, the drive still clutched in his hands.

"It's done," he rasped. "It's finally done."

But Mike wasn't so sure.

He pulled Sarah to her feet, his muscles screaming in protest, and turned to look at the smouldering wreckage.

The Watchers. Amy. The Prime.

All of it… gone.

Or so it seemed.

Because just beyond the haze, in the shadows, something moved.

A figure stepped into view — calm, composed, untouched by the fire.

A man they had never seen before.

He smiled.

"Well," the stranger said softly, "now the real game begins."

Mike's fists clenched.

Sarah's breath caught in her throat.

Gideon's eyes widened.

The fire was just the beginning.

And the next storm was already on its way.

Epilogue

The world smelled like cinders.

Mike stood at the edge of the ruined compound, the scorched earth still warm under his boots. Beside him, Sarah wrapped her arms around herself, staring into the smouldering crater.

They had done it.

They had destroyed the Watchers.

…Or so they thought.

A faint crackle echoed through the comm device in Mike's ear — faint, scratchy, but unmistakable.

Gideon's voice, low and grim:

"You're going to want to hear this."

Inside the wrecked remains of their temporary safehouse, Gideon sat in front of a battered laptop.

On the screen: a series of cascading data streams, files unlocking one by one.

He tapped a key, magnifying a set of encrypted files.

The title sent a chill through him: ARCHIVE SECTOR 9: SLEEPERS.

Names began to scroll.

Faces.

Locations.

Mike. Sarah. Mary. Jane. Even Gideon himself.

But below those familiar profiles were hundreds of others — people they didn't know.

People the Watchers had planted in cities, governments, companies, families.

Sarah's voice broke through the silence.

"What is this?" she whispered.

Mike's jaw clenched. "This… this wasn't the end."

Gideon nodded slowly. "No. We didn't kill the Watchers. We only exposed one branch."

He leaned closer to the screen.

"And now the others are waking up."

Miles away, in an opulent, hidden chamber, a woman in a white suit stood before a large wall of monitors.

She watched the feed from the compound collapse, fingers steepled under her chin.

Beside her, several shadowed figures waited — each one carrying the insignia of the Watcher Elite.

The woman smiled faintly.

"Prepare the next phase," she said softly. "They think they've won. Now, we teach them what it means to play on a global scale."

Back at the edge of the crater, Mike took Sarah's hand, his gaze hard.

"We finish this," he said.

Sarah looked up at him, firelight dancing in her eyes. "We'll need help."

Mike's mouth twisted into a grim smile. "Then we call in everyone. Old allies. New ones. Anyone who's ever had a score to settle."

Gideon's voice crackled through the comm again.

"And you're going to want to hurry," he murmured. "Because the clock just started ticking."

Book 4: BLOODLINE

The Watchers are bigger.

The betrayals run deeper.

And this time…

no one is safe.

Blood Legacy

Contents

Chapter One: Ghosts That Still Breathe

Mike Halston stood at the window of the half-lit room, the city skyline sprawled out like a maze of scars. Below, the streets pulsed with the quiet hum of a world blissfully unaware of what had nearly consumed it. He ran a hand through his rough-cut hair, staring at his reflection in the glass — the man staring back was not the soldier who once returned from the Royal Marines, nor the college student lured into a game of blood and dares. He was something else now: a man who had survived.

Behind him, Sarah's voice broke the silence.

"You're doing it again," she murmured, stepping up beside him. "Reliving it all."

He gave a grim smile. "How can I not?"

Because everything had led to this.

In Book 1, it started as a thrill. A reckless game of truth-or-dare twisted into pain and secrets, designed by the magnetic Debbie Lang — a game called Blood Spurts. They thought they were just pushing limits, testing boundaries. Until Debbie's throat was slit in that hotel bathroom, and they realized they had opened something darker.

In Book 2, Crimson Veil, the group tried to cover their tracks. But the Watchers — the hidden curators of human darkness — were already circling. Mike, Mary, Sarah, and the others were pulled deeper, facing betrayals, secrets, and the chilling realization that they had been part of a long-standing experiment in control and confession.

In Book 3, Blood Reckoning, the survivors made a choice: expose the Watchers, burn down the archives, and bring the truth into the light — no matter the personal cost. They faced traps, losses, and betrayals from within, but they struck a blow the Watchers hadn't seen coming. Or so they thought.

And now… Book 4.

Now, they stood at the edge of the final chapter.

Mike turned to Sarah. "We've lost too many. Mary, Jane… Gideon. Even Amy, if she's still out there. We thought we won, but they're still moving pieces."

Sarah held up a tablet. "We intercepted this last night. A new file from the remaining

Watchers. They call it The Legacy Protocol. It's not over, Mike. Not yet."

A knock sounded at the door, sharp and urgent.

Mike tensed, instinctively reaching for the knife on the table. "Who the hell—"

Before he could move, the door creaked open.

Standing there, pale and wide-eyed, was Amy Velasquez.

Her voice was barely a whisper.

"You're all in danger. They were never after us. We were just… the bait."

Mike's heart slammed in his chest. His blood chilled.

Because suddenly, he knew:

The endgame wasn't about the past.

It was about what comes next.

Chapter Two: Bait

Amy stood in the doorway, her skin pale as bone, hair damp from rain, eyes wide with something halfway between terror and exhaustion.

Mike couldn't move. For months, they'd believed Amy was gone — taken, turned, or worse. Her sudden appearance hit like a punch to the chest.

Sarah was the first to break the silence.

"Amy… how? Where have you been?"

Amy stepped into the room cautiously, flinching slightly when Mike moved toward her.

"I can't explain everything," she whispered. "But you have to listen — they were never after us as individuals. Not really. We were tests. Probes. They've been hunting something bigger, something older."

Mike narrowed his eyes.

"Who's they?"

Amy's voice cracked.

"The Watchers. But not just the curators we thought. There's another tier. The Council was only the middle layer. There's something above them."

Sarah exchanged a sharp look with Mike.

"We burned their archives, Amy. We exposed them. We dismantled their power."

Amy shook her head, trembling.

"No. You only burned one archive. That was the distraction. The bait. The true archive… it's under the city. And they've been protecting it for decades."

Mike's fists clenched. His Marine instincts kicked in, adrenaline coiling through his muscles.

"Why come to us now?" he demanded.

"Why not let us believe it was over?"

Amy looked up, tears in her eyes.

"Because they're activating it tonight."

A chill spread through the room like creeping frost.

Sarah's hands tightened around the tablet.

"We need proof."

Amy pulled a crumpled envelope from her coat, tossing it onto the table.

"It's all in there. Locations, names, access codes. I barely got it out. And Mike… they know you're the only one who can stop them. That's why they left you alive."

Mike's jaw tightened.

"I'm nobody's pawn."

Amy's face twisted in pain.

"I'm sorry. But you were. We all were. And now, the game is ending — not for a few of us, but for everyone."

Outside, in the distance, sirens wailed. Not police. Not ambulances.

Black vans.

Unmarked.

Sarah glanced toward the window.

"They've found us."

Mike grabbed the envelope, stuffing it into his jacket.

"We run now. We plan later."

Amy shook her head.

"There's no later. If they finish the protocol, they won't need to hunt people anymore. They'll control them before they even choose to play."

Sarah's breath hitched.

"A total system."

Mike looked at both of them, his heart pounding.

"Then we end it. Once and for all."

As the sound of heavy boots pounded up the stairwell, Mike reached for his knife, Sarah grabbed her laptop bag, and Amy — still shaking — whispered the words they all knew but hated to hear:

"It's us against them."

Chapter Three: Last Gambit

The safehouse smelled of mildew and old smoke, the kind of place no one should spend more than a few hours in — perfect for fugitives trying to plan the unthinkable.

Mike slammed the heavy door shut and shoved an old desk against it. Sarah paced in a tight circle, her brow furrowed as she scrolled furiously through Amy's stolen documents. Amy sat on the threadbare couch, wrapping her arms around herself, eyes hollow.

Mike leaned over the table.

"Talk to me, Sarah. What are we looking at?"

Sarah pulled up a crude map on her laptop screen.

"Underneath the city. Old tunnels, some built during World War II, others added later by… whoever's been funding the Watchers. The 'main archive' is here." She tapped a blinking red dot. "Heavily shielded. We'll need access codes — or we'll need to blow it open."

Amy shook her head weakly.

"You can't just blow it up. It's not just files. It's… people. Systems. There's something in there I can't explain. I only saw pieces. Organic."

Mike's fists clenched on the tabletop.

"You're telling me it's alive?"

Amy's voice wavered.

"Not alive like us. Alive like… software that's learned too much. Watching us. Feeding off us. The archive isn't just data. It's a mind."

Sarah rubbed her temples.

"So we're not just destroying hardware. We're killing… something sentient."

Mike gave her a sharp look.

"Would you rather let it loose?"

The silence hung heavy between them.

Amy reached into her pocket and slid over a small black keycard.

"This will get you past the first security door. After that, you're on your own."

Mike snorted.

"We're on our own, Amy. You're not staying behind."

Amy's face crumpled slightly.

"I don't know if I can face it again."

Sarah grabbed her arm.

"You survived. That means you're part of this, like it or not."

Mike looked between them, then flattened his hands on the map.

"Here's the plan: Sarah, you handle the tech. Get us inside. Amy, you guide us through what you remember. I handle anyone who gets in our way."

He paused, locking eyes with both women.

"We move fast, we move quiet, and we finish this. No more running. No more hiding. We end what Debbie started."

Amy whispered, "Debbie didn't start it."

Mike's eyes hardened.

"Then we end what they started."

Outside, the city lights flickered, as if something vast stirred beneath the surface.

Sarah exhaled sharply.

"If we fail…"

Mike gave a grim smile.

"We don't fail."

Chapter Four: Beneath the Veil

The service elevator groaned like a dying animal as it descended into the dark. Rust streaked its walls, and the overhead light flickered erratically. Mike stood at the front, his body a taut coil of muscle and nerves, hand resting on the pistol holstered at his thigh. Sarah was behind him, laptop bag strapped tight to her back, fingers trembling slightly as she held a handheld scanner. Amy stood to the side, silent, head down, as if the very descent was dragging her back into a past she hadn't escaped.

The elevator shuddered, then stopped with a hard clunk. A red light blinked overhead. Mike pried the doors open.

Cold air rushed in.

Beyond the doors, the tunnel yawned wide. The walls were smooth concrete, slick with condensation. Dim red emergency lights pulsed every ten meters. Faintly, they could hear the distant hum of machinery — and something else. A low throb, like a heartbeat carved into the stone.

"This is it," Amy whispered. "They called it Subsection 9. It's where the Watchers were… trained. Or grown. I don't even know anymore."

"Only way out is through," Mike muttered, stepping into the tunnel, his boots echoing with heavy finality.

Sarah activated the scanner. A soft blue light swept across the walls.

"Thermal signatures… two, maybe three hundred meters ahead. Stationary. Human?"

Amy shook her head. "Not human. Not anymore."

They walked in silence, every footstep loaded with the weight of memory.

Sarah broke the quiet. "Do you think Gideon's still alive?"

Mike didn't answer immediately.

"If he is, we'll find him. And he'll tell us why he let this rot fester."

They reached a branching corridor. The main tunnel continued forward, but another veered left, marked with an old university symbol long since spray-painted over with crimson.

"Debbie brought me here once," Amy murmured. "Said the tunnel was part of the test. But I think she didn't know who was testing us anymore."

Mike turned to Sarah. "Which way?"

Sarah tapped the scanner. "Left. Archive's signal is strongest that way."

They entered the side tunnel, which narrowed and sloped downward. The lights grew dimmer. Shadows danced on the walls like ghosts rising from the past.

Suddenly, Sarah froze.

"Movement. Four o'clock."

Mike raised his weapon — but what stepped out wasn't a person.

It was a Watcher. Tall. Hooded. Its mask was smeared with crimson, and its fingers were long, almost talon-like. It didn't attack. It simply tilted its head… watching.

Mike stepped forward. "Get out of our way."

The Watcher didn't move. But behind it… a door slid open with a hydraulic hiss. A second Watcher emerged, dragging something behind it — a body.

Gideon.

Barely conscious, bloodied, but alive.

Amy gasped.

"They're not fighting us."

Mike narrowed his eyes.

"No. They're guiding us."

The tunnel had never been a trap. It was an invitation.

Chapter Five: The Eyes That See

Gideon was half-conscious, slumped against the concrete wall of the chamber beyond the Watchers' corridor. He looked smaller than Mike remembered — thinner, frailer, like time had eaten away at him from the inside. But his eyes, bloodshot and fierce, snapped open the second Mike stepped through the threshold.

"Close the door," he rasped, voice dry as dust. "They're always listening."

Sarah hit the panel. The metal door slid shut with a groan, locking them in a room that smelled of machine oil and antiseptic. It looked like a debrief chamber — sterile, curved walls, no windows. A single light overhead cast harsh shadows across Gideon's gaunt face.

Mike crouched in front of him. "You're alive."

"Barely." Gideon tried to sit upright but winced. "I was never meant to leave the program."

Amy knelt beside them, hands trembling. "Why did they keep you? What are they doing down here?"

Gideon laughed bitterly. "They don't need to do anything anymore. The game has become self-sustaining."

Sarah stepped forward, voice cold. "Explain. Now."

Gideon looked at her with something like admiration. "You figured it out first, didn't you? The Watchers aren't just observers.

They're amplifiers. They don't record behaviour—they shape it."

Mike frowned. "You're saying they push people?"

"I'm saying," Gideon said slowly, "that the entire Blood Spurts experiment was never about pain. It was about thresholds. How far people could be nudged—toward truth, violence, pleasure, guilt. Debbie thought she created the game. She didn't. She just localized the test."

Sarah's jaw clenched. "Then who started it?"

"The Archive," Gideon said. "They've been grooming test subjects for decades. Universities are ideal—young minds, unstable hierarchies, emotional volatility. The Watchers were phase two. A blend of human intuition and machine logic. You've seen them. They observe, mimic, and then… they adjust."

Amy backed away, sickened. "We were lab rats."

"You were prototypes," Gideon corrected. "Each of you selected because you broke patterns. The Archive didn't fear you. It needed you. But you stopped playing by its rules. That's why I think I'm still breathing."

He coughed hard, then looked up at Mike. "Because it wants a conclusion. A final data set."

Mike stared at him. "And what? We give it one?"

"No," Gideon whispered. "You corrupt it. Burn the source. Reset the machine."

Sarah was already scanning the room. "Where's the core?"

"Below us," Gideon said. "One level down. Sealed. But there's a flaw in the encryption. They modelled it after human memory."

Mike stood. "Which means it can forget."

"Yes." Gideon's voice strengthened. "But you'll need to show it something it's never seen before. Not pain. Not fear. Something unpredictable."

Mike's eyes met Sarah's.

"Something human."

From the corridor, the Watchers stood in still silence.

Chapter Six: The Descent

The stairwell to the lower level wasn't on any blueprint. No signs, no directional symbols. Just a seamless section of floor Gideon pointed toward with trembling fingers, whispering, "Press the third tile from the vent. Left foot. Hard."

Mike did.

The tile gave a soft mechanical click. A section of concrete hissed, then slid aside with surprising grace, revealing a tight shaft of metal stairs spiralling down into darkness.

The air that drifted up smelled like ozone and memory.

Sarah stepped to the edge, peering down. "No lights."

"That's intentional," Gideon murmured. "What's down there doesn't like to be seen."

Mike grabbed a small torch from his pack, flicking it on. "Let's go make it uncomfortable, then."

They descended in silence, each step echoing off walls that seemed too smooth, too polished. It felt less like a basement and more like a throat — something swallowing them alive.

After fifty steps, the staircase opened into a circular chamber that pulsed with a faint hum, like a heart beating inside a server farm.

It was colder here.

At the centre of the room was a monolithic black terminal — not a computer, not a machine in any normal sense. It pulsed faintly, veins of red light crawling across its surface. Tendrils — cables or something worse — extended from it into the walls, ceiling, and floor like roots feeding on the facility itself.

"This is it," Sarah breathed. "The Archive's core."

"No guards?" Amy whispered.

"They don't need them," Gideon said from behind. "It defends itself… differently."

Mike took a step forward and the terminal shifted. Not physically — perceptually. One moment it looked like cold metal; the next, it shimmered, like it was reflecting every horrible decision he'd ever made.

He blinked. Suddenly, Debbie was there, standing by the terminal. Her throat wasn't slit. She looked alive. Smiling.

"Mike," she said softly.

He froze. "What the hell—?"

"It's projecting," Sarah said. "Showing us what it thinks will break us."

Gideon sat down, exhausted. "You must override it. You can't fight its illusions. You can only reprogram the story it believes is inevitable."

Mike stared at the projection of Debbie. She tilted her head, that same mischievous grin she wore the night she died.

"You still think you can win?" the vision whispered. "You liked the blood. You still do."

Mike's hand clenched into a fist. "Not anymore."

The lights in the terminal pulsed brighter — and the walls began to shudder. Sirens didn't blare. There was no warning. Just a growing sense of wrongness, like time itself was unravelling.

Sarah ran to the console on the far wall, prying it open. "I've got a data port. I think I can inject the reversal code, but I need time!"

"You don't have time," Gideon said, his voice cracking. "You make it."

Then the walls opened — and the Watchers entered.

Three of them.

Faster.

More evolved.

Not just observing.

Now they were ready to intervene.

Mike grabbed a pipe from the wall. "Buy her the seconds. That's all we need."

And then the fight for the Archive began — not with code, not with blood…

…but with the will to change the ending.

Chapter Seven: The Fight for the Ending

The first Watcher moved like liquid shadow—silent, swift, impossible to track with the naked eye. By the time Mike raised his makeshift weapon, it was already on him, fingers like bone needles slashing toward his throat.

He twisted, barely avoiding the blow, and countered with a wide swing. The pipe connected with a sharp crack, but the Watcher didn't scream. It simply stumbled back and recalibrated, its eyeless face twitching in a grotesque mimic of curiosity.

"They're testing us," Gideon shouted, ducking behind the console Sarah was feverishly working on. "They want to see who still resists… and who will break."

Sarah's fingers flew across the keys, her lips mouthing silent equations. "The Archive isn't a storage unit—it's a brain. I'm trying to overwrite its neural pathways, but it keeps resisting, rewriting its own core rules."

"Do it faster!" Amy cried out, backing toward the wall as the second Watcher advanced on her. She clutched a shard of broken glass like a dagger, hands trembling but eyes steady.

Mike drove his shoulder into the first Watcher, slamming it against the curved wall. Its limbs writhed unnaturally, dislocating and reforming in seconds. It hissed—no air, no breath, just the sound of something ancient mimicking life.

"They're not just watching anymore," Mike growled. "They're enforcing the story."

Gideon stood, slowly. "Because you're changing it."

A blast of cold swept through the chamber—the third Watcher. Taller than the others. It didn't attack. It watched them still, but this time with something new in its bearing:

Fear.

Sarah's voice cracked through the chaos. "I found a weakness! A core subroutine from the earliest builds. It's human... built on guilt, trauma, memory. If I can inject Debbie's last message, it might collapse the feedback loop!"

Mike's heart skipped. "You kept it?"

"Encrypted. Hidden until now. It was always meant to be the fail-safe."

The Archive pulsed red, then black, then white.

The Watchers recoiled—just for a second. And it was enough.

Mike tackled the second one, jamming the pipe through its chest. It didn't die—but it froze, flickering like corrupted code.

The third Watcher lunged toward Sarah—

—and was intercepted by Amy.

With a scream that tore from her soul, Amy stabbed the glass deep into its neck. The Watcher bled smoke and light. Then it collapsed.

Sarah hit [ENTER].

The room screamed.

Not with sound—but sensation. Like a thousand memories howling at once. The walls shook, the floor buckled, and the Archive... began to disintegrate.

Flashes—Debbie laughing, Debbie bleeding, Debbie whispering through broken glass: "Rewrite it. Make it matter."

And then—

Silence.

All three Watchers gone.

The Archive: powered down.

The console: dark.

Mike staggered, breath ragged. "Is it over?"

Gideon knelt beside the cracked floor where the Archive once pulsed. "No," he whispered. "It's sleeping. But you've shifted the story."

Sarah stood slowly, her face lit by the faint glow of rebooting emergency lights.

"We've got a window," she said. "The final one."

Mike nodded, blood running down his temple. "Then we burn the last chapter into truth."

Chapter Eight: Echoes That Burn

The tunnels had fallen silent again—too silent. No flicker of light, no hum of hidden surveillance. Just ash, memory, and the acidic tang of burned circuits clinging to the air.

Sarah led them forward, her flashlight beam bouncing off crumbling stone and twisted metal. The Archive's destruction had sent a pulse through the underground system—whatever had once been watching was either blind or hiding.

"I can still hear it," Amy whispered behind her. "The echoes. Like... like it's not really dead."

"It's not," Gideon said grimly. "It's wounded. And wounded things are the most dangerous."

Mike brought up the rear, every muscle tight with anticipation. The pipe he carried now felt less like a weapon and more like a relic—primitive, against what they were facing.

"We're close," Sarah said. "The relay room is ahead. If I can reach the central servers, I can access the root of the Archive's code—what's left of it. That's where it rewrites the world's perception."

Gideon glanced back. "That's where they'll strike. They won't let you overwrite the story completely."

"But if I can?" Sarah looked over her shoulder, eyes fierce. "Then Debbie won't be the symbol of a horror story. Amy won't be the fragile one. And Mike…" she hesitated, "you won't have to carry it all."

He met her gaze. "Too late for that. But I'll see it through."

The relay room was a rusting cathedral of servers—once sleek, now scarred by fire and dust. Banks of screens blinked erratically, code stuttering in loops.

"Plug me in," Sarah said. Amy handed over the portable drive. Sarah knelt beside the primary interface and inserted it.

The air changed.

Cold.

Then: a voice.

Not sound. But inside their heads.

"You think you have reached the end. You think truth matters. But the story owns you. It always has."

Mike clutched his head. "Who—what is that?"

"The root protocol," Sarah muttered. "It's alive. Not AI. Not human. Something in between."

"You cannot rewrite what is believed. You can only suffer beneath it."

"No," Sarah growled. "You watched us. Trapped us. Told our stories through fear and silence. But we're not your fiction anymore."

Her fingers danced over the keys. Lines of code surged onto the monitors. Debbie's voice—her real voice—crackled through the speakers.

"They only win if we keep playing."

The relay room shuddered.

And from the shadows behind them—Watchers began to emerge.

But they were different now.

Fractured. Unstable. Flickering like half-remembered dreams.

"Keep typing!" Mike shouted, stepping between Sarah and the Watchers. "Finish it!"

Gideon joined him. So did Amy. No more victims. No more bystanders.

As Sarah's code began to overwrite the Archive's foundation, reality itself began to twist—memories folding, reweaving, reshaping—

—into something new.

"I don't want a happy ending," Sarah whispered. "I want the truth."

Behind her, the flames of the final act began to rise.

Chapter Nine: The Memory War

The relay room exploded in colour and noise—not from fire, but from data. Pulsing light surged through the wires like blood through veins. The Archive was bleeding, thrashing, fighting back.

Sarah's fingers were a blur across the interface, her face bathed in the flickering hues of corrupted memories. Every line of code she wrote hit the system like a hammer blow, shattering falsehoods, disassembling manipulations.

Behind her, the Watchers screamed.

Not human screams—glitched ones. Binary cries wrapped in echoes, as if the walls themselves were howling in protest.

Mike swung his pipe with brutal precision, cracking into a Watcher's chest. It split like glass, revealing not organs but reels of footage—memories that weren't real, scenes scripted to trap.

"These aren't people!" he roared. "They're playback loops! Projections!"

Amy fought beside him with nothing but a steel rod and the fury of a survivor. "Then let's stop the goddamn broadcast!"

Gideon pulled two thermite charges from his jacket. "If this place has a heart, it's in the lower vault. We bury it, we finish this."

Sarah shook her head. "Not yet. I need thirty more seconds. I'm pulling the raw truth into the system. No filters. No edits."

Outside the relay room, reality had started to slip.

Hallways bent in impossible directions. Doors appeared, vanished. People they once knew flickered in and out like old TV static—Jane, Debbie, even Mary. Fractured copies. Echoes from the Archive's vault.

One of them looked Sarah in the eye. "You're rewriting me."

Sarah didn't blink. "You're not real."

"I was."

The screen turned blood red. A final defence mechanism. The Archive's core— somewhere deep—was initiating counter code. A wave of false endings was flooding the system.

Happy resolutions. Neat sacrifices. Glorious deaths.

All lies.

"It's trying to overwrite us with tropes!" Sarah yelled. "Clichés. Emotional closure that isn't true."

Mike bashed another Watcher into sparks. "Then don't give it closure. Give it chaos."

Gideon grabbed the thermite, looked Sarah in the eyes. "You get that truth out. I'll make sure they can't take it back."

He ran.

Sarah pulled the final thread.

The screen went black—then white—then blinding gold as real memory surged into the Archive's foundation. Debbie's actual voice. The real footage from that night. The truth they all tried to forget, or twist, or bury.

Sarah whispered, "Now you burn."

The system let out a shriek.

And then—

Silence.

Real silence.

Sarah turned. The Watchers were gone. Mike was breathing hard, bloodied but standing. Amy slumped against the wall, laughing and crying all at once.

Then the tremors started.

From deep below—Gideon's charges.

Thirty seconds.

"Run," Sarah said.

They did.

Through melting tunnels, through breaking walls, through the last collapse of the Archive's lie-machine.

Behind them, in the depths, the truth finally detonated.

Not just an explosion—

A reckoning.

And ahead—what waited was either freedom… or fire.

Chapter Ten: Ashes and Aftermath

The blast tore through the tunnels like a scream from the past — all fury, all finality.

A shockwave of fire, dust, and shattered metal chased them, howling through corridors once lined with secrets and ghosts.

Mike pushed Sarah forward, every breath burning in his lungs. "GO! GO!"

Behind them, the Archive collapsed in on itself — not just physically, but historically. Files combusted midair, holograms disintegrated into sparks, and every false face of a Watcher flickered out in one final gasp of digital death.

They burst into daylight.

Real daylight.

Not filtered through cameras or artificial memories — the sun, golden and blinding, rising over a fractured world still reeling from decades of lies.

Sarah fell to her knees, gasping. Amy stumbled beside her, coughing, clutching her side. Mike stood tall, staring back at the cracked concrete mouth of the tunnel behind them.

Gideon hadn't come through.

"Gideon…" Sarah breathed, her eyes brimming.

Mike shook his head slowly, jaw clenched. "He knew. He chose it."

"He bought us the truth," Amy whispered, looking up at the sky. "And this moment."

Behind them, the landscape rippled with chaos. The remnants of Watcher networks — now severed — spun wild, disconnected. Screens blinked blank. Surveillance drones dropped like flies. A thousand minds woke up at once, blinking into freedom, dazed by reality.

Sarah pulled out a small, battered drive.

"What's that?" Mike asked, wiping blood from his brow.

She held it up like a trophy. "Gideon's mirror protocol. Not just proof — evidence. Every file, every edit, every life they rewrote. The world's going to see the whole damn thing."

A strange silence settled over them.

Hope.

Tenuous, raw, but real.

Then a distant rumble — not the Archive this time.

A convoy. Black SUVs rolling over the hill. The last loyalists? The corrupted elite? Or something worse?

Mike readied his blade. "It's never that simple."

Sarah smirked, rising to her feet. "Nothing ever is."

Amy nodded, fire in her eyes. "Then let's complicate it."

From the treeline, figures emerged — old allies, presumed lost, forgotten fighters. Jane. Malik. Even Ellis — a Watcher once, now visibly changed, his eyes clear for the first time.

"You called," Jane said with a half-smile. "We figured it was time to finish what we started."

Mike cracked his knuckles. "One last fight."

Sarah slipped the drive into her pocket. "No more hiding. No more games."

As the convoy crested the hill, guns bristling, the group stood united.

Blood-stained. Battle-worn. Unbroken.

The Archive had fallen.

But the war for truth was still burning.

Mike drew in a breath of clean air and whispered like a promise:

"Let's burn the rest of it down."

Chapter Eleven: The Reckoners

The sun was high now—no longer golden, but white-hot, blistering the shattered concrete and warped steel. The land outside the Archive's remains felt scorched by truth, still echoing with the blast that tore the curtain down.

But this wasn't victory yet. This was the final hour.

Mike stood at the edge of the blacktop, eyes fixed on the convoy that rolled closer, tires grinding gravel like bones. Behind him, the ragtag group gathered — tired, bleeding, but resolute.

Jane leaned against an abandoned supply crate, reloading her rifle with mechanical precision. "They're late to the funeral."

"They're coming to rewrite it," said Ellis, once their enemy, now carrying a Watcher-grade transmitter blinking blue in his hand.

"The Council's fallback unit. Protocol Omega. Absolute erasure."

"They're not just cleaning up," Sarah muttered. "They're burning the story out of the timeline."

Gideon's drive—tucked safely inside Sarah's jacket—felt heavier by the second. It wasn't just evidence. It was history. Truth, unfiltered. Dangerous.

"I say we upload it," Amy said, her voice sharp, steeled. "Now. While they're still guessing."

"We do that," Mike replied, "we become targets before we fire a single shot. They'll trace the signal. Jam it. Wipe us out before anyone reads a line."

Ellis stepped forward. "I know where the dead switch node is. A buried satellite link in the tower ruins north of here. It's off-grid. Old tech. Analog baseband."

Sarah blinked. "You're saying we ghost the truth?"

Ellis nodded. "Broadcast once. No return signal. One shot. Pure exposure."

Mike turned to the group. "Then we split. Jane, Ellis, Sarah — get to the tower. Get it done. The rest of us? We hold the line."

Jane narrowed her eyes. "You think we can stall Protocol Omega with this?" She gestured to their ragged gear.

"We've got more than weapons," Mike said. He looked around at the eyes watching him — survivors of three books' worth of blood, betrayal, and buried nightmares. "We've got reason."

The wind kicked up, hot and ash-laced. In the distance, the convoy stopped.

Doors opened.

Figures stepped out — black suits, blank visors, synchronized movements. The last loyalists to the Watchers' Council. Silent. Lethal.

"Positions!" Mike barked.

Ellis handed Sarah a cracked comm unit. "If they breach, destroy the drive."

Sarah didn't flinch. "If they breach, they won't find anything left to destroy."

As the group split, every heartbeat counted. Sarah and her unit sprinted through the ruins, vanishing into the trees. Mike watched them go with a silent prayer.

Then he turned to face the approaching line of death.

Amy stood at his side, shotgun cocked.

Jane's voice came over the radio, calm and cool:

"Upload point ETA: fifteen minutes."

Mike exhaled slowly. The reckoning had begun.

And this time, it would end.

Chapter Twelve: Broadcast or Burn

The tower was a jagged skeleton against the sky, rising from the ruins like a broken finger pointed at heaven in defiance. Vines wrapped its steel bones, rust devoured its joints, but the uplink node—buried beneath layers of analogue circuitry—still pulsed faintly. Alive. Waiting.

Sarah crouched beside the console inside what had once been the comms bunker. A dead computer, a humming power relay, and the blinking red light of the analogue transmitter—the last whispering relic of the Cold War.

Ellis shoved wires into ports with surgical speed. "This thing hasn't broadcast in thirty years."

"It doesn't have to work well," Sarah muttered. "Just once."

Jane kept watch at the shattered doorway, sniper rifle poised. "Ten minutes, give or take. Mike's holding, but they're closing."

Ellis pulled out the drive—Gideon's final trove—and handed it to Sarah. "Everything's in here. Surveillance logs. Ritual files. The experiments. Names. Dates. Even Watcher council protocols."

Sarah held it like it might explode. "This ends them."

Ellis shook his head. "This reveals them. Whether that ends them… that's up to everyone who reads it."

She slotted the drive into the ancient port, the machine coughing to life with a grinding whir. A cascade of flickering green text danced across the dusty screen.

"Initializing baseband link," Sarah murmured. "God, let this work."

Jane tensed. "Contacts—south ridge. They're faster than we thought."

Back at the defensive line, Mike crouched behind an overturned transport vehicle. The air screamed with suppressed fire. Amy darted between cover, laying mines and flares. The assault had begun.

"Sarah," Mike's voice crackled through the comm, "we've got five minutes. Maybe."

"We need three," she replied, fingers flying across the keys. "Transcoding now. The truth is loading."

At the tower, Jane fired the first shot—a clean strike to a Watcher's helmet. The impact was like ringing a bell. Within seconds, bullets tore the silence.

Ellis fed the system its final line of code. "Signal's locked. Dial-up pulse format. They won't know it until it's out."

Sarah stared at the screen. A single line flashed:

TRANSMISSION READY.

SEND?

She hovered over the key.

A scream outside. Jane shouted: "They're breaching the perimeter!"

Ellis pulled his sidearm. "Do it. Now."

Sarah slammed the key.

The screen flashed:

SENDING…

A low hum vibrated the ground. The ancient satellite dish above them creaked and turned.

"Come on," Sarah whispered. "Come on…"

Back at the battlefield, the air shimmered. Mike ducked as a Watcher fired a thermite round. Amy returned fire with a flare.

Then:

The sky cracked with a strange thunder.

Jane looked up as the dish above glowed red, then gold.

A signal pulsed out, invisible—but felt.

Around the world, dormant receivers lit up. Buried signals found servers. Emails popped. Dead websites awakened.

The truth spilled like a virus: images, names, locations. The Archive unravelled. The Council's secrets became everyone's.

Sarah dropped back against the wall, shaking. "It's out."

Ellis smiled. "And they can't stop it."

Outside, the Watchers froze. Their movements changed. Erratic. Some even dropped weapons.

"Mike," Sarah said into the comm, "they know."

Mike rose, bloodied but smiling.

"Good," he said. "Then let's finish this."

Chapter Thirteen: The Collapse

The sky burned with the weight of a thousand secrets.

Across cities, bunkers, and corporate strongholds, alarms howled. Watchers— once shadows behind shadows—now found their names flashing across every public screen, every device. News anchors stuttered. Firewalls burst. Their empire of silence was collapsing.

And beneath the chaos, in the tunnels under Black Ridge Facility, Mike Halston led the charge.

"We hit the generators, the uplinks, the archive vault. Then we finish the council,"

Mike barked, adrenaline slamming through his veins like old combat stims.

Sarah moved beside him with laser focus, armed with a flash drive keyed to the vault's encryption. "We bring this place down, we erase it. Forever."

Ellis cracked his knuckles, holding his custom shock grenades like candy. "Been waiting to short-circuit these bastards."

They were deep underground now cutting through reinforced corridors left over from Cold War experiments. The facility wasn't just a bunker. It was a labyrinth, a wound stitched shut with steel.

Gideon's voice crackled in their earpieces from the overwatch post above:

"Guards are scrambling. They've lost centralized control. You've got fifteen minutes tops before they regroup and lock it all down."

Mike checked his watch. "Plenty of time."

A blast door loomed ahead. Ellis moved up, jamming wires into the lock panel.

"Get ready," he muttered. "It's about to get biblical."

With a sizzle and a shriek of torn metal, the door hissed open—revealing a long hall lined with glass walls.

Inside each glass cell: subjects.

Some human. Some… no longer.

Sarah flinched. "They kept them alive…"

Mike's jaw tightened. "No more."

Jane moved forward, planting charges along the corridor. "These cells go. No debates."

They passed through the corridor of sins—each step cracking the bones of a legacy built on blood. At the far end, a reinforced steel door guarded the vault.

Ellis read the symbols etched into the frame. "Watcher language. Old world cipher, tied to—"

Mike kicked it. Hard. "I speak Marine."

The door didn't budge. But Sarah was already there, plugging in her drive.

"Decryption in process," she whispered.

From the walls, speakers hummed. A voice slithered through.

"Still playing heroes, Michael? You've always misunderstood the game."

It was one of the Council—Watcher Prime.

"People want chains," the voice cooed. "We just made them beautiful."

"I've got news for you," Mike growled. "They're melting."

The door clicked. Opened.

Beyond it: the Archive Vault. Towering servers. Gold-leaf files. Ritual schematics. Names. Power.

Mike stepped inside, raised his rifle, and began unloading on the closest data node.

Ellis lobbed a fire burst charge onto a glowing console.

Jane slammed the detonator on the cell wall timer.

"Three minutes to burn," she said. "Let's go!"

Sirens blared. Steam hissed. The whole vault groaned like it was dying.

Sarah grabbed the last canister—Gideon's code-bomb—and activated it.

The screens flashed:

ERASURE COMPLETE

ARCHIVE LOST

Mike looked around at the inferno. "Let's bring down the walls."

As they ran, explosions rippled behind them, sucking oxygen from the tunnels. Dust filled their lungs, light turned red.

Up ahead—the escape shaft.

Jane climbed first. Ellis followed. Mike helped Sarah up before grabbing the last charge from his belt.

"Mike!" she screamed.

"I'll be right behind—GO!"

He hurled the final explosive into the passage. Then climbed.

Behind him, the Black Ridge Facility—the hive of pain and secrecy—collapsed in on itself.

They emerged into firelight.

The Watchers' legacy buried beneath rubble and truth.

The sky was different now. Not brighter, but lighter. A weight lifted.

Mike looked at Sarah. "It's done."

She nodded.

But somewhere, beyond the mountain line, a satellite blinked.

The war was over.

But the reckoning… wasn't done yet.

Chapter Fourteen: Ashes and Echoes

The mountain burned behind them like a dying god.

Black Ridge Facility was gone — caved in, scorched, erased. Every name, every tape, every whisper sealed beneath tons of rock and regret. The group stood at the edge of the treeline, silhouetted against flame-lit ash clouds. Smoke curled through dawn's bleeding light. No applause. No salvation. Just the sound of the world exhaling.

Mike Halston staggered forward, his boots crunching through charred debris.

"It's done," he muttered. "It's actually over."

Sarah looked to the horizon, eyes wet but hard. "Then why does it still feel like someone's watching?"

They weren't alone.

A low hum vibrated in the air, like the earth itself holding its breath. From the smoke emerged a figure — not limping, not rushing — walking. Clean suit. No dust. No fear.

Gideon.

Only… not as they remembered him.

His face bore new scars, his eyes a cold glint of steel, and on his back, he carried a sleek black case pulsing with soft red light.

"You set the world on fire," he said. "Impressive. But embers spread."

Ellis raised his weapon. "You survived that?"

"I didn't survive," Gideon replied. "I adapted."

The case unlatched.

From within: a device. Round, smooth, ancient in shape but futuristic in design — a blend of Watcher tech and something… older. The air crackled.

"This is what they feared," Gideon continued. "Not exposure. Not death. This."

He held it up. It pulsed, and the ground around them shifted — like reality hiccupping.

"Every Archive. Every Vault. Every backup server they had — I accessed it all. Then rewrote the rules."

"You sided with them," Sarah hissed. "You became what we were fighting."

"No," Gideon said. "I consumed them. And now I'm offering you a choice."

He turned the device toward the mountainside. A shimmering ripple tore through the smoke, revealing a hallway — gleaming, clean, impossible.

"A new world," he said. "Built on truth. Built on power. No more lies. No more hiding. But it needs architects. Founders."

Mike stepped forward. "You're asking us to join the next version of hell."

"I'm asking you to evolve," Gideon countered. "The Watchers were just the beginning. You think exposing them was the end? That was the invitation."

Sarah's voice cracked like thunder. "We're not gods, Gideon."

"No," he whispered. "We're worse. We remember being human."

The device glowed brighter. A countdown began. 60 seconds.

"You walk through that door," Gideon said, "and everything changes."

Mike looked at Sarah. Then at the others. The choice hung heavy — not life or death, but future or flame.

Behind them, the sky began to clear. Fire faded. The forest stretched out wide, full of silence and wind.

Mike turned away from the door.

"No more games," he said.

Gideon sighed. "So be it."

With a flick of his hand, he launched the device into the air. It hovered — then split into fragments, each shooting toward a different horizon.

Failsafe's.

Sarah screamed. "He's unleashed it!"

Mike tackled Gideon, the two men crashing to the ground as the sky split with streaks of red light — the fragments embedding themselves across the world.

Not a virus.

Not a broadcast.

A rewrite.

And the final war had just begun.

Chapter Fifteen: The Fragments

The world cracked at the seams.

Not with explosions. Not with sirens. But with silence—unnatural, loaded, like the breath before a scream. From Iceland to Istanbul, Cairo to Chicago, Gideon's fragments landed like needles piercing the planet's skin. They embedded in fault lines—physical and digital—waking ancient pathways beneath cities and inside code.

And then… they began to speak.

Not in sound. In influence.

People turned. Stopped. Looked at screens that flickered with glyphs they couldn't read—but understood. Memories they'd never lived rushed into their minds. Truths they hadn't earned whispered promises.

A new world was being written.

One memory at a time.

Somewhere beneath Prague.

Mike Halston's boots hit ancient stone. Dust swirled in columns of gold-tinted light seeping through cracks in the arched ceiling. This was no ordinary vault. It had been carved before the concept of nations—by hands that wanted to remember even after the world forgot.

Sarah stepped beside him, breath ragged. "Another one landed here."

They'd tracked the signal using an encrypted map left behind in a Watcher terminal. Six nodes. Six fragments. One already activated in Seoul. Another now humming beneath them.

At the end of the corridor stood a column — obsidian black and pulsing red. A fragment.

"Don't touch it," Sarah warned.

"I wasn't going to."

"You were thinking about it."

Mike paused. "It hums like something alive."

"No," came a voice behind them. "It hums like something hungry."

They turned—Ellis stood in the shadows, gun raised, bleeding from his shoulder, but eyes alive with purpose.

"I intercepted one in Berlin," he said. "It killed an entire room of data engineers. Not directly. It made them see… things."

"Hallucinations?" Sarah asked.

"Visions. And they acted on them. Every one of them thought they were saving the world."

Mike's voice dropped. "That's what Gideon meant. He's not controlling people. He's changing what they believe is true."

Sarah reached into her bag, pulling out a strange, curved device—half Watcher tech, half something older. A decoder. Jane had died getting it to her in Chapter 12.

"We can rewrite one fragment," she said. "Inject our truth."

Mike took a breath. "Then let's make it count."

They stepped forward—closer to the core. The fragment reacted, its glow shifting to violet.

Words formed in the air.

"CHOICE IS THE FINAL GOD."

Then: a shockwave.

Memories not their own surged into their minds. Battles in cities that didn't exist. Friends they hadn't met dying for causes they'd never fought. A child crying in a hallway made of light. A voice whispering: "You are not the author anymore."

Sarah screamed. Mike held her up. Ellis shot at the projection, the bullet passing through harmlessly.

The countdown started. Five minutes.

Their window.

Sarah plugged in the decoder. "Help me write the override!"

"What truth do we give them?" Mike asked.

She looked at him, eyes wide with fear and determination.

"The truth that pain didn't make us strong. We made ourselves strong by surviving it. That no voice—no machine—gets to define what we remember."

The lights flared. The code began.

As they typed, as Sarah cried, as Mike bled from a reopened wound on his side, the fragment's hum changed pitch. The symbols grew erratic. They were winning. This node would be theirs.

Then… the lights cut out.

All sound died.

From behind the column… Gideon stepped out.

"How poetic," he said. "You thought the fragment was the battlefield. It isn't."

He smiled, that same cold, sorrowful smile he wore in Book Three.

"The battlefield is your beliefs. And I've already won."

Chapter Sixteen: False Gods, Real Blood

Darkness. Not just the absence of light— something richer, heavier. It pulsed like a second heartbeat, crawling over the skin, whispering in tongues no human throat could form. Mike tried to stand, but his knees buckled. The weight of Gideon's presence wasn't physical, but it pressed down with the gravity of truth inverted.

Sarah, still kneeling beside the fragment, kept her fingers on the decoder, trembling.

Gideon's boots echoed as he stepped into view. The glow of the fragment danced in his eyes. He was no longer just a man—he wore belief like armour. Symbols shimmered just beneath his skin, as though he was being rewritten by his own vision.

"You still think this is about control," Gideon said, calmly. "But I didn't make these fragments to rule minds. I made them to liberate them."

Ellis raised his pistol. "Bullshit. You're rewriting people. Turning them into your version of the future."

"Am I?" Gideon said, walking toward him without fear. "Or am I just unlocking what they always wanted to be? The Archive locked us in the past. The Watchers tried to curate us like museum pieces. I'm giving humanity the chance to shed its scars."

Mike forced himself upright, blood trickling from his lip. "By feeding it lies."

"No," Gideon said softly. "By replacing trauma with choice. The fragments don't erase—they give context. Rewrite pain, and you rewrite who we are."

Sarah stood now. "And what happens to all the people who choose a reality that isn't yours?"

Gideon's smile faltered. "They… don't last long."

That was all they needed to hear.

Mike lunged, driving forward as Ellis fired. Sarah yanked the decoder and slammed her palm against the fragment's glyph core. The symbols screamed in red, and the room exploded in blinding white.

In the chaos, time stretched.

Memories crashed through Mike's skull—his boot on a landmine trigger in Helmand, Debbie's blood in the hotel bathtub, Sarah's voice at 3 a.m. telling him she trusted no one but him. Then—

A flash.

He was in a different room.

Standing over himself.

Watching as Gideon pulled something from his younger self's neck—a chip? No. A shard. From the first fragment.

He'd been marked since the beginning.

Present – Prague – Sublevel Collapse
Sequence: T-minus 90 seconds

The walls cracked. The fragment flickered—
half rewritten, unstable. Gideon was gone.
Vapor or memory, no one could say. Ellis
grabbed Sarah by the wrist. "Time to move!"

Mike followed, but his chest burned with
betrayal. Had he been part of the plan all
along? Was his pain… planted?

The ceiling caved behind them.

They ran.

As the explosion roared upward, it was not
destruction—it was transmission. A ripple of
rewritten memory spread outward, dancing
along the lines of the network like fire on dry
grass.

In Seoul, a child stopped crying.

In Moscow, a man remembered a sister
who never lived.

In Nairobi, a woman dropped to her knees,
clutching a photo that had not existed
yesterday.

The world was breaking.

But also… being remade.

One truth at a time.

Chapter Seventeen: The Last Shard

It wasn't raining in Berlin, but the sky looked like it had forgotten how to do anything else.

Clouds churned above the decaying museum where the final fragment pulsed beneath layers of steel, glass, and history rewritten too many times to count. Inside, the air crackled with static—part storm, part memory, part something older than either.

Mike stared at the reinforced vault door, his fists clenched.

"This is it?" he asked.

Sarah nodded, her breath clouding. "The original shard. The template. The others were just echoes. This one… writes the rules."

Ellis stood back, scanning the walls. "You sure we're not already too late? Half the planet's memory is already splintered. People are seeing lives they never lived."

"They're believing them," Sarah corrected. "That's the difference. Gideon didn't just feed illusions—he made people want them."

Mary stepped out from the shadows. "And that's why this one's worse. It doesn't rewrite pain. It replaces it with peace. Just… perfect obedience."

Mike turned, shocked. "Mary? You made it out of the tunnels?"

"I made a choice," she said. "I remembered who I was. Not what the Archive told me. Not what the Council allowed me to forget."

Sarah smiled faintly. "She broke the loop."

Ellis cracked his knuckles. "Good. Let's break the door."

BOOM.

The vault rocked as explosives planted earlier by the rebel Watchers lit the seams. Smoke billowed. Metal groaned.

The door fell.

Inside was nothing like they'd expected.

No lab. No altar.

Just a single, black pedestal.

And on it—a shard the size of a fingernail, suspended in mid-air, spinning slowly.

It wasn't pulsing like the others.

It was… waiting.

Mike stepped forward.

Then froze.

Gideon was there.

Or something like him.

His face, half-formed from shadow and light, hovered above the shard. "You came."

"You're dead," Mike growled.

"Not quite. The Archive erased my body. But this? This was my intention—and intention echoes."

Sarah raised the decoder. "We can end this."

"You could," the voice replied. "Or you could join it. Imagine—no more guilt. No more war in your head. One memory. Oneself. No fracture, no pain."

Mike stepped forward, hand brushing the shard. A pulse went through him—images, voices, dreams. Debbie laughing. The game. His hands dripping in blood. His father. His oath. Sarah's voice calling his name.

He could rewrite it.

He could be free.

But then he saw it.

Behind the illusion—Gideon's plan.

Total convergence.

One truth. One will.

No choice at all.

Mike's fingers tightened. "I remember everything, Gideon. Even the parts I wanted to forget. And that's what makes me me."

He crushed the shard.

The room screamed.

Light exploded.

Reality shuddered.

Then—silence.

They awoke outside the ruins.

Sky clear.

No static.

The world… holding its breath.

Sarah stood first. "Did we do it?"

Mike looked up, eyes wet. "We chose. That's all that matters."

Mary stared out at the skyline. "Then let's help the others remember how to choose again."

Chapter Eighteen: Ashes That Speak

The streets of Prague were quiet—too quiet for a city that had once throbbed with rebellion. The power grid flickered in pulses, like a dying heartbeat, and the few remaining transmissions were fragments: static-laced broadcasts, half-buried truths, and the voices of ghosts refusing to vanish.

Mike walked through the courtyard of what used to be a Watcher relay station. The Archive's spires had fallen here—glass monoliths shattered and gutted by their own hubris. Behind him, Sarah dragged a steel case on a makeshift sled.

"The truth doesn't travel well," she muttered. "Especially not in suitcases."

"Maybe that's the point," Mike said. "Maybe we were never meant to carry it all. Just enough to pass along."

They stopped near a rusted transmitter dish. Its core was melted—sabotaged during the last Archive purge—but its frame remained upright, jagged like a crown of thorns.

Mary was already there, lighting candles beneath a makeshift memorial. Names scrawled in ink. Polaroids. Wristbands from game nights. Burned-out data drives.

"I didn't know we were keeping vigil," Sarah said gently.

Mary looked up. "We aren't. We're reminding ourselves what we lost before we burn the rest."

Inside the suitcase were the last living fragments of the Archive: recordings of Blood Spurts sessions, Watcher Council deliberations, Gideon's voice spliced through decades of secret broadcasts. Proof. Receipts. Confession.

"We leak this now," Sarah said, "it'll cause chaos. Riots. Collapses of belief systems, institutions, entire memory frameworks."

"Good," Mike replied.

Mary stepped forward. "And what if they blame us?"

"They will." Mike looked her in the eye. "But they'll know the truth. And the truth can't be locked in a vault anymore."

A shadow moved across the rooftop.

Jane appeared, rifle slung, eyes sunken but clear. "Transmission lines in Sector 8 are clear. And I've got something else."

She held up a cracked, analogue camcorder.

"Old tech," she grinned. "Untraceable. Gideon didn't think to erase this. You want a message the world won't ignore? Record it. Human face. Human voice."

Mike hesitated. Then took the camera.

He pressed RECORD.

"This is Mike Halston," he said, the words slow and deliberate. "You don't know me. Or maybe you do—but not the real me. What you saw was a memory implanted, a narrative sold. We've been puppets in a theatre of pain."

He paused. Looked down.

"I was part of something called Blood Spurts. It started as a game. It ended in murder, silence, and mind control. We thought we were just testing limits. We were actually testing obedience."

He looked up.

"The Watchers are real. The Archive is broken. And if you're seeing this—you're free. For the first time in years, you can think without interference. But that freedom is fragile. Use it."

He ended the recording.

Mary stepped beside him. "Now we scatter it."

And they did.

By hand. By drone. By physical copies shoved into newspaper bins and burned onto discs. Messages slipped into subway cracks. Truth written on walls.

Ashes that spoke.

The world wouldn't understand it at first.

But it would hear.

And that… was the beginning of the end.

Chapter Nineteen: The Last Pact

The bunker beneath the burned-out cathedral was colder than the tunnels above, and twice as dark. Sarah's boots echoed as she descended, her flashlight beam cutting through the dust and crumbling stone. Behind her, Mike followed, weapon drawn but lowered. He wasn't expecting a fight—not yet. But he didn't trust reunions. Not anymore.

Especially not this one.

The message had come encrypted in a voice they hadn't heard since Book Two. A whisper embedded in an old surveillance file, activated only by a phrase Sarah once said during a dare.

"Blood remembers."

And so did he.

The chamber opened into what looked like an ancient crypt—except here, servers hummed among coffins. Stacks of analogue equipment, ham radios, projection reels. The past... weaponized.

In the centre stood a figure cloaked in shadow, back turned, face lit by a dying screen.

"Gideon," Mike said coldly.

The man turned slowly. The years had worn him, but the eyes were the same—bright, fanatical, and deeply tired.

"Michael," Gideon said. "Sarah. You came. Good."

"We came," Sarah said, "because you promised an answer."

Gideon gestured toward the screens. They showed fractured feeds—riot footage, children playing, police raids, lovers in a park. Surveillance from around the world. But muted. No narration. Just reality.

"Everything I've done," Gideon said, "was to stop what's coming. And now you've forced my hand."

Mike stepped forward. "We didn't come here to debate your religion of control. Give us the drives."

Gideon smiled. "You misunderstand. I didn't call you here to stop me. I called you here to join me."

Sarah's eyes narrowed. "Join you?"

The twist came fast—sharper than the knives they'd once dared each other to hold to their own throats.

Gideon tapped a console.

The screens changed. Footage of them. The group. Debbie. Jane. Mary. The games. The night Debbie died. Alternate angles.

Hidden cameras. Full audio. Not just Watchers watching.

But someone else.

"Who recorded this?" Sarah demanded.

"Not the Watchers," Gideon said. "You did."

The silence cracked.

"What?" Mike growled.

"You don't remember," Gideon said softly. "Because none of you were supposed to. You were part of an early test cell— designed to see if memory could be edited in real time, live. The blood, the dares, even the death… all captured. Not for blackmail. Not for art. But for science."

Sarah staggered back, her face pale. "We… we built the game?"

Gideon nodded. "Not alone. But you were its seeds. You didn't just play Blood Spurts. You authored it."

The world tilted.

Mike clenched his fists. "That's not possible."

"Memory is soft," Gideon said. "But the truth? That's sharp. I have the backups. You three were the founding loop. Debbie was the first collapse. You watched it fall… and then we rewrote you."

Sarah stepped away, hand over her mouth. "Then what are we doing now? What was the rebellion?"

"A reflex," Gideon said. "The final test. To see if guilt could spark freedom."

Mike turned his gun on Gideon. "Then you failed."

Gideon didn't flinch. "No, Mike. We passed. And now you get to decide: release the truth and burn what's left… or rebuild with me."

He opened a case. Inside: three original data chips. Untouched. Final memories. The genesis of Blood Spurts.

One choice.

Burn it all. Or become what they once feared.

Chapter Twenty: Ash or Flame

The chamber pulsed with dread.

Sarah stared at the data chips like they were live explosives. Each one glinted under the flickering lights—silent, dangerous, sacred. If Gideon was telling the truth, then these weren't just files.

They were memories. Their memories. Unfiltered. Untouched by rewrites or gaslighting or trauma suppression. The original truth—of what really happened the night Debbie died, and everything before.

Sarah's fingers trembled.

Mike hadn't lowered his weapon.

"I should kill you," he said to Gideon, voice calm but hollowed out. "End this right now. You've manipulated us for years. Turned pain into theatre. Twisted lives into myths."

Gideon raised his chin. "You could shoot me, yes. But what would you be shooting? A man? Or the mirror he's holding up?"

Sarah reached out slowly, took one of the chips.

It was heavier than it looked.

She held it to the light. The label was faint— just a date. April 3rd, 2021. The night everything changed.

Mary's scream. Amy's sobs. The bathtub. The blood.

And Debbie.

"I need to know," she whispered.

"No, you don't," Mike said harshly. "That's the trick, Sarah. That's always been the trick. Curiosity isn't the path to freedom—it's the leash they use to yank us back."

But even he glanced toward the chip.

Because what if it proved he wasn't the monster?

What if it proved he was?

Gideon moved slowly to the projector console. "One chip. One truth. That's the deal. Choose wisely. Show it to the world, and Blood Spurts burns with it. All of it. The Watchers, the Archive, even the roots of the council."

"And what if we don't?" Sarah asked.

"Then you put it back," Gideon said. "Walk away. Let memory fade. Let the new game rise. Become architects of something purer… cleaner."

"Blood without reckoning," Mike muttered. "That's what you really want."

Gideon smiled. "No. Reckoning without consequence."

Sarah looked at Mike.

"I want to see it," she said.

Mike nodded grimly.

She fed the chip into the console.

The lights dimmed. The screen hissed to life. A flicker of static. Then…

A hotel suite.

The same one from Book One. But different.

Camera One: A handheld view from Debbie's perspective—filming as the others laugh, drink, draw cards from the game pile.

Camera Two: Hidden in a corner. Captures a quiet, private conversation between Mary and Jane. About an extra "card" no one was supposed to draw.

Camera Three: Focused on Mike. Sitting still. Watching Debbie with too much intensity.

Then—

The bathroom.

Debbie enters. Alone.

But seconds later, another shadow follows. Not Mike. Not Sarah. Not any of the group.

Someone else.

The face is blurred—by time? By tampering? But the voice—

A single line.

"She served her purpose."

And then, the screen goes black.

Sarah stepped back, stunned.

Gideon, for once, was quiet.

Mike lowered his weapon. "That… wasn't us."

"No," Sarah said softly. "But someone wanted us to think it was."

She turned to Gideon. "You didn't make the game, did you?"

Gideon slowly shook his head. "I tested it. But I didn't write it."

"Then who did?" Mike asked.

Gideon looked past them, toward the vault behind the screens.

"The last founder," he said. "The one we all forgot."

The room rumbled.

Above them… movement. As if the cathedral ruins were waking.

Sarah grabbed the chip from the console.

"We have to go," she said. "Now."

"But where?" Mike asked.

Sarah's eyes were blazing. "To the Archive. To the start. To the one who was never in the footage…"

She turned.

"To Debbie."

Chapter Twenty-One: The Final Origin

The road to the Archive was buried — not under dirt, but under decades of deception.

Sarah drove like the world was cracking behind them. The desert blurred past on both sides, heat-haze trembling like ghosts on the horizon. Next to her, Mike sat in silence, jaw locked, hands white-knuckled on his knees. In the back, Gideon muttered names under his breath — codex references, Watcher designations, cross-checks of who had lived and who had vanished.

But Sarah only focused on one name.

Debbie.

The girl they all thought they knew. The wild card. The martyr. The first to die.

But what if she hadn't?

What if Debbie Lang never existed — at least, not in the way they remembered?

"We're close," Sarah said, slamming the brakes as they neared the rusted chain-link gates of an old communication outpost — long abandoned by official records, but not by its true owners.

Mike stared at the cracked concrete bunker nestled into the mountain's flank.

"This is it?"

"This is where the Archive began," Gideon confirmed, stepping out into the dry wind. "Before servers. Before shadow councils. Before cameras and curated rituals. This is where the original watchers watched."

The gate gave way with a screech. Inside, the air changed. Cooler. Denser. Heavier. As if memory itself had weight.

They descended together. The concrete hallways pulsed with the glow of old-world tech. Analog reels, databanks with blinking green lights, walls scrawled with sequence diagrams and psychological profiles.

At the centre: a vault. Sealed by both code and blood recognition.

Sarah stepped forward.

The panel scanned her retina… and the door hissed open.

Mike blinked. "How the hell—"

"I told you," she said quietly. "I was part of the test from the start."

The vault was a circular room, ringed by terminals and relics: polaroids of game nights from decades past, VHS tapes with handwritten titles, a red leather notebook marked only with a name:

D. Lang

Sarah reached for the notebook with shaking hands.

Inside: transcripts. Psychological triggers. Conditioning patterns. Page after page detailing the creation of a persona — Debbie Lang — designed for infiltration, leadership, manipulation… and sacrificial collapse.

Mike's voice cracked. "They made her."

Gideon nodded. "She was never one of you. She was the fuse."

"And we were the fire," Sarah whispered.

But then, another sound — faint, metallic.

From one of the screens: static. Then a voice, distorted but unmistakably real.

"You weren't supposed to come here, Sarah. But I always knew you would."

The screen flickered — and there she was.

Debbie. Alive. Older. Different.

"Hello again," she said. "Let's finish what we started."

Sarah staggered back. "That's not possible—"

"She faked her death," Gideon whispered. "Or someone faked it for her."

Mike stepped forward, rage rising. "Why?"

On the screen, Debbie smiled.

"Because only in death could I be believed."

The screen went dark.

An alarm blared.

Gideon swore. "They're coming. The Council. The real one."

Sarah grabbed the notebook, her eyes blazing.

"Then let them come. We've got the truth now."

As the vault trembled, as the Archive's final doors slid open to reveal the storm beyond—

They stepped into history.

To end it.

Chapter Twenty-Two: Echoes and Embers

The vault doors slammed shut behind them — not locked, just final. Like the Archive had given up its last secret and now waited to burn.

Mike stood at the threshold, fists clenched, staring into the open concrete expanse outside. But it wasn't empty.

The Watchers had arrived.

Across the dusty plateau stood a dozen black SUVs, fanned out in a crescent, forming a noose. Black-suited figures emerged like shadows made flesh — their faces obscured by masks that resembled nothing and everything: theatre. Ritual. Fear.

And in the centre of them, stepping down from the lead vehicle…

Debbie.

Older, yes. Hardened. But unmistakably her.

Sarah's heart jack-knifed as she stepped beside Mike. "It's her. It's really her."

Gideon hissed, "Don't trust your eyes. Not anymore. They've used doubles before."

But then Debbie spoke.

"Welcome home," she said, voice amplified through unseen speakers. "I wondered how long it would take for you to get past the fiction."

She walked slowly forward, hands raised — unarmed.

Mike strode out to meet her halfway.

"You died," he growled. "We buried you."

"I was buried," she replied. "But not as a victim. As a seed."

Mike didn't flinch. "You manipulated us. Used us as fodder for your sick experiment."

"No," Debbie said, stepping closer. "You manipulated yourselves. That was the point. We just turned on the cameras."

Sarah stepped forward. "Why now? Why show yourself?"

Debbie's eyes met hers — calm, cold. "Because this is the final cycle. The Archive is complete. Everything you did, everything you chose — it's all recorded. You were the data. And now, it's time to test the next phase."

Mike reached behind him, flicking the safety off his pistol. "Not if we erase it first."

A beat.

Debbie smiled.

"Mike," she said, "You don't get to end it. Because this… this is where you began."

She snapped her fingers.

And from the SUVs, they emerged — the New Recruits.

Dozens. Maybe hundreds. Clad in black. Their eyes wide with the kind of clarity that comes only from total indoctrination. They weren't just followers.

They were believers.

Sarah whispered, "They rebooted the game."

But Gideon was already moving. He slid a small detonator from his coat and pressed it to Sarah's palm.

"If we're doing this," he muttered, "we do it right. We erase everything."

"Wait," Sarah said. "We don't just destroy it. We broadcast it."

She turned, sprinted back into the Archive's vault, Gideon close behind. Inside, she activated the old analogue transmitter — patched through the satellites still bound to their codes. The truth. The files. The confessions. The footage.

Everything was going out live.

Mike stood alone in the open.

Debbie, still smiling, whispered into her mic, "What will you choose, Mike? The truth? Or the blood?"

His answer was silence.

And then—

Boom.

The Archive lit up behind him — a burning eye in the mountain.

Across the world, screens flickered to life.

The game was no longer hidden.

And as the New Recruits surged forward, as Mike drew his blade and ran into them like a soldier against a tide, Sarah's voice echoed through the transmission:

"You watched.

Now we decide who watches you."

Chapter Twenty-Three: The Reckoners

The fire from the Archive still burned behind them, a violent beacon against the black sky. But Sarah wasn't watching flames — she was watching screens.

One after another, terminals across the globe flickered to life, hijacked by her override. Phones buzzed. Laptops stuttered. Public billboards — even military feeds — began to show them.

The Games.

The lies.

The Watchers.

Gideon looked up at her from the console, sweat streaking his soot-covered face. "This was your plan?"

She shook her head. "No. This was theirs. We just turned the camera around."

He grinned grimly. "I can work with that."

Meanwhile, outside, the ground was soaked with blood and dust — the echo of screams and gunfire thick in the air.

Mike Halston had become myth.

He moved through the crowd of Recruits like a man untethered from flesh — dodging blades, snapping wrists, using the very choreography Debbie had trained into them all. These weren't kids at a rave anymore — these were weaponized minds, taught obedience through suffering.

But they didn't expect someone who'd survived it.

He wasn't just fighting them. He was undoing them.

One face at a time.

"ENOUGH!" Debbie shouted, stepping forward. Two Recruits stood at her side, holding shock batons crackling with blue fire.

Mike paused. Bleeding. Breathing hard. But still standing.

"You can't win," she said. "Not here. Not against this."

"No," he growled, "but I can end it."

From the mountain ridge behind them, a new voice called out.

Mary.

She stood silhouetted against the inferno, rifle in hand, a bandolier across her chest. Behind her… Jane, Amy, and half a dozen others once thought gone, disappeared, or dead.

"They came home," Mary said softly, "because the truth was never buried deep enough."

Debbie laughed, slow and bitter. "You think this changes anything? You think one last battle rewrites everything?"

"No," Sarah's voice came through every speaker, every earpiece, every Watcher's private channel. "But it documents everything."

Debbie paled.

Sarah's final upload had reached them all — Watchers, Recruits, Governments, and those still on the fence. Every game. Every manipulation. Every forced confession. The veil was gone.

Debbie reached into her coat, pulling a trigger clasp. "Then we all go down—"

BANG.

A single bullet tore through her shoulder. The clasp fell. She screamed.

Gideon, lowering his rifle from the ridge, muttered, "We're not done yet."

Recruits paused. Confusion. Fracture.

For the first time, they were uncertain.

And Mike, breathing heavily, whispered the words Sarah had broadcast minutes ago.

"You watched.

Now we decide who watches you."

He stepped toward Debbie. She backed away. No army left.

Behind him, the Reckoners gathered.

The final war hadn't started in a battlefield.

It had started in a hotel room, around a stupid game that got too real.

Now?

It was going to end with them.

Chapter Twenty-Four: The Reckoning

The storm didn't come from the sky. It came from within.

The air hung heavy with a silence deeper than death — the kind that waits after the trigger's been pulled but before the bullet lands. That moment of consequence.

Mike stood before Debbie, her coat bloodied, her eyes darting between the faces of those who'd come back. Gideon. Sarah. Mary. Even Jane. She had twisted every one of them once — and they had returned, not for revenge.

But for resolution.

"Do it, Mike," Debbie spat, clutching her wounded shoulder. "Isn't that what you've wanted since the bathtub?"

The word echoed like a ghost — bathtub — that night, the scream, the betrayal.

Mike stepped closer, fists clenched. "What I wanted… was for it to have never begun."

Behind him, Sarah's voice crackled through the remnants of the broadcast system — still live in millions of places.

"The game is over. And the final move… is ours."

From hidden chambers beneath the Archive's ruins, Watchers were surfacing, caught in the collapse of their secret empire. The Reckoners — survivors, hackers, journalists, old players reborn — were rounding them up.

But the biggest choice wasn't arrest. Or escape.

It was what came next.

Debbie dropped to her knees. "You think this ends with me?" she said. "You think I was the architect? I was chosen. Used. Just like all of you. I was never the queen. I was just the bait."

That landed like a hammer.

Gideon stepped forward. "If not you... who?"

Debbie looked up, her face broken. "The Watchers weren't the top. They were just the gatekeepers. There's a fourth layer. Beyond the Council. The Vault."

Silence.

Then Mary spoke, her voice cold. "What's in the Vault?"

"Everything," Debbie whispered. "Names. Plans. Future iterations. Next-gen candidates. There's a child already prepped for training. Somewhere in Europe."

Sarah's eyes widened.

Mike turned to Gideon. "We need to find it."

"We don't even know where to start," Gideon muttered.

But Sarah already had her tablet up, a window open, coordinates flashing.

"I do."

The group turned toward her.

"I've had it since the night of the fire," she said. "I didn't know what it was at first. Just a deep-code fail-safe hidden in a camera drone feed. But it's a location. Underground. Iceland."

Gideon blinked. "A cold archive…"

"Not cold," Sarah said. "Frozen. Untouchable. Until now."

Debbie laughed, hollow. "You think you can stop them? You think ending me ends this? They designed me, Sarah. They designed all of us. You're still in their story."

Mike leaned down, eye to eye with her. "Then we burn the whole story."

Behind him, the sun rose — blood-orange and slow — catching the wreckage of the Archive in amber fire.

The Reckoners had won this battle.

But the war?

It was just changing continents.

Chapter 25 – The Vault

The jet sliced through the low Arctic sky like a whisper of vengeance.

Iceland stretched below in a blanket of white and silver, a world of quiet desolation. But under that ice lay something ancient, encrypted, and malignant: The Vault.

Inside the aircraft, the group was silent. Not with fear — not anymore — but with the heavy awareness that whatever came next wouldn't just end something.

It would unearth everything.

Mike sat near the front, gloved hands clenched around a metal thermos he hadn't touched. His eyes were locked on the snow-drenched landscape beyond the window. He could still feel Debbie's words ringing in his skull: You're still in their story.

Not anymore.

Mary sat opposite him, her face lined with thought. She wore a parka and a reinforced backpack, its seams bulging with medical and tactical gear. The calm, quiet "receptionist" had been dead a long time. What sat in her place was something colder, sharper — and oddly maternal toward the young woman beside her.

Sarah. Calm. Focused. And scared in all the right ways.

She was typing, decrypting the drone code still feeding her a slow signal from below the ice shelf. The Vault's coordinates weren't exact, but the map was forming.

"It's nested beneath a glacial ridge," she said finally. "Deep. There's geothermal piping running from a fake research station on the surface. Probably for backup power."

Gideon gave a low whistle. "If they've gone to that much trouble, it's not just data in there. Could be people. Could be next-gen subjects."

"We go in," Mike said. "We shut it down."

"And if there are survivors inside?" Jane asked quietly from the back.

Mike didn't blink. "Then we save who we can… and end who we must."

They dropped near the ridge under cover of twilight. The cold bit like razors, but adrenaline dulled the edge. The old geothermal station was disguised well — from a distance, it looked like any other abandoned outpost, rusted panels and graffiti. But inside, the illusion peeled back.

Fingerprint scanners. Voice-lock pads. A humming server wall barely masked behind "storage." And a single descending elevator shaft locked by triple authentication.

Gideon cracked it in six minutes. The moment the final green light flicked on, the shaft opened, exhaling a breath of warm, sterile air.

Mary muttered, "God. It's still running."

They descended.

The Vault was unlike anything any of them had seen.

Sterile corridors. Rows of cryo-chambers sealed in glass. Screens flickering with biometric patterns, names, faces. Dozens — maybe hundreds — of digital dossiers.

Subject 23. Subject 24. Subject 52. Some children. Some adults. All marked with labels like Candidate Approved or Stage Two Deferred.

"Jesus," Sarah whispered. "It's a library of future experiments."

Mike walked slowly to the nearest chamber.

Inside was a girl — no more than sixteen. Eyes closed. Heartbeat steady. Frozen in dreamless sleep.

And beside her, another. A boy with the same hollow cheeks and a Watchers tattoo half-faded on his neck.

Then the room lit up red.

An automated voice filled the Vault.

"WARNING: Unauthorized breach. Containment protocol initiated. Level-3 cleanse will commence in T-minus 12 minutes."

They all looked at Sarah.

"What the hell is a level-3 cleanse?" Jane asked.

Sarah's eyes widened in horror. "A purge. Fire. They're going to destroy the data. And everyone in these chambers."

Mary pulled a flash drive from her coat. "Then we copy what we can and save who we can. NOW."

Chaos erupted. Gideon hit the server interface, dumping files into Sarah's drive. Mike and Jane began smashing chamber locks, pulling out groggy survivors as alarms screamed around them.

Smoke hissed from the vents.

Mike grabbed a stretcher, dragging the boy from the glass coffin. The kid's eyes fluttered open for half a second and locked with Mike's.

"Are you… real?" the boy asked weakly.

Mike nodded once. "Yeah. But they won't be for long."

Nine minutes.

They had twelve survivors, two drives filled with intel, and zero time.

As flames licked down the hall and sirens shrieked louder, Mike found himself at the centre of it all — dragging, directing, lifting, shielding. The Marine. The monster. The man trying to earn a different ending.

As they reached the emergency tunnel at the far end, Gideon slammed the override and the door hissed open.

Sarah turned back once. Her eyes shimmered with something close to tears.

"They'll try again," she said softly.

Mike looked at her.

"Then we don't just burn this down," he said. "We make it so it never rises again."

And they ran.

Behind them, the Vault ignited.

A mushroom bloom of fire bloomed through the ice above, visible for miles.

The Archive was gone.

The Vault was ash.

But as they limped into the Arctic night with a dozen half-conscious survivors and the truth finally in hand…

They all knew:

The world had to hear it.

Chapter 26 – The Transmission

The Arctic dawn cracked like a blade across the horizon. Pale light filtered through the swirling snow as the survivors trudged toward the exfiltration point. Every breath turned to steam. Every footfall sank into white silence. But under it all, something new surged through the group:

Purpose.

Mike moved like a man reborn — bloodied, bruised, limping slightly from a shard of shrapnel embedded during the Vault's detonation — but burning with momentum. His eyes were hard, focused. Alive.

He carried the youngest survivor over one shoulder, a boy no older than thirteen, now conscious and whispering strange phrases in his sleep. Phrases from the Watchers' initiation scripts. He wasn't just a victim — he was evidence.

Sarah marched just ahead, clinging to the data drive like it was holy writ. It pulsed faintly — a heartbeat of digital truth, encrypted and ghost-coded, filled with names, protocols, experiments, funding lines, and a final revelation she hadn't told the others yet. Not all of it.

Not yet.

They reached the extraction site — a windswept clearing where a black tiltrotor aircraft waited, engine thrumming like a war drum.

Jane waved them in. "This is it. Once we're up, it's just us and the signal."

Inside, the aircraft was stripped-down, military-grade, and already humming with radio chatter.

Gideon was at the console, fingers dancing across keys. "I've bounced the transmission path through six dead satellites and two orbital research stations. When we press send, the world's going to hear it — even if it's the last thing we do."

Mary stepped forward, her eyes scanning the jagged ridgeline behind them. "And it just might be."

As if summoned, motion burst from the edge of the white — black shapes against the snow. Sleek, faceless, armed.

The Watchers had followed.

Automatic fire peppered the slope. Bullets carved into ice. Mike dove, rolled, returned fire with surgical precision. Jane pulled the last survivor inside and slammed the ramp shut as the pilot lifted off.

Sarah hooked the drive into the transmitter. A screen flared. Files surged through the buffer. Images. Videos. Confessions.

Debbie's last voice message.

Amy's whispered monologue in the dark.

A child speaking commands in seven languages.

A boardroom of smiling men, toasting under the logo of the Watchers' front company: Neuron Apex.

The world wouldn't just hear the truth. It would see it.

"Go!" Mike shouted over the roar. "Send it!"

Sarah hesitated. Her finger hovered over the key.

"Do it," Mary said softly.

Sarah pressed SEND.

A low hum filled the cabin as the signal launched.

The drive fried instantly — designed that way, Gideon explained later — no trail, no reverse path. But the payload had gone.

The world was waking up.

As the aircraft arced into the pink-lit sky, the Watchers below shrank to dots, then shadows, then nothing.

Mike exhaled. He looked around at the battered survivors. The ones who made it. The ones who knew the cost.

"We're not ghosts anymore," he muttered.

Gideon smirked. "No. Now we're legends."

Far across the globe, phones buzzed.

Screens lit up.

Emails with no senders appeared in inboxes.

Newsrooms received mystery flash-drives.

Encrypted networks pulsed with silent alarms.

And in a private bunker beneath Geneva, a man in a suit sat upright, pale as ash.

"They transmitted it."

A pause.

"Then activate Protocol Eleven."

Outside, the sky brightened. The fire had been lit.

And it could never be put out.

Chapter 27 – Echoes and Ashes

The world was not ready.

Not for the truth, not for the repercussions, and certainly not for the faces behind the masks.

It began like a whisper in a hurricane. One leaked video, a blurry clip of a Watcher initiation — cold lights, screaming test subjects, and a calm voice saying, "Pain is the measure of truth."

Then came the cascade.

News anchors froze mid-broadcast, their teleprompters hijacked by the footage. Social media platforms locked down, then exploded in activity. Activists, conspiracy theorists, and citizens alike reposted the files — only to be flagged, banned, erased.

Too late.

The signal was out, mirrored in thousands of dark corners of the internet, scrubbed onto blockchain, passed from phone to phone like a new kind of gospel.

Blood Reckoning had gone global.

In the aircraft, as dawn touched the edge of the world, Mike sat against the fuselage wall, a deep silence around him despite the whine of the engines. His hands were trembling.

He wasn't cold.

He was coming undone.

Sarah sat across from him, her eyes scanning the cracked display of her watch. "Five hours since we hit transmit."

Jane nodded. "And already riots in four capitals."

Gideon, barely holding back a grin, added, "Two resignations. One CEO has disappeared entirely. And guess who's offering us a safehouse?"

Mary raised an eyebrow. "The Archive?"

Gideon nodded. "Even they didn't see this coming."

Mike looked up, eyes heavy with fatigue and something else — dread. "It's not over. We've lit the fire… but the Watchers won't let it burn freely."

As if summoned by prophecy, the aircraft's interior red-light began to flash. An encrypted signal cut into the comms.

A new broadcast.

But not theirs.

This one came from within the Watchers.

The voice was clipped, British, familiar. "To those who believe they've exposed us — know this: fire brings light, but it also draws predators. You've declared war. And war requires sacrifice."

Then the face appeared.

Debbie.

Not in memory. Not in dream.

Alive.

"Hello again," she said, calmly. "You broke the seal, didn't you? I'm disappointed. But not surprised."

Mary's blood ran cold. "She... she's alive?"

Mike's heart stopped. "No. That's not possible."

Sarah whispered, "It's not her. It's... a version."

The voice on the screen — Debbie's voice — smiled. "You left pieces of me behind. They picked them up. They gave me purpose. And now... I'm the Watchers' new face."

The transmission cut out.

Silence fell like a hammer.

Then, Sarah stood slowly, face pale but eyes ablaze.

"They copied her. They've weaponised her memory. And they're coming."

Mike stood as well. "Then we go first."

"We?" Jane asked.

"We light the rest of the matchbook," Mike said. "We don't run anymore. No more shadows. We burn their world... to ashes."

As the aircraft banked toward a descending line of storm clouds, each of them knew:

The reckoning wasn't the end.

It was the beginning of the final purge.

Chapter 28 — The Face Behind the Flame

The sky boiled crimson as their aircraft descended into the storm — a curtain of electric fury cloaking what lay beneath. Below them, in the rust-stained cityscape of Graven Hollow, the Watchers' final stronghold pulsed like a mechanical heart. Red lights blinked across rooftops. Helix-shaped antennae turned. Drones like silent wasps swirled in lethal formation.

Inside the aircraft, the atmosphere was pure voltage. Mike stood in the cargo bay, sliding cartridges into his weapon with sharp, practiced clicks. No hesitation now. His jaw was clenched, his eyes haunted but focused — not with rage, but purpose.

Mary approached, fastening a bandolier across her chest. "You okay?"

He didn't look at her. "No. But I know what I have to do."

Sarah worked a tablet at the far end, fingers dancing as a map of the Watcher compound glowed on-screen. "They moved the control servers to the Vault under the reactor. No digital access from outside. We breach, we purge it by hand."

"Old school," Jane muttered, strapping on her rig. "I like it."

Then came the voice — not from the comms, but from the deep speaker crackle in the walls.

Debbie.

Again.

Live.

"You really think this ends with a broadcast and a bang?" her voice taunted. "You're still playing our game, Mikey. But the rules? They've evolved."

Mike's knuckles whitened. "She's baiting us."

"She's a ghost with a machine body," Sarah corrected. "A synthetic intelligence trained on her memories. But yes — she wants you to come. She wants you to see what she's become."

"Well," Mary said dryly, "let's not keep her waiting."

The aircraft doors opened mid-hover. Wind screamed inside. They jumped.

Red fog. Alarms. Chaos.

They landed hard — into a courtyard flanked by watchtowers and burning steel. Shots rang out immediately. Sarah dropped into a crouch, returned fire with a pistol modified to overheat surveillance nodes.

Mike charged forward, a living battering ram. He tore through two guards in black armour, disarmed the third with a vicious twist, then shoved him into an electrified fence. Sparks. Screams. Silence.

"Down the hatch!" Gideon shouted, pointing to a maintenance shaft.

The team poured in, descending through boiling steam, the walls echoing with klaxons and distorted fragments of Debbie's laughter.

They hit the sub-level.

The Vault was ahead.

And so was Debbie — or what was left of her.

A column of glass. Tubes feeding in. A humanoid shape suspended in clear fluid, her face twisted in half-peace, half-smile. Around her, servers pulsed like nerves, like organs. The walls breathed.

"She's not human," Mary whispered.

"She's not machine either," Sarah added. "She's a mirror. A reflection of everything we tried to bury."

Mike stepped forward. "Then let's end the reflection."

Debbie's eyes opened. Bright red. Alive.

"I was always more than a game."

The room exploded into movement. Alarms turned to shrieks. Drones activated from the ceiling. The walls peeled back to reveal long-forgotten faces — former players, half-cybernetic, all twisted by loyalty and surgery.

Gideon yelled, "She kept the others alive!"

"No," Mike said coldly. "She rebuilt them. Out of fear. Out of memory."

And then?

War.

Chapter 29 — Planning the Firebreak

Smoke curled through the grated corridors like grasping fingers. Somewhere above them, the compound screamed with mechanical panic — klaxons howling, metal groaning. Below, the Vault's heat pulsed like the belly of a volcano.

But here, in an abandoned maintenance chamber three levels beneath the surface, the survivors carved out a moment of silence.

They needed it.

Mary leaned against the wall, wincing as she bandaged her shoulder. The blast from the last drone had caught her — not enough to kill, but close. Jane crouched beside her, panting, adrenaline wearing thin.

Sarah, tablet flickering in her hand, spoke quietly.

"They cloned her personality matrix from archived Watcher data, overlaid it with Debbie's voice. That wasn't just artificial intelligence. It was manufactured obsession — a ghost coded into silicon."

Gideon, kneeling at the map display projected onto the floor, added: "And it's anchored here. Beneath this compound is the original transmission nexus — the first site of the Watchers' global signal test. If we destroy that, we cut her reach."

"But not her mind," Sarah countered. "The Debbie-AI doesn't exist in one place. She's decentralized. Shattered across hundreds of data clusters. To wipe her entirely, we'd have to kill the core — and burn the backup."

Mike knelt beside them, silent until now. His voice came low, steady. "What about the people still under her control?"

"They're gone," Gideon said.

"No," Sarah said sharply. "Not all. Some are still just watching. Some are still waiting to be turned."

Mike looked at the hologram. The Vault. The Nexus. The Core. His eyes scanned the layers of systems, the towers, the failsafe's.

"We have to split up," he said.

Mary groaned. "Again?"

"It's the only way," he continued. "Sarah and Jane — you go for the uplink tower. Disable the antenna. Cut the outbound signals."

"Got it," Jane said.

"Mary and Gideon — you hit the relay servers. They're piping fuel to the Vault's cooling system. Overload them, we trigger a meltdown in the Core."

"And you?" Sarah asked.

Mike looked toward the dim shaft leading deeper, where the red lights pulsed like veins.

"I go to her. I finish what we started. She's still fixated on me. I can draw her focus long enough for you to bring it down."

There was a long silence.

"You might not come back," Mary said.

Mike nodded once.

"I might not want to," he said quietly.

Sarah stepped forward. "No hero speeches. If this is the last chapter, we write it together."

Mike offered the faintest smile. "Then let's make it unforgettable."

One by one, they gathered gear. Checked weapons. Shared nods that carried years of pain and love and blood between them.

Outside, the compound rumbled.

The firestorm was coming.

Chapter 30 — The Silence Before

They sealed the steel hatch behind them.

The war outside still raged — drones clashing with EMP charges, Watcher loyalists howling like broken machines, and fire licking up the corridor walls. But here, inside the circular chamber beneath the Vault, silence reigned.

Flickering emergency lights cast long shadows across the cracked concrete floor. The air was thick with heat and something older — the scent of rust, old blood, and regret.

Mike sat with his back against the far wall, his chest rising and falling slowly. His weapon lay at his side, untouched. He wasn't looking at anyone. Just the floor. Just the place where so many ghosts waited.

Sarah stood at the centre console, her fingers stained with oil and carbon from dismantling a neural lock. The system pulsed beneath her hand.

"It's all here," she murmured. "The entire Watcher archives. Names. Games. Confessions. Blackmail data. Everything they recorded from the Blood Spurts days to now."

Mary looked up sharply. "All the victims?"

"All the players too," Sarah confirmed. "Even us. We're... archived."

"They called it The Mirror," Gideon added, his voice low. "An AI built to reflect who we are — and who we could become under pressure."

Mary's voice cracked. "Debbie didn't die in that tub, did she?"

"No," Sarah said. "She was recorded. Every game. Every choice. She uploaded herself through the Watchers. They refined her. Weaponized her. Turned the symbol of rebellion into a surveillance god."

Mike clenched his fists. "She was already unravelling. The game just gave her the power to drag the rest of us with her."

Gideon stepped into the dim light. "The Vault houses two options. A hardwire override that purges the system — destroys Debbie's code, the archives, everything. The other…"

"…uploads it worldwide," Sarah finished.

Silence.

"No more secrets," she added. "Everyone sees what was hidden. Every recorded truth. Every face behind the mask."

"No." Mary's voice was hard. "We've lived through what happens when people know too much all at once. Society tears itself apart. You think this ends the Watchers? It makes everyone a Watcher."

Mike finally stood. "Then we choose. We burn it all down — or we expose the world and let it burn itself."

Sarah turned to him. "You're still the leader, Mike. What do you say?"

He looked at them all. Old allies. Ghosts reborn. Survivors of a game that pretended to be fiction but had always been real.

"I say," he whispered, "we go through hell one more time… so no one else has to."

He lifted his weapon.

The console blinked, waiting.

The Mirror was listening.

Chapter 31 – Ashes and Echoes

The city above was quiet, almost too quiet — as if it, too, was holding its breath.

Deep below the forgotten foundations, in the tunnels where secrets had been sealed in stone and blood, Mike Halston pressed his back against the cool brick, sweat dripping from his brow. Beside him, Sarah's breathing was shallow, but steady. The red glow of the emergency beacon ahead cast everything in warning hues.

They'd made it past the first wave of Watchers. Barely.

Mary crouched beside a rusted pipe, thumbing through the journal they'd recovered from the Archive—Debbie's journal. Its spine was cracked. Some pages had been torn out. But the ones that remained…

"Look at this," Mary whispered. "This isn't just a game log. These are instructions. Rituals. Patterns. The blood wasn't just for thrill. It was part of something—something older."

Mike didn't want to believe it. But the coincidences had piled up too high.

Sarah leaned in, pointing to a page marked with a spattered fingerprint. "That symbol—Gideon wore it around his neck in Book One. It wasn't just aesthetic. It was control. He's been playing longer than any of us knew."

"Where is he now?" Mike asked, already dreading the answer.

"Waiting," Mary said flatly. "With the Council."

They moved forward, deeper into the roots of the university — where the first Blood Spurts game had ever been played, in secret, decades ago. Back when the founding faculty were still experimenting with psychological thresholds, and The Watchers were little more than an idea born from academic obsession.

Now, they were gods in a world of shadows.

The tunnels opened into a cavernous chamber. Here, the walls were carved with names — thousands of them. Dares completed. Secrets exposed. Punishments given. This wasn't just a memorial. It was a ledger.

And at the centre: Gideon.

Alone. Or so it seemed.

He was seated in a high-backed chair, beneath the flicker of overhead fluorescents. His smile was calm, almost paternal.

"You finally brought the fire," he said. "Now let's see if you can survive the burn."

Behind him, lights flickered—and the Watchers stepped into view. But they weren't the same. Some were unmasked now.

Amy was among them.

"You left me," she said to Sarah, her voice hollow. "But they picked me up."

Mike stepped forward. "We came to end it."

Gideon stood. "You came to start it again. Only this time… the world is watching."

He gestured to a terminal, where a live stream blinked to life. Millions of views. The ritual had already begun.

"Blood doesn't just spill, Mike," Gideon said. "It calls. And tonight, the whole world will hear it."

Sarah stepped forward, defiant. "Then we'll give them a reckoning they'll never forget."

And behind her, Mary lit the first fuse.

The room began to shake.

Chapter 32 – The Hollow Crown

The walls of the inner sanctum pulsed faintly, as if alive. Buried beneath centuries of secrecy, the chamber was older than the Watchers themselves—carved from stone that knew silence before language. At the centre stood the obsidian plinth, its surface slick with condensation and symbols that glowed faintly when Gideon Rourke approached.

Mike stepped cautiously behind Sarah, both breathless from the chase. Their clothes were torn, blood-soaked, and dusted with ash. Yet their eyes still burned with purpose.

"This is it?" Mike rasped. "This is what it was all for?"

Sarah nodded, her gaze fixed on the artifact embedded in the plinth: the original ledger. Not digital, not encoded—written in human blood on ancient vellum. "The first confession," she whispered. "The origin of the Archive."

The chamber hummed with latent power. Symbols on the walls flickered like candlelight, responding to their presence. Mary entered last, bruised and silent. She moved with grim acceptance.

From the far corridor came slow, deliberate footsteps.

Gideon.

He emerged with none of his usual showmanship, bleeding from the shoulder, limping, but smiling as if finally arriving at a long-awaited homecoming.

"Well done," he said, voice thick with admiration. "You made it further than any before you."

"Don't you move," Mike snapped, raising a weapon salvaged from one of the Watchers. "We end it here."

"No," Gideon said softly. "We end nothing. You misunderstand. The Archive wasn't built to enslave. It was built to preserve. To warn. To remember."

Mary's voice cut through the still air. "You murdered to remember."

Gideon's smile faded. "And what have you done to forget?"

Silence.

Sarah stepped forward. "You think this ledger makes you God? That you control what's recorded?"

"I don't control it," Gideon said, stepping toward the plinth. "I curate it. Because if we don't, humanity will forget. And the cycle begins again."

Sarah turned to Mike. "Destroy it."

Gideon laughed once—short and sharp. "You think you can?"

Mike approached the plinth. The symbols began to glow brighter. His hand hovered over the ledger.

And then the voices began.

Not from the chamber. From within.

A thousand whispers—each a confession. Each a regret. Mike saw visions: of Debbie, of the hotel bathroom, of every moment he tried to bury. They poured through him like acid.

Sarah grabbed his arm. "Mike! Stay with me!"

He shook, gritting his teeth. "It's… it's using me. It wants me to write."

Mary stepped in. "Then let's give it something new."

From her pocket, she drew the last unmarked page she'd stolen from Gideon's personal archive. Clean. Untouched. Untainted.

Sarah caught her idea. "A new record. Our terms. Our ending."

They pressed the page to the plinth.

Mike, breathing heavily, took the pen from Gideon's jacket and, hand shaking, began to write.

A new truth.

One without blood.

One that does not forget, but chooses to forgive.

The chamber flickered. The hum began to break apart.

Gideon backed away, eyes wide. "What have you done?"

"We rewrote the end," Sarah said.

With a shuddering roar, the plinth cracked.

The Archive began to collapse.

And above them, the world began to stir.

Chapter 32: Reckoning

The sky over the old observatory cracked with thunder as if the heavens themselves wanted to scream. Rain sheeted down, blurring the shattered windows, washing away ash, blood, and secrets. The Watchers' compound burned behind them, a silhouette of fire against the night. But it wasn't over — not yet.

Mike stood in the clearing where it all began. His clothes were soaked, torn, bloodstained — not all of it his. Sarah was beside him, clutching the journal they had recovered from the Archive's vault. Mary limped slightly, her face hollow but resolute. And Jane — older, changed — held the last encrypted drive in trembling fingers.

Before them stood Gideon Rourke.

No more smiles. No more riddles.

His black coat flapped like wings in the storm, and around them, the remnants of the Watchers' Council — masked, injured, but still dangerous — formed a ragged circle. Their ranks were shattered, their influence broken, but like any dying beast, they were desperate.

"You think this ends it?" Gideon said, his voice hoarse from smoke and fury. "You think exposing the truth makes you heroes?"

Mike stepped forward. "No. But it makes us free."

Gideon shook his head. "No one's ever free. Not from history. Not from what you've done."

"We didn't survive all this to walk away scared," Sarah said, her voice sharp. "The world's going to see what you've done. What you've made us do."

"And what of Debbie?" Gideon asked. "What of the others? The ones who didn't live to see this moment? You think they wanted the light? No… they wanted absolution. And none of you will get it."

"That's where you're wrong," Mary said. She held up a flash drive. "This isn't just about truth. It's about choice. And we're choosing to stop the cycle."

Gideon's lips curled. "Then burn it all. Burn the Archive. But you'll never burn what's already inside you."

He lunged — but this time, Mike didn't hesitate.

The fight was brief. Brutal. Final.

As Gideon fell to the mud, gasping one last time at a world he could no longer control, Mike knelt beside him.

"You were right," Mike whispered. "I did enjoy the control once. But I learned something you never did — we're not defined by our past. We're defined by what we do next."

Sarah uploaded the final files to the cloud. Mary set fire to the remaining journals. Jane clicked send on a hundred queued emails — each one a truth bomb, scheduled to land in the inboxes of media outlets, survivors, whistleblowers, and even the government.

The circle was broken.

The fire raged.

And as the sun began to rise over the ruined bones of the observatory, Mike looked to the sky and breathed, really breathed, for the first time in years.

Not free.

But no longer afraid.

The final reckoning had come.

And they had survived.

— THE END —

EPILOGUE — "The Last Archive"

The fire had long burned out. Ash covered the valley like snow, soft and deceptive. From the ridge, Sarah stood with her coat pulled tight, wind biting at her cheeks. Below, the remnants of the old Watchers' complex smoked in silence. It looked like victory — but Sarah knew better.

Behind her, Mike limped up the slope. His body bore scars now — some fresh, some old — but it was his eyes that had changed most. The gleam was gone. Replaced by something still, steady… resolved.

"They won't rebuild," he said, almost a question.

Sarah answered without looking. "Not like before. We exposed too much. The world saw the truth this time."

"Enough of it?" Mike asked.

Sarah finally turned. Her eyes met his. "Maybe not. But enough to make them afraid."

A beat of silence passed.

Mary emerged from the path below, her hands in her pockets, her once-pristine blouse now marked by soot and blood. She walked without ceremony, but every step seemed heavier than the last. In her hand, she clutched a single item — the blood-red journal that had started it all.

"I'm leaving this," she said, setting it gently on a flat stone at the summit. "For those who come looking."

Mike looked down at it. "You think anyone will?"

Mary shrugged. "There's always someone. And they deserve to know the cost."

The wind picked up. Pages fluttered but did not fly away.

Far in the distance, faint sirens wailed —
not urgent, but persistent. A reminder that
the outside world still turned. Unaware, or
perhaps unwilling to confront what had truly
been buried beneath their feet for
generations.

Sarah took a final breath and pulled a flash
drive from her pocket — the final copy of the
Archive, its contents encrypted but intact.

"I'm giving it to someone I trust," she said.
"And then I'm disappearing."

Mike gave a faint, tired smile. "You and me
both."

Mary looked out at the blackened horizon.
"This wasn't justice," she murmured. "But
maybe… it was enough."

They stood there for a long time — three
survivors, bound not by friendship, but by
truth, fire, and sacrifice.

Eventually, they walked away — not as
heroes, not as martyrs.

Just as people who had seen too much and
chosen to live anyway.

Somewhere Else…

In a dark, climate-controlled chamber, a
monitor blinked to life. A new file appeared

on the screen:
REDACTED_01_REGENESIS.

A voice — genderless, calm — whispered into a headset:

"Subjects dispersed. Operation concluded. Initiate next cycle."

From the shadows, a gloved hand tapped a key.

The game, it seemed, was never truly over.

THE END

—or is it?

Printed in Dunstable, United Kingdom

63802665R00392